The
Governess

The
Governess

Wendy Holden

WELBECK

Published in 2020 by Welbeck Fiction Limited,
part of Welbeck Publishing Group
20 Mortimer Street London W1T 3JW

A CIP catalogue record for this book is available from the British Library

Hardback ISBN: 978-1-78739-466-7
Trade Paperback ISBN: 978-1-78739-470-4
E-book: 978-1-78739-475-9

Typeset by Palimpsest Book Production Ltd., Falkirk, Stirlingshire

Printed and bound by CPI Group (UK) Ltd., Croydon, CR0 4YY

10 9 8 7 6 5 4 3 2

House of Windsor

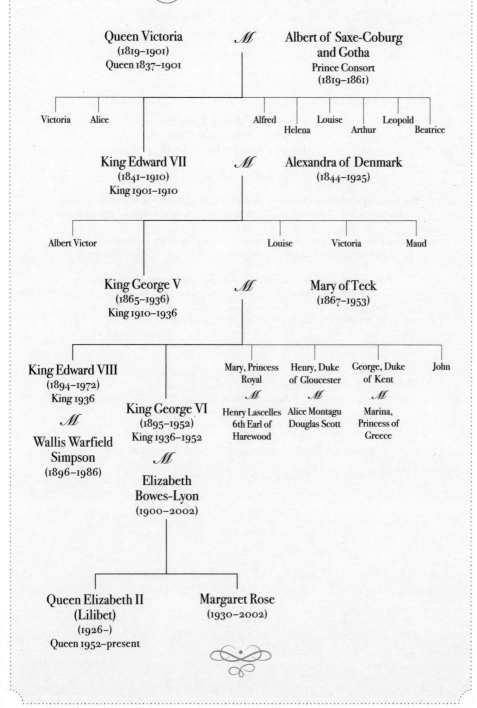

Queen Victoria
(1819–1901)
Queen 1837–1901

M

Albert of Saxe-Coburg
and Gotha
Prince Consort
(1819–1861)

Victoria   Alice   Alfred   Louise   Leopold
                   Helena   Arthur   Beatrice

King Edward VII
(1841–1910)
King 1901–1910

M

Alexandra of Denmark
(1844–1925)

Albert Victor   Louise   Victoria   Maud

King George V
(1865–1936)
King 1910–1936

M

Mary of Teck
(1867–1953)

King Edward VIII
(1894–1972)
King 1936

M

Wallis Warfield
Simpson
(1896–1986)

King George VI
(1895–1952)
King 1936–1952

M

Elizabeth
Bowes-Lyon
(1900–2002)

Mary, Princess
Royal

M

Henry Lascelles
6th Earl of
Harewood

Henry, Duke
of Gloucester

M

Alice Montagu
Douglas Scott

George, Duke
of Kent

M

Marina,
Princess of
Greece

John

Queen Elizabeth II
(Lilibet)
(1926–)
Queen 1952–present

Margaret Rose
(1930–2002)

Prologue

Aberdeen, Scotland
July 1987

EVERYTHING was ready. The mahogany table in the dining room was spread with a white lace cloth. Sunlight streaming through the wide bay window set the gold rims of the china cups ablaze. Plates had been set out with little white linen napkins. Silver cake-forks had been removed from boxes and polished. Sugar tongs, a silver cream jug and silver spoons all shone brilliantly.

In the cool of the kitchen, sandwiches waited on best plates. Smoked salmon, chicken, ham and cucumber, all with the crusts removed. There were the circular jam sandwiches, 'jam pennies', that had always been a favourite. There were scones and muffins and a magnificent chocolate cake.

There were flowers everywhere, bought specially for the occasion. Vases and jugs rescued from dark cupboards had been washed and restored to use. Pastel summer petals foamed on every surface and the rich scent of roses mingled with that of beeswax polish.

On the other side of the hall, in the high-ceilinged drawing room, a tall old woman in a pale pink dress stood straight-backed at the window. Pearls glowed at her neck and on the decoration pinned to her bosom. On either side of her nose, large, sloping eyes burned with anticipation. She was breathing rapidly and her knuckles were clamped to the sill. Her entire being was focused on the end of the street, where it met the busy main road. It was along there that her visitors would come.

They had not been here before, to her fine big villa on one of the city's best streets, built of the local grey granite. In dark weather it looked sombre, but in sunshine, against a blue sky, it glittered. Today, the end of July, was one of those beautiful, glittering days.

The light through the drawing room's big window fell on the elegant stone mantelpiece. On it stood a row of silver-framed photographs. One was of two smiling little girls, dressed identically in red tartan kilts and jerseys. The elder held a brown dog with pointed ears, which the younger was petting. They stood against a tulip border, and behind them were castle towers.

The photograph next to this one showed the same girls in coronets. They looked immensely serious in long white dresses, fur-edged cloaks flowing round like a velvet river. Behind them stood a man and woman, also in cloaks and in crowns heavy with jewels. The man looked apprehensive but the woman's gaze had a steely strength.

In the quiet of the drawing room, the old lady continued to wait. From time to time she gave an excited sigh, as if a long-held dream was to be realised. Perhaps this year, finally it would be fulfilled. She never ceased to hope. It was hope that, annually, led her to polish the silver, select the flowers with care, cut the sandwiches.

The only other sound was the tick of a grandfather clock. Flames danced in the fireplace between the arched alcoves. Summer it may be, but big Scottish houses could be cool, Scottish castles even cooler. Few people knew that better than she did.

Now, the woman held her breath. The moment had arrived. Along the main road from the airport a limousine had glided into view. That would be the police escort. Her guests would be in the one directly behind. The old hands gripped the sill harder. She thought she could see, in the rear, the pale flash of a familiar face.

In the front of the second car, a fogeyish young man opened an attaché case. He was new to the job, and his movements betrayed his nervousness. He took out a piece of paper and twisted his pinstriped body to the rear. Here sat two dark-haired middle-aged women between whom there was a strong sisterly resemblance.

One was heavily made-up, deeply tanned and wore a bright coral frock with theatrical white jewellery. The other, more conservative, wore a fawn twinset, a kilt and a double string of pearls. Her hair rose from her forehead in a dark wave.

The new equerry respectfully cleared his throat. 'If I might mention it, ma'am. We are about to pass the road where a former employee of the Royal Household lives.'

The woman in the twinset had been gazing out the window. Now she looked at the equerry.

'Her name is Marion Crawford. She says she was Your Majesty's governess for seventeen years. I'm told she writes every year, offering Your Majesty the opportunity to take tea with her on the way to Balmoral.' The equerry paused. 'I thought perhaps . . .'

The woman with the tan burst in, shrilly. 'Letters from Marion Crawford should be handled with a *very* long pair of forceps!' She looked agitatedly at her sister. 'Lilibet?'

There was no reply. The chauffeur gently pressed the brake. A blue street sign signalled the end of the old woman's road.

Up in the house, behind the gleaming drawing-room window, the wrinkled hand was waving frantically. The cars had slowed! Finally, after all these years, they would turn up the avenue and into her drive! She had opened the gates, as she always did.

'Lilibet!' demanded the woman in the bright coral frock.

PART ONE

EDINBURGH, 1932

Chapter One

The classroom was gloomy. Everything was brown, from the desks with their lids and inkwells to the wooden forms and floorboards. Brown was the heavy Bakelite clock and brown the picture frame surrounding a bulge-eyed King George V and a flint-faced Queen Mary. A brown leather strap, or tawse, jiggled in the schoolmaster's bony hand. It looked well-worn, as if often used.

The sight of it made Marion wince. Corporal punishment, in her view, had no place in modern classrooms. Nor, for that matter, had Dr Stone, the gaunt and black-gowned schoolmaster whose lesson she was sitting in on. 'I was expecting someone much older,' he had growled at her in greeting. 'And *male*.'

Marion could not imagine why Miss Golspie, the college principal, had sent her to observe such an establishment. Glenlorne was Edinburgh's most expensive private prep school. It was for the sons of the city's wealthy citizens, who would go on afterwards to the major public schools. As Miss Golspie well knew, none of this appealed to Marion. Her interests were at the other end of the social scale.

It didn't help that Dr Stone kept staring at her hair, and addressed all his remarks to it, as if making some satirical point. The new short crop was supposed to look chic, fashionable and emancipated. But did she actually resemble a skinned rabbit?

'Sit at the back,' Dr Stone told her hair.

Marion rallied. She had had enough of this. At least she *had* hair, short though it was. His ghoulish yellow cranium, on the other hand, had a mere few greasy strands plastered across it. 'If you don't mind,' she crisply informed him, 'I'd prefer to observe from the front.'

Looking for an unoccupied chair, she spotted one in the shadowy corner, seat turned to the wall. Through the wooden struts of the chair-back a tall white cone was visible. As she approached, she saw a letter 'D'. She blinked. Was it possible? In this day and age?

'You are proposing to sit on the *dunce*'s chair?' The master's tone dripped acid amusement.

Marion did not reply. She picked up the humiliating headgear with her fingertips and dropped it lightly on the floor. Then she took the chair, sat down calmly and gave the class a smile. Two rows of boys stared back, round-eyed.

There was a sharp crack as Dr Stone slapped the tawse on his palm. The boys jumped slightly in their seats. 'This,' he said with obvious reluctance, 'is Miss Crawley.'

'Good morning, Miss Crawley,' chorused the boys.

'Craw*ford*,' she corrected gently. She had fully expected to loathe them, these little Scottish Fauntleroys. Instead she felt sorry for them. They looked so sweet, in their little grey blazers. They deserved better than this old sadist.

Another slap of tawse on palm. Another jump. 'Miss Crawley is studying to be a teacher and is observing our geography lesson as part of her training'. There was a contemptuous emphasis on 'teacher' and 'training'.

From beneath their crested caps, the boys continued to stare at her curiously. Marion continued to smile brightly back. *Take no notice of that rude old fossil,* said the smile. *Women can take degrees now, they can train for the professions. Tell your sisters! Tell your mothers!*

Dr Stone, having temporarily laid aside the tawse, was writing something on the blackboard. The chalk screeched with the movement of his bony yellow hand. *The British Empire,* announced the untidy scrawl. From the desk below the blackboard, a long thin stick was now produced. A collective intake of breath suggested this too had dispensed painful punishment in its time.

The cane rapped the glass covering a large map of the world. 'Can you,' Stone snarled, 'see a colour that appears everywhere?'

Several hands went up. 'Is it pink, sir?'

There was a triumphant glint about the steel spectacles. 'Indeed it is! Pink is the colour of the British Empire! There is no continent on Earth in which our great and glorious nation does not own territories!'

Marion shifted in her seat. Old-fashioned jingoism of this sort made her uncomfortable.

'So even if you are *here*' – the cane landed on the west side of Africa – 'you are a British subject.'

'They're the same as us, then, sir?' ventured a small boy. He flinched as the master rounded on him furiously.

'Not at *all* the same as us! *They* are *colonial subjects*!'

'But what's the difference, sir?'

'They,' snarled Dr Stone, 'are *uncivilised*.'

Back at Moray House Teacher Training College, she hurried straight to the principal, heart pounding with indignation, heels clattering down the beeswax-scented corridors.

'Come in.'

Miss Golspie's office was light and modern, panelled with pale oak, lined with close-packed bookshelves and lively with colourful rugs, pictures and vases. The principal, as contemporary as her surroundings in a floaty frock of bright abstract print, looked up from her desk. From within a well-cut grey bob, her handsome, intelligent face expressed surprise. 'My dear Marion. You look pale.' She raised a brightly patterned cup. 'Tea?'

'Yes please.'

Miss Golspie poured another cup from her Clarice Cliff teapot, handed it over then gestured to the large tangerine sofa in the window bay. 'Sit down and tell me all about it.'

Marion sat down and told her all about it. She had been appalled by everything, but the *uncivilised* remark most of all. 'It's so *wrong* to talk about people like that,' she fumed. 'We're all equal – or should be. How many other teachers are telling children such old-fashioned, prejudiced things?'

'Quite a few, I daresay,' Miss Golspie said drily. 'In those kinds of schools anyway.'

Marion's large eyes blazed. 'I'd never work anywhere like that!'

The principal replaced her teacup in its saucer. 'My dear, you can't ignore certain attitudes because you don't like them. Otherwise those attitudes prevail. If you want to change things you must stand up and defend the right.'

'You make it sound like a war,' Marion muttered.

'What else is the fight against ignorance?'

In the silence that followed, Marion sipped her tea. It had an unusual, smoky scent. 'Lapsang souchong,'the principal said with a smile, seeing the question on her face. 'I grew very fond of it when I taught in China.'

Miss Golspie's previous life had clearly been full of adventure, which in turn had informed her exotic tastes and engaged personality. She was the most interested and interesting person Marion knew, full of energy and ideas, a constant inspiration to her students. She was probably the same age as Dr Stone, but there the resemblance ended. It was amazing to think they were on the same planet, let alone in the same city and profession.

'Why did you send me to Glenlorne?' she was calm enough now to ask. 'It's hardly my kind of place.'

The principal regarded her with bright dark eyes over the patterned rim of her teacup. 'No, your kind of place is the slums.'

Marion looked at her quickly. Miss Golspie had always supported her ambition to teach there. 'Yes,' she said firmly. 'Someone has to.'

Three years after the Wall Street Crash and the economic hardships that had followed, the belief endured that the condition of the poor was largely their own fault. But even if that were true, which Marion doubted, it certainly wasn't the fault of the children. Sheer professional curiosity had first led her into the stinking passages of Grassmarket, one of Edinburgh's most notorious slums, but pity and outrage had sent her back every Saturday ever since. The squalor and stink were bad enough, but it was what poverty did to the mind that took her breath away. Slum children had difficulty concentrating, their comprehension was slow and a near-starvation diet led to bad eyesight and impaired hearing. It took them ages to get through one simple book. The literacy rate was near-nil, meaning that their chances of ever emerging from Grassmarket, getting a job and having anything resembling a rewarding life, were near-nil too. Unless she did something about it.

Miss Golspie was looking at her with thoughtful dark eyes. 'I understand why you feel the way you do. But what about the other end of the scale?'

'The rich?' Marion was puzzled. 'They don't need my help.'

'You're sure about that?'

'Of course. They're the elite. They have every advantage.'

'They have Dr Stone,' the principal pointed out. 'And you just said you felt sorry for the children in his class.'

'I do. Very.'

'So what sort of advantage is that?'

Marion considered this. 'I'm not quite sure what you're getting at,' she said eventually.

Isabel Golspie leaned back in her chair and smiled. 'What I'm getting at,' she said, 'is rather radical. I'm trying to suggest that, admirable though it is for you to want to help the very lowest class of society, the top of society need you too. And if you can help them, they can help the others.'

Marion was completely lost now. But if Miss Golspie was suggesting she go to work at Glenlorne, she could forget it.

The principal calmly sipped her tea. 'You've seen what it's like at an elite school. Those little boys will have power one day. And one of their main childhood influences will have been Dr Stone. How do we grow a just society out of that?'

Marion stared down into her teacup, at the brown pool of tea, whose name she could not now recall. But she could remember the tawse, the dunce's cap, the fear on the little boys' faces. 'I want to work in slums,' she said, stubbornly.

'Which is precisely why you should teach the wealthy,' suggested Miss Golspie. 'Who else is going to tell them how poor people live? About feminism, equal opportunities, social justice and all the other things you care about? Not Dr Stone, you can be sure of that.'

Chapter Two

The next day was Saturday, the day when Marion went to visit the slums. As always when she visited Grassmarket, she dressed up. The children living there saw enough dirty rags. She wanted to raise their sights and cheer them up by wearing her smartest, brightest clothes.

Her new pink frock swirled satisfyingly about her knees. You would never know the pattern had come free with a magazine. Her mother was clever with her needle, and the drop waist fell perfectly. The hem was just the right length to show off her slim legs.

She hurried along, as if sheer speed would outpace the words of Miss Golspie, which had sounded in her dreams all night. She could see the principal's argument, which was a typically ingenious one. But her commitment to the poor of Edinburgh was total.

About to cross the road, she stepped back just in time. A car swept past, all shining panels and royal crest. A recent heavy downpour had left puddles in the gutter, which the tyres now ploughed through. A wave of muddy water rose upward, scattering her skirt and stockings.

Marion swore under her breath. She looked after the car, now gleaming in the distance, heading towards the palace at Holyrood. On both sides of the road, people were staring at it. Were the royal family making one of their periodic visits? She remembered George V on Dr Stone's wall. Had the pop-eyed king-emperor ruined her dress? She felt a stir of passionate anti-royal feeling.

'This any use?' The voice came from behind her. A young man was holding out a crumpled handkerchief.

'Thanks.' She took it hastily, without looking. The frock was her priority. But as she dabbed, her gaze kept wandering from the dirty fabric to the footwear beside her on the pavement. The brown leather was scuffed, and one lace was undone. But the shoes were good ones; expensive.

'I should introduce myself,' he said. 'I'm Valentine.'

'*Valentine?*' She stopped dabbing and looked up. A pair of bright dark eyes looked back. 'As in the card?'

'Everyone says that,' he replied equably. 'As in one of the Two Gentlemen of Verona, actually.'

She straightened. 'I've never seen that play.'

'Everyone says that as well. What's your name?'

'Marion.'

'As in Maid?'

'Everyone says that.' They didn't, actually, but he wasn't to know.

He grinned. He was very attractive. There was a crackle about him, an energy. He was shorter than her – most men were – but looked strong. His hair was thick and dark, and a shining hank of it dangled in one eye, giving him a boyish look, although she guessed he was about her age, twenty-two. The scruffy shoes were matched with a battered tweed jacket, creased flannels and a red scarf that glowed like a flame. He was carrying a large green canvas bag, with a flap over the top. Whatever was in it looked bulky and heavy. Books?

'Are you a student?' she asked him. The university was full of bumptious young men who strode about the streets as if they owned the place.

He nodded. 'Guilty as charged.'

'English, I'm guessing.'

'Actually, I'm studying history.'

She rolled her eyes. 'I mean you. *You're* English.' His accent definitely was, but not the cold, clipped sort. His voice was low, warm and had a crack in it that was very attractive.

He looked disappointed. 'Is it that obvious?'

'Well you don't sound Scottish.'

'The accent's quite hard,' he said, deadpan. 'Even for Scots. People in Glasgow seem to struggle with it terribly.'

This made her laugh. He looked pleased.

'I'm from London,' he said. 'Ever been there?'

She shook her head. She had never been out of Scotland. Suddenly, she felt confined and provincial. She handed back the handkerchief. 'I have to go.'

'Can I walk with you?' he asked.

She looked at him. 'Why?'

'Because you're beautiful?'

That made her laugh again. What a flatterer. She was not beautiful. She had good big eyes and nice chestnut hair, even if it was now nearly all shorn. Damn that accursed crop. It only drew attention to the fact her nose was on the large side and she was both too tall and too thin. 'A long drink of water,' her mother called her.

Oh well. She did not intend to make her living through her looks. Women had more choices these days.

'I like your hair,' Valentine said, sending a huge, helpless wave of relief through her. She smiled her thanks and started to walk off.

He fell into step beside her. This was unexpected, but not unwelcome.

'Where are you going?'

'Grassmarket.'

The dark eyes widened. '*You* . . . live *there*?'

She was tempted to tease him, but found herself telling the truth. 'No, I teach there in my spare time.' Now, surely, he would leave her alone. Her interest in the slums shocked most people.

He stayed where he was, however, and hitched the heavy bag on to his other shoulder. 'I'm wildly impressed.'

Something in the overstatement made her defensive. 'You don't need to be,' she returned stiffly. 'I'm studying to be a teacher. Underprivileged children are my area of special interest.'

Now, surely, he was bound to leave. He kept up, however. 'Really?' he said brightly. 'That's absolutely fascinating.'

'That's one word for it,' she agreed.

They had almost reached the top of the Royal Mile now. The weather had cleared completely and become blue, bright and beautiful. To the north, the Firth of Forth sparkled like a carpet of sapphires. To the south, the great bare bulk of Arthur's Seat rose over the towers and spires. Above the great black stone gateway of Edinburgh Castle, the motto on the coat of arms shone gold in the sun: 'Nemo Me Impune Lacessit.'

'No one provokes me with impunity,' Valentine translated easily.

'Or,' said Marion, 'as the Scots would put it, "Dinna mess wi me, or else!"'

'But they *were* messed with,' he pointed out. 'Mary Queen of Scots and Charles I lost their heads. And James II and Bonnie Prince Charlie lost their kingdoms. That lot down there' – he nodded towards Holyrood, at the other end of the long street – 'need to watch out.'

Marion glanced at her dress. The damp hem, edged with a greyish border of mud, clung to her bony knees. 'They do,' she agreed. 'Look what they did to my frock.'

'I don't mean that,' he said. His bantering tone had gone and he now sounded slightly impatient.

Beneath the rearing dark hair, his face had become serious. His features were beautifully moulded, she saw, his lips full and shapely, his cheekbones pronounced.

'What do you mean, then?' she asked. 'What do they need to watch out for?'

'For the international proletarian revolution,' he declared.

She felt a thrill of shock. 'You're a republican?'

'You're getting close.' The dark eyes gleamed. 'The monarchy's an outdated institution. How can a system where privilege, power and position come from a mere accident of birth ever be justified? It has no place in the modern world.' He paused, before adding, in stirring tones, 'As the spring must follow the winter, the triumph of the workers over the ruling classes is historically inevitable.'

She felt her mouth drop open. 'You're a Communist!'

'And what if I am? What if I'm a red under your bed?'

His amused gaze was locked on hers. The thought of him under her bed, and even in it, jumped into her head. She tried to push the image away, but it was too late – something sharp had pierced her, low in her belly.

He had flipped back the flap of the bag now. Inside were piled, not books, but a great many newspapers. They bore a red hammer and sickle and the title *The Daily Worker*. He grinned at her. 'Can I interest you in a copy, madam? Something sensational to read on the train?'

She stared at him. 'You're selling *those*? *Here*?' Respectable Edinburgh wasn't an especially left-of-centre city.

'All members of the party have to. It's our socialist duty. Spreading the word.'

'And what is the word exactly?' Marion was curious. She was interested in politics but knew little about Communism, which was something she associated with fierce, bearded Russians, violent uprisings and murdered czars. Not well-brought-up young men from England.

'Well.' He hesitated. 'Do you believe in the equality of the sexes?'

'Absolutely.'

'And do you agree that everyone should enjoy equal social and economic status?'

She nodded vehemently.

'Do you believe in love rather than money?'

'Er . . .' She looked at him. He was grinning, and a wave of heat rushed up her neck. Just being close to him was exciting. She had never met anyone like this before. She searched for a smart reply, failed to find one and decided she'd had enough of this disconcerting stranger.

'I have to go,' she muttered, then turned and clattered down the dark stairs leading from the castle rock. She half-expected to hear him clatter after her, and her relief that he didn't was mixed with regret. She realised, feeling the lump in her pocket, that she still had his handkerchief.

At the bottom were dirty cobbles and dark, rotten entries. These broken houses with their tall gables had once been home to the city's aristocracy. Now Grassmarket sheltered – if that was the word – its opposite extreme. She took a deep breath and plunged into the warren of gloomy passages.

The McGintys' door was on the first floor, up a broken and banisterless staircase.

The battered portal threatened to collapse at her knock. A small pale face appeared in the gap, its initially suspicious expression flaming with sudden delight. 'Miss Crawford!'

It was Annie who had first brought Marion to Grassmarket, the previous winter. She was eight, but looked three years younger. Her father was an organ grinder who did the rounds of the Edinburgh streets, taking his daughter with him. The day had been freezing wet and the child's naked feet had looked cold and vulnerable on the shiny pavement. And yet she had sung *'Loch Lomond'* with a sweet gusto.

Marion's own coat was old and her shoes had seen better days. But she was nonetheless grateful for them as she sheltered under a nearby shop awning and pretended to study displays of gleaming silverware. Her chance came when the organ stopped grinding. She turned; the father had stepped away, so she approached. 'Why are you not at school?' she gently asked, flinching as she saw the bruises on the child's thin arms. Beneath her dirty hair spread what looked like a healing gash across her forehead.

Fear had filled Annie's large eyes. She would, she said, have liked school, but whenever her father went out with the organ, out she must go too. It was at this point that the father had reappeared out of the doorway of a low-looking pub. He had the small, mean eyes of a fighting dog and was wiping his mouth with the back of a dirty hand. He spoke roughly to the child and dragged her off down the street, wresting from his daughter's thin fingers the sixpence Marion had slipped her. She had followed, at a discreet distance, and found not only Grassmarket, but what she now felt was her vocation.

McGinty was not here now, thankfully. Annie's mother, a wan, wasted creature who worked as a seamstress, was lying on the bed, eyes closed. A piece of dirty flannel was tied round her head. 'Ma's head is bad,' Annie said.

Marion looked at her, wishing she could help. But she was not a doctor, much less a plumber, glazier, carpenter, electrician or any of the other trades that, combined, might make this wretched place vaguely habitable. She was only a teacher, and a not-quite-qualified one at that.

But that was something. If Annie learned to read and write, and add up a bit, she could get a proper job. Escape from this miserable hovel. Hopefully take her mother with her.

There was a nudge from Annie. 'Are we gan to read, Miss Crawford?'

'Sorry, Annie. Of course we are.' Marion hurriedly got out *The Princess and the Pea*.

It now struck her as an unfortunate choice. But Annie didn't seem to compare her circumstances with those of the more fortunate. She just loved the pictures of the beautiful carved four-poster with its piles of patterned mattresses.

' . . . she was a *real* princess!'

As the spindly child spelled out the simple words, Marion felt a hard ache in her heart. This was what she wanted to do – help children like this rise up and escape their circumstances. Not the scions of the rich, who could look after themselves. Until the revolution, of course. She smiled, thinking of Valentine and his fiery philosophy.

She agreed that a revolution was needed. Just not the big, violent sort he espoused, pitting a nation against itself. Her revolution would make more money available so schools could have the books currently in desperately short supply. She had spent evening after evening repairing old ones, gluing pages back in, trying to make them readable. But there was nothing she could do about the leaking roofs, clapped-out boilers and pathetic lack of pens and pencils, or even blackboards. During her training, she had several times drawn maps on the brick walls of playgrounds to explain geography to a crowd of shivering children. The funding of the education budget was a national disgrace. But the housing budget was even more of one. The slums should be destroyed; it was appalling, in 1932, that children like Annie lived in conditions that would have shocked Dickens. What chance did they have, apart from her?

Miss Golspie, Marion decided, was wrong. Her future was not with the wealthy and powerful, but here, with the poorest of the poor.

Chapter Three

She stayed longer than she had intended. Golden evening light was spreading stickily over the Old Town as she made her way home. It was the city's ancient heart and where its dark glamour seemed most intense.

'Marion Crawford?'

A red-cheeked young woman, smartly dressed, her smooth dark hair twisted into a bun, was staring at her curiously. 'Marion Crawford? Is it really you?'

'Ethel.' Marion had finally placed the homely face from the back row of a long-ago schoolroom. She and Ethel McKinley were the same age. But not, it seemed, the same anything else. There was a wedding ring, and a sleeping baby dribbled on Ethel's smart coat.

Ethel was looking at Marion's hair. Or at where it had been until recently. 'Have you had it all cut off?'

Marion flushed. As she pulled off the white cloche to reveal the short brown side-parted crop, Ethel's dark eyes rounded.

'It's the fashion,' Marion said defensively. 'It's an Eton crop.'

'Eaten?' Ethel's smile was satirical. 'Eaten by what?'

This shaft of wit made Marion impatient. Who was Ethel to poke fun? What had she done with her life except get married? And have babies? Anyone could do that.

'*Eton*,' she elucidated. 'It's a school. An expensive boys' school, near London. I see you're a mother,' she added, to change the subject.

Ethel was, like herself, only just twenty-two. Too young to be married with children, especially when there was so much else one could do. Women these days had careers; did Ethel not know?

'This is Elizabeth,' Ethel said grandly. She shifted the enormous child in her arms.

'Lovely,' Marion said politely.

'After the little princess,' Ethel prompted.

'Oh . . . yes.'

Princess Elizabeth, along with her baby sister Margaret Rose, was the daughter of the Duke and Duchess of York. Along with the rest of the nation, Marion had seen pictures of them in the newspapers: white-socked, blue-eyed, golden-haired, frilly-dressed. She didn't follow royalty, however. She felt an interest in them was for the older generation, not her own. She felt Ethel was rather pitiable.

Annoyingly, Ethel seemed to have the same view of her. 'Not got married, then?' She was staring at Marion's naked ring finger.

'I want a career, not a man and a ring!' Marion wanted to shout. Instead she said, patiently, 'I'm studying. At Moray House in Edinburgh. It's a teacher training college.'

'Going to be a teacher, then?' Ethel deduced brilliantly.

'That's right.'

'At an expensive one, like that you just mentioned?'

'Eton?' Marion suppressed a snort. 'Not exactly. I'm intending to work in the slums, as it happens.'

'The slums!' As expected, Ethel looked staggered. She made her excuses, and hurried off.

Grinning to herself, Marion walked on. She passed the end of a street in which a group of young men had gathered. They were shouting and laughing and were, she realised, kicking something on the ground. Or someone. Was that not a person in the middle of all the black-trousered legs and shining boots? They were kicking with all their might. They would kill him.

She didn't stop to think. She raced down the alley, whose floor was thick with scattered newspapers. She could see, between the thrusting legs, a young man curled in the foetal position. He looked dead already.

The nearest thug whirled round and saw her. His oiled hair was smoothed to his scalp and centre-parted above a cruel, handsome face. His eyes were sharp, with a dead, metal glint. 'It's not the police,' he said, scornfully. 'It's just a woman.'

Any urge to stand her feminist ground faded as Marion now found herself closed in by black-clothed men with sinister expressions. Tall though she was, they seemed taller.

'Look what we've got here,' one said, mockingly.

As she tried to back away, something shot out and grabbed her. A hand in a black leather glove. It gleamed malevolently against the innocent pink of her dress sleeve.

'What's the hurry, love?'

'Fancy a drink?'

'Come on!'

Terror pounded in her temples. 'Let go of me!' She tried to shake off the leather gauntlet, which now moved to her breast.

'Want to go home to your boyfriend?' The man was fleshy and brutish. She could smell his meaty breath. His nose, with its spots and pores, was almost pressing against hers. His hand twisted her breast, and pain shot through her. 'I'll be your boyfriend. Give us a kiss!'

Marion was revolted, but also terrified. She glanced round. She was right down the entry, in its darkest part. No one passing would see. They could push her down, do what they wanted. With a colossal effort of will, she summoned a steady voice. 'Let go of me!'

There was laughter at this, and some contemptuous imitations. The meaty-breathed one now released her and another of the men took charge. 'Come on.' He touched her lips with a leather-gloved finger. 'Pick one of us.' The finger traced the line of her jaw. The metallic eyes glittered. 'Or we'll pick for you.'

Instinct took over. She raised her knee hard and suddenly and watched his eyes widen with pain and fury. He reeled away, cursing and roaring. The meaty-breathed one now gripped her harder. He lifted his other fist, and Marion saw the knuckleduster glitter in the overhead light. She closed her eyes, bracing herself for the sickening impact of hard metal on soft flesh and delicate bone.

It never came. There were sudden shouts at the end of the entry and the sharp blast of police whistles. The men in black disappeared in an instant, into the shadows at the bottom of the alley. She heard, as if from a great distance, boots in steel toecaps clattering up what might have been fire escapes. On the dirty brick floor, the young man lay still, dark-haired, his white shirt stained with blood. There was something familiar about him.

'You're brave, Maid Marion,' said Valentine.

'Stupid, you mean,' she muttered.

Half an hour after the frightening skirmish found them sitting in the pub nearest to the alley entrance. It was a rough place, but that was an advantage; no one batted an eyelid when she half-carried, half-dragged Valentine in and bought him a glass of whisky, for shock. She had bought herself one too.

He was in much better shape than had first seemed humanly possible. She had come, it seemed, at precisely the right time, before the beating had got properly underway. The blood covering his front had turned out to be his red scarf. 'The trick is to make like the hedgehog,' he said. 'Curl into as tight a ball as possible. So they can't kick your head.'

His head had survived quite well, it seemed to her. He had a black eye, split lip and swollen cheek, but his teeth had survived. His smile remained wide and sunny. 'You sound like you're used to it,' she said.

'Occupational hazard.' He cocked his head at the newspapers. She followed his gaze. She had gathered up the clean ones from the dirty floor of the alley and shoved them in the bag she had found at the foot of the wall. 'Not everyone's a fan of Communism. The fans of Mussolini especially. Know who he is?'

His slightly patronising tone stung, especially after what she had just done for him. 'I do read the papers,' she snapped. 'He's the leader of Italy's Fascists.'

He grinned. 'Very good. He's also the inspiration for our own dear Mr Mosley, who's just founded his own British Union of Fascists in tribute. It was from their friendly embrace that you just plucked me, in fact.'

Marion was curious. 'Why don't Fascists like Communists?'

She expected a long, fluent explanation, but Valentine hesitated. 'It's about the state, basically,' he said, after a pause.

'The state?'

'With Communism the state runs everything.'

'I see. And Fascism?'

'Well, that puts the state first. Basically, that's the difference.'

Marion frowned. 'Is that a difference?'

Valentine drew hard on his cigarette and let the smoke fall out of his mouth. The effect was curiously erotic. He rubbed his forehead. 'Look, normally I'd be all over this. But my head, you know?'

She felt guilty. He'd been injured. Embarking on ideological debate probably wasn't very fair, given the circumstances.

He was looking at his empty glass. 'Another drink? It's really helping with the pain. I'll go to the bar. Er, lend me a couple of shillings?'

Waiting, she leafed through the *Daily Worker*. He returned with two glasses of whisky in each palm. 'Thought I'd save myself the trouble of going back,' he said, sliding the four tumblers rather carelessly onto the table. Shooting out a hand to steady them, Marion tried not to dwell on the fact that they represented the last of her money. She had been rather counting on the change.

'Do you sell many of these?' she asked, gesturing at the *Daily Worker* as Valentine knocked back his first glass in one.

'That's better! Sorry, what did you say?'

She repeated the question, adding, 'It doesn't look very interesting.'

'If by that you mean there's none of the corruption and entertainment of the popular press, that's deliberate.'

'Really? Why?'

'So as not to distract the masses from the struggle, of course.'

'But what if they want to be distracted?' She turned the pages, bemused. 'There are no cartoons here, no fashion. You don't even have any racing tips.'

'Racing tips won't pull down the citadels of the bourgeoisie,' Valentine said sternly. 'Or fashion, for that matter.'

She closed the paper. 'Well, the revolution doesn't sound like much fun to me.'

He shrugged and held up his second whisky glass. 'Workers of the world, unite!'

She put the first of hers to her lips. The merest sip sent a coarse and fiery path down her gullet. He had clearly gone for quantity over quality. 'What work do you do?' she asked, suddenly aware she had no idea.

'I'm a student,' he said, slightly defensively.

'So you've never actually worked? Never had a job?' A smile tugged the corners of her mouth.

He shrugged. 'From each according to his abilities, to each according to his needs.'

'What does *that* mean?'

He reached over. 'It means I'll have your spare whisky if you don't want it. Down with the bourgeoisie!'

Chapter Four

She had expected her mother to be in bed. But as she hurried up the little street, a crack of light divided the front-room curtains. She slid her key into the lock and entered the cramped hall.

'Marion?'

She went to the threshold of the tiny sitting room. The bright rays of a table lamp outlined the comfortable figure of her mother, sitting sewing in her chair by the fire. She felt a wash of deep affection at the familiar scene. 'Hello, Mother. Sorry I'm late.'

Mrs Crawford's plump, homely face was not, as usual, smiling. It was drawn with worry and bright with indignation. 'You're *terribly* late! We couldn't imagine where you were!'

'We?'

'Well, Peter was here. Or had you forgotten he was coming?'

Peter! Her friend from the year above at teaching college. They had been going to a concert together; *The Mikado*. She sank down in the opposite chair, covered her face and groaned.

'He waited right up until the last minute,' Mrs Crawford went on. 'He only left because he thought you might have gone to the concert to meet him there.'

Marion pictured Peter's head on its long neck switching anxiously about in the foyer crowds, his pale, myopic eyes squinting through his spectacles. 'Really, Marion. How can you treat him like this? He's such a nice boy. And devoted to you, of course.'

'No he *isn't*, Mother. We're just friends.' She was fond of Peter, but that was all. It was her mother who loved him. Earnest, polite, hard-working and trustworthy, he was perfect son-in-law material. But the thought of marrying him, of sharing his bed, no!

Her mother gave a shuddering, horrified gasp. 'What's happened to your *dress*? I've only just made it for you. Is that *blood*?'

'Well, yes. There was a fight, you see, and – '

'*Fight?*' interjected Mrs Crawford, in a yelp.

'Not *me*. I was just helping someone who was hurt.' She bent over and hugged her seated mother. 'Just think of it as a good deed,' she urged, smiling. 'Marion the Good Samaritan.'

'You're incorrigible,' said Mrs Crawford, but fondly, to Marion's relief. Her mother rarely, if ever, got angry. Since the death of her father the two of them had been everything to each other. But it had been a close-run thing and probably a sign that seeing Valentine again was a bad idea. She had only just met him, and already he had caused her nothing but trouble.

Next day, the world seemed somehow brighter and sharper. She felt a lightness in her heart that was almost a giddiness. This faded as she realised she now had to face Peter and apologise.

He would be wonderful about it, of course. The fact that he was wholly good and kind made it all even worse. If only she could love him as she knew he loved her. They were, as her mother never tired of pointing out, unusually well-matched.

They had met during the first term, two years ago. As well as their teaching interests, they shared a love of walking and of music, literature and art. They came from similar humble backgrounds: Marion's father, now dead, had worked on the railways, while Peter's was a postman. His aim was to be the first postman's son to go to Eton, albeit in a professional capacity. He was determined to teach at the Great Public Schools, as he called them, from which poverty had barred him as a boy. Marion admired his ambition, but not his aspiration. Certainly not after the Glenlorne experience.

She headed into the college, hurrying along the green-tiled corridors with their herringbone wooden floors. She found Peter in the library, harmless in his pale blue pullover, frowning earnestly over his books. He looked delighted to see her, increasing her guilt a thousandfold.

'I'm so sorry about last night,' she began.

'Shhh!' said the librarian.

'Yes, it was a shame,' Peter whispered mildly. 'You missed the most marvellous Nanki-Poo.'

'*Shhhhhhh!*'

'Another time,' said Marion, not wanting to linger. Miss Golspie's class on Dr Froebel was about to start.

'Actually, are you free later? I have something to tell you.' Through his very clean round spectacles, Peter's pale eyes blazed with uncharacteristic excitement. 'Let's go to Jenners for tea,' he added, with equally uncharacteristic impulsiveness.

Jenners was Edinburgh's smartest department store, with restaurant prices to match. The something he had to tell must be important.

Round the corner of the bookstack, the librarian loomed. 'Do you *mind?*'

Marion was packing up her books at the end of the Froebel class when Miss Golspie dipped by. 'Enjoy that? You looked as if you did. Your hand was a blur throughout, making notes.'

Marion smiled at her teacher. 'What an amazing man. I had no idea he invented the nursery. And believed that every child has an inner life, which careful nurturing brings out.' Her words were tumbling over one another in her enthusiasm. 'I particularly loved his conviction that childhood is a proper, precious state in itself, not just a preparation for adulthood.' She had thought about Annie during that section of the lecture, and burned with indignation and pity for her. Annie's childhood was already over, if it had ever happened at all.

'Froebel's my favourite, I have to say.' Miss Golspie tossed an aquamarine scarf over the shoulder of a red velvet pinafore. 'It's all so unlikely, a German chap from the early nineteenth century having all those ideas about the importance of play and learning through nature. There are men now, a hundred years later, who still have no idea about that.'

Their eyes met. There was no doubt as to whom she was referencing, but Marion carefully did not react. She was not to be drawn down that road again.

Miss Golspie smiled. 'Could you come and see me later, in my office?' Her tone was casual. 'There's something I want to talk to you about.'

Marion watched the brightly clad figure leave and wondered at the coincidence. Peter too had something to tell her. Two people on the same day.

Later, Marion entered the principal's oak-panelled realm. The scent of Lapsang Souchong filled the air. 'Sit down, do. Tea?' Miss Golspie waved a cup.

'No thank you. I'm going to tea at Jenners after this, as it happens.'

'At Jenners! I'd better get straight to the point, then.' Miss Golspie looked at her through a pair of outsized lime-green reading glasses. She had many artist friends, one of whom had presumably made these. Perhaps the same one who had made the new cushion shaped like a pair of red lips. Marion stared at it as she settled into the squashy depths of the orange sofa.

'Lady Rose Leveson-Gower has written to me,' Miss Golspie announced. 'Her husband is the commanding admiral at Rosyth.'

Rosyth was the Royal Navy base in Edinburgh. Marion nodded in understanding of this eminence, but failed to see what it had to do with her.

'She wanted me to recommend someone to teach her daughter, Lady Mary, over the summer. I thought of you.'

'Me?' Marion stared at her. 'But you know how I feel about teaching aristocrats.'

Miss Golspie did not, as her pupil half feared, display any anger or impatience at this. 'Quite so,' she said briskly. 'You made it perfectly clear. And it is, of course, entirely up to you whether you take the job or not. I am merely the messenger. Lady Rose asked for my best pupil, which you undoubtedly are, and I thought the money would come in useful.'

Realising she was being ungracious, Marion reddened. It was, she could see, a huge compliment. The best pupil, when she was not even in the final year! And the money most definitely would be welcome, there was no question about that. But she didn't want to do it, even so. She looked up, intending to say so.

Miss Golspie was watching her over the lime-green glasses, her expression one of calm interest. 'So you'll think about it?'

Marion, about to deliver a categoric 'no', found herself reluctantly nodding instead. 'I'll think about it.'

Later, at Jenners, she and Peter sat amid silver teapots, groaning cake stands and potted palms. A little orchestra played waltzes. The evening was hot, and above the tinkle of china and conversation, teak ceiling fans stirred the soupy air. All you needed was a couple of elephants, Marion thought as she fanned herself with her napkin. She grinned as, right on cue, two broad-beamed Edinburgh matrons paraded past in stately pachyderm fashion.

Peter was pink with the heat. His pale hair stuck to his forehead. He reached for an egg sandwich. 'I've been offered a job,' he announced. 'A permanent teaching job.'

'That's *wonderful*, Peter!'

He took a bite and eyed her. 'It *is* rather good, isn't it?'

'Where? Eton?'

He shook his head. He was to be a junior classics master somewhere near Inverness. 'But it's a start.'

'Congratulations,' Marion said warmly, wondering why he was staring at her. He seemed anxious, for some reason.

'I wondered . . .' he said. 'That is to say, I wanted to ask . . .'

'What?' she urged. He had altered position, and the potted fern behind him now seemed to protrude from his head. It was hard not to laugh. 'Out with it, Peter! You're making me nervous.'

'Will you marry me?' Peter blurted.

Marion crashed her cup down into the saucer and gripped the

arms of her chair. She felt off balance, as if she had been drinking gin, not Earl Grey. Marry? She was only twenty-two. Life, with all its potential, stretched ahead like a shining road. 'But you're going to work at this school,' she said, stupidly.

'More tea, madam?' An obviously eavesdropping waitress hovered with a silver teapot.

'Yes! You'd come with me,' Peter said when she had gone. He looked relieved, as if he had let go of a burden. He bit happily into his egg sandwich. 'We'd live at the school.'

Marion, to whom the burden had been passed, imagined the shining road of her life disappearing up the drive of some stuffy establishment surrounded by mountains, cut off by lochs, very possibly with the likes of Dr Stone on its staff. And with Peter, whom she liked but could never love. There wasn't an atom of physical attraction there.

'What do you say?' He was smiling encouragingly; a piece of cress was lodged between his teeth.

She took a deep breath. 'I'm very flattered, Peter.'

She saw hope flash in his pale eyes and felt terrible. 'But the truth is,' she added hurriedly, 'I'm not thinking about marriage to anyone just yet. My work comes first and I've got another year of college to go.'

Peter looked down. 'I understand. Your work's very important to you. And you're such a good teacher, Marion. You're Miss Golspie's best student, everyone knows that.'

She felt moved. He must be hurt, but he was being so generous. He was such a good man. If only she could love him. But love didn't seem to work like that. The most suitable person wasn't necessarily the one who attracted you. As a pair of wide dark eyes glowed in her mind, she reddened.

They parted outside Jenners. She watched him walk off down Princes Street, gave him a few minutes and then set off home the back way. There was no danger of him seeing her there, and the back streets had cooling shadows.

As she passed the front of a pub, a familiar figure came out. 'Maid Marion!'

His appearance was too sudden for her to stop an instinctive smile of joy.

He was wearing the same clothes as yesterday. There was beard growth on his chin. The red scarf was still round his neck; the same blood-spattered shirt; the same mud-smeared jacket. But the energy she remembered was there too – the spark and the fizz and the black fire in his eyes. She was filled again with the sense that here was someone thrilling, unpredictable, exciting.

'How are you?' she asked. Better, by the looks of it. He had emerged from the pub with quite a spring in his step.

In reply, Valentine clutched his arm. 'It comes and goes,' he said, wincing. 'If you could help me back to my rooms, that would be great.'

She stared, wanting to laugh. He was ridiculously audacious. He seemed unabashed, however, staring back imploringly with wide, round eyes. 'Please?' he begged, looking suddenly so like a helpless little boy that resistance was useless. She groaned, and gave in.

'What were you doing in the pub?' she asked as she helped him along. The memory of her lost shillings was still raw. It had been embarrassing to let Peter pay for the tea instead of splitting the cost, especially after what she had said to him.

He had taken her arm and was leaning on her heavily, emitting the occasional soft moan as if in great pain. 'Pub?'

Marion half turned, pointing with her free hand. 'That one. Whose public bar I just saw you coming out of.'

He pushed a hand through his uncombed hair. 'Oh, *that* pub,' he said, as if seeing it for the first time. 'We weren't in the bar, we were upstairs. Having a meeting.'

'We?' She looked at him closely, not entirely convinced.

He stared boldly back, his dark gaze unflinching. 'The university Communist Party.'

'The pub lets you have Communist Party meetings upstairs?' It sounded most unlikely to her.

His hair flopped forward with the vigour of his nod. 'Absolutely.

Where we plot the death of imperialism and the epoch of international proletarian revolution. When men and women who struggle in their workplaces and in their communities for the defeat of capitalism will finally achieve a more just and equal society.'

The drama and force of this speech, and the dazzling smile with which it ended, had the effect of stunning her from all further thought. By the time she had recovered her faculties and was framing more detailed questions, Valentine had begun to sing. It wasn't a song Marion recognised, but the tune was catchy and the lyrics striking. Something about workers arising from their slumbers. She wondered what time Valentine had risen from his slumbers. He looked as if he had slept in his clothes.

The song had many verses, during which time they approached the university area. The streets became grander, more neoclassical, all domes and porticoes, fluted columns and elegant wide steps.

'So comrades come rally/And the last fight let us face/The Internationale/Unites the human race,' Valentine finished, with a wave of a clenched fist. 'Ooh,' he groaned, as if suddenly remembering he was meant to be injured.

As they passed a porter's lodge, a bowler-hatted figure within rose to his feet.

'Mackenzie!' Valentine slapped the college servant convivially on his dark-suited shoulder. 'And how are you this fine evening?'

The college servant looked unmoved by this blast of charm. 'I'd be better if you'd pay those fines you owe, sir.' He rolled a jaundiced eye up and down Marion. 'No young ladies staying the night again either.'

Flashing him an uneasy smile, Valentine hurried off across the lawns, his limp miraculously eased. Marion hurried after him. 'What does he mean, no young ladies staying the night again?'

'Haven't the faintest idea. Got me confused with someone else,' Valentine threw over his shoulder as he picked up speed. They were practically running now. The grassy quadrangle was surrounded with imposing grey buildings. He hurried up the steps into one of them – a hall of residence, Marion guessed, seeing pigeonholes in the hallway.One seemed particularly stuffed with cards and invitations.

Valentine paused and shoved the entire handful into his pocket before clattering up a flight of wooden stairs.

His room was disgusting. A wardrobe door hung open, revealing a confusion of papers. His clothes were on the floor, all looking more dirty and creased even than those he had been beaten up in. There were newspapers everywhere, empty bottles lying on their sides along the skirting board, heaps of books and overflowing ashtrays. Above it all hung the horrible vinegar stench of stale smoke.

'Can't you open a window?' she asked, using the challenge to conceal her awkwardness. What was she doing here? She had vaguely intended to leave him at the porter's lodge, but somehow she had followed him in.

He pushed back the half-drawn curtains. The way he rattled and struggled at the pane suggested this was the first time he had ever tried. She went over to help. 'You have to move this back,' she said, operating the lever holding the sash down. 'It won't open otherwise.'

He seemed as unabashed by his lack of practical knowledge as he was about the general mess and lack of facilities. 'I don't have any tea,' he said, rummaging in the bottom of a half-open drawer, 'but I can offer you this.' He produced a bottle of whisky and waved it at her.

She looked at it doubtfully. 'Haven't you got any glasses? Cups?'

He shook his head, airily. 'They're a bourgeois construct. We'll just have to drink straight from the bottle.'

He passed it to her. She braced herself and took a swig. It was even worse than what they had drunk in the pub, but after the initial scorch of contact, a warm, relaxed feeling spread through her. Her awkwardness vanished. She looked around, taking it all in.

Beyond the mess, the prevailing aesthetic was Soviet culture. Posters of muscular peasants waving spades or sitting on tractors were stuck haphazardly on the walls.

'Do sit down.' Valentine interrupted her thoughts.

She glanced around and laughed. 'Where? You don't have any chairs.' They, too, were a bourgeois construct, presumably.

'Plenty of room here.' He was sitting on the bed, which was unmade, the sheets twisted, the blanket half-disappeared underneath. He patted the mattress beside him invitingly. 'Come on.'

The outrage she felt was mild compared to the accompanying violent pang of longing. She backed against the wall, folding her arms tightly, trying to appear insouciant. 'No young ladies staying the night again, remember.'

He rose to his feet, exasperated. 'He got me confused with someone else, I tell you.'

'All the same, I'm going.'

He was close to her now and, quite suddenly, he kissed her. No one had ever kissed her like this, with a tenderness that became urgency. She clung to him. When her lips left his, they felt twice their usual size. His already were, of course, thanks to the beating. 'Didn't that hurt?' she asked, when the power to speak returned.

'Not at all. Desire is an anaesthetic. Don't you find?'

'I'm . . . not sure.'

His dark eyes had a wolfish gleam. 'Don't you want to find out?'

She found herself being led back towards the twisted bed. Before she knew it, he had pulled her down and nudged her knees apart.

'Stop!' cried Marion, sitting up with difficulty. Her cheeks burned and her heart crashed in her chest. She glanced at him hotly from under her hair.

He grinned at her from the pillow, hands behind his head. 'Sorry. My mistake. I thought you were an independent woman. Making your own decisions.'

'I am!' she said, crossly. 'And one of my independent decisions is not to let you do that.'

She buttoned herself up and, flustered, stepped over the rubbish towards the door.

There was a small stone bust on the mantelpiece. Passing, she glanced at it. It was of a stern-looking bearded man.

'Vladimir Ilyich,' said Valentine, still lounging on the bed.

'Who?'

'Lenin. The greatest revolutionary leader the world has ever seen.'

She stared at the carved face. 'Really? Why was he so great?'

Lenin had been in charge when the czar and his family were shot in the cellar. She recalled the ghastly details: the diamonds sewn in the corsets, the girls' shorn hair, the frightened little boy.

'It would,' Valentine said loftily, 'take me far too long to explain.'

She glanced at him suspiciously, remembering the Fascist-Communist discussion. How much did Valentine really know about revolutionary politics?

'What was so great about murdering the Romanovs?' she asked.

'They were enemies of the people.'

'But why?' They had been teenage girls, most of them. The thought made her stomach churn.

'They just . . . were.'

She was about to impatiently accuse him of ignorant dogmatism when Miss Golspie slid into her mind, glowing scarves, green glasses and all. She recalled the conversation earlier that afternoon in which she had declared herself uninterested in teaching aristocrats. Perhaps she was guilty of dogmatism herself.

She stared into Lenin's sharp little eyes. Perhaps she should take the job with the Leveson-Gowers. There were good reasons to do so: the money, the compliment from Miss Golspie it represented and all those earlier, ingenious arguments about how the children of the wealthy needed to know about the poor, for the benefit of society in general. She considered the Bolshevik leader's hard, intransigent face. Had that happened in Russia, perhaps Lenin wouldn't have been the greatest revolutionary leader the world had ever seen. If indeed he had been.

Chapter Five

She took the job with the Leveson-Gowers. It was a beautiful daily walk along the lochside to Rosyth, with the Forth flashing silver through the trees. The path through the woods was fringed with wild flowers: blue cranesbill, pink campion, white stitchwort, herb Robert. Marion loved the expectant way they turned their faces up as she passed. She liked to pick them and put them in her hat.

'You're working for the oppressors of the poor,' Valentine had sneered, predictably. 'The aristocratic overlords. The capitalist running dogs.'

Marion rolled her eyes. 'They're not like that at all,' she insisted. The Leveson-Gowers, in fact, seemed to lead a simple life. Good manners were high on the agenda and she had never heard a haughty remark from any of them. Nor had she heard anyone swear. None of which could be said of Valentine.

'They've got no idea how most people live,' he blustered. Marion looked him sternly in the eye.

'Yes they have.' In line with Miss Golspie's exhortations, she took her new responsibilities seriously. Her new pupil, Lady Mary Leveson-Gower, was, as a consequence, fully appraised of recent scientific, political and social developments.

'Don't you feel like a servant?' he taunted, next.

She laughed. 'Actually, the servants at Admiralty House don't feel like servants.'

He stared. 'What do you mean?'

'They're far grander than the family.'

It was strange but true that those working for the Leveson-Gowers seemed to appropriate their employers' status to themselves. The cook especially never missed an opportunity to trumpet the family's grand connections. As Marion passed through the kitchen on her way in and out of the house, Cook regaled her with gossipy snippets. Did Marion know that Lady Rose Leveson-Gower's sister was the Duchess of York? She did not. Did Marion know that Lady Rose called her sister 'Buffy'? She did not care. Did Marion know that Lady Rose's husband, the Hon William Spencer Leveson Gower, was 'Wisp' to his friends? Actually, this was quite funny. 'Wisp' suggested insubstantial, and the Admiral was easily seventeen stone.

According to Cook, Lady Rose could have done even better than the Commanding Admiral at Rosyth. This was not hard to believe. Lady Rose was a lush, romantic beauty with a full, oval face and skin like thick cream. She had elegant dark brows, a slim, straight nose and shining blonde hair. Her eyes were especially extraordinary – a dewy violet.

'Oh yes!' Cook's round eyes bulged with excitement. 'They say Her Ladyship was proposed to more than twenty times! They say that she used to be admired by *the Prince of Wales himself*!'

'Gosh,' said Marion, knowing Cook would completely miss the irony.

Mrs Crawford, agog for details about aristocratic goings-on, loved all this, however. And so Marion told her as much as she could remember. After her mother's despair at Peter's departure – she had never known about the proposal, fortunately – it was a relief to see her basking in the warm sun of near-royal association. No friend, neighbour or butcher's queue was ignorant of her daughter's new proximity to the great and the good.

Her daughter's new proximity to Valentine was rather less cause for celebration. Mrs Crawford was not only impervious to his charm but resented his familiar manner. Peter would never have dreamed of breezing in without warning, addressing her as 'Mrs C' and helping himself to whatever was in the larder. Marion would listen to her complaints while thinking that there were many other things Valentine did that Peter would never have dreamed of, all of them entirely delightful.

She had still not given in to him, although by now it was virtually a technicality. As they kissed, his hand would find its way beneath her blouse or up her skirt almost without her realising. She had never really believed in love before, not in the head-spinning, lightning-bolt sense of romantic novels. But now she wondered whether heart-thumping passion was real, after all. She would drift dreamily about the house, her mother's grumbles having as little impact as water on the back of the proverbial duck.

'He talks all the time about the working classes but he's never done a day's work in his life.'

While Marion thought this exact same thing, she felt compelled to defend him. 'He's a student, Mother.'

'But what are his intentions?' demanded Mrs Crawford.

The defeat of capitalism would obviously not be an acceptable answer. Marion turned to bluster instead. 'Mother! This is 1932. Girls don't need men with intentions. They have intentions of their own.'

But Valentine's intentions were not of the sort Mrs Crawford would approve of. The fact that she did not approve of him either drove the two of them for walks in the hills in all weathers. Here the intentions revealed themselves on sunny beds of heather, or in caves during sudden bursts of rain. Marion fended them off – with increasing reluctance, it had to be said.

One afternoon they had taken a picnic and were following a sandy path through scented heather and sun-warmed boulders. Their way wound up past silver birch trees and flaming yellow gorse. They stopped for lunch under cerulean skies, in which birds wheeled and a warm sun shone. Below them stretched the Firth of Forth, its surface wrinkled like blue silk and shuddering at the touch of the wind.

'I've got a present for you,' Valentine announced. She was surprised. She was the gift-giver, normally. Fresh shirts, a new pair of trousers, two second-hand chairs for his room.

He rummaged in his jacket pocket and produced a brown paper bag containing something hard and rectangular. 'I hope you'll find it useful.' His face was serious but he was obviously suppressing laughter.

Marion slid out a small book with a pale grey cover. *The Complete Book of Etiquette.*

'Now that you're moving in such elevated circles, you need to know which class of butter knife to use with which class of bishop.'

She knew it was victory of a sort that he had lowered his attacks to jokes. And this was a good one. She turned a couple of pages and laughed. 'A gentleman should *never* wear a lounge suit on the beach.'

'Only black tie.' Valentine snorted. 'Complete with spats and a top hat.'

'And absolutely *no* jewellery on the dunes.'

'Perish the thought. Ever seen a tiara at Blackpool?'

'Ha ha!'

'Hee hee!'

'No one, unless they be a complete snob, will think the worse of you for inadvertently using the wrong fork at table.'

'That's a relief. Give it here, my turn. Oh, here we go. To refer to someone as a gent or a bloke is very bad form. One should always strive to avoid the repetitive use of slang and meaningless ejaculations.' Valentine hooted. *'Meaningless ejaculations!'*

Marion had the book now. 'Nearly everyone knows the story of the two men who spent twenty years on a desert island not speaking to each other because they had not been introduced.' She wiped her streaming eyes. 'Do they?'

'Oh, absolutely.'

'Ha ha.'

Valentine was unpacking the picnic, laying it out on the rock. There were hard-boiled eggs and lemonade in the rucksack, and slices of cake swiped from the larder when her mother's back was turned. Mrs Crawford, who had regularly plied Peter with her baking, would never have allowed Valentine access to her Victoria sponge.

'On entering a restaurant, the senior man of the party will go in first so he can bespeak a table.'

Marion placed one of the sandwich packets on her head. 'An erect carriage and dignified bearing are central to correct form.'

Valentine indicated the boulder. 'Would madam like to be seated?'

'Why, thank you, kind sir!'

After lunch, they lay stretched out. The warm air was scented and heady as wine. When Valentine began to kiss her, she rolled away. She watched his face slump in disappointment then stiffen in surprise as she unbuttoned her dress and removed her underwear. She stood above him, stretching in the sunshine.

He stared up at her. 'Are you sure?'

She nodded. Never had she been so sure about anything.

Afterwards, they lay in the heather. Suddenly curious, she asked him about his childhood and he told her he had been to a succession of boarding schools, many of which had expelled him.

'Didn't your mother mind?' She could hardly imagine what Mrs Crawford would have said.

'She hardly noticed.' His tone was scornful. 'Too busy running around Monte Carlo with her second husband.'

It sounded like a life from another world. She returned to the subject of most interest. 'So why did the schools throw you out?'

He waved his cigarette in the air. 'Let me count the ways. First we refused to join the Officer's Training Corps. Then we painted a statue of the king with red paint.'

'We?'

'Me and Esmond,' he said, as if the name would immediately resonate with her.

'Esmond?'

'My cousin. We were at school together. One of the schools, anyway. He got me into Communism, in fact.' That he hero-worshipped this Esmond was obvious.

'On Armistice Day, we put anti-war leaflets in all the prayer books. They fluttered down during the Two Minutes' Silence, causing a row of unimaginable proportions.'

'I can imagine. But why go to those extremes?'

'Because public schools perpetuate an evil and outdated class system' was the answer. His glib tone infuriated her. He seemed to have no awareness of his privilege.

'Slums do the same,' she snapped. 'But unfortunately they're not so easy to leave.'

Valentine propped himself up on his elbow. 'Don't be so pompous. You're working for the Duchess of York's sister.'

'Only for the summer. Some of us have to make money, you know. We don't all have privilege handed to us on a plate.'

'Some of us are using our privilege to raise the consciousness of the workers. Not pretending to be egalitarian feminists whilst becoming lickspittles to the aristocracy.'

She gasped. 'How *dare* you?'

His laughter was low, triumphant. 'You're beautiful when you're angry.'

She glared at him, but felt herself melt. He was so absurdly handsome, and these arguments excited both of them. She rolled onto her back and only pretended to fend him off when he leaped on her.

'And how are you getting along with Mary?' the much-admired Lady Rose enquired charmingly after a few weeks had gone by. It was the end of the day and she had called Marion into the sitting room, whose air pulsed with perfume from the vases on every shining surface. Lady Rose loved flowers, and there were roses in every size and shade of pink.

'Very well,' Marion said, and meant it. Mary was a delicate, fair-haired child who compensated for a lack of physical vigour with a powerful interest in her lessons. 'She's a clever girl,' she added.

'She tells me you've been teaching her about the suffragettes.' Lady Rose toyed with a long rope of huge pearls.

Marion looked at her. Was Lady Rose shocked? 'Modern women need to know about the modern world,' she said firmly. 'We were talking about the vote and I felt she should know that it was largely through the suffragettes that women eventually got it.'

The violet eyes twinkled. 'Indeed. It appears you have quite fired her up. She has been sternly lecturing her father on the principle of equal rights.' Lady Rose gave one of her silvery laughs. 'And, of course, she's very taken with the spectre stalking Europe. She's done some simply terrifying drawings of it.'

Mary had indeed been struck by the opening of *The Communist Manifesto*, although her questions had been less about dialectical materialism than what the stalking spectre looked like. Was it a skeleton?

'And she's been telling me all about those clever boffins in Cambridge splitting the atom.'

'Cockcroft and Walton, yes.' Mary, who had a scientific bent, had been fascinated by the sensational recent experiment's power and speed. 'Had you thought about sending Mary to school?' she asked. It seemed the obvious thing, once she herself had returned to college in the autumn.

But now it seemed she really had said something shocking. Lady Rose's beautiful violet eyes widened in amazement. For a second, her lovely oval face went blank before it resumed its customary charming expression. 'Goodness, Miss Crawford. I hardly think that is necessary, do you? When I was growing up my sisters and I only had a governess. And we all married well.' Lady Rose paused. 'One of us *very* well,' she added, significantly.

Marion stared at Lady Rose. Had no one told her that marrying well, as she put it, was no longer the route to an interesting life? If indeed it ever had been. Women could take degrees now, have careers. Lady Rose was stuck in the Dark Ages.

A week or so later, Mary greeted her governess in the schoolroom full of excitement. 'Great news, Miss Crawford! Aunt Peter is coming here tomorrow.'

This strange name suggested a mannish woman in a trouser suit and monocle. 'Lovely,' she said. She picked up the slim volume on the table. 'Now, are you sitting comfortably? Shall we see what Alan Breck and David Balfour do next?'

They were soon absorbed in *Kidnapped*. Would she have been a Jacobite? Mary asked her governess.

'Most definitely not. They were terribly misled.'

'I would have followed Bonnie Prince Charlie!' Mary said fervently.

'He let his people down,' Marion pointed out. 'They gave him their hearts, but he betrayed them and went abroad. He never came back.'

Mary reflected gloomily on this poor example of royal behaviour. 'I'm glad princes don't behave like that any more.'

Later, Marion picked up her hat for her walk back. The morning-gathered flowers lay limply over the brim. Lady Rose appeared, apparently about to go out. She wore a perfect pearl-grey cloche, trimmed with a matching feather. 'Miss Crawford!' she exclaimed. 'I'm so very glad to have caught you.'

Marion paused, cautiously. Had her uncompromising views on Charles Edward Stuart been transmitted? Some Scots, definitely, would find them controversial.

'We have visitors tomorrow,' said Lady Rose.

Marion nodded, the limp adornment on her hat brim nodding with her. 'Mary mentioned Aunt Peter.'

To her surprise, Lady Rose burst out laughing. 'Her real name is Elizabeth. The children couldn't pronounce it so they called her Peter.'

Aunt Elizabeth. There was only one Aunt Elizabeth Marion could think of. The most famous Aunt Elizabeth on the planet.

Lady Rose's blue eyes twinkled. 'These days, of course, we must all call her Her Royal Highness the Duchess of York.'

Marion waited to be told that, as the family was dealing with royalty, her presence was not required. Well, good. She could use the time studying for the new term in autumn.

'I would like you to meet them,' Lady Rose concluded.

Chapter Six

Next day, Mary was in unusually tearing spirits, which Marion happily indulged with games on the lawn. Back in the house for elevenses, they were cut off at the pass by one of the housemaids. 'Yer wanted in the drawing room.'

Remembering, suddenly, the royal visitors, Marion looked down at her frock. It was wet at the hem and bore magnificent grass stains. She raised her chin. They must take her as they found her.

The drawing room was long and rectangular. Pictures in gold frames hung from the rail, and bay windows at the end overlooked the sea.

Lady Rose wafted up to her, smiling. 'Miss Crawford! Come and meet my sister.' She found herself taken by the arm. 'It's Your Royal Highness when you first meet her,' Lady Rose went on. 'But ma'am after that is fine. Ma'am as in jam, remember. Not ma'am as in smarm.'

The Duchess of York sat on one of the window seats. She looked much like her sister, although with darker, stronger brows, darker hair and a wider face. Her skin had a porcelain perfection and her eyes were piercingly blue. Her hands and feet were as small as a doll's, the former sparkling with diamonds, the latter in pale, high-heeled shoes. Her dress was of blue chiffon, and ropes of pearls gleamed softly against it.

Marion felt suddenly acutely aware of her stained skirt and her stout, serviceable shoes.

The duchess exuded an impish glee. 'The famous Miss Crawford!' She spoke in an excited, high-pitched voice, with emphasis. 'Rose has been telling me how far you *walk* every day! Simply *miles*! You're as strong as a *horse*, she says.'

It was difficult to know what to make of such exuberance. 'I enjoy walking,' Marion replied. 'Your Royal Highness,' she added quickly, to which the duchess gave a roguish, couldn't-matter-less wave of the hand.

'And the countryside round here is *very* beautiful. O Caledonia stern and wild!' The girlish little figure in blue leaned forward. 'We Scots must stick together!'

Marion tried not to look surprised. She hadn't even realised the duchess was Scottish. She didn't sound it.

'I daresay you've passed lots of absolutely beastly exams, Miss Crawford?'

'Some,' Marion admitted. 'Marm. *Mam.*'

'I only ever took one exam. In a *horrid* place called Hackney. They made me eat tapioca and it still makes me *boil* with rage to think that I forced down that rubbish for nothing! I didn't pass, you see,' the duchess confided. 'Whisper it soft, but intellectual giant I am not.'

She was like something out of P. G. Wodehouse, Marion thought, just as, right on cue, the duchess waved and called, 'Bertie!'

Marion turned. Bertie was a slim, dark-haired man talking to Admiral Leveson-Gower. He hurried over immediately. He too was exquisitely dressed, in a perfectly cut tweed suit. Smoke streamed from the cigarette between his thin fingers.

He looked at the duchess adoringly. 'Darling?'

'This is the amazing Miss Crawford!' enthused his wife. 'She walks literally *hundreds* of miles every day and has passed *thousands* of fiendish exams!'

Prince Albert seemed quite accustomed to his wife's exaggerations.

'Good m-m-morning, Miss Crawford,' he said, after several aborted efforts to achieve the phrase.

His wife regarded him gleefully. 'I was just telling her how irredeemably *thick* we both are!'

'Oh, terribly d-dim,' agreed the duke. 'I was p-p-placed sixty-seventh out of sixty-eight in my class at Osborne Naval College.'

'But it wasn't his fault.' The duchess turned to Marion. 'My husband's youth was *blighted* by a succession of elderly tutors. Is that not so, Bertie?'

The duke drew hard on his cigarette and nodded. 'Madame Bricka was the f-f-first. She'd taught my m-m-mother when she was a little girl, but she was quite o-o – ' He started to cough.

'Old, Bertie.' His wife reached and tugged the sleeve of his suit. 'Remember Mr Logue. Let's-go-gathering-heather-with-the-glad-brigade-of-grand-dragoons.'

This evidently was a breathing exercise of some sort. Marion watched the duke attempt to repeat it. 'Glad brigade of g-g-g— Oh, *blast*!!'

His wife kept up her reassuring smile. 'Remember to *breathe*.'

The duke remembered to breathe. It seemed to work. 'And very fat. Always hanging around with her blasted F-F-French and German primers.'

The duchess was giggling. 'And what about the one with the *huge* moustache?'

The duke took another deep drag of his cigarette, sucking his thin cheeks into the bony hollows of his face. 'That was H-Hansell. Wore tweeds and smoked a pipe and was a c-c-con— Oh, *blast! Blast!*'

'Conservative?' the duchess supplied serenely. 'Breathe *deeply*, Bertie!'

The duke shot her a grateful glance, then tried again. 'No, a con . . . con . . . *connoisseur*. Of ec-ec-ec . . . Oh *blast it*!'

'Ecclesiastical architecture' took some time to establish. The struggle didn't seem to upset the duchess in the least. 'And tell Miss Crawford about the one who ate *tadpoles*!'

'Oh yes! Mr H-h-h . . .'

'Hua!'

'That's right. My brothers and I went fishing in the pond at Sandringham. We got lots of t-t-tadpoles and got the cook to serve them to him as a s-s-savoury, on t-t-toast.'

'*Bertie!*' The duchess was shrieking with laughter now. 'What must Miss Crawford *think*?'

*

Mrs Crawford was full of questions when Marion arrived back home. 'What was Her Royal Highness wearing?'

'Blue,' said Marion shortly. She felt exhausted. The royal visit had necessitated a longer than usual day, which she was glad to see the end of.

'*Blue?*' repeated her mother. 'Is that all?'

Marion obediently summoned up the details. Once the initial excitement had subsided, she had noticed that, for a young woman, the duchess had dressed like someone much older. Her frock, while of luxurious material, was unfashionable; no doubt because she was plump and the flat-chested, drop-waist style would not have flattered her. Her mother hung on to every word.

'Hair?' she demanded, when the clothes report was concluded.

That had been slightly old-fashioned too: a fringe with a bun at the back. Marion thought this a missed opportunity. The duchess, presumably, could afford the very finest hairdressers.

'Were the little princesses there?' Mrs Crawford wanted to know next.

Marion suppressed a yawn. 'They were at Balmoral with the king.'

'Balmoral!' Mrs Crawford looked dazzled.

'And the duke? What was he like?'

Marion made a final effort. 'A side parting that looked done with a ruler and shoes that shone like mirrors. Oh, and he has a speech impediment.'

'Good heavens! A stutter?'

Marion could have kicked herself for opening up this fresh line of enquiry. She edged towards the sitting-room door. 'I'm afraid that's all I can remember, Ma. Our brush with royalty is over.'

The Leveson-Gower household gradually recovered from the excitement. The housemaids twittered for a few days afterwards and Cook repeatedly relayed her short conversation with the duchess. 'I asked her how old the princesses were now,' she went on, like a gramophone record with the needle stuck. 'And Her Royal Highness just looked at me, like I'm looking at you now, and said "Six and one!" Six and one!' Cook shook her fleshy jowls in wonder. 'Six and one!'

*

One afternoon when Marion was about to leave, Lady Rose appeared in the hallway. 'May I have a word, Miss Crawford? In the sitting room?'

Lady Rose's sitting room was filled with an abundance of roses. The scent was sweet and strong and mingled with cedarwood from the fire, which burned even on the hottest days.

Sinking gracefully on to a silk-striped sofa, her ladyship tucked a strand of dark gold hair behind an ear. 'It seems,' she said, in her soft voice, 'that you have made an impression, Miss Crawford.'

'Impression?'

'My sister would like you to undertake the education of her daughters.'

Marion stared at her. Her mind had gone absolutely blank.

Lady Rose flopped back against the sofa and burst into peals of laughter. 'Miss Crawford! Your face!'

The warmth and the flower scent seemed suddenly overpowering. 'You mean,' Marion asked slowly, 'your sister the Duchess of York?'

'Indeed I do,' twinkled Lady Rose.

'Her daughters Princess Elizabeth and Princess Margaret?'

'The Princess Margaret *Rose*, yes,' corrected Lady Rose. 'My sister thinks you would be perfect.' The diamonds in her ears glittered in the sunlight coming through the windows. 'What do you say, Miss Crawford?'

Chapter Seven

Marion took a deep, stiffening breath and tried to gather her whirling thoughts. There was no question, obviously. She had other plans, entirely different ones. 'I'm very honored to be asked – '

'Obviously!'

' – but I'll have to turn the duchess's offer down.'

'What?' All colour drained from Lady Rose's face. 'Turn it . . . down?' Her tone was one of absolute disbelief.

'I have other commitments,' Marion said, steadily. 'My college course. After which I intend to work with the poor.'

It was Lady Rose's turn to look amazed. 'The . . . ?' The word wouldn't come out. She tried again. 'The . . . ?' Her eyes bulged and she swallowed.

'In the slums,' Marion added, for good measure.

A silence followed, interrupted with occasional snaps from the fire. Lady Rose stared into it. Then she turned her head to Marion. Her expression was calm again, even if her eyes held traces of shock.

'Miss Crawford. You clearly feel you have a vocation, but what higher vocation could there be than serving your king and his family? What greater honour or more important task than to be shaping the young minds of the next generation of imperial rulers?'

Marion stared at her. This was an unexpectedly skilful move. She had played the commitment card, but Lady Rose had played it back, acing it with flattery. Her words also held echoes of Miss Golspie. *You should teach the wealthy.* But she had spent the summer doing that. She had done her duty.

'You would enjoy living in London,' Lady Rose added, moving

to secure her advantage. 'A pretty young girl like you would have a wonderful time there.'

Marion suppressed a pang of longing. The fact that Valentine came from the capital made her wish she knew it better. But there would be time to travel later, in the vague future. For now, her plans did not include working with royalty. Her vocation was with society's exact opposite extreme.

'I'm afraid I can't,' she said, firmly.

Lady Rose stood up. The violet eyes were resigned. 'Very well, Miss Crawford. I will let my sister know.'

As she walked back through the trees, Marion reran the amazing conversation through her mind. Had she done the right thing? From her own point of view, definitely yes. As for Lady Rose and the Yorks, the inconvenience of her refusal would surely be tempered by the knowledge that every other governess on the planet would jump at the chance.

Her mother, on the other hand, would be devastated. A cold dread slithered through Marion's stomach at the thought.

Mrs Crawford's interest in the royal family had recently become a mania. She had hung portraits of them in the sitting room and filled several scrapbooks – large, home-made brown-paper affairs held together with string – with pictures cut from newspapers. The Little Princesses had a scrapbook all to themselves.

No, she could not go home yet. Her mother would sense her guilt and cross-examine her with a barrister's ruthlessness. She needed time to compose herself.

On the edge of the woods Marion hesitated. The weather was hot and close, with a thunderous weight to the air. Between the rasping, restless leaves, the light was a dirty yellow.

She would, she decided, go and see Valentine. He was not expecting her, but it would be a surprise. She would not tell him about the Yorks; not yet, anyway. There was no need: lacking her mother's perception, he was unlikely to suspect anything, while volunteering the information would only invite his triumphal glee.

By the time she reached the city, great black towers of cloud had gathered in the sky. All hell was clearly about to break loose. She hurried down Princes Street. She needed to get inside with all speed. The same thought had obviously occurred to everyone else. People were casting doubtful looks upward before redoubling their pace.

The rain fell faster and faster. In no time at all it was a heavy grey curtain, drumming on the pavements and gurgling down the gutters. Marion's hat, soaked through, hung over her face, irredeemably ruined, with soggy flowers hanging off the end. Her hair stuck to her neck and her skirts clung to her legs. The water in her shoes bubbled and squelched and her heels skidded on the slippery stones.

Few other people were in the streets now. The rain had made it so dark that the few passing vehicles had switched on their headlights. They shone like yellow eyes through the hissing rain. Above, the thunder rolled and crashed.

Eventually, the university came into view, its outlines grey and vague in the downpour. Still holding on to her ruined hat, Marion ran across the wet grass, feet squelching, heels sinking in the mud. The great steps of the central building poured like a waterfall.

She ran down the passage and up the wooden stairs. His door loomed before her. She twisted the knob and threw it open.

Her merry salutation died in her throat. Two people lay on the bed amid the familiar twisted sheets. One was Valentine, eyes closed in ecstasy as he ground his body between a pair of white thighs.

She stared, frozen to the spot. But something moved on her face, something warm. A hot tear was slowly threading down her cheek.

Chapter Eight

It was like falling into a void. Like drowning, over and over again. Then, after the black despair, came a fiery ache in her heart, which hurt when she moved. It was, she realised, anger. It was there last thing at night, when finally, briefly, she went to sleep, and back in the morning when, heavy-eyed, she woke up.

The anger was largely directed at herself. She was a fool. And Valentine was a fraud. He cared nothing for the masses, only himself. She never wanted to see him again. Let him rot along with all the other entitled, pretentious pseudo-socialists. So much for tearing down the citadels of the bourgeoisie. What he really wanted to do was tear off their knickers.

Her mother, to whom an edited version of events had been given, did not help. 'I *told* you so,' Mrs Crawford said, rubbing great handfuls of salt in Marion's wounds. 'I *never* trusted him.'

Her indignation was given added vehemence by the discovery of the job her daughter had turned down. She blamed Valentine for this too, and there was no reason not to let her.

Marion buried herself in her books, preparing for the new term. But it was hard to concentrate. Her mother's criticisms and Valentine's betrayal made Edinburgh a difficult place to live. Out in the city, every street reminded her of her shame and humiliation, while home, formerly a haven, was full of frozen silences and martyrish sighs. The portraits of the royal family did not help matters. They looked down from the walls with blue eyes full of rebuke. Her shattered spirits meant that visiting Annie, and Grassmarket, was out of the question. She simply did not have the strength.

The urge to escape, temporarily at least, grew within her. In her desperation, she was even thinking about Peter; perhaps his offer of marriage was still open. But, quite apart from the romantic aspects, was a boarding school in the Highlands really the answer?

The job with the Yorks, so easily refused, now seemed to have had distinct possibilities. She could have gone to London, at least for a while. And it would have been exactly the sort of job Miss Golspie had recommended at the beginning of the summer. *You should teach the wealthy.* Lady Rose had reiterated it. *What greater honour or more important task than to be shaping the young minds of the next generation of imperial rulers?*

A missed opportunity, then. But it was too late now. Someone else would have been appointed. As her mother never tired of saying, the whole world would want to look after the famous Little Princesses.

Marion was mulling miserably, once again, on these gloomy reflections when, to her utter amazement, Valentine appeared one afternoon, letting himself into their house as if nothing had happened. He had, through deliberate management or, more likely, good luck, chosen a time when her mother was out.

She was sitting with her teaching manuals at the little fold-down table. The sitting room was too small to have one up all the time. When Valentine flopped down in Mrs Crawford's fireside armchair and lit a cigarette, she was too surprised to stop him. He regarded her with a wide, earnest gaze. 'I don't want to lose you,' he said.

The wild urge to laugh gripped her, mixed with a longing to hit him with a vase. 'It's a bit late for that, isn't it?' she said, as calmly as she could. 'I caught you with someone else.'

'Yes, but that doesn't affect anything.'

She blinked, disbelieving. *'Doesn't affect anything?'*

'It's possible to love two people at the same time.'

'What!'

'I call it "rethinking conventional relationships."' His smile was bright and eager. 'A new way of loving, for the modern age.'

She felt her mouth fall open.

'I can love both of you,' he went on, as if it were the simplest thing in the world. 'Why not?'

Marion was lost for words. Someone else, however, was anything but.

'Get out!' It was her mother who had spoken. Neither of them had heard her come in. Mrs Crawford, radiating fury in the doorway, appeared like some vengeful creature from legend. She glared at Valentine with glittering eyes. 'You've done enough damage,' she snarled.

Valentine did not need telling twice. He fled, taking his new ways of loving with him.

'Good riddance to bad rubbish!' Mrs Crawford yelled after him, not caring, for once, what the neighbours might say. The door slammed. A picture slid sideways on the wall. It was one of the new ones, of the queen.

'This was on the mat. Must just have arrived in the post.' Her mother pushed something into her hand. 'Looks important. Apart from the mud, that is. Your friend managed to stomp all over it as he came.'

'He's not my friend.' She took the envelope crossly. As well as the advertised black boot-print, it bore an embossed coronet. Marion opened it and pulled out two thick, smooth pages covered in large, looping handwriting . . . The address was in embossed capitals: 'The Royal Lodge, Windsor Great Park.'

She read it, and her sense of unreality deepened. 'It's from the Duchess of York,' she said slowly.

Mrs Crawford's fury became violent excitement. 'What does she want? What does it say?'

Why not come to us for a month, and see how you like us, and we like you? the duchess had written.

She was being given a second chance after all.

PART TWO

145 PICCADILLY

Chapter Nine

Marion stared out of the window as the train thundered south through the countryside. Dark shaggy hedges and heavy green trees bordered the rolling gold meadows of late summer. The trackside was gay with yellow ragwort and purple berberis, overlaid with the rags of engine steam. Marion wondered if she would know when they crossed the border. Would she feel a tug within? A sign to the true-bred Scotswoman that she had left her native land and was in alien territory, the country of the English?

Above, on the rack, sat her suitcase. It contained mostly old clothes. Her pale blue coat was worn as well. New things had been beyond their budget; the royal family were not paying much either. Her mother had wanted to buy patterns for ballgowns. 'I'll be working, Mother,' Marion had teased her. 'Not dancing. And for only four weeks, it's not worth making anything new. Besides, if they wanted me in smart clothes they should have paid me smart money.'

They were in fact paying even less than Lady Rose had, as Marion was living in. She would have a room in the Yorks' weekend home – Royal Lodge at Windsor – and in their house in Piccadilly during the week.

'Two houses!' she had said to her mother.

'They're royalty,' said Mrs Crawford, as if this explained it.

'They're royalty,' Miss Golspie had agreed, when Marion went to see her. The principal's eyes gleamed over her coloured reading glasses.

'So you don't mind if I delay returning to Moray House?' Marion had almost been hoping that she would. Now that arrangements were well underway, she was wondering if she was doing the right thing after all.

Beneath the portrait of the Girton pioneer, the principal linked her fingers and rested her chin on them. 'Not at all. On the contrary, I regard it as secondment. An extension of your duty to bring everyday life to those whose lives are, shall we say, a little remote from it.' Miss Golspie smiled.

Marion replied with an uncertain nod. 'Remote' was not exactly the word. As the most cursory examination of Mrs Crawford's scrapbooks showed, the distance between Princess Elizabeth and ordinary life was that between Earth and a particularly distant planet. She did not even look like a little girl, but like a gold-and-white doll, neatly brushed, in a fussy ruffled frock.

Her full name was Elizabeth Alexandra Mary. She was born in London in April 1926, the third in line to the throne, and her arrival was greeted by a twenty-one-gun salute from the Tower of London and congratulatory telegrams from nine reigning kings, a reigning queen and an emperor. At the age of one, she had received three tons of toys from the people of the Antipodes. The people of France, not to be outdone, later gave her two dolls whose 150 accessories included pairs of gloves, jewel cases, beaded bags, fans, sunshades, tortoiseshell hairbrushes and their own monogrammed writing paper. All over the Empire, her image was on flags, stamps and toffee tins. There was a figure of her in Madame Tussaud's, children's hospital wards bore her name and a flag had recently risen above Princess Elizabeth Land in northern Canada. None of this seemed to encourage a well-balanced view of either herself or anyone else.

'But what can I do with her?' Marion asked Miss Golspie in panic. 'How can I show someone like that what is normal?'

The principal waved a hand with a large blue Bakelite ring. A row of wooden bracelets rattled. 'Use your imagination, my dear!'

'But.' Marion blinked at her.

'Take her out! London is one big outdoor classroom! Take her on the bus. Into the parks! To Woolworths!'

'*Woolworths?*'

Miss Golspie's eyes gleamed impishly. 'And why not? You can be sure she has never been there. It would be a royal first!'

Marion considered. Once the surprise and panic had faded, she could see what was meant. A very different curriculum; a set of lessons that no royal child had ever received before.

Even with these intentions, saying goodbye to Annie was difficult. In the weeks since she had last visited, Grassmarket seemed, if it were possible, to have got even more decrepit.

'Sit doon, Miss Crawford, do,' said Annie's mother, attempting a wincing smile in which her lack of teeth was sadly evident. The flannel was still tied around her head. Perching on the one bed, which doubled as a sofa, Marion glanced round the room for Mrs McGinty's tailor's dummy. Usually it stood by the window, to catch what dim light struggled into the courtyard. The family had sold it, she now discovered.

'Ma's eyes are too bad noo,' Annie explained sadly. 'She canna do the fancy sewing nae more. So she lost her situation.'

Marion felt anguished for them. How would they manage?

'I can do rough sewing.' Annie's mother gave a brave smile. 'Mending dresses for neighbours.'

'And I've been charring,' her daughter added proudly. 'Takin' in washing. Standing at the close end with mae dolly tub.'

A child of six, charring and doing laundry! As a great wave of guilt and doubt crashed through her, Marion battled to control herself. She must remember what Miss Golspie had said. She was tackling all this from the other end.

She had decided not to say where she was going. The contrast was too cruel; the explanation too complicated. And the parting would, anyway, only be temporary. 'I won't be away long,' she had promised.

Annie had leaned close. The smell of her unwashed little body nipped Marion's nostrils. 'Miss Crawford, can I chum ye?'

'Come with you,' in Edinburgh dialect. Marion had placed her clean forehead against the child's dirty hair. 'Oh, Annie,' she said softly. 'How I wish you could.'

*

The train rattled down the country, stopping and starting, always in the worst areas of every town. Durham. York. Leeds. Doncaster. The factory chimneys and rows of blackened terraces all looked the same. So many poor people, Marion thought. And here she was, off to serve the richest. It was crazy, really.

But she gritted her teeth, remembered Miss Golspie and channelled her doubts into planning her alternative curriculum. It would include a bus ride and shopping at Woolworths, as Miss Golspie had suggested. And, perhaps, to give some insight into how the nation was run and protected, they would visit Parliament – but strictly the public gallery – and a police station. The London docks, for trade. The Bank of England, so Elizabeth might learn about how it worked, that substance of which her family had so much and most people so little.

Having made her notes, Marion reached for the *Teacher's World* she had bought at the station. It was her favourite of the professional magazines because of the columnist Enid Blyton. While its purpose was to interest children in animals, her weekly '*Letter from Bobs*', supposedly written by her pet fox terrier, was one of Marion's guilty pleasures. Bobs this week had been chasing the postman and causing ructions in Enid's flower beds. It made Marion smile in spite of herself. Blyton was a talented writer. She would be wonderful at children's books.

Would Princess Elizabeth enjoy '*Letter From Bobs*'? Did the Yorks even have dogs? She knew so little about where she was going, Marion thought.

She dozed and read as the hours passed. People came and went. She must have fallen asleep, because suddenly she woke to see the 'King's Cross' sign sliding past the window. They were arriving in London.

She had been looking forward to seeing it. But now the necessity of moving bags, finding tube lines and making connections supersceded all else. She made the Windsor-bound train by a whisker, and an hour or so later, as it rounded a bend, she saw, in the distance, a vast mass of turrets, walls and towers. Against the garish stripes of sunset, battlements showed like black teeth. A flag fluttered.

She had travelled most of the length of England, and now she was nearly here.

Windsor and Eton station was quiet and dark. As she tugged her case onto the platform, someone in a dark green uniform bowled up.

'Miss Crawford? Blimey, young, aintcha? Was expecting someone ancient. This yer luggage?' His cawing London accent fell unfamiliarly on her ears.

'Yes, yes and yes,' said Marion, amused.

She had never travelled in a car before. It was exciting, if noisy and smelling strongly of cigarettes. They soon left the town behind. Peering outside, she could see nothing but darkness and the faint outlines of trees.

'We're 'ere,' said the driver, as a pair of white-painted gates flashed past. Ahead was a large building blazing with yellow lights.

A dignified figure in a tailcoat appeared in the doorway, light gleaming on his silver hair. 'Miss Crawford? I am Mr Ainslie, the butler. Their Royal Highnesses the Duke and Duchess of York are in London this evening.'

Relief swept Marion. She could go straight to bed in that case. She was by now so tired she could have lain down on the floor.

'However,' Mr Ainslie continued gravely, 'Her Royal Highness the Princess Elizabeth wanted to wait up for you. If you would follow me upstairs?'

As all hope of rest vanished – in the immediate future anyway – Marion stumbled crossly after Ainslie through a vast, ornate room. Things now were beginning to take on the aspect of a dream. Faces loomed from gold-framed oil paintings on the wall. A row of huge arched windows looked into the black night.

After several passages and flights of stairs, Ainslie stopped at a white-painted door that opened immediately upon his knock. A large black-clad figure loomed in the entrance. It had a square jaw and a glinting eye, which looked Marion up and down coldly.

'Miss Crawford, Mrs Knight. Princess Elizabeth's nanny.' Ainslie then shot off as if he couldn't get away fast enough.

Marion watched the glinting eye take in the details of her worn old coat. Then the broad black back had turned and the solid legs in their sensible shoes were stomping off. Marion followed her through a pink-walled day nursery with a table and chairs, bookshelves and cupboards lining the walls. Were the three tons of toys in those, and the French dolls with their writing paper?

It was simpler than she had expected, similar to what she had known at Rosyth. The night nursery was indeed almost identical: a soft brown room with a fireplace before which stood a clothes airer, rug and armchair. Opposite it, in a small, iron-framed bed, a small figure with a mop of curly hair was sitting up.

Marion stared at her in surprise. The world's most famous six-year-old looked different than the frilled doll of the photographs. She wore a simple nightdress patterned with small pink roses and held two dressing-gown cords in her hands. They were attached to the ends of the bedknobs and she was jerking and pulling them vigorously. 'Trot on!' she commanded in a high little voice.

It was an unexpectedly comical sight. 'Do you usually drive in bed?' Marion asked.

The blonde curls nodded. 'Oh yes. Always. I go once or twice round the park before I go to sleep. It exercises my horses.'

Mrs Knight now stepped forward. 'This is Miss Crawford.' She sounded as if she were announcing something dreadful.

The princess dropped the dressing gown cords. She looked at Marion properly for the first time. She had her mother's keen, rather piercing blue eyes. 'Why have you no hair?'

There was a muffled snort from Mrs Knight. Ignoring her, Marion pulled off her hat. 'I've enough to be going on with. It's an Eton crop.'

The princess seemed satisfied with this explanation. She nodded and picked up the reins again. She negotiated what was evidently a dangerous and difficult corner before asking, in her direct way, 'Are you going to stay with us?'

Marion hesitated. 'For a little while at least.'

Mrs Knight now barged forward. 'Time for us to go to sleep,' she said sternly.

The princess allowed herself to be tucked away. Then, suddenly, she bounced up again and looked straight at Marion. 'Will you play with me tomorrow?'

'Er, yes. Of course.'

A huge grin flashed across the child's face, changing its serious appearance completely. The effect was dazzling. Marion was still recovering when the princess added, happily, 'Good night. See you tomorrow.'

Chapter Ten

Marion slept deeply. She awoke slowly, like someone surfacing from the depths of the ocean. She found herself in an unfamiliar bed, staring at a strange white ceiling. Where was she?

In a tremendous flash it all came back. Royal Lodge. A dragon in the nursery. Once around the park before bedtime.

She swung her legs from beneath the blankets and headed to the window. Behind the flower-print curtains, sunlight burst through leafy branches. A lawn stretched beyond, leading to flower beds. Birds hopped about.

A noise, faint but definite, caught her ear. A child's shriek, perhaps. Alarmed, she pulled on her ancient dressing gown and headed to the door. The corridor was empty but the noise was louder. Screams, definitely. Thumps and yells.

She thought of the little girl in the bed driving her team. The monkey-like grin. Was she in danger? Why were there no staff about? Barefoot as she was, Marion hurried down the corridor towards the sound.

Downstairs and round a bend, an open doorway gave into a large bedroom. In the middle of a blue carpet, back turned, stood a child in a rose-patterned nightdress. She held a large, lace-edged pillow.

'Elizabeth?'

The princess whirled round, the colour high in her cheeks and her blue eyes shining with excitement. 'Miss Crawford!' she exclaimed, just as a smaller, plumper child appeared from behind the door.

With a howl of triumph she thumped her sister hard with a pillow.

'Margaret, you *beast*! I wasn't looking!'

As the elder princess, yelling vengeance, gave chase to the shrieking younger, Marion now noticed the big wide bed. Beneath a blue silken bedspread huddled two large, shaking lumps. As pillows were now smashed against them, two protesting red faces emerged from under the covers.

She was looking at the Duke and Duchess of York, Marion realised in astonishment. 'Surrender!' the younger princess was demanding, threateningly waving her pillow at her parents.

'Never!' The duchess was mimicking a dramatic film heroine, the back of her hand to her forehead, dark hair tumbling about her cheeks.

'Beg for mercy!' Elizabeth commanded her father, who was covering his face with thin hands as she thwacked him with all her might.

'N-n-never!' he gasped, before descending into a fit of coughing.

A pillow hurled by Margaret now slammed into the polished dressing table, sending all its contents onto the floor. A crystal perfume bottle smashed against a silver-backed brush. A silver lid fell off a jar, spilling talcum powder. Squeals of delight greeted this destruction.

Marion stood, inhaling the heavy scent rising from the stain on the carpet. She had no idea what to say. The duchess now spotted her. 'Miss Crawford! What *must* you think of us?'

The duchess wore thick silk pajamas. Marion briefly wondered what she thought of her, in her threadbare dressing gown, her large pale Scottish feet bare on the carpet.

The duchess burst into peals of laughter. 'I should have mentioned that we always romp in the morning! We want our girls to have as normal and ordinary an upbringing as possible!'

As Marion returned to her room, the shrieks, whoops and yells echoed down the corridor behind her. It was all rather unbelievable, the duchess's explanation most of all. Was it normal and ordinary to thwack your parents with pillows first thing in the morning? And who tidied up the bedroom after these romps? She was glad it was not her.

Her confused spirits rose when she saw that a large brown tray had been left outside her door. On it was arranged, with exquisite precision, a silver teapot, crested china cup and saucer, two boiled eggs, a silver toast rack and butter stamped with the royal crest. There was a snowy napkin in a silver ring and a newspaper that seemed to have been ironed.

Inside her room, Marion spread out the paper on her small but serviceable desk and read it as she ate. The news was not good. The unemployment figures had risen yet again and were now approaching three million. The north of England, her native Scotland and the valleys of South Wales were the most depressed areas. Benefit cuts were making matters worse and several hunger marches from all over the country – Scotland, South Wales, the North, anywhere that unemployment and poverty were biting the hardest – were marching to London in order to draw attention to their desperate plight and demand the abolition of the hated Means Test. Introduced in 1931 as part of a sweeping general austerity package, this granted minimal unemployment benefit only after an invasive and humiliating examination of the applicant's entire household. Pensions, savings, even family possessions were taken into account. Marion read of the little bands of walkers, many dressed by the collective efforts of their families – the father's trousers, the brother's coat, the uncle's boots – and felt a wave of hot anger. How could people still be living like this, in 1932?

She looked at the silver knife in her hand, and the butter with its royal crest, and felt her previously keen appetite fade away.

She had just finished dressing when the door to her room burst open. 'Miss Crawford! I've come to take you to the Little House!'

Princess Elizabeth wore a pink dress with laces up the front and white cap sleeves. The effect was vaguely Tyrolean, and very fussy. Her hair was impeccably brushed and her shoes shone like mirrors. Two white socks were pulled up to spotless knees.

She looked an entirely different child from the pillow-hurler in the bedroom.

'What's the Little House?' Marion asked.

'The people of Wales gave it to me,' the princess said airily. 'Wasn't that nice of them?'

Marion glanced at the newspaper, with its pictures of the pinch-faced people of the principality. 'Very.'

'Come on!' urged the child, excitedly.

Outside in the garden, flowers were in full bloom that were yet buds in Scotland. Royal Lodge in the daylight was, Marion saw, not white at all, but painted a pale pink. With the row of arched French windows and the finials on the balustrade it looked unexpectedly exotic, especially surrounded by many-coloured rhododendrons and with a background of soft green trees.

'I bet you enjoy climbing those trees,' Marion remarked as they passed a magnificent Lebanon cedar.

'I've never climbed a tree, actually.'

'Never?'

'Alah wouldn't like it. I'm to stay on the paths and not get my clothes dirty.'

'Allah?' What did the God of Islam have to do with it?

'Mrs Knight,' said the princess. 'Look! Here's the Little House.'

The Little House was actually quite big, much bigger than Marion had imagined. It was in fact an entire house, built to scale for a six-year-old girl. It had a small square chimney and walls of palest blue, into which, on the ground floor, two large white lattice bay windows protruded. Three further windows were set at first-floor level beneath an undulating roof of golden thatch. Before the house were a low brick wall and a sundial in a circle of grass. There was an elegant front door, above which words were painted in black Gothic letters.

'It says "Y Bwthyn Bach",' explained Elizabeth. 'That is Welsh for The Little House. Do come in. Mind your head!'

Stooping, Marion followed Elizabeth through the little front door and looked around in amazement. The scaled-down world was complete in every detail. There were little chairs, a child-sized grandfather clock, blue chintz curtains at windows that really opened.

Elizabeth was flicking the lights on and off. 'It has electricity.'

Marion remembered the newspaper. The Hunger Marchers. Carefully she said, 'Did you know that most people in Wales don't have that?'

A pair of earnest blue eyes were turned on her. 'But they've plenty of *coal*, Miss Crawford. Granny told me. She's been down lots of mines.'

Marion blinked. The child clearly hadn't the foggiest idea how some people lived. It was time she found out. 'Most of the mines have shut now,' she said flatly.

Elizabeth clapped her hands. 'Goody! The miners must be very pleased.'

'Er, not exactly.'

The wide blue eyes looked accusing. 'But Granny said it was a horribly dirty job. Isn't it?'

'Well yes, but – '

'There you are, then.' With an air of abundant satisfaction, the princess went skipping off into the tiny kitchen.

Marion hesitated before following. She felt rather stunned. With such lack of awareness, where did one even start?

Perhaps with the draining board. 'Speaking of horribly dirty.' She drew a finger through the thick dust. 'Why don't you clean it?'

'Clean it?' The princess looked surprised. 'I don't know how.'

Marion looked at her. 'Oh dear.'

'What's the matter?' This was uttered anxiously.

'The people of Wales would be upset if they knew how dirty it was. The people of Wales might ask for it back.'

'Oh, Miss Crawford!' The princess was jigging from foot to foot in panic. 'What shall we do?'

Marion was opening the tiny cupboards in the kitchen. An array of brushes lay within, plus a scaled-down mop and bucket. 'Clean it, of course.'

The princess proved to be a gifted housewife. She particularly enjoyed making the windows squeak as she rubbed them down with newspaper. She plumped the pillows on the child-sized four-poster bed upstairs and even sprinkled the little lavatory pan with a minia-ture canister of Vim. In the kitchen's miniature sink, she got to work on the sticky crockery from the miniature oak dresser. 'This is such *fun*,' she gasped, grinning her huge monkey grin, her arms up to the elbows in soap suds.

'Isn't it?' agreed Marion, trying not to think of Annie McGinty, forced out charring with her mother.

Chapter Eleven

It was lunchtime at Royal Lodge and Marion was standing behind a chair in a dining room with a fine view of the garden. She had been surprised at the invitation to eat with the family. 'Their Royal Highnesses are very informal,' Ainslie had instructed. He seemed unaware of the contradiction that sounded like.

Informal! The waiting Marion took in the polished table set with gleaming glasses engraved with the lion and the unicorn. The charger before her was ringed in gold and painted with an exquisite rendering of a pheasant. She turned it over. 'Meissen, 1787'. The plate was set with military exactness between a full set of gleaming silver flatware, which spread out like wings on either side. Flanking a carved sideboard heavy with silver were two footmen. Marion tried not to stare. She had not realised, outside of fairy tales, that footmen actually existed. These ones were very tall, and looked similar, as if they had been picked to form a pair. They wore black tailcoats and breeches, scarlet waistcoats, brilliantly white shirts and stockings and buckled pumps. And was their hair actually *powdered*? It was strangely white, and stiff.

She tried to concentrate on her file of notes. She had taken great pains over her curriculum. Every morning would consist of three half hours of different subjects, followed by a break for games in the garden. Then reading.

But the most important lessons would be in the afternoons, after lunch, when the programme of Elizabeth's education in real life would begin. After the footmen and the lunch plates, but most especially after meeting the princess, it now seemed more vital than ever. She was a real little girl, in the most unreal of settings.

Marion flicked through her notes. She had slipped in, almost as an afterthought, a copy of *Teacher's World*. She found '*Letter From Bobs*' and read it again.

Princess Elizabeth now whirled into the room. 'Why are you laughing, Miss Crawford?'

Marion showed her. The princess's eyes widened as she read it. 'I *love* Bobs!' she exclaimed.

Her fervency was striking. 'Do you have a dog?' Marion asked.

Elizabeth shook her head sorrowfully.

'Perhaps you should get one. There's plenty of room here. We could take it for walks.' Then she remembered that by the time any dog arrived, she would be gone.

Fortunately, they were now interrupted. Voices could be heard approaching.

'Yes, but you know P-Papa,' the duke was saying. 'He's used the same c-collar stud for fifty years, and the same brushes, with only one re-b-bristling.'

As she saw her daughter, the duchess beamed. She wore a dress of misty blue, with white high-heeled peep-toed shoes.

Above his snowy collar, silken tie and immaculate tweeds, the duke looked fragile. Perhaps the pillow-battering this morning had taken its toll. He seemed wearier than Marion remembered him being at Rosyth. He held a cigarette in his thin fingers, streaming smoke.

'Good afternoon, Miss Crawford,' said the duchess. 'Or should I say "*rebonjour*", like the French?' The blue eyes twinkled.

Marion sidled out from behind her chair and gave a nod-jerk intended to cover all curtseying eventualities. 'Your Royal Highnesses . . .'

The duchess waved a white hand. 'Oh, sir and ma'am will do, and Lilibet, of course. We must think of a nickname for you, Miss Crawford. We four are great ones for nicknames.'

We four. It sounded close-knit and loving. And they wanted to include her too, with a nickname. Marion felt a warm glow of pleasure, then remembered. She was going. Not staying.

The princess rushed to them, all excitement. 'Mummie! Papa! Miss Crawford thinks we should get a dog!'

The duchess looked surprised, then smiled. 'Well, we must think about it, my darling.'

Ainslie appeared. Champagne was poured but Marion declined. At the first lunch with her new employers, however short-term, alcohol seemed unwise.

'Oh, do have some, Miss Crawford!' urged the duchess, and Marion could only watch as Ainslie filled up the glass at her place. She took a sip; it fizzed startlingly on her tongue and had a rich, yeasty taste. She felt instantly relaxed. It was like magic.

The duke now addressed her directly for the first time, speaking in his slow, careful way. 'And what do you think of the Royal Lodge, Miss C-Crawford?'

'It's beautiful, sir. I very much enjoyed seeing The Little House.' Marion smiled at Elizabeth. The child stopped spooning in her soup immediately.

'Miss Crawford was surprised that it had electric light, Papa. She said that most Welsh people don't have that!'

Marion's face flamed so violently she felt her cheeks might turn to ashes.

There was silence for a few seconds, and then the duke said, 'As a matter of fact, Lilibet, Miss C-Crawford is quite right. There are t-terrible problems in Wales, and we must do what we can to help.'

The duchess beamed. 'My husband is very interested in the condition of the working man, Miss Crawford. He is in fact the first member of the Royal Family to visit a trade union!'

'The Amalgamated Engineering Union, P-Peckham, to be precise,' put in her husband. 'It has 1,800 branches and 320,000 m-members.'

The duchess now spotted Marion's notes. 'And what is in that impressive folder, Miss Crawford?'

Marion gratefully passed it over. 'Some ideas for what Princess Elizabeth and I might do in the schoolroom.'

The duchess looked at it as if it might bite her. 'Miss Crawford. You mustn't work Lilibet too hard. We want her to *enjoy* her education. To have a normal, *happy* time!'

Marion felt bemused. Even Lady Rose had taken more interest

than this. 'We will be doing quite a lot of reading,' she said, rather desperately. 'Do you have any recommendations?'

She was relieved to see the duchess's wide, porcelain complexion split into a beaming smile. 'As a matter of fact, I do! The very greatest writer in the English language!'

Marion waited. Brontë? Dickens? Austen? She planned to introduce them all, in small, carefully selected excerpts.

'P. G. Wodehouse! There's simply no one better to cheer you up when you're a bit flat!'

Marion was scrabbling for a reply when the duke interrupted. 'I don't quite understand.' He was holding up '*Letter From Bobs*'. 'Seems to be c-correspondence from a d-dog.'

As a laughing Princess Elizabeth clapped her hand over her mouth, Marion hastily explained about Enid Blyton.

'Thank you, Ainslie,' the duchess murmured faintly as the butler topped up her champagne from his linen-swathed bottle.

Lunch continued, with the duke and duchess talking among themselves. Marion decided to return to the subject of books with the princess and asked whether she had read *Peter Pan* – for her money, one of the finest children's books ever written.

'No, but my Grandpapa Scotland knows Mr Barrie very well. He often comes to Glamis.'

Thanks to Cook at Rosyth, Marion knew this to be a great medieval fortress amid the golden fields of Angus. It was here, as the youngest daughter of the Earl of Strathmore, that the duchess had been brought up. It was so grand that, instead of a common or garden ghost, it had its own monster, which dragged itself about the passageways, groaning and clanking its chains.

Her glance now fell onto the princess's plate. Her eyes widened. Elizabeth had carefully cut her meat into neat little rectangles and arranged her vegetables into separate areas.

It was obviously a highly developed ritual. The princess put her knife and fork absolutely straight on either side of her plate while she counted five chews of mutton. She then picked up her fork and ate five peas before cutting a carrot into five equal pieces and eating that. Then she would return to the mutton again. Every time she took a sip, from a silver christening mug with an engraved flower on the front, she replaced it in exactly the same position, with the engraved flower facing her.

Shortly afterwards, the door of the room pushed open and a small chubby face appeared round it, surrounded by a halo of golden hair. A tall, gloomy presence behind pushed the child gently into the room, then disappeared.

'Margaret!' exclaimed the duke, grinding out his cigarette into a small silver ashtray.

'Wan' eat sugar!' announced the littlest princess, toddling over on her short fat legs and holding out a plump hand. As he was clearly expected to, the duke took a spoon and dug it into the bowl of sugar crystals. Margaret unhesitatingly crammed the lot into her mouth.

Elizabeth, on the other hand, sorted out her pieces in size order, lining them up precisely with the exact same space between each before eating them carefully, one by one. For the first time, Marion noticed how very bitten her nails were. They were red raw, gnawed down to the quick.

The duchess dabbed at her scarlet lips with a napkin and announced. 'The king and queen are coming this afternoon for tea.'

'Are they coming to spy on Miss Crawford?' asked Elizabeth. Her face was bright with interest now.

Now Marion felt apprehensive. The idea of being examined by George V was uncomfortable, and also hardly imaginable. He was a profile on a stamp, or a poster on the wall. Not a person. And he always looked so grumpy.

She was told to wait in the garden, where she walked nervously about, full of a restless energy. The lawns led to a small wood in which several venerable oak trees stood. They were of course the national tree, and on a whim she started rehearsing her curtseys to the broad trunks.

They were such a stupid gesture, she thought, and difficult to perform in the grass without toppling. Satirically, she bowed her head and mouthed a respectful 'Your Majesty' before sinking into the deepest swoop she could manage.

Twittering birds hopped about the branches. They seemed to enjoy this ironic display of courtesy. But now Marion's ear picked up a sound that no bird could make. She turned to see, descending the broad steps towards the lawns, the instantly recognisable figures of the Defender of the Faith and his consort. Had they seen her curtseying to the oak trees? She watched as, like photographs come to life, Queen Mary and King George made their slow, deliberate way towards her.

Chapter Twelve

Queen Mary was enormous, as tall as Marion herself. She came to a halt and stood absolutely erect, radiating a freezing dignity. She wasn't a photograph come to life, as Marion had first thought. She was something much stranger. In pictures, where all was monochrome, her preference for the fashions of last century seemed less obvious. But in real life her lavender outfit looked utterly bizarre.

Her neckline met her chin and her sleeves were massive leg of muttons, tightly buttoned at the gloved wrist. Her long skirts fell to ankles welded with feet at ten and two. Her bosom was vast and featureless, as if a pillow had been stuffed there. Her huge toque hat was thick with mauve flowers and looked like a planter on her head. But what astonished Marion most was that the curly grey front of her hair was false, attached with pins.

The king, in grey, looked more like someone from the here and now – although there was something of a former age about the white gardenia in his buttonhole and the fact that his trousers were pressed at the sides, not the front. Compared to his vast wife, he looked small and vulnerable. His eyes were big, blue and watery, like his son's, although he lacked the duke's graveyard pallor. Above his beard, whose grey was mixed with yellow, possibly from tobacco, his cheeks were a brilliant, fiery red.

The queen leaned forward on her rolled mauve silk umbrella and watched with a critical air Marion's wobbling curtsey. 'You are Miss Crawford?' Her accent was strongly German. 'You are ze governoss?'

'I am, Your Majesty.'

The queen's face was powdery and whiskery. Her eyes were small, but very bright.

'I remember my olt governess so well,' she declared, puckering her lips in a wistful smile. 'Madame Bricka.'

The name rang a bell. The fat one with the blasted primers. Marion remembered.

The queen continued, her powdery face quite transformed with memory. 'I was such a curious pupil! So eager to learn! I used to ply my dear Bricka with questions about everything under the sun! And keep her searching too, ja, until she found the answer.'

Marion could just imagine the put-upon governess rummaging through reference books in some vast and shadowy library.

The king, who had been standing at his wife's side emitting the occasional grunt, now bashed the lawn with his stick. 'FOR GOODNESS' SAKE, TEACH MARGARET AND LILIBET TO WRITE A DECENT HAND, THAT'S ALL I ASK YOU,' he boomed, making Marion start violently. She had been wrong to think him vulnerable. He was terrifying. His voice was shattering, deafening, echoing round the garden like the aftermath of an explosion. He had been in the Navy, she remembered.

'NOT ONE OF MY CHILDREN CAN WRITE PROPERLY!' the monarch roared next. He was clearly referring to the endless handwriting exercises beloved of Victorian schools, where small hands had been forced to learn perfect, painstaking copperplate. Teachers these days thought there were better ways of using classroom time. Pupils were encouraged not to labour over script or passively recite times tables but to find out things for themselves. They were taken out of the classroom to use the resources of nature. They climbed hills so that contours could be picked out and visited parks so plants and pond life could be studied.

Marion wondered whether it was worth saying any of this, or whether the words would come out if she tried.

'AND YOU'LL TEACH POETRY?' the king added suddenly. 'ALWAYS LIKED THAT ONE ABOUT THE BLEAK MIDWINTER. VERY GOOD, THAT!'

'A potent simile,' Marion politely agreed.

The royal ear turned towards her. 'DAMN SILLY? YOU THINK SO?'

Actually, she did think so. Not Christina Rossetti, but certainly the outmoded educational straitjacket the king seemed to favour. Thank goodness he lived a safe distance away at Buckingham Palace and was unlikely to interfere in her programme. As the king and queen abruptly turned their backs and stomped away, the duke and duchess now appeared on the terrace. It was like a play, Marion thought. One group of actors left, another came on.

The Yorks seemed to be playing different parts now. They had changed their clothes. The duke wore a filthy blue boiler suit and the duchess rubber boots and an old tweed coat tied with string. They looked like a couple of tramps.

Marion waited to be asked how the interview had gone, but the duchess had other priorities. 'I *do* hope you've got green fingers!' she called merrily.

As it dawned on her that she was expected to garden, Marion felt a mixture of indignation and despair. She hadn't come to London to grub about in flower beds. She had come to see the high life, the galleries, the cultural opportunities.

An hour later, her one good suit had been badly pulled about by brambles, as had her stockings. The latter were ruined, effectively, and everything stank of smoke from the Duke's ever-larger pyre of burning rubbish. Marion remembered, crossly, the vast wardrobes in the duchess's bedroom, and the tiny cupboard in her own.

'Eau de Bonfire!' cried the duchess, stomping past. 'There's no scent *quite* like it!'

Especially not if you can't get rid of it, Marion thought, staring at her hands in despair. She had broken all her nails in the effort to pull up dandelions, some of whose roots had parsnip-like proportions. Her initial impression that the Yorks were odd had become the conviction that they were insane. Delusional, at the very least. She thought of the newspaper reports she had read only that morning, which seemed like years ago. People all over the country were jobless and starving, and here was the king's son, with his house full of footmen, parading around in wellingtons like a latter-day male Marie Antoinette. Ridiculous.

There was a soft laugh from behind her; the duchess again. 'Robert Louis Stevenson once said that there was *nothing* so interesting as weeding!'

Robert Louis Stevenson was wrong, Marion thought darkly. Or, more likely, joking. She sat back on the muddied heels of what had been well-polished court shoes and observed her colleagues, none of whom looked thrilled to be made to garden either.

Ainslie the butler was piloting a wheelbarrow with all the dignity he could muster, and the chauffeur was raking leaves, his chipper manner considerably subdued. Not far from him, the duke could be seen sawing like a man possessed. On the ground surrounding him lay huge branches he had already lopped off. Scattered about were his tools, an array of implements so sharp you could cut yourself looking at them. She thought of Marie Antoinette again. These people almost deserved an angry mob descending on them.

'Play ball, Miss Crawford?'

Princess Elizabeth was behind her, holding a red ball expectantly. Unlike her parents in their tramp garb, she still wore the fussy outfit from earlier. It now looked even fussier; a large white ribbon had been added, presumably in honour of her grandparents. Had she no outdoor clothes? Marion wondered. But then she remembered that Elizabeth had never climbed a tree, and was expected to stay on the paths and not get dirty. That was ridiculous too, and sad. Children needed to act like children, not prissy miniature grown-ups.

She struggled up, wiping her hands on her skirt. It made little difference now, it was so muddy.

The red sphere flew back and forth between them. The princess kept dropping it. 'Butterfingers!' Marion teased.

Elizabeth carefully inspected her hands, with their bitten nails. 'There is no butter on my fingers, Miss Crawford.'

Marion laughed. 'No, I mean you're not very good at catching.'

They began to throw the ball again, but with hardly more success. Picking it up once more, Marion saw that Elizabeth was fixing her with a thoughtful blue stare.

'What's the matter?'

'I'm trying to think of a nickname for you.'

'Why?'

'Everyone has nicknames in our family.'

'Can't we stick to Miss Crawford?'

The golden curls shook in disapproval. 'You have to have a nickname. Alah is Alah, and my sister is called Bud because she's too little to be a proper rose, really. What's your Christian name?'

Marion told her.

'I suppose I could call you that,' Elizabeth mused. 'I call Grandmama's ladies-in-waiting Cynthia and Helen.'

Marion felt strongly that she did not want to be grouped with whatever fearsome old bats attended Queen Mary. But nicknames seemed a waste of time to her. When the month was up, she would be gone.

The princess dropped yet another ball. 'Oh, Crawfie!' she wailed in despair. Then the little face brightened. '*Crawfie!* That's what I'll call you! Crawfie!'

The day ended as it had begun, with a gigantic rumpus. First there were violent card games in the sitting room, which wound both girls, especially baby Margaret, to a pitch of crazed hysteria just at the time they should be calming down for bed. Then came the high jinks in the bathroom. From her bedroom on the floor below, Marion, writing to her mother, could hear the Yorks and their daughters splashing and shrieking.

My bedroom is small, and has a single bed with a white counterpane. The floor is lino, but there's a rug, and a little wardrobe, which I opened to find, to my absolute amazement, that all my things had been hung up, and all my underwear put in the drawers! Given the state of some of it, I'd have rather done that myself, but apparently someone unpacking your my bag is quite normal when you stay with royalty.

I've got a little armchair and a fireplace with a three-barred electric fire. There's a little desk at the back where I'm writing to you now. As there won't be many chances for me to use this special Royal Lodge notepaper, I'm making the most of it.

She paused and noticed that the yelling had stopped. Through the half-open door she saw the parents merrily go by, arm in arm. A soaked succession of housemaids followed, carrying sopping towels. Marion wondered how they dried their clothes and shoes, or whether, given they were on duty, they actually could.

She tried to catch their eye as they passed, but none of them looked at her, let alone returned her smile. They did not seem to want her sympathy; still less her friendship. She had encountered this at Rosyth too. With the chatty exception of Cook, the others below stairs seemed to shun her.

She decided not to worry about it. She would be gone soon; what did it matter? And in the meantime, bathrooms, so much work for housemaids, were for her a blessing. She, who had never had one of her own, now had a private one across the landing.

My very own little white-tiled bathroom has electric light and running hot water and — you'll never guess, Mother, you'll never, ever guess — my very own lavatory!!! No more going out in all weathers to shiver with the spiders and pull newspaper strips off a nail! Well, not for four weeks anyway!

Chapter Thirteen

Two enormous, shiny royal limousines were required to make the journey back from Royal Lodge to the Yorks' London home in Piccadilly. The duke and duchess swept off in the first. Marion and the princesses went in the second, along with Mrs Knight, who had been largely avoided until now but who took the front-facing seat as if it were her right. Plonked proprietorially on her lap and dressed in more white frills than a rack of lamb was Princess Margaret. Despite being the littlest and youngest of the family, she was clearly both too large and too old for such treatment and was squirming violently . . .

Sitting on the jump seat with her back to the driver, Marion battled nausea by asking Elizabeth about her reading. 'Have you read *Alice in Wonderland*?'

'Yes, and it's silly.'

Nanny Knight, who had possibly encouraged this view of Carroll's masterpiece, snorted.

'Do you like fairy tales?'

Two serious blue eyes met hers. 'They're silly as well, Crawfie. They're all about princesses. I'm a princess and they're nothing like me.'

Marion laughed. 'It's hard to argue with that.'

It was raining when they got to the city. Their big, dry warm car drove past wet Londoners hurrying down the steps into the tube stations. Elizabeth's face pressed hard against the glass, staring out. It had a longing expression, which gave Marion an idea.

'Have you ever been on the Underground?' she asked.

The child looked at her. 'No, Crawfie. Have you?'

'Yes. When I came from Scotland and had to change trains. It was fun.'

'I shouldn't think it is,' Mrs Knight said, immediately.

Marion wondered what the grim-faced nanny thought fun was, exactly. Or was she jealous? The princess's lavish use of 'Crawfie' seemed to have induced further tightening of the already-tight lips and a harsher glint to the gimlet eyes.

She opened her handbag. Somewhere in its depths was the new map of the Underground she had picked up at King's Cross station. It was ingenious, something of a work of art, showing each stop and the various lines in different colours. The lady in the ticket office, handing it over, had been very proud of it.

'Here,' she said, passing it to the princess. 'It's so clever. This map takes all the Underground stations in London, which are dotted about everywhere, and puts them all on lovely straight lines, at the same distance apart.' Anything more likely to appeal to Elizabeth's strong sense of order was hard to imagine. 'So it's neat and tidy and easy to use,' she finished.

Elizabeth took it immediately and stared at it hard. After a few moments there was a gasp of excitement. 'I *see*! If I am at Hyde Park Corner and I want to go to Elephant and Castle – what a *funny* name that is!' She looked up, grinning her monkey grin.

It was like being touched by a flame; Marion felt something inside her light up and glow. She smiled back. 'Yes, so how would you get there?'

The golden head bent down again. 'I would go to Piccadilly Circus and change to the Bakerloo.'

'Don't read in the car; you'll feel sick,' admonished Mrs Knight.

Marion watched the princess move her finger around the map, delightedly pronounce the unfamiliar names. 'Tooting! Like a horn! Barking! Like a dog!' It seemed incredible that she lived in the centre of her grandparents' mighty imperial capital and yet knew next to nothing about it. Marion realised she was looking at her first opportunity to bring the real world to the princess. She leaned forward with a smile.

'Perhaps we could go on the Underground,' she suggested. She would rather like to explore it herself. Her experience had been brief, just from one major terminus to the other.

Elizabeth looked up, blue eyes blazing with excitement, but it was Mrs Knight who spoke first. 'A ridiculous suggestion!' she snapped, her eyes glinting angrily beneath her hat brim. 'Taking a small and precious child into such a place amid who knows what dangers!'

'Dangers!' gasped the princess, clearly thrilled. Marion was tempted to say something, but the furious look the nanny now threw her suggested discretion was the better part of valour.

One forty-five Piccadilly, where they arrived soon afterwards, was the centre of a graceful classical terrace rising four grey stone floors above wide pavements. Marion had seen from her city map that the house was close to the main museums and galleries, as well as the parks and of course the shops. She felt a stir of excitement. This was more like it.

The house had double-glazed windows, an electric lift and planters of blue hydrangeas on the front windowsills, a decorative touch Marion had not seen before. At the top was the nursery floor, where, under a large glass dome, a circular gallery ran. All the way round it, tails to the wall, stood a collection of toy horses. There was something familiar and slightly alarming about the absolute precision with which they were arranged, all neatly spaced, saddled and brushed.

Marion was glad to find her room was at the front, over the street. She would be able to see everything that went on. As she pulled up the window sash and leaned out, a great burst of excitement filled her. London, with all its noise and bustle! However strange the circumstances, and for however short a period, at least she was here at the centre of the Empire, in the greatest city in the world. She stared down at the great wide thoroughfare, fascinated.

It was so full of life. The buses roared by, bells dinging, colourful adverts plastered on the sides, passengers packed in their tops. There were cars, heavy horses and carts, people on bicycles.

On the opposite side of the road, behind smart black railings, was a park. The rain had stopped now and a late sun emerged, the final flourish of evening. It sparkled on the grass and glimmered on the trees. Blackbirds were singing. Beyond the tree branches, Marion could see the gold top of a familiar monument and a long colonnaded facade. She felt a little jump in her chest. Was that Buckingham Palace, so close?

It was strange to think that she had actually met the king and queen. And even stranger to remember what they had been like. Ordinary people had no idea, but, of course, few ordinary people ever met the royal family. Perhaps it was just as well. Valentine's predicted revolution might be much closer if they had.

A rumble now reached her ears; it sounded like people singing. It seemed that a procession was coming up Piccadilly. Excited, she leaned farther out.

It looked big, and was moving quite rapidly, like a dark tide, across the width of the road. Tall red things waved above it – banners. It seemed like a demonstration of some kind. There was an air of excitement, of agitation. Men in dark blue uniforms were hurrying along either side of it; policemen, she realised. Behind them, also hurrying, were ordinary men and women; Londoners, gawping at the marching figures in the road as though they were a curiosity.

What was going on? The middle of Piccadilly was a sea of caps. There was shouting. Men's voices, yelling slogans she could not make out. They were singing something; she recognised the tune. Valentine had taught it to her the first time they met; it was 'The Internationale', the socialist anthem.

'So comrades come rally
And the last fight let us face
The Internationale
Unites the human race.'

Her hand flew to her mouth. This was one of the hunger marches she had read about in the paper. One of the desperate deputations of the jobless from towns where industry had drained away. Her heart sped up when she saw, white against the red, the hammer and sickle on some of the banners.

'LANCASHIRE YOUTH CONTINGENT.
FIGHTING AGAINST STARVATION.'

'MANCHESTER CONTINGENT.
FIGHT THE STARVERS.'

Her throat was dry. She felt full of a desperate pity. She could see the marchers clearly now; they were men of all ages in shabby clothes. They had bony, hungry faces. The young ones especially moved her; they walked straighter and there was about them a defiant pride. Their eyes switched about, looking at the grand houses with a mixture of derision and awe. A tall, broad-shouldered young man with a camera caught her eye. He did not seem to be part of the procession but rather to be recording it as he ran alongside.

The procession was right underneath her now. She could see how the men in the police line, on either side of the marchers, were jeering and pushing at them. They had sticks and truncheons, with which they were poking their victims. They seemed determined to provoke a reaction, presumably so they could then condemn the marchers as men of violence, bent only on causing trouble.

It was outrageous, Marion thought. These people had a right to peaceful protest. They and their families were suffering. Why else would they walk hundreds of miles, sleeping under hedges, taking what food was given as they passed through the towns?

She was looking at the rear of the procession now, the last of the banners and flags, the poor, shabby clothes. They were still singing bravely, their voices still audible above the hoots and honks of the traffic that followed slowly behind. They turned the corner into the park and were gone.

Marion sat on the bed and put her head in her hands. All her excitement had gone. She felt now only anger, pity and guilt. Her sympathies were entirely with the marchers, but those who had looked up and seen her would have thought they were the opposite. Here she was, in the house of a royal duke. What was she doing here?

A high, piping voice pulled her from these turbulent thoughts. Princess Elizabeth was outside on the gallery landing. She could also hear the low rumble of Mrs Knight. Marion padded to her door and eased it open. She felt too agitated to show herself properly.

In the golden evening light pouring through the glass dome, the princess presented the very picture of perfect childhood. Her well-brushed hair shone and she looked warm and protected in a pink dressing gown and matching slippers.

She was kneeling before one of her toy horses with a small brush. She seemed to have a particular way of brushing it. Then, with equal ceremony, she combed its mane and tail. The final touch was to slide a small basket over its face. 'Your nosebag, Blitzen,' she said, patting it. 'Enjoy your feed.'

She moved to the next, carefully removing its saddle and bridle and brushing and combing in the same way as before. Surely, Marion thought, she wasn't going to do this to all of them? There were thirty at least. It would take *hours*.

The same thought seemed to have occurred to Mrs Knight. 'Now come on, Lilibet,' she chaffed gently. 'It's time to wave to Grandpapa England across the park.'

'But, Alah, you know I have to groom *all* my horses.' A note of panic sharpened Elizabeth's voice.

'You don't want to miss His Majesty. You know he always watches for you from the palace with his binoculars.'

'But have all those men outside gone?' Elizabeth removed the next saddle and bridle. Her movements were faster now, and more agitated.

'Quite gone,' Mrs Knight said comfortably. 'The nice policemen have taken them all away.'

'What were they doing, Alah?'

'Causing trouble.'

'Why?'

'Because some very bad people told them to.'

Marion gasped. The urge to burst out of her room seized her, but deep down she knew ranting on the landing would achieve nothing. She would have to enlighten the princess in other ways.

Chapter Fourteen

Lessons began the next morning, in a somewhat hastily arranged venue. No one, it emerged, had thought about a schoolroom. The Piccadilly house had reception rooms, a library and conservatory, storage rooms, kitchens – but that Marion needed a place to teach seemed not to have occurred to anyone, right up until yesterday evening when she first raised the subject.

'Her Royal Highness says to use her boudoir,' Ainslie had intoned, when Marion, desperate, sent him to ask.

Marion was in the boudoir some half an hour before her pupil was expected. She looked around with a groan. How could this fussy ground-floor room, full of silk-upholstered furniture, mirrors and clocks, be turned into a sensible place for study? The only remotely desk-like item rioted with gold carving and inlaid marquetry. There was something about its squat, bulging shape and bow legs that reminded Marion of the rear end of a bulldog.

The lessons were supposed to start at nine, but the scrolled-gold clock on the carved mantelpiece had chimed a silver quarter-past and still no one had appeared.

She stared at the boudoir's long windows. Between the looping layers of silk curtains, blue sky was visible. She looked at the heavily gold-framed oils on the walls – landscapes, mostly – and drummed her feet in frustration. When half past tinkled she got up and marched crossly out into the hall.

This was large and dim and dominated by two enormous elephant tusks hanging on the wall and the statue of an African servant in ornate livery. Neither seemed to Marion especially relevant to the twentieth century. She listened hard. Was that Elizabeth's laugh?

She mounted the stairs slowly, her heels sinking into the soft peach carpet. The Yorks' bedroom was on the first floor, she knew. The sound was louder now: children shrieking with excitement. Marion stopped dead, realising what it was. The morning romps of Royal Lodge went on here as well. Irrespective of any governess's timetable.

A good hour later, Elizabeth appeared, resplendent in her usual white lace. 'Good morning, Crawfie.'

Marion bit back the snappy retort that hovered on the tip of her tongue. It was not the princess's fault she was late. Rather, it was the fault of her parents or, more probably, the large black shadow that had ushered her into the room before retreating and closing the door with a triumphant click. Had Mrs Knight even given the duke and duchess the timetable?

Elizabeth was sitting at the makeshift desk, the ornamental pug one. To reach the required height, Marion had piled up several pink silk cushions in the middle of a pink silk sofa. Elizabeth's feet, in buttoned satin slippers, swung between the carved gold legs. Noticing this, Marion thought that this was all so exactly the opposite of anything she had ever intended doing. How could Miss Golspie possibly be right? If organising a normal lesson was this difficult, how could her alternative timetable even begin to happen? It was tempting to give up altogether.

Then she reminded herself that it was only for a few weeks, and that Mrs Knight clearly wanted her to feel defeated before she had started. Why, though? They were doing different parts of the same job; cooperation would make much more sense.

Something about Elizabeth's frock now caught Marion's eye. The frills looked as if they all been hand-pressed – *goffered*, even, with special irons – which must take Mrs Knight hours. Hundreds of fiddly covered buttons stretched down its back. Buttons only a nanny could manage. Was there an agenda here, to do with longevity of employment?

'We'll start with Shakespeare,' she announced, brightly. As

Elizabeth's face fell, she imagined the child's grandmother frowningly waving a vast volume and suspected that any possible love for the national poet had been all but destroyed already. But there was more than one way to teach him, of course.

'Just a tiny poem, but very charming,' she said. 'Close your eyes and count all the beautiful pictures in it.' She then recited, from memory, the lovely verses from *A Winter's Tale*.

When all around the wind doth blow . . .

When she got to the verse about Marian's nose being red and raw, she stopped and tapped her own. As she had hoped, the princess giggled. Greasy Joan had a similar effect.

After half an hour, they switched to science. Elizabeth had no idea what this was. 'It's how everything works,' Marion explained.

There was puzzlement in the blue eyes. 'Doesn't God make everything work?'

The young teacher hesitated. She was treading on delicate ground here. 'He has a bit of help,' she smiled. 'Now get out your pencils.' The pencils were her own. Asking Mrs Knight to supply some was a battle for another day.

She noticed that the princess was arranging the pencils in precise lines, with exact spaces between them. It was an echo of her behaviour with the lunch plate yesterday, and the sugar. Marion, whose training encompassed child psychology, now realised she was looking at obsessive compulsion: the behaviour of those trying to control uncontrollable circumstances. This cossetted, regularised environment was the very last place she had expected to find it.

'Why do you do that?' she asked Elizabeth.

The princess looked up, staring at her with candid blue eyes. 'Because it makes me feel safe.'

'Safe?' echoed Marion. 'Safe from what?'

Before the child could reply, the door swung open. A pair of merry blue eyes appeared beneath a feathered hat and above a powder-blue fur stole.

'Ma'am.' Marion rose to her feet and dipped a curtsey. The duchess's eyes were on her daughter, however. Lilibet sat at a table, frowning as she drew a small plant brought from the garden.

'An art lesson. How delightful.'

'Actually, ma'am, we are studying science.'

'But Lilibet is drawing,' the duchess smilingly pointed out.

'Quite so, ma'am. But she's likely to learn the principal facts of plant biology more effectively this way.'

Almost imperceptibly, the smile wavered. 'But . . . science. Don't you need a blackboard? And facts? That's certainly the way I was taught.'

'These days,' Marion explained gently, 'it is thought that a child learns better with activity and experience.'

'How extraordinary . . .' The blue eyes blinked rapidly. 'Well please don't forget that Lilibet has a dancing lesson at Madame Vacani's this morning.'

'*Dancing* lesson, ma'am?'

Elizabeth of York was disappearing back through the ornate door. 'Lilibet *so* adores her dancing, Miss Crawford,' she threw over her blue-befurred shoulder. 'And of course it is *such* an important skill for a young lady. Balls will play a *huge* part in her life.'

Into Marion's indignation now came a wild urge to laugh. This faded instantly with the duchess's parting shot. 'And the class will be the most marvellous opportunity for you to get to know Alah better!'

'Mrs Knight is coming too?' Why were two fully grown women required to chaperone one small girl?

But the duchess had gone.

During the subsequent hour entirely spent waiting in the hall, Marion thought angrily about her curriculum. This morning was to have been maths. She had planned to use sweets to demonstrate simple adding and subtracting. Then history, which would have been a perusal of current affairs via *The Children's Newspaper*.

She had studied every detail of the African servant's livery by the time Elizabeth reappeared. A white swansdown cape had now been added to the frills. A black looming figure followed the girl.

Mrs Knight got into the car first, holding the princess firmly by the hand as if to demonstrate that she was her property.

The gleaming Daimler glided off, slowed down almost immediately and turned through a large white gatepost on which the word

'IN' was painted in big white capitals. Inside was a large cobbled courtyard filled with shining black cars just like theirs. The cars were moving slowly forward and disgorging children in frilly dresses similar to Elizabeth's on a wide flight of stone stairs that led up to the pillared front of an enormous house.

Marion stared up at it through the windows. This was the dancing class? She had a sudden, piercing memory of Annie McGinty, forcing a barefoot jig on the frozen pavement.

Inside all was red carpet, chandeliers and loud chatter. The lobby was teeming with children: girls in white frills, bronze sandals and ribbons in their hair and boys in dark knickerbocker suits with rounded white collars. Her initial impression was that there were a lot of them but a closer look revealed at least half the crowd were black-clad nannies like Mrs Knight and nervous-looking women with old-fashioned bun hairstyles and badly fitting suits. Governesses, possibly.

She looked away from this unwelcome reflection and about her at the fluted pillars and marble statues, the gilded mirrors and glowing pictures, the tall stone urns foaming with powerfully scented flowers, and thought that Buckingham Palace itself could scarcely be less grand.

On the other hand, at least Elizabeth was mixing with children her own age. Then Marion noticed the carpet. There was a good two feet of space between the princess's white satin shoes and those of everyone else.

The other children were openly staring at her, as if she were an animal in a zoo. The grown-ups gawped as if at a movie star. Elizabeth looked back shyly, but also as if she were used to it.

Marion felt a mixture of outrage and pity. Even if she was the most famous six-year-old in the world, featuring on stamps and sweet tins the length and breadth of the Empire, the princess was still a six-year-old. And this was a private event, among peers. She glared at the nannies, who in particular should have had a more sensible attitude. But they were too busy staring at Elizabeth to notice her. And behind the princess stood Nanny Knight, basking in reflected glory like a seal in the sun.

But now, it seemed, things were about to happen. The children and nannies began slowly moving up a great wide staircase, thick with red carpet and bordered with lacelike gilt balustrades. At the top was a reception committee. A woman with dark hair, long pearls and a silver frock in the fashionable drop-waisted style stood by a haughty-looking boy to whom she bore a strong family resemblance. Were these the dance teachers? They looked to Marion like the owners of the house.

She was right. The woman curtsied so low to Elizabeth that Marion felt she might kneel on the floor. 'Your Royal Highness,' she said, fulsomely. 'We are honoured that you could come to our humble home.'

But it's only a dance class, Marion wanted to scream. As for the 'humble', that was ridiculous. The level of obeisance was appalling.

But Elizabeth seemed entirely used to it. 'Good morning,' she said in her light, clear voice. She turned to the boy. 'Hello.' He bent his smooth, side-parted head and bowed even lower than his mother had curtsied. The gesture was rendered comic by the necessity of keeping a finger on the bridge of his glasses.

Neither the child nor his mother took the slightest notice of Marion, although a murmur was made at Mrs Knight, who inclined her head grandly in reply. The three of them moved on, through a vast and ornate doorway.

The room inside was as enormous as it was palatial. The walls were panelled with pale blue scrolled with silver and interspersed with mirrors. Children scampered about, pursued by their nannies. Elizabeth watched, rather longingly it seemed to Marion, as if she would like to join in but did not know how.

A plump woman, her white hair set in precise waves, stood smiling at the front of the room. She held a long wooden cane in her hand. A few feet away was a magnificent black lacquered grand piano, at which a woman with a beaky nose turned pages of music.

'Are you with Princess Elizabeth?' A breathless voice was at her elbow. Marion turned. One of the crumpled women was staring at her with an eager, toothy face.

'Well, yes,' Marion admitted, adding, so there should be no confusion with Mrs Knight, 'I'm her governess.'

'I'm a governess too,' the woman said dolefully. She looked very tired. Her large eyes had beneath them dark, exhausted circles, matching her drab suit.

'Don't you enjoy teaching?' Marion was curious.

'Enjoy teaching Lord Peregrine and Lady Annabel?' A wild expression briefly lit up the tired eyes, as if she were about to burst into hysterical laughter, or scream. She leaned forward; the movement sent out a strong whiff of mothballs. 'It's a bit like teaching a pair of animals,' she whispered. Her teeth stuck out alarmingly.

The children named were currently capering around the ballroom, presumably. 'Oh dear,' Marion said, sympathetically.

The woman now steered the subject back. 'But you are Princess Elizabeth's governess! That must be so wonderful!'

'It's a job,' Marion said. 'And the princess is a six-year-old girl.'

Her point was that her charge was just a child, like any other, and the duties of a governess were the same everywhere. But this was clearly not how her words were interpreted. The exhausted eyeballs shone. 'Yes! And what a job! To live with the royal family!'

'I'm not one of them,' Marion countered, with a smile.

'No, but you know what really goes on! You're on the inside and everyone else is on the outside.'

'I'm here to *teach*.' Marion felt impatient. This downtrodden creature with her protuberant teeth made her uncomfortable. Obviously lonely, probably unmarried, clearly unvalued, she made her feel trapped, almost as if she were looking into her own future. 'And it's only temporary, anyway,' she added, firmly.

The white-haired dance teacher now thumped on the polished wooden floor with her cane. The sound bounced off the mirrors. 'Good morning, children,' she declaimed operatically.

The chatter stopped. The young faces looked up, some nudged to do so by their nannies. 'Good morning, Madame.'

'Take your partners, the class is about to begin!' She gestured at the henpecked woman. 'Music please, Miss Bird.'

Miss Bird struck up. At a nod from his mother, the host moved in purposefully on Elizabeth. Perched on one of the decorative chairs that lined the walls, Marion watched in amazement as about twenty small children went through the intricacies of a waltz, their every movement accompanied by the thud of Miss Vacani's stick. *'One* two three, *one* two three.'

What on earth could be the point of this? What preparation was this for modern life?

The next dance was a quadrille, which made Marion think again of *Alice in Wonderland*, where it was performed with a lobster. As this progressed haltingly through its paces, with Madame Vacani shouting encouragement or offering correction ('Yes, Algernon! No, Celia!'), a group of footmen appeared carrying trays of glasses and plates, which they took to a table at the back of the room. Their costumes, erect carriage and gliding movement made them look more like dancers than the children.

A minuet followed. Marion had to hand it to Madame Vacani, the children seemed well-disciplined, performing the movements accurately, if without marked enthusiasm. Only one child seemed to be behaving badly, clowning around in the back row and pulling faces.

Then came a break. From the chairs around the room's edge, the nannies rushed in like a crowd invading a football pitch and milled around their charges.

'Do you want to do something? Do you want to go to *the place?*' they whispered urgently. They meant the loo, Marion realised scornfully. So why not say so?

Elizabeth did not seem to need the place. She was edging towards the table of food at the back. Here were plates of sandwiches – triangular ones of egg, sardine or honey, or circular ones made of strawberry jam – and plates of tiny cakes: heart-shaped, star-shaped, circular or three-cornered, iced with chocolate or lemon and orange-flavoured icing, all copiously decorated with silver balls. There were big crystal jugs of lemonade and orangeade, all evidently freshly made. For a break in a dance class, it was unexpectedly lavish. Marion wondered if all this, too, had been especially contrived to impress Elizabeth.

If so, it looked as if it might fall on stony ground. As the princess hovered over a plate of chocolate biscuits, Mrs Knight's large square form loomed behind her. The little girl turned. 'Can I?' Her tone was imploring.

But the nanny shook her head. 'We stick to bread and butter.'

'Not even a jam penny?' the princess pleaded.

Mrs Knight's large, square face turned stern. 'We have our acid tum.'

Seeing Elizabeth's face fall, Marion tried to come to her rescue. 'Does she really have an acid stomach?' she asked as Mrs Knight pointedly ignored her, and Elizabeth, resigned to her fate, took a plate and dolefully transferred a piece of bread and butter to it, while all around other children piled theirs gleefully with sardine sandwiches and chocolate biscuits.

A few minutes later, Mrs Knight disappeared. Marion looked around and eventually spotted her halfway down the room, the centre of what seemed to be an admiring circle of fellow nannies. Seeing Elizabeth's golden head bent obediently over her restricted tea, Marion stepped close to her. 'I don't think one chocolate biscuit would harm. Do you?'

The big blue eyes looked wonderingly up at her. She seemed about to reply when someone else butted in.

'Lilibet!'

A girl had come up. She had tousled mouse-coloured hair, a very straight, long nose and possibly the wickedest eyes Marion had ever seen. It was the child who had been behaving badly during the dancing.

The princess turned. 'Oh, hello, Magdalene.'

'I say, I'm starving.' Magdalene grabbed a plate and piled it with everything she could lay hands on. Elizabeth watched admiringly as an unsteady tower of sardine sandwiches and jam pennies began to rise.

Magdalene spoke through a mouthful of jam penny. 'Show me your toes, Lilibet.'

'Why?'

'Because the girls at my school say you've got webbed feet.'

'The girls talk about me *at your school*?' Elizabeth sounded surprised as she obediently peeled off a sock. Marion looked round swiftly. Mrs Knight was still nowhere to be seen.

'Everybody talks about you all the time, silly,' Magdalene said matter-of-factly. 'And even more about your uncle.'

'Which uncle?'

'The one who's heir to the throne and won't get married.' Magdalene took another chomp of sandwich. 'I heard the rentals talking about it. *Parentals*,' she added, before Elizabeth could ask. 'Georgie and May are very worried, apparently.'

Marion interrupted. 'Magdalene, it's not very respectful to refer to Their Majesties as – '

The long-nosed child gave her a contemptuous look before turning back to the princess. 'They're quite beside themselves,' she went on unrepentantly. 'All your family are.'

Grinning, Magdalene shoved in yet another jam penny. The princess, meanwhile, frowned and stared at her bitten nails. Then came the thump on the floor and the class began again.

Watching from the side chairs, Marion wondered whether this exchange in any way explained Elizabeth's obsessive orderliness. *Because it makes me feel safe.* That might make sense, if there was a deep-seated worry within the family?

But who would have imagined that worry to be the golden Prince of Wales, heart-throb of an entire Empire? The thought was an amazing one. To the outside world, Prince Edward, handsome as a film star and with the charisma to match, was the absolute epitome of the perfect heir to the throne. To hear, especially in these circles, that he was not sent a strange excitement churning through Marion. This was how it must feel to be on the inside of things, to know the truth. As the downtrodden governess had said.

The thought made her pull herself together sharply. She remembered how less than impressed she had been when the Rosyth cook had described Lady Rose's brief princely entanglement. She must not, she reminded herself, become dazzled by the royal family. As she had told the governess earlier, she was not one of them. Far from it. She was here to do a job. And Magdalene was only a child, and an obviously naughty one. She was probably talking absolute rubbish.

*

Later, Marion was in her room when a commotion downstairs sent her outside to the banister rail. Someone had just come through the front door. Someone with side-parted golden hair and a suit of a check so loud you could hear it four floors up.

A hot tide of excitement flooded right to Marion's toes and fingertips. Here he was in the flesh. The famous Prince of Wales! The Empire's darling! The thrill was so strong it made her head spin, and it took some seconds to remember that she was not supposed to be impressed.

'Shop!' shouted the idol on whom the sun never set. *'Shop!'*

The duchess appeared in a pale, glittery evening gown. She had a cocktail in her hand, and the hall chandelier gleamed on her bare arms and shoulders. She kissed her brother-in-law warmly, even lingeringly.

'Elizabeth!' He took out the cigarette to kiss her back. 'How's my favourite girl? Been stunting?'

She giggled. 'Always stunting. Tomorrow I'm making a speech to the League of Women Helpers.'

Stunting? In the gallery, Marion frowned. Was that what they called their official duties?

The prince gave a bitter-sounding laugh. 'Well, I hope you find some women to help me!'

'You're incorrigible! You just need to find a nice princess and settle down!'

The prince responded to this lively chaffing with a groan. 'Don't. Papa's drawn up a whole list of them. Ranging from Ingrid of Sweden to Thyra of Mecklenburg-Schwerin, who is literally fifteen! And I'm expected to pick one! God, how I *hate* being the Prince of Wales!'

Up in the gallery, Marion felt a ripple of surprise. She could see now why his parents and family might be worried. Magdalene had not been making it up after all. A whole *list* of princesses?

The duchess seemed less surprised. She had clearly heard it before. 'You know you don't mean that,' she said briskly.

'I do! It's all silly princing and stunting. The older I get the bigger a fool I'm made to look, and God knows that's not too difficult. Why should anybody care? I'm no better than anyone else!'

'Perhaps not,' returned his sister-in-law, lightly, 'but the monarchy rather depends on people thinking it's better than they are. A better version of themselves.'

Marion's fingers tightened on the banister rail. *Irredeemably thick* was how the duchess had described herself at Admiralty House. Hardly. She seemed to have a firmer grasp of the royal role than the heir to the throne did.

The prince snorted derisively. 'Well, I'm not a better version of anyone! Some men are chained to their desks! I'm chained to the banqueting table! In this last week alone I have inspected the Welsh Guards, awarded prizes at the Police Boxing Tournament, opened the new premises of the Chartered Auctioneers and Estate Agents' Institute and awarded certificates to the Society of Apothecaries.'

'And,' said the duchess, as this amazing speech ended, 'I'm sure they were absolutely thrilled.'

'But it's so boring!' The prince sounded resentful and frustrated. 'So relentlessly bloody *boring*.'

His sister-in-law gave a silvery giggle.

'Nonsense. It's easy. You just have to act.' She began to walk about the hall, hand outstretched, greeting invisible admiring crowds. 'Have you come far?' she asked the grandfather clock. Then, to a sidetable. 'How old is your delightful baby?'

'You see! You're so much better at it than I am!'

'What a nice coat!' the duchess complimented the front door. 'Goodness, the weather's cold today, isn't it? And you're a *plumber*?' This, to a window. 'But how utterly too *fascinating*. I've always absolutely *longed* to know how pipes work!'

She really was brilliant at it, Marion, from above, conceded. The prince refused to be placated, however. 'Tomorrow I have to open a hospital ward,' he sulked. 'I *hate* hospitals. *Beastly* places.'

'No, no, no, darling,' the duchess gaily corrected. 'You're quite wrong. We're the British Royal Family. We *love* hospitals!'

Quite suddenly, the prince seemed to brighten. 'You know, I've just had the darndest idea. You and Bertie should be king and queen. Not me and whatever unfortunate Mitteleuropa archduchess I'm forced to pick off Papa's wretched list.'

The duchess's humour had drained away. 'Not even in jest!' she admonished.

The duke appeared now, also with a cocktail, and with the usual cigarette streaming from his fingers. His brother clapped him on the back. 'Bertie! How's the Foreman?'

The blow to his shoulder blades had made the duke cough hard. 'It's t-t-too bad of you to c-c-call me that.'

'Not at all,' his brother teased. 'Papa was banging on only the other day about some trade union you'd descended on.'

'The Amalgamated E-E-Engineering Union, yes. It has eighteen h-hundred b-b-branches and over th-th-th . . . oh *blast* it!'

'Three hundred and twenty thousand members,' put in the duchess swiftly.

The prince did not seem to be listening. He was looking around the hall. 'You know, I do love coming round here. Such a jolly little setup. Wish I had something like it.' His tone was wistful. 'You're a lucky blighter, Bertie.'

He was so ridiculously sorry for himself, Marion thought. Suddenly, he looked up, sending her leaping back in alarm. Had she been spotted?

He then raised his strange, high voice, still looking up towards the higher floors. *'And where are my favourite girls?'*

His listlessness gone, he sprang up the stairs with such speed that Marion had no time to move. She was still rooted to the spot when he spotted her, stopped and stared. Meeting his gaze was like looking into a blue sun. 'I say! Who have we here?'

Marion found that she couldn't speak. Something had tied her tongue. Despite all she had just seen and heard, she was overcome, dazzled.

'Oh, it's Crawfie.' The duchess, climbing after her brother-in-law, now caught up, slightly panting but still clutching her cocktail. 'The new governess,' she added, looking quizzically at her employee.

'Governess, eh?' His strange, darting gaze raked her up and down. 'Know anything about books?'

'Yes, sir.' She had started to recover herself now. He was very small, she noticed. Tiny, actually. He and the duchess were almost the same size.

He was fumbling in the pocket of his check suit. 'Lady Desborough gave me a rum little book today. Ever heard of it?'

Marion raised her eyes to the cover of *Jane Eyre* and burst out laughing at the unexpected joke. It was good of the prince to put her at ease, like this. Then she realised he was staring at her. Far from smiling back, he seemed puzzled.

Yells now broke the peace of the upper storey. Two small figures, one on all fours, came tumbling out of the nursery, Mrs Knight in hot pursuit.

Chapter Fifteen

The next day, Marion avoided the boudoir.

'We'll have lessons in the garden,' she decided. They were less likely to encounter interruptions and it was more in line with the outdoor principles of Dr Froebel.

'But I'll get dirty,' the princess gasped. 'Alah will be cross.'

'You really don't have any playclothes?'

She would talk to the duchess about it, Marion resolved. The child could not spend her entire life in goffered ruffles. 'Right,' she said, fishing several small white paper bags from her handbag. 'Lesson one. Mathematics.'

She had slipped out early that morning to find a sweetshop. The nearest one was in Victoria Station, a half-hour walk from the Piccadilly house. The results of her foray were supposed to illustrate the principles of addition and subtraction. But Lilibet's interest was in the sweets themselves. 'What is it?' she asked, handling a liquorice allsort curiously.

It emerged that she had never had one before, or a bull's-eye. Nor did she have any conception of what a gobstopper was. Her idea of sweets was the elaborate Victorian confections made by the royal kitchens: violet creams, gilded marzipans and the like.

'So you have ten sherbet lemons,' Marion began, 'and if you take five away, what do you have left?'

'Sherbet lemons?' Elizabeth was staring at the yellow sweet. 'Is that what they're called?'

Marion repeated the question.

'Do they have sherbet in them? What is sherbet? I've heard of Schubert, but you can't eat him.'

Marion smiled. 'I'll let you taste one if you do the sum.'

Something now made her look up. Between her and the sunshine stood the short, fussily dressed figure of the duchess. She wore a fur stole in powder blue and a matching hat whose turned-up brim sprouted tall feathers. Together with the heels, they were, presumably, intended to add height. But somehow they had the opposite effect.

Several rows of pearls glowed softly at her throat, while diamonds flashed at her fingers and wrists.

'Eating sweets! How *too* delightful!'

'Actually, ma'am, we are studying mathematics.'

The periwinkle eyes blinked rapidly. 'Goodness. These modern methods. Well, you are to take Lilibet to Mr Adams. He is expecting you.'

Marion frowned. 'No one mentioned this to me.'

'I expect they forgot.' The duchess beamed brightly. 'Come on, Lilibet!'

She was clearly expected to come on too. But Marion stood, or rather sat, her ground. 'Who's Mr Adams?'

'Takes photographs. Flash bang wallop!' The duchess flashed her teeth briefly. 'Jolly little man. Chop-chop, Lilibet.'

'But we've only just started our lessons,' Marion pointed out. Why was being photographed more important than being educated?

The duchess's beam remained unwavering. 'You can eat your sweets later. Owen is bringing the car round.'

''Ere we are,' the chauffeur announced. Already impatient at the interruption, Marion now felt ludicrous as she stepped out of the Daimler a bare two minutes after getting in. Before her was an imposing carved-stone facade. 'The Children's Studio', said a polished brass plate to the side of a shining door. She eyed it with dislike. What a waste of time. Elizabeth should be learning, not posing for pictures.

That the reception area, which she had expected to be polished and gloomy, was a cheerful yellow and blue was the first surprise. The second was the apparition who came suddenly through the door, tall and beaming, a short white dustcoat buttoned over his suit and a shock of wild white hair framing a vivid aquiline face dominated by an enormous dark moustache.

'Good morning!' He extended a hand to Marion and grasped hers warmly. 'I'm Marcus Adams. Come in, come in.'

There was something fantastical and eccentric about him, but also reassuring and likeable. Beneath dramatic black eyebrows he had bright, twinkling eyes.

He led the way back through the door he had just entered by. Beyond was what looked like a large playroom. There were shelves of toys, a carpet, cushions. Lilibet went instantly over and got down a model horse. Marion glanced about her curiously.

Adams chuckled. 'You're looking for the camera? You won't see it yet. I spent a year designing my children's studio so there isn't any paraphernalia about. No dazzling lights, no big lenses and in particular no horrible black cloth to disappear under and terrify the little ones. I want my young sitters to feel completely at ease.'

Marion stared. A royal photographer's studio was the last place she expected to find the play-centred principles so beloved of Dr Froebel. 'You have an excellent understanding of the character of the child.'

The extraordinary Mr Adams flexed his amazing eyebrows. 'Photography, my dear, is ninety-five per cent psychology and only five per cent mechanical. If your sitters feel happy, happy pictures is what you'll get.' He looked at Elizabeth, contentedly galloping her horse over the carpet. 'Ready, my dear?'

The princess beamed and nodded. Adams went to the back of the room, where he swung round a large box on wheels. On top of it was a metal frame with another box mounted within it. The second box was a camera, Marion saw now as he turned it. But it was not like any camera she had ever seen before. It was an eccentric structure with a length of rubber tubing attached to a rubber bulb.

'Built it myself,' Adams announced, pushing it across the carpet. 'Means I can go anywhere in the room, and because it looks like a toy the children regard it as one.' He smiled at Marion. 'Off you go then, my dear.'

The delighted feeling abruptly vanished. 'Go?'

Adams gestured to the back of the room, whose far wall was a glass screen with some chairs behind it. 'Holding pen for the parents. Or, as they usually are, nannies.' He gave her a keen glance. 'How is our dear Mrs Knight, by the way?'

'Very well.' Marion kept her face carefully straight.

'So I see, judging from all those bows and buttons. But I'll do what I can to make her look like a real child rather than a doll.'

In the parents' pen, Marion watched through the glass, expecting the photographs to begin immediately. They did not, however. Lilibet continued playing and Adams leaned against his camera, chatting to her.

'Cup of tea?' someone asked politely from behind. Marion twisted round. She was looking into the face of a young man so handsome it made the heat rush to her face. He was tall and broad with wavy fair hair. His rolled-up white sleeves revealed strong tanned forearms and he had spots of pink in his cheeks. She knew him from some-where, but where?

He held out a hand. 'I'm Tom Parker, Mr Adams' assistant.'

There was something warm and rolling about his accent. It was English, but not London, she thought. Nor monied upper-class, like the Yorks.

'Funny handshake you've got,' he said. She realised that, flustered, she had given him the royal handshake. Palm up, limp, and, according to Ainslie, who had taught it to her, 'on no account must you ever squeeze.'

'One lump or two? The tea?'

'Two,' Marion blurted, though she didn't usually take even one. She now remembered, with a shock, where she had seen him before. Of all places, the procession of unemployed. He was the one with the camera, running alongside.

'I saw you,' she told him. 'At least I think I did. At the march on Piccadilly two days ago.'

The pink drained from his face. 'You were there?'

'My window looks over the street.'

He knitted his brows and said nothing more. She had the uncomfortable sense of having unearthed something intended to be hidden. They stared out through the glass of the parents' pen. Mr Adams was moving his peculiar camera around, and Lilibet was looking delightedly up at it. That the photographs would be wonderful was obvious.

'He's brilliant,' Marion observed.

'A great artist,' Tom agreed.

This interested her. 'You think photography's art?'

'One of the great art forms of the twentieth century,' he said simply. 'What Mr Adams does is the modern equivalent of all those people in the National Portrait Gallery.'

'I've never been to the National Portrait Gallery,' she said, slightly wistfully. 'I've only just arrived in London.'

The grey eyes kindled. 'In that case,' Tom said gallantly, 'let me be the first to take you.'

The opportunity came two afternoons later, when Elizabeth had gone to someone called Lady Cavan for singing instruction. It was, after the dancing lesson, all too easy to imagine. Marion was torn between shuddering at the very thought and relief she wasn't expected to go too, and could escape.

The gallery visit with Mr Adams' assistant was an intriguing prospect. There was a mystery to Tom. Why work for a royal photographer but take pictures of hunger marches? The gallery, too, would be interesting. She would learn something, which she could later share with Elizabeth. And Tom was good-looking, of course, although romance, after Valentine, was the last thing she wanted.

All the same, she could not help comparing them. Valentine, for instance, had notoriously never been on time for anything. But there Tom stood, waiting as he had said he would be, under the carved stone entrance of the National Portrait Gallery. She hurried towards him, suddenly shy beneath her smile. For the first time since coming to London she wished for better clothes. Her one good suit was not only battered by the Royal Lodge garden, but also exuded a strong scent of Eau de Bonfire.

Tom, more dashing even than she remembered, and neat in ironed flannels and a well-brushed tweed jacket, did not seem nervous in the least. He greeted her with a warm smile and showed her through the revolving doors – another contrast to Valentine, who always barged in first. She glanced around, impressed, at the mosaic and marble. 'Quite a place.'

'As befits somewhere containing the pictures of the nation's most inspirational figures,' Tom returned, going on to explain that the genesis of the collection lay in the idea that the public, presented with images of the great and good, might become great and good themselves. 'Admittedly, not all of them were terribly morally upright,' he added. They had walked through the galleries and were standing before a picture of a smiling dark-haired woman with a cat whose paw was in a bowl of goldfish. 'A very famous courtesan.' Tom grinned. 'Her name was Kitty Fisher. As symbolism goes, it's a bit literal.'

His clear eyes met hers and the idea of a courtesan, with its associations of erotic pleasure, seemed to hang in the air between them. Marion was relieved when they moved on. 'This is what I wanted you to see,' Tom said, stopping in front of an enormous picture. 'The Marcus Adams of the sixteenth century.'

They were looking at Hans Holbein's great sketch of Henry VIII, all broad shoulders, powerful legs, massive chest, challenging gaze. Marion frowned. The thrusting masculinity before her and sugary pictures of a laughing Princess Elizabeth seemed to have little in common to her.

'An absolute master at creating the royal image,' Tom went on.

He could say that again, thought Marion, eyes fixed helplessly on Henry's enormous codpiece. 'You mean Holbein?' She was confused.

'Yes, and Mr Adams. They do exactly the same thing.'

She turned to him, bemused. 'But it's entirely different, surely.'

He shook his head. 'Being royal is all about image. The Tudors knew that better than anyone. Come over here.' He took her arm, sending a great judder of pleasure straight to her heart, which seemed to suddenly burst into light.

Once she had recovered she found herself staring at a picture that seemed to be an explosion of sorts as well: lace, gold, satin, pearls and lavish embroidery. The face in the centre of it wore a tight, calm smile.

'Elizabeth the First,' Tom said. 'The most brilliant royal manipulator of her image until Elizabeth of York.'

Marion stared at him. 'What?'

'The duchess. She's streets ahead of the rest of them. A genius at PR, Mr Adams says.'

'PR?'

'Public relations. Controlling people's view of you. Making sure they see what you want them to see and think what you want them to think.'

He had to be joking, and yet she could see he wasn't. 'But why would she want to do that?'

He looked at her, amused. 'Power, in a word. Monarchs don't lead the nation into battle any more. We've moved on from the divine right of kings. The throne is a form of celebrity these days. And your duchess knows that better than anyone. Why else have her daughters photographed so much, and supply the papers with the pictures?'

Marion could see what he meant now, and that it might even be true. She remembered the scene in the hall with the Prince of Wales. 'I had no idea,' she said.

Tom gave her a reassuring smile. 'Don't worry. You're not supposed to. But it's only one of the reasons why photography is the most important art form of the twentieth century.'

She looked at him consideringly. 'You really believe that, don't you?'

He nodded. 'One day photographers will get the recognition they deserve. Perhaps one day a princess will actually marry a photographer, not just sit for one.'

Marion laughed. 'Now you really are joking.'

'Perhaps. Anyway, are you hungry? There's a good tearoom downstairs.'

Being the object of Tom's interest was like sitting in warm sunshine. Over coffee and sticky buns, he asked more questions in half an hour than Valentine had the whole time they had known each other.

She told him about her training, and Annie. His broad, clear face was incredulous. 'You wanted to work in the slums? So what are you doing with the Yorks?'

She took a deep breath and explained about Miss Golspie, and her mission to introduce the princess to the ordinary. She had feared that he wouldn't understand, or might even laugh. But he looked interested, even sympathetic. 'I'm in quite a similar situation,' he said, pouring them both more tea. 'Mr Adams is teaching me how to photograph the royal family, but that isn't really what I want to do.'

She remembered now: the hunger march, him running alongside with his camera, his caginess when she brought the subject up at the studio. The excitement and revelations of the gallery visit had pushed all this from her mind. She smiled at him. 'You don't want to take pictures of princesses?'

The grey eyes that met hers were serious. 'Don't get me wrong. Mr Adams has been wonderful to me. Everything I know about photographs and cameras I've learned from him. But I want to take it in a different direction.'

'What direction?'

'Photojournalism.'

'What's that? I've never heard of it.'

He smiled. 'I've made it up. The word, I mean. It's journalism, but with photographs. You record events like reporters do. But you use pictures, not words.'

'You mean things like the way the police were pushing? To annoy the marchers?'

'Exactly.' His eyes shone; he looked pleased. 'Tell the truth about something. Find the telling detail. A picture can say so much.'

'Or so little,' Marion said, thinking of the perfect royal portraits.

He smiled. 'Well, quite. The thing about photojournalism is that it's not pre-planned. It's spontaneous, on the spot.'

She considered this. 'What do photojournalists do with their pictures though?'

'Same thing journalists do with their words. Sell them to newspapers and magazines.'

This surprised her. 'But who wants pictures of police hitting marchers?'

'Actually, there's a growing market for them. Some newspaper editors want to show what is really happening in the world. Not just be part of a royal public relations exercise.'

A horrible possibility now dawned on her. 'You wouldn't be a Communist, by any chance?' She wasn't sure she could bear another.

He was midway through biting into a scone. The laughter this provoked made him snatch for his napkin. His broad shoulders heaved. 'Nothing of the sort,' he gasped, eyes streaming. 'As a matter of fact, I don't trust extremes.'

'Good.' This was a relief. 'But you still don't want Mr Adams to know about . . . your other interests.' That was certainly the impression he had given.

'Not really.' There was a flash of anxiety in his grey eyes as he looked at her. 'You won't say anything?'

She smiled and patted his arm. 'Don't worry. Your secret's safe with me. And anyway, as you said, we're doing similar things. You're working with the royal photographer but doing your photojournalism and I'm working with the royal family but trying to connect them with real life.'

His broad, handsome face cleared. 'Yes. We make a good team.'

Something flashed through her at that. Sternly, she reminded herself that she was not looking for love. What was the point? She was headed back to Scotland before much longer.

Chapter Sixteen

The invitation from Queen Mary came out of the blue. Her Majesty wished Marion to come to the palace for tea. She hoped this would be convenient and would Marion please telephone at once to her lady-in-waiting, Lady Cynthia Colville?

Marion lifted the heavy black receiver with trepidation. She had met Lady Cynthia; a terrifying old dragon with a huge nose, fierce eyes and a mouth twisted in permanent disgust. When not waiting on the queen, she presided at the London Juvenile Court. The predicament of any felon up before her would be unenviable to say the least.

'Her Majesty means just me, and not the princess?' a puzzled Marion asked her.

'Her Majesty does. Kindly be on time. Her Majesty is never late for any engagement, public or private. She expects the same punctuality from others.' With that, Lady Cynthia rang off.

Marion went to consult the duchess, who chuckled. 'My mother-in-law has strong views on education! Prepare to be instructed in *thorough* Teutonic fashion!'

But what business was it of Queen Mary's? Marion wondered. Elizabeth was the duchess's daughter. Any instructions should come from her, surely? She felt mildly offended, but also fascinated. Tea with the queen-empress would be extraordinary – and what would Buckingham Palace be like?

She set off a good half hour earlier than necessary, as the walk from Piccadilly through Green Park to Buckingham Palace was ten minutes at the most. The buses roared by to nearby Hyde Park Corner, bells dinging, adverts plastered on the sides, passengers packed in their tops. There were cars to dodge too, heavy horses and carts, and still a number of boys on bicycles, even though morning deliveries were long over.

Green Park, lovely in summer, was sprinkled with flowers and tourists. They sat in deckchairs or lay on the warm grass. They were content, it seemed, to be near to the gold-topped black railings of Buckingham Palace, from whose pillared central portico the Royal Standard fluttered. The gilt figure atop the Victoria Memorial blazed against the blue sky. She could see the soldiers, magnificent in their bearskins, with the gold on their red jackets flashing in the sun. A sense of excitement gripped her. She was going where very few people ever went.

At 4:50 p.m. precisely she walked through the black gates of Buckingham Palace. Under the eyes of several observers, she approached the policeman, who seemed to expect her; he nodded her through and directed her to a black doubled-fronted door on the right-hand side of the facade. As she approached, the doors opened as if by magic; up a wide, shallow flight of steps and Marion was inside.

The palace interior was like the grandest of grand hotels. Great carpeted corridors flowed like red rivers between white panelled walls scrolled with gold. Vast chandeliers blazed from the ceilings, dripping with faceted glass. It was all very quiet.

'Your coat, madam?'

'Thank you.' Marion handed the pale blue jacket over to a tall figure in black tails. His waistcoat was a brilliant scarlet and his collar stiff and white.

'This way, madam.' He set off along one of the corridors, walking well to the edge of the carpet. Hurrying alongside him, Marion walked in the middle. Passing several other black tailcoats, all of whom looked at her askance, she asked what she was doing wrong.

'Only royalty walk down the middle?' she gasped, torn between amusement and its opposite.

'A freshly brushed carpet is fit only for royal feet.'

She stared at him. Was he serious? His delivery was absolutely deadpan, but beneath his powdered hair, his black eyes sparkled. 'This way, madam.'

Madam followed. The palace was almost fantastically ornate. One would never have imagined it from the austere outside. The rooms were massive, built on a giant scale; there seemed not an unfestooned square inch. Walls were of shimmering damask and ceilings blazed with gold. Layers of swagged curtains at colossal windows were restrained by thick silken ropes. There were enormous gold-framed mirrors, huge portraits and shining sofas whose bloated silk cushions threatened to burst from their carved gold frames. Everywhere Marion looked there were painted medallions, gilded mouldings, blank-eyed statues striking attitudes in alcoves.

'Madam!' The footman claimed her attention. She saw that he had stopped dead and turned swiftly to the wall.

A short young woman in a white frock was walking down the dead centre of the carpet. As she passed, she swept Marion, who had not turned, a haughty glance with some familiar blue eyes. She turned the corner and was gone.

'Who was that?'

'Her Royal Highness the Princess Royal, miss.'

King George's only daughter, Marion knew. The sister of the duke and the Prince of Wales. 'Why did you turn to the wall?'

'We're supposed to avert our gaze, miss.'

'*What?* But that's *ridiculous*.'

Who did these people think they were? They may be king-emperor and queen-empress, but this was the twentieth century.

They had reached a wide, red-carpeted staircase where an elegant gentleman in an even more elaborate outfit awaited in the dead centre of the carpet at the top. Behind him, two closed white doors heavy with gold decoration were set in a tall gold and white door-case.

Marion's thoughts flew back to *Alice*, only this time it was *Through the Looking-Glass*, with the Fish and Frog Footmen. Apart from the wet look conferred by his brilliantined hair, the first footman bore no resemblance to a fish. But there was certainly something of the frog about the bulge-eyed functionary she was now approaching, resplendent in his red tailcoat and patent pumps with silver buckles. 'Her Majesty's personal footman,' the first footman muttered under his breath, before turning away.

Emanating tremendous dignity, the frog footman smiled a courtly smile at the precise moment a series of silvery tinkles from unseen clocks announced that the hour was exactly five. As the last stroke died away, he intoned, 'Her Majesty is waiting.'

Turning his red-tailcoated back on her, the frog footman seized the round gold knobs of doors. As he pulled them open, the vista exposed was of an opulent sitting room. But this was mere hazy shining background. It was what stood in the foreground that occupied the attention.

Queen Mary stood proudly erect, her ankles touching, her feet at ten to two, her gaze drilling straight into Marion's. The scene was completely silent but felt somehow full of noise, like a blare of trumpets. It was a tremendous *coup de théâtre*.

'Miss Marion Crawford, Your Majesty,' announced the footman, before ushering Marion into the room and withdrawing. On silent, oiled gold hinges, the doors behind her closed. There was no escape. A sense of panic swept through Marion.

Queen Mary had been imposing enough in the Royal Lodge gardens. But inside Buckingham Palace the effect was tremendous. She loomed above Marion like a vast statue topped with a face of frowning resolve. Her pale grey gown and the width of her bust suggested the palace frontage. As ever, her high collar and leg-of-mutton sleeves recalled the Victorian era, as did her hair, supplemented at the front with that strange little pelmet of false grey curls.

Awed and rather terrified, Marion dropped into the deepest curtsey her shaking knees allowed, then limply, without squeezing, shook the proffered hand, which bristled with diamonds. She had expected now to be offered a chair but the royal ankles remained welded together while the royal expression, frowning and expectant, suggested that something else was required. Marion wobbled carpet-ward in another curtsey.

The statue now moved. 'Let us have tea first and then ve can haf a talk,' said the queen in her guttural voice.

Only now did Marion look about herself. The walls of the predominantly red room had a satin shimmer, and the great looping curtains at the colossal windows were restrained by silken ropes.

The queen was leading the way into another, smaller room furnished in grey-blue silk. A faint creak accompanied her, as of much whalebone corsetry. A fire glowed in the depths of a marble fireplace despite the sun outside the silk-draped window. A table stood by it, draped with a white cloth edged with lace. Arranged upon it were pink cups and saucers, a plate of muffins and scones and a large fruit cake. The queen was standing up and fiddling with a silver kettle hanging over a methylated spirit lamp. It bore the monogram VR.

'Zis kettle belonged to Queen Victoria,' Queen Mary remarked needlessly as the water boiled and was decanted into a silver teapot marked with the same royal monogram. 'Zis teapot too. And you see zis bracelet?' She extended a glittering hand to Marion. The links of the bracelet seemed to be painted with eyes. It was rather horrible.

'Zey are the eyes of all Queen Victoria's chiltren!' Queen Mary declared triumphantly.

Tea began. The queen ate with great relish, looking about her as she chewed and making approving little noises deep in her throat. Raisins and crumbs tumbled down the palatial frontage. Marion picked nervously at a scone and darted occasional looks at her hostess. Queen Mary had a bristly chin, she noticed. An ornate gold clock could be heard softly ticking on the mantelpiece.

Having demolished a muffin and a slice of cake, the queen dabbed her wide mouth with a linen napkin, gave a grunt of satisfaction and looked Marion squarely in the eye. 'Now ve vill haf our discussion.'

She began fiddling in a basket on the floor. Her hand emerged, holding what looked like a heap of dirty string. 'Vaste not vont not,' pronounced the old lady as she began to unravel the cord. 'I never throw anything avay. Never! Packing string, post string, it is alvays useful. I keep it all. Also the paper and envelopes. We must not vaste money.'

Marion clenched her jaw. The risk was that it would drop open at the sight of a woman surrounded by gilded splendour, to whom she had been conducted by two footmen and curtsied to twice, untangling used parcel string and rolling it into neat little balls.

'You are enchoying teaching the bambino?'

The chance, Marion thought, would be a fine thing. 'We haven't had many lessons,' she admitted.

The queen did not seem to hear this. 'Ja, she reminds me so much of myself! I vud read for six hours every day!'

Marion thought this sounded rather excessive. 'I was aiming for an hour for Princess Elizabeth. Children need variety and exercise, especially at her age.'

Queen Mary looked up from an especially tricky knot. 'My torter-in-law tells me that you haf some unusual ideas about education, Miss Crawfort.'

'Not unusual,' Marion corrected, smiling. 'Just modern.'

The small eyes glinted. 'I too haf ideas about education. You must teach Lilibet history. Children are very interested in genealogy. Royal genealogy in particular.'

Marion suppressed a gasp.

'History is by far the most important subject,' the queen proclaimed. 'It is for instance far more faluable than arithmetic.' The bright eyes peered hard at her over the glasses. 'You are teaching Lilibet arithmetic?'

'Yes.'

The wide old mouth twitched sceptically at the corner. 'Lilibet does not need to study arithmetic. She vill never have to run a household budget!'

'But – '

'Chography, though, that is worth doing. Chorge's empire covers a very large part of the globe. You must ask Mrs Knight.'

'Mrs *Knight*?' What did she know about geography?

Queen Mary went on to explain that among the toys in the nursery was a set of building blocks made of fifty different timbers grown in various parts of the king's vast realm. It had been presented to Their Majesties during the 1911 Durbar.

'Vot an occasion!' The old queen was misty-eyed now. 'Ve vere treated like gods! Ve rode on elephants and I vore the biggest diamond in ze vorld!' The old hands continued to wind the grubby little bits of string.

Marion shifted on her padded seat. It was time to stand up for herself. 'Your Majesty,' she began, firmly. 'It may be that for a truly rounded education, the princess might additionally benefit from an awareness of social conditions – the difficulties faced by a great many of Your Majesty's people, the poor.'

A sort of whinnying harrumph came from the seat opposite. 'Ze poor!' exclaimed Queen Mary.

Marion braced herself for a royal thunderstorm. The frog footman would be summoned to throw her out of the palace gates. If so, let him. She would have at least gone down fighting.

The queen stared at her indignantly. 'But I too am very interested in how poor people lif and vork. I know a lot about the vorking classes as I have always been surrounded vith servants.'

As there seemed no answer to this, Marion did not attempt one. Nor, it seemed, was one required. 'I haf taken tea vith miner's vives,' Her Majesty went on, 'and vonce when ve vere staying in Yorkshire there vos a terrible pit accident. Ve vent straight to the pit cottages and comforted ze veeping vidows.'

Marion eventually stumbled out of the audience clutching a set of Happy Families playing cards where the families concerned were the Plantagenets, Tudors and Hanoverians. How happy had any of them actually been? Her brain teemed with Queen Mary's reading recommendations: the classics and the Bible, as well as poetry by heart – 'Vonderful memory-training! And you simply must read Harrison Ainsvorth.'

Marion had never heard of a novel called *Harrison Ainsvorth*. But she had barely been back at 145 Piccadilly before a car swept up from the palace containing a large box of books. The entire works of Shakespeare, Dickens and Jane Austen were topped by a small leather-bound volume whose gold-stamped spine read *Windsor Castle*, by Harrison Ainsworth.

Marion flicked through it. There were a lot of 'thees' and 'forsooths'. She groaned. Really, this was the most uphill of uphill struggles. However, it would soon be over.

Elizabeth keeps asking me to call her Lilibet, she wrote to her mother. *She said that everyone else in the family does. But I can't really encourage her to think of me as family when I'll be gone soon.*

But the weeks went by and the end of the month passed, and nothing was said.

Had the Yorks forgotten? Should she say something herself? But her job was hardly finished yet. Elizabeth loved outside learning, her obsessive compulsion seemed much diminished and she now almost had fingernails. But the programme of 'normal' adventures, which had always been the point, hadn't even got started.

Permission was hard to obtain; the duchess, especially in London, was always rushing off in a whirl of furs to a waiting car, and the duke was either out or shut in his office. Marion had asked herself many times why she was even trying. She should just leave, surely. Enlightened principles, modern ideas – they had no place here. The dancing class and, especially, the audience with Queen Mary had shown her what she was up against.

But now that she knew Elizabeth better, stepping away was harder. Besides being a joy to teach, she was a loving little girl it was impossible not to love in return. If she left now, Marion wondered, would the prison gates ever open? Or would the child be condemned, like some princess in a tower, to spend the rest of her days in lonely privilege? She thought of Buckingham Palace, heavy and hushed, with that feeling of being cut off from the rest of the world, even though the whole of London was going about its business just beyond the brocade-draped windows.

Had the princess been an insufferable prig, it might have been easier. But Elizabeth was soft-hearted and sensitive. Her compassion, especially for animals, was striking. Standing with the child at the window as she looked down on Piccadilly below, Marion listened to her concerns about the horses pulling the brewers dray that stopped every evening at the traffic lights. Her anxiety if the horses were late was touching, as was her concern for weary little ponies trotting home with their carts. Their owners would have been amazed to know the extent of royal concern and sympathy they roused from that upper window.

'Oh, Crawfie!' Elizabeth cried one day, watching with burning eyes a particularly sad little specimen staggering away from the traffic lights pulling a huge cart. 'If I am ever queen, I will make a law against all this. Horses should have a rest too!'

'But you aren't going to be queen,' Marion pointed out. 'Your uncle is the heir to the throne.'

Elizabeth did not seem to be listening. 'And I shan't let anyone dock their pony's tail!'

If she left, Marion wondered, who would play with Elizabeth as she did? She had encouraged the serious princess to be silly by being silly herself. Elizabeth could, at first, hardly believe that Marion would allow her to slip a pair of red reins with bells on over her shoulders and gallop her round the house. 'Alah would never let me do this to her!' she whispered.

'Really?' A smile tugged at Marion's lips. 'You do surprise me.'

'Paw the ground, Crawfie! With your hoof! Like this!' She demonstrated with her small foot on the carpet.

Deliveries was the other favourite game. The bells on her reins jingling, Marion would allow herself to be driven round the garden to the rear of the Piccadilly house, 'delivering groceries'. She would be patted, given her nosebag and jerked to a standstill as the princess stopped at imaginary houses, handed over imaginary goods and held long and intimate conversations with imaginary customers. She seemed to have an advanced understanding of customer service, and the importance of keeping clients happy. In a different life, Marion thought, she would make a great saleswoman. Or perhaps the head of a large business. But without her help, would Elizabeth ever know these other lives even existed?

And in this life, anyway, she needed sensible clothes to play in. Marion had tackled the duchess on the subject but was told to ask

Mrs Knight about it. Mrs Knight had advised her to ask the duchess. And so it had gone on, even though the sooty bushes behind the Piccadilly house left streaks and smears all over the lace and chiffon.

Then there was Tom. He didn't want her to leave either. He made a comic sad face. 'I'll miss you.'

'Aww!' She made a comic sad one in return, to hide the fact she would miss him too.

The first outing to the National Portrait Gallery had led to others. The British Museum, the Victoria and Albert, walks across the parks and, today, tea in his flat. It was in a small, shabby apartment block near King's Cross Station but, in an inversion of Valentine's foul room in its magnificent university building, was pin-neat. The tiny rooms were immaculately clean, and the coverlet on Tom's narrow bed was so straight and taut you could have bounced a penny on it.

'What's that noise?' she asked. There was a thundering sound above, as of a jangling piano on a wooden floor, and people stamping and shouting. Tom's windows were rattling with the force of it.

He rolled his eyes. 'The upstairs neighbours.'

She stared. There was no noise like this in Piccadilly. 'Can't you tell them to stop?'

He gave her a wry grin. 'Be my guest. But I wouldn't recommend it. They're not usually entirely sober this time of day.'

'But how do you sleep?'

He shrugged. 'I'm used to it.'

'Can't you move?'

'I could. If I had the money.'

Marion, reddening, wondered why she had assumed that everyone in London lived like the Yorks did, amid the carpeted peace of many-roomed mansions.

On a shelf near his bed was a photograph of a pretty young woman. Her insides clenched. 'Who's that?' she asked, attempting insouciance.

'My sister, Kate.'

'Does she live in London?'

He shook his head. 'I'm from Cornwall.'

So that was the accent. 'How romantic,' she said, thinking of craggy rocks dashed by turbulent seas, of picturesque villages in the folds of rolling hills.

'Not if you're Kate,' Tom said shortly. 'She's got TB.'

Marion's hands flew to her face. She stared back at him, aghast. 'I'm so sorry. How absolutely dreadful of me.'

'You weren't to know.' His eyes were on his sister's face. 'But you're right, it is dreadful. Everything I earn here goes towards her treatment. That's one reason I'm doing the photojournalism, to get some extra money for Kate.' He smiled at her. 'Want to see my latest, by the way?'

The miniscule bathroom, in which two people could hardly stand together, doubled as a darkroom. It had a red bulb, and lines of drying photographs were strung up near the ceiling. He took them down and showed her some of the pictures he had taken recently: poor children in the East End of London, stick-thin, sunken-eyed and shoeless. She looked at him with brimming eyes; his face was right next to hers. 'They're very powerful.'

He pulled her to him and kissed her. She clung to him as if he were the answer to every conundrum and contradiction swirling within her. She allowed him to lead her into the little bedroom, gently undress her and make love to her. He was unhurried in all the ways Valentine had been abrupt. Generous as Valentine had been selfish. Desire thundered within her, drowning out even the piano music coming from above. When it was all over, she lay in his arms. She felt calm, and complete, as if something long searched for had finally been found.

Tenderly, he nuzzled her hair. 'Don't go,' he said.

Marion now felt pulled in any number of different ways. To help her decide, she made a list of pros and cons. The best pros were Elizabeth, Tom and 'Operation Normal', as he called her programme of outings. The worst cons were the continuing absence from college, from Grassmarket and from her mother. She added Queen Mary,

Alah and the lack of direction from the duchess. Without support, what could she do?

She looked at the list when she had finished it. The pros and cons seemed fairly evenly balanced. Perhaps she should just leave things as they were. Let events take their course. They were drifting, but not unpleasantly.

Then she squared her shoulders and raised her chin. She was not here to drift. She had come here with a mission. But as she was not allowed to perform it, she should just go back.

That weekend, at Royal Lodge, she went to the duchess's study. It was a charming, octagonal room with tables heaped with books and panelled walls hung with paintings. An air of comfort pervaded, along with the powerful scent of roses. Within a green marble fireplace, a fire flickered calmly.

At the back by a tall, pink-curtained window, a big mahogany writing desk was crowded with photographs and personal effects. 'Crawfie!' The duchess looked up, her ivory skin glowing in the light of a fringed lamp. 'Do you want to talk to me?'

Marion hesitated. The strong, clear words in strong clear tones that she had rehearsed in her bedroom had deserted her. All the power in the room had shifted, or so it seemed, to the woman at the desk. But it was hers, surely, Marion thought. She was the one leaving. 'It's just . . .' she began.

The shining head behind the desk graciously tilted. 'Just?'

Marion stared down at her hands, twisting together. 'My trial period is over, ma'am.'

'Is it *really?*'

'Yes, ma'am. I . . .' But the words about returning to Scotland and her intended career path died in Marion's mouth. The blue eyes fixed on her had a mesmerising power.

'But of course you must stay,' the duchess said mildly, as if the whole affair had been settled long ago and couldn't be more obvious or simple.

Marion made an effort to rally. 'But, ma'am. I – '

The telephone on the duchess's desk now shrilled. She picked it up and exclaimed, with delight, 'Hello, you old fruit!'

The interview was clearly over. It was, Marion thought as she left the room, almost as if the duchess had a button under her desk to arrange convenient telephone interruptions.

She returned to Edinburgh, ostensibly to collect her things but really to think it all over again. 'I'm really not sure,' she said to her mother. 'I always meant to leave after a month.'

Here in Scotland, with almost the length of England between them, the duchess's strange, blue-eyed power had no dominion. Tom, on the other hand, did. She desired him and admired him equally; his pioneering photography was fascinating and his devotion to his sister touching. She would have liked to inspire his devotion herself, but she had to be sensible. Attractive though he was, she hardly knew him. She could not base a decision this important on the strength of a few dates. Her previous romantic experience attested to that.

The worst pull was Elizabeth. But now, back in the city of Annie McGinty, there was no real contest. With so much misery and poverty, how could her work with the Yorks be justified? Even if she got permission for them, what difference would a few tube trips make? How could she return to London?

She would stay in Scotland, Marion decided, and do what she wanted, what she had always intended: go back to college, to the children in Grassmarket. Take up where she had left off. Her mother, royalist as she was, had surely had enough of living alone now. She would be glad to have her only child return.

'You should go back to them,' Mrs Crawford said, to Marion's astonishment.

They were standing in the little stone-flagged galley kitchen. Mrs Crawford was frying bacon and eggs for breakfast. On the scrubbed wooden table next to the green enamel cooker, two plain white plates stood ready. It was, admittedly, very different from the Meissen and footmen of life with the Yorks, not to mention food cooked by a professional chef. Marion pushed this reflection aside.

'Don't you want me home, Mother?'

'Of course I do.' Her mother sighed, then knit her brows determinedly.

Marion was exasperated. 'Mother, I'm not staying in London just so you can tell the butcher's queue that I work for the royal family.'

'It's not that. You said yourself that you haven't finished the job with Elizabeth. You've hardly started, in fact.'

'You sound like Miss Golspie,' Marion said sulkily, regretting she had admitted these details.

Mrs Crawford nodded. 'As a matter of fact, Miss Golspie's been to see me.'

'*Has* she?'

'She was just passing, she said, and dropped in for coffee.'

Marion raised an eyebrow. This seemed unlikely. Moray House College and the Crawfords' little terrace were on opposite sides of the city.

'I mentioned that you were coming home. We had quite a chat.' Her mother's eyes were bright with the remembered importance of being sought out by so great a person.

Marion folded her arms. 'And?'

There was a hiss as Mrs Crawford lifted the bacon from the pan. 'They need you, the Yorks. The princess in particular needs you.' She picked up the plates and carried them into the tiny sitting room, where the folding table had been put up.

Marion followed with the teapot, which she set down next to a copy of *The Times*. Its presence was unexpected; her mother's preferred reading matter were picture papers.

The front page described how another hunger march, reaching London, had had the petition it carried, intended for Parliament, confiscated. Scuffles were reported. There was a photograph of police on horseback armed with long batons; another of a group of officers dragging a young man along the ground. She wondered if Tom had taken it. A powerful longing went through her.

'This is a dangerous situation,' said Mrs Crawford, nodding at the paper. 'The country's becoming divided between the haves and the have-nots.'

Marion could hear Isabel Golspie's voice in this. The principal had clearly been working on her mother. The newspaper was there on purpose, part of an argument. 'But what can *I* do?' she asked, stubbornly. 'I've tried my best.'

'So try again! Get that wee bairn out from behind those palace walls,' her mother instructed. 'Like Miss Golspie told you to.'

'But they won't let me!' Marion cried.

Her mother's eyes flashed. 'So make them let you! You've got to show her how ordinary people live. She's the future of the royal family. But if they go on like this, they might not even have one.' She waved a reddened hand at *The Times*.

'You don't seriously think there'll be a revolution?' Remembering her mother's contempt for Valentine, she almost wanted to laugh.

'Well, it happened to the czar! And he was the king's own cousin!'

Marion's insides froze. She thought of Elizabeth. She knew, from the romps, what shrieks in the Royal Lodge corridors sounded like.

She felt manipulated. Cornered. 'But my vocation's here,' she began, and stopped. She sounded unconvincing, even to herself. 'I want to work in Grassmarket. Get *that* wee bairn out from behind *those* walls. Slum walls, not palace ones.'

Her mother gripped her hand. 'It's time to make your vocation somewhere else. Make a different sort of a difference.'

Next day, on her way to Grassmarket, Marion mulled over this exchange. Her mother, obviously backed by Miss Golspie, had made a powerful case. Could she really do more good in London than here?

She was thinking so intently that she did not notice the figure approaching her in the street. And when it did, recognition was slow to come.

'Ethel?' Her old classmate was barely recognisable. Previously plump, glossy of hair and bossy of manner, she seemed like a balloon with the air gone. She was thinner, her shoulders were slumped and the formerly shiny bun was straggly and uncombed. The once-bright brown eyes were faded, and there hung about her an air of exhausted defeat. Had she been ill?

'How's the family?' Marion asked.

'Jock's minding Lizzie,' Ethel said.

'Good.' More men should share the childcare burden, Marion felt. But why was Ethel's stare so hostile?

'It's *not* good,' she blurted. 'He's lost his job. The shipyard cut back – he's a ship riveter – and . . .' She bit her lip hard.

'Well, that's hardly his fault,' Marion robustly assured her.

'No, it's not,' Ethel agreed, heatedly. 'But a lot of folk seem to think it is. Talking about lazy idle loafers on the dole.' She stopped, her eyes glistening.

Marion stared. The right thing to say seemed suddenly elusive. Ethel did not especially seem to expect it, however.

'We've had to throw my mother out.' Her voice was choked with anger. 'That bloody Means Test.'

'What do you mean?' Marion knew the Means Test assessed household income by means of invasive, humiliating questioning. But why would Ethel have to eject her parent?

'They deducted money because they said she was a lodger. But she wasn't paying anything. She doesn't have anything. None of us do.' Ethel raised a reddened hand to her mouth.

Marion stared at the pavement. She had no idea what to say, except that on no account would she be revealing who she worked for.

But Ethel seemed to know. She felt her hand being seized, suddenly. The other woman's defeated expression had changed to one of sudden, violent hope. 'I'm sure the king would help us,' she said desperately. 'Will you put in a good word? Please?'

Marion went on to Grassmarket with a sinking heart. It was like living in a nightmare; other people's nightmares, but nightmares all the same.

At the McGintys', things were not only as bad as anticipated, but worse. McGinty had returned with his barrel organ, but brought no new prosperity. Rather, he drank away what little his daughter and her mother brought in. 'He's like a de'il when he's been out smelling the cork,' Annie reported.

Thin before, she was skeletal now. Her cheeks sported the accumulated dirt of weeks and her rusty hair stuck out in all directions. Her thin cotton gown was all but worn out and her shawl was threadbare. When she walked she shuffled along in case her large men's slippers, found on a rubbish heap, should slip off her feet. Mrs McGinty, formerly an assiduous mother, was now clearly too ill to be one. She was almost blind and suffering from neuralgia. To help with the pain, she had tied a dirty scrap of flannel round her head, but clearly it made little difference.

Back at home, with her mother, Marion flung herself on the sofa in despair. 'It's so *unfair*! I want to do something about it!'

Perching on the sofa arm, Mrs Crawford stroked her daughter's troubled head. 'But you can't do anything. Not here.'

True, Marion knew. She could not get Jock his job back, and even teaching Annie was out of the question now, given her charring obligations and the return of her obstructive father.

'I'll visit them for you,' her mother promised. 'I'll keep an eye on Annie.'

Marion raised her head. 'Really?' Her mother had never set foot in Grassmarket in her life. She was amazed and touched. 'You'll do that? For me?'

Her mother nodded. Her eyes were glistening. 'For you, for little Elizabeth. So you can do what you meant to do. Marion, you *have* to go back.'

Chapter Seventeen

She travelled back south through a lush late-summer landscape. On the rack above her seat was a suitcase with a new outfit. Marion herself was in need of a replacement wardrobe, but these clothes were not for her. They were many sizes too small and for someone else entirely.

She had exacted this price at least. If she was to go back, it would be with a set of playclothes for Elizabeth. Running up a hard-wearing tartan skirt on the Singer and knitting a warm red jersey in the armchair had been no problem for her nimble-fingered mother. On the contrary; she had set about it with delight.

And of course, Marion thought, looking out at the sunny fields, there were other advantages too. She would not have to leave the princess, and she would see Tom again.

And as for Annie McGinty and her teaching course, well, she *would* return. Just not straight away. Fate, in the unlikely combined form of Miss Golspie, Ethel McKinley, her mother and the Duchess of York, had decreed otherwise. Fate had also made her task clear, and she planned to put it into action the instant she arrived at Piccadilly.

'*Crawfie!*'

She had barely got through the door when Lilibet, who had clearly been waiting for her, hurled herself across the hall and clasped her in a hug. But something had hurled itself after her – something low-slung and ginger-coloured. The princess threw herself on the carpet with a scream of rapture. Her absence, Marion saw, had coincided with the arrival of the long-hoped-for dog.

'His name is Rozavel Golden Eagle!' Lilibet gasped, excitedly. Marion had never seen her so utterly delighted. She was now sitting up, laughing as the rough-haired ginger animal licked her face.

'That's a very long name.'

'The kennels called him Dookie! Because they knew he was going to live with the Duke of York!'

Not everyone shared the princess's joy at this arrangement, Marion guessed. Ainslie was edging round the hall walls, a nervous smile on his face. A housemaid hobbled past, face pale with pain and annoyance. She hurled a gaze of hot loathing at the dog, who was now running over the princess's stomach as she lay on her back, fondling the animal's large ears and tickling its barrel-like body. It was not a breed Marion recognised.

'He's a corgi!' Lilibet cried happily. She stared at Marion's luggage. 'Is that a pirate chest out of a story?'

'Absolutely.' Marion played along immediately. 'A pirate gave it to me.'

Actually, the little polished curved-lid box had been a farewell gift from her mother. The wood had, in a former life, been the panelling in the wardroom of a German battleship scuttled by her crew in Scapa Flow. It was bound with brass fittings and had an 'M' set in lighter wood into the lid.

She smiled at Lilibet. She looked beautiful with her shining eyes and the huge monkey grin that transformed her serious face. She had grown taller even in the past week, and lost some of her childish plumpness. Marion hoped the playclothes would fit.

She must go and hand them over immediately. There was no way round it. Mrs Knight was in charge of clothes and dressing, and the princesses' wardrobes were her kingdom.

The exchange was done on the nursery threshold, over whose boundary no representative of the schoolroom could cross. Looking unimpressed, Mrs Knight took the parcel and began to open it.

Marion glanced past her into the green-painted nursery, where Margaret, as usual, was standing up in her cot, gripping the wooden bars and staring at the budgerigars in the cage by the window. It was possible she shared with them a fellow feeling.

She really must have a word about this, Marion thought. But that was a battle for another day.

'And what might these be, Miss Crawford?' The nanny's thick fingers had reached the tartan skirt and jumper.

'Playclothes, Mrs Knight,' Marion said pleasantly. Against the unrelieved black of the nanny's uniform, the little red outfit struck an optimistic note. 'If you could dress, er, Lilibet in them for lessons, that would be lovely.'

The nanny raised her square chin in challenge. The child's nickname had been, until now, her prerogative. Marion met the flinty gaze without flinching. *Yes, Mrs Knight. Things are about to change round here.*

Later, having failed to locate the duchess, she approached the duke's ground-floor study and knocked. Unexpectedly, a gale of laughter greeted this. She twisted the knob and popped her head round the door. 'May I come in?'

The Yorks were both there, sitting on either side of a fireplace with a large oil painting of cows above it. The evening sunshine fell on the duchess's diamond rings and glowed on a double row of large pearls. 'Oh, it's you, Crawfie.'

As if, Marion thought, she had simply gone round the corner and not the entire length of Britain in order to rethink her whole future. Not to mention theirs.

'Yes, it's me, ma'am. I'm back from Scotland.'

The duke held a cut-glass tumbler of whisky and the duchess a glass of champagne, almost empty. 'And how is my dear homeland?' she asked.

'It seemed fine, ma'am.'

Marion wondered how long had they been drinking. The duchess's eyes were misty. Her glass was now completely empty. 'My ain countree!' she declaimed. 'How I *long* to live in some far wee croftie next to the shining river!'

The door opened and a footman entered with a silver tray, on which stood a full flute of champagne. Glasses were exchanged. 'Thank you, Fotheringay.'

Watching Fotheringay bow and retreat backward out of the room, Marion reminded herself that she had returned with the express purpose of connecting these people with ordinary life. It was clearly going to be an uphill struggle. But she may as well get on with it. 'Ma'am?'

The duchess took a hearty swig of champagne. 'Wonderful calves,' she remarked vaguely.

'Calves?' Marion glanced at the cows above the fireplace.

'Used to be frightfully important in a footman. In my grandfather's day the butler actually measured them with a compass to make sure they were all the same size.'

Marion took a deep breath. 'I would like to ask permission to take Princess Elizabeth on the Underground.'

The Yorks stared at her in amazement. It was as if she had suggested taking their daughter to the moon.

'I thought it would be good for her to see the . . .' Marion stopped. She had been about to say 'normal world', but that implied that the one Lilibet lived in was abnormal. 'Real world', similarly, seemed to set up unfavourable comparison with 'royal'. 'The ordinary world,' she said, eventually. 'To see how . . .' Marion paused again. 'How *other* people live.'

She looked from the wide, creamy face to the grey and drawn one and waited for the light to dawn. For them to see that she was trying to help them, not to mention their daughter.

Eventually, the duke spoke. 'It m-m-might be a g-good idea, darling,' he said to his wife.

'But Bertie! The *Underground*.' The duchess clenched her champagne flute for support.

'They don't have to g-g-go far. They could visit Mama and Papa.'

Marion felt impatient. To go from the Piccadilly mansion to Buckingham Palace hardly counted as exposure to the real world. But she had anticipated this, and had a plan. 'I thought, perhaps, the new central YWCA?'

Elizabeth of York looked blank.

'I believe you opened it, ma'am? It's on the Tottenham Court Road?'

'Oh yes. Vaguely. A new building, by Mr Lutyens? Rather modern?'

'Exactly, ma'am.' This was part of the plan too. Lilibet had probably never been in a building more recent than the mid-nineteenth century. 'Very modern. It has a cafeteria where you serve yourself.'

Right on cue, Fotheringay now returned. He took a new glass of champagne from his salver and placed it by the duchess. She sipped, musingly. 'Serve yourself? What *marvellous* fun!'

Chapter Eighteen

On the morning of the Underground outing, Lilibet spent a long time getting ready. Or rather, Mrs Knight spent a long time getting her ready. Deliberately, Marion guessed as she paced round and round the upstairs gallery. The glassy-eyed stares of Lilibet's horses only added to her agitation. It was a relief when, at long last, the nursery door swung open. But almost as soon it became disappointment.

'She can't wear this, Mrs Knight!'

Lilibet, hopping from foot to foot in excitement, the Underground map flapping in her hand, was resplendent in satin shoes and lace ruffles. 'She's going on public transport,' Marion went on. 'What's happened to the playclothes?'

They hadn't been seen since the moment they were handed over, almost a week ago now. Mrs Knight always had an excuse, none convincing. Convincing was obviously not the point.

Now there was an impassive shrug from the broad, black-clad shoulders. 'In the laundry, possibly?'

'But, Mrs Knight, they're not dirty.' She forced herself to sound calm. She wouldn't reveal how hurt she felt on her behalf of her mother, who had worked on the clothes so hard and with such good intentions. 'Lilibet hasn't worn them.'

She had expected anger about the clothes, even a scene. But that Mrs Knight would simply refuse to dress Lilibet in the little skirt and jersey had never crossed her mind. Now, she could not think why it hadn't. That this would be the response was obvious. Had she just been too hopeful? Naive?

But the ghastly woman would not get the better of her. She had a larger goal in mind; it would not be derailed so easily. She tried hard to maintain a pleasant manner. 'Perhaps you could look again, Mrs Knight? Or I could look for you?'

At this, the gimlet eyes narrowed. That would never be allowed.

Marion sighed. In order to win the war, she must accept she had lost this battle. 'Perhaps a coat and beret then, Mrs Knight?' Anything to cover up all those frills. And that silly satin ribbon.

Finally, after much more unnecessary delay, they set off along Piccadilly. Behind them was Cameron.

Cameron was the Yorks' detective and just as disobliging as his colleague in the nursery. Perhaps they were even in cahoots. Certainly, as far as being a detective went, Cameron was a liability. A bespectacled, mackintoshed Scot with a thin moustache, homburg hat and theatrically suspicious manner, he was the visual embodiment of his profession.

Was he out to undermine the expedition? In Hyde Park Corner Underground, he marched ponderously about, hands behind his back, darting searching glances from under his hat brim into the corners of the station ceiling. He drew attention from all quarters. People stared at him, and it seemed only a matter of time before they noticed Lilibet too.

Especially as Marion had encouraged her to buy her own ticket, which proved to be a slow business. She now stood at the counter in her coat and beret, fumbling in a little embroidered purse and counting out the unfamiliar coins with frowning concentration. Marion was on tenterhooks, expecting her to exclaim, any moment, 'But that looks nothing like Grandpapa!' This had been her reaction to the back of the thrupenny bit.

The ticket lady was doing her best to help, and so far had not recognised her small customer. Finally, the princess turned away from the kiosk with a small piece of pasteboard and a smile as triumphant as if she had invented the Underground, and wasn't just riding on it.

Marion felt her worries fall away and a wave of joy roll through her. For all of the aggravation, it was worth it, it really was.

She glanced at Cameron. The great detective had his back turned and was currently investigating some posters advertising the south coast. It was tempting to sneak off and leave him there. But then he whirled round, rolled a cartoonishly distrustful eye and marched after them towards the platforms.

A cut-glass scream from Lilibet. 'Crawfie! The stairs are moving!'

Marion did her best to place herself between her charge and the amused Londoners for whom the new escalators were already old hat. Lilibet gripped the moving handrail and gasped with delicious fear as she sailed down into the depths of the station.

On the platform, she took a keen interest in the other passengers. 'Don't stare quite so much,' Marion muttered.

'I'm not staring!' replied the high, clear voice. 'What's that *awful* smell?'

Marion moved them down the platform, away from the malodorous tramp. The train now arrived, amid much rushing and noise. 'It's magic!' Lilibet exclaimed, as the doors sprang open by themselves.

The feeling of delight seized Marion again, just as long as it took to see that Cameron, staring intently in turn at every occupant, his arms belligerently folded, again threatened to ruin everything. She clenched her fists in frustration. Even she, a newcomer to London, knew that on the train you looked at the floor. Or else at your paper.

Lilibet wasn't really helping. She was talking to her neighbour, a large, red-faced woman who looked quite spellbound. 'Oh, Crawfie,' the princess said happily, 'this is Mrs Simmons. She's a charlady from Muswell Hill. Isn't that just *too* marvellous?'

The hall at Piccadilly came back to Marion; the duchess's acting class for the Prince of Wales. It seemed that Lilibet had had the same instruction as her uncle.

'Do you really use a bucket?' the princess was asking her neighbour. 'I *love* buckets. You can make the most wonderful sandcastles with them.'

It was a relief when the train slid into the station and the magic words Tottenham Court Road appeared on the tiled wall. They had arrived!

Lilibet loved everything about the YWCA, from the imposing

double staircase that led to the red-brick entrance to the big café dining room with its practical chairs and tables.

Most exciting of all had been the tea; the thick cups and saucers, the bread-and-butter of doorstep proportions – so different from the wafer-thin slices she was used to – and the thrilling moment when, assuming that everything would be brought to her, the princess left her teapot on the counter. The woman at the till had leaned on her meaty forearms and bawled after her. 'This is self-service, you know! If you want it, you must come and fetch it!'

'Such a loud shout!' Lilibet reminisced, blissfully.

They had been seated a mere ten minutes. The little girl had positioned her crockery, cut her bread and butter into eight absolutely equal pieces and was beginning to alternate eating them with swigs of sugary tea. But then, suddenly and without warning, they had been bundled by Cameron into the YWCA manager's office. As they sat on a row of hastily arranged office chairs in front of the excited official's desk, a call was placed to 145 Piccadilly, requesting a car.

'What's going on?' Marion had demanded of the detective. 'Just what do you think you are doing?'

Cameron's little round glasses flashed as he looked at her. 'Miss Crawford. You are underestimating the very real dangers posed by Irish republicanism. There are terrorists everywhere.'

'Terrorists?' echoed Lilibet, clearly thrilled.

'But no one knows she's here!' Marion argued. 'It's a completely secret visit.'

Cameron looked at her. 'Someone knew. There were press photographers outside.'

Marion glared at him. She didn't believe this for a moment. If word had got out and their cover had been blown, the most likely culprit was Cameron himself. He had, from the moment of arrival, paraded pompously about the café, ostentatiously taking notes and examining the furniture in the most ridiculous fashion.

Her arguments were in vain, however. The car had arrived soon after and they were rushed out as if the whole place was about to explode. The return trip on the Underground was abandoned.

She had got Lilibet out of the gilded cage only to see her dragged back in and the door swiftly shut. Marion looked out with hot eyes as the shops of Oxford Street passed by. She thought of Mrs Knight's enmity, the duchess's incomprehension, Cameron's incompetence. Her disappointment gave way to despair. Really, what was the point?

She felt a strange sensation in her fingers. A small hand, its once-white gloves stained with YWCA butter, was pressing hers. She turned her head. An eager little face was looking up at her.

'Never mind, Crawfie,' Lilibet said reassuringly. 'It wasn't your fault.'

Something hard rolled up Marion's throat.

'It was such fun,' the princess went on, looking wistfully at the little pasteboard tube ticket she held in her other hand. She was clearly wondering when, if ever, she would be allowed back into the ordinary world.

Watching her, Marion felt galvanised. A new determination spread through her. *Soon,* she silently promised the princess. *Soon.* And she'd get those playclothes back as well.

Chapter Nineteen

Marion gazed at Tom fondly over the café's sticky table-top. It was a frequent evening rendezvous, round the corner from both their places of work. Small, cheap and unglamorous as it was, it had the quality of magic for her. Tom was in it, and that was enough.

Was she in love? After the trauma of Valentine, she was reluctant to think of it as such. She had been in no hurry to surrender her heart again, even to someone as handsome and interesting as Tom. Fun and companionship were fine, of course. But no more than that.

But Tom had insinuated himself in her life so quickly. She saw him most evenings now and had almost come to depend on him. He was so supportive, so interested. He encouraged her to unburden herself, and after a day dealing with the caprices of the duchess, or the petty meanness of Mrs Knight, it was a relief to do so.

He never seemed bored. Rather, he sympathised and asked questions. He seemed to understand how difficult and strange her work could be, how demanding and wearing all the different personalities. Of course, he knew some of them personally, which helped. No detail seemed too small to interest him. He seemed to find it all fascinating and, by extension, her. She loved amusing and amazing him. 'Really?' he would say. Or 'You *are* joking?' Complaining had never been so much fun.

Just now she had been telling him about Mrs Knight and the play-clothes. She had expected his usual riveted attention but for some reason it seemed elsewhere. 'Am I boring you?' she teased, nudging him.

He looked at her as if he were coming back from somewhere very far away. 'Sorry. A bit distracted, that's all.'

'Work?'

He shrugged. 'Can't complain. Mr Adams is good to me.'

'The photojournalism, I mean.'

He looked down. He had competition, she knew. Others were catching up. The picture she had seen in Scotland had been not by him, but someone else.

'Is is Kate?' she asked, gently.

But Tom did not seem to want to talk about his sister. He made an obvious effort to cheer up and concentrate. 'How's Operation Normal going?' he teased.

Marion rolled her eyes. 'We're confined to the garden at the moment. The scare at the YWCA put the kibosh on things for a while.' She buttered her scone agitatedly. 'So ridiculous, Cameron saying there were photographers. No one knew she was there.'

As Tom stared into his tea, she thought again of his sister and how ridiculously small her troubles were in comparison. Really, why should he care? She should just deal with it, confront the old bat about the missing outfit once and for all. Mrs Knight was obviously intending to hide the clothes until Elizabeth was too big to wear them. Well, she would not succeed.

'Miss Crawford?' Mrs Knight's tone was predictably hostile. Over her arm, she had one of Margaret's long white nightdresses, which she was in the act of folding.

Marion was pleasant, but direct. 'It's about Lilibet's play outfit.'

Mrs Knight did not reply. She turned and went back into the nursery. A faint sound caught Marion's ear. The nanny was humming to herself as she continued folding the nightdress. A small smile was playing about the thin lips.

Marion stepped over the sacred threshold and into the room. The nanny stopped humming immediately, whirled and glared at her. She met the glare steadily. 'Where are the clothes?'

Flinty eyes met hers. 'I haven't seen them.'

'But they must be here. Where else would they be?'

The nanny said nothing. And she could do nothing, Marion knew.

This was Mrs Knight's domain. It was out of the question for her to start rummaging in every drawer. She turned angrily on her heel and left.

Even hampered by frills, Lilibet had improved at games. Her catching was now expert and her double-skipping of salt, mustard, vinegar, pepper, within the turn of a rope tied to a tree, was now dazzlingly fast. She jumped the hopscotch course with the grace of a Highland dancer.

'And now let's play Deliveries, Crawfie!'

It was the day after the encounter with Mrs Knight. They were in the garden for the mid-lesson break. Marion shot an apprehensive look towards the railings that separated it from the park. There had been unhelpful developments here, too.

Some days ago, a picture had appeared in one of the newspapers of Lilibet playing on the lawn. Small knots of sightseers had started to gather as a result.

How the picture had got there, Marion had no idea. The duchess had been outraged. 'He must have been hiding in one of the bushes!'

'Surely not, ma'am. Who would do that?'

The blue eyes flashed. 'Well, it better not happen again, Crawfie. You know what Alah and Cameron say. There are some dangerous people out there.'

Marion heard the unmistakable sound of a gauntlet being thrown down. If more pictures appeared, the duchess was saying, that would be an end to garden games. This was infuriating in itself; but what was she, Marion, to do? It was hardly her fault.

More exasperating still was the double standard. As she knew from Tom, the duchess actively sought newspaper space for Marcus Adams' pictures of her daughters. But anyone else's were considered a gross breach of privacy.

'Come on, Crawfie! Paw the ground! Like this.' The small satin shoe, besmirched with mud, stamped on the grass.

Lilibet had not yet commented on the faces that now lined up daily behind the garden railings to watch her. It was possible she had either not noticed them or, as she had at the dance class, accepted being stared at as her lot.

But Marion, a grown woman in jingling bells and red leather straps, felt not only ridiculous but protective. The princess had so little freedom. Pushing for more was an uphill struggle as it was. Her eyes flicked about the crowd. If someone here had a camera, she would act.

The small collection of people looked harmless enough. She looked closer and harder. Still nothing.

'Crawfie!' cried Lilibet, jingling the reins. 'Do gallop faster!'

She had no choice but to comply, and to charge about, neighing and pawing. But was that, now, in the garden corner, at the edge of the shrubbery – a flash of light on glass? 'Go to the garden door,' Marion whispered to her charge.

'But, Crawfie!'

'Go!'

As soon as Lilibet was safely by the house, Marion charged over to the shrubbery. Still in her harness, bells jangling with fury, she wrenched back the branches. As she had suspected, the lens of a small camera stared back at her.

'How dare you!' she yelled. 'This is a private garden! You are invading the princess's privacy! Have you no shame?' The idea of someone making money out of her innocent charge, and imprisoning her yet further in the process, filled her with a violent anger. 'You are disgusting!' she screeched at the hapless cameraman, who had now lowered his lens to expose his face. Shock barrelled through her as she saw, looking back at her, a pair of level grey eyes: Tom's eyes.

'You!' she gasped, staggering backward. She clutched at the bush to stop herself falling. The world stopped for a moment, immobilised by the sheer impossibility of it all. Then it started again and got faster and faster as not only did she realise it was happening and real, but that the duchess was quite right; this probably was all her fault. Tom knew every movement of her day, after all. Only one aspect was unexplained: why? What on earth had possessed him?

'Are you mad?' she yelled. He stared back at her, his face expressionless, but something in his eyes, something hard and defiant, gave her the clue. A cold surge of horror rose within her.

Cameron had not been imagining it. There really had been a photographer outside the YWCA. Tom. He had known all about the planned trip. He knew everything, and that was why he had cultivated her. He had never cared for her. He had deliberately seduced her. When she had thought he was sympathising, he was merely intelligence-gathering. All he had ever wanted from her was information. She had been deluding herself. Yet again.

The realisation made her dumb. She could only watch him turn and walk rapidly away, then drop her eyes to the sooty grass. A great wave of self-pity broke over her; her vision blurred and she wanted to fling herself on the ground and howl. But she had Lilibet to think of, and so she raised her chin, blinked hard and forced a smile as she hurried to the garden door, the bells tinkling ridiculously as she went.

In the hallway, Lilibet was beaming. 'Crawfie, you were *savage*!' she said in delight. 'I'm sure he thinks now that Crawfies bite!'

Later, Marion was in the lift. It being a Friday, they were going to Royal Lodge and she needed to collect her few things. There was another passenger – a young woman with a turned-up nose and pert air. Marion knew her by sight well enough; she was a housemaid, and one of the group that travelled between Piccadilly and Royal Lodge. She had an idea that her name was Ivy, but along with her colleagues, the maid had never said a single friendly word.

Accordingly, Marion avoided looking at her. This was easy to do as the girl was a good foot shorter than she was. She fixed her gaze high on the gleaming panelling and abandoned herself to her miserable thoughts. The first shock had given way to disbelief. He had seemed so genuinely fond of her. And he was a photojournalist, crusader for truth, devoted brother of a sick sister. It was incomprehensible.

Tears swam before her eyes; she blinked them back. Feeling confused was a luxury she could not afford. She had to think. This could get her in a lot of trouble. She was implicated; she had been intimate with Tom, told him things. Should any of this be discovered, she might even be dismissed. The fact that she had been entirely innocent, her only crime being to trust him, would count for nothing with her mistress. Beneath her soft exterior, there was something ruthless about the duchess. 'Y'all right?' came an unexpected voice from below. 'If yer don't mind me sayin' so, yer look in a right two and eight.'

Marion looked down into a pair of sharp black eyes. 'A what?' she asked, coldly. When she first came to this house, she would have been glad of a friendly word from a colleague. But now, what did it matter? What did anything?

The girl grinned, showing small wonky teeth. 'State. Condition of considerable agitation.'

'You could say that,' Marion said shortly.

'So what's the matter? That old bat Knight upset you?'

This was a surprise. Marion had imagined complete solidarity behind the nursery door.

'Bloody old tartar,' Ivy went on, resentfully. 'Got more airs and graces than the bloomin' duchess 'erself. Won't even pick up anything off the floor. Muggins 'ere 'as to scrabble about after 'er if she as much as drops 'er 'anky.'

'She says she doesn't know where Lilibet's playclothes are,' Marion said, dully. Ivy put out a narrow finger and pressed a button in the gleaming brass panel. The lift juddered to a stop immediately.

'She bleedin' well does. Saw 'er shove 'em in the Mother 'Ubbard meself.'

'Mother 'Ubbard . . . Hubbard?'

'Cupboard. She's 'idden 'em, the old bitch.'

Marion narrowed her eyes. Just as she had thought.

'Want me to get 'em back for you?'

Marion stared at Ivy. '*Could* you?'

The sharp face had a resolute look. 'Reckon so. Don't think she saw me watchin'. I'll just wait for 'er to spend a penny. She always takes ages.'

'Why are you helping me?' Marion asked. 'No one's as much as spoken to me until now.'

Ivy shrugged. 'Reckon it's a bit unfair, meself. You don't seem a bad sort to me.'

Given her current troubles, it felt like a vote of confidence. Marion smiled back, grateful.

But nothing had happened, either about the clothes or the photographs, by the time, that afternoon, they set off for Royal Lodge. All the way there, as Lilibet chattered, Marion churned inwardly with self-recrimination and dread.

How could she have got Tom so wrong? How could he do this to her? It might cost her her career. The papers' late editions must be out by now. What if a picture of Lilibet had appeared? Possibly with her in it too, complete with bells and reins. What if the duchess thought she and Tom had colluded, for money? The thought made Marion feel sick.

The loss of Tom seemed nothing beside the loss of the job. Now that she risked losing it, she wanted desperately to keep it. She had planned to leave in the past, of course. But that was entirely different from being sacked in shameful circumstances. What would her mother say? Miss Golspie? They would be so disappointed. And the thought of never seeing Lilibet again was unbearable. That was the worst thing of all.

Later she sat in her room, trying to read, but her eyes slid off the lines on the page. She expected a knock at any moment. When one finally came, she almost shot ten feet into the air. She composed herself as best she could and opened the door to receive her fate.

'Wotcha!' Instead of Ainslie, come to escort her off the premises, Ivy stood there, her pinched face flushed, a red jumper and a tartan skirt in her arms.

Marion stared at her. Compared to what she had been expecting, the friendly gesture meant as much as the clothes. Inexpressibly moved, she flung her arms around her. 'Thank you!'

Ivy looked surprised, but pleased. 'Anything to get one over on that old cow. Pain in the Khyber, she is.'

'Khyber?' repeated Marion, struggling with her emotions.

'Khyber Pass. Arse.'

Marion laughed. 'I've never heard of that.'

'Why would yer? You're pimple and blotch.'

Marion raised her hands to her face, indignant. Her skin was excellent, or so she had thought.

Ivy cackled. 'Scotch, I mean. Don't yer know rhymin' slang? You speak it if you're born in the East End. Like me. I'm one o' nine bin lids.'

'Bin . . . ?'

'Kids.'

'Ha.' Marion was beginning to get the idea now. She felt encouraged by Ivy's friendliness. 'Want to come in?' she asked, holding her door open. It suddenly felt like a long time since she had talked to someone her own age.

Ivy came in and sat down on the bed. 'So 'ow d'you like it 'ere?' she asked.

'I'm getting used to it.'

Ivy snorted. 'There's a lot to get used to.' She flicked Marion a sharp glance. 'Got a young man, 'ave you?'

The almost brutal directness was a relief. A more sympathetic approach might have been an invitation to throw herself on Ivy's scanty bosom and confess all. As it was, Marion shook her head vehemently and stared at the lino. 'Absolutely not.' And that, she was quite determined, was the way it would remain.

Ivy was stepping out with a footman from Buckingham Palace. 'You've met 'im,' she said. 'When you went to see Queen Mary.'

'Oh yes!' Marion smiled at the memory. 'We had to turn to the wall when Princess Mary went past.'

Ivy cackled. 'Unbelievable, ain't it? Alf says that even when they're eating on their own the queen wears her tiara.'

Marion shook her head. 'Ridiculous.'

'Word to the wise, though.' Ivy shifted closer to her on the bed. 'If you fancy a bit of the other, make sure 'e's someone from inside.'

Marion tried, and failed, to decode this remark. 'What?'

'Boyfriends. Make sure they work for the royal family. Know the rules. That way, you won't get into any trouble.'

Marion tried to look suitably grateful, and not at all as if she had learned this lesson the hard way.

When Ivy had gone she looked at the little tartan outfit and felt warmed. She had that. She had a friend. She had Lilibet. She would put Tom behind her and forge on. If she was allowed to.

It looked as if she would be. She was down first thing to monitor the papers as they arrived, perusing them to the screams and thumps of the early-morning romp. To her vast relief, there was nothing.

The Royal Lodge day unfolded in the usual way: lessons, followed by playing in the Little House, now shining and clean in every respect. Lilibet set about polishing her set of scaled-down silver cutlery stamped with her monogram, an 'E' with a crown above it, while Marion admired the miniature oil painting of the Duchess of York above the tiny fireplace in the sitting room. The artist had rendered beautifully her subject's vivid colouring. 'Mummie really is so pretty, isn't she?' Lilibet said lovingly. 'She's quite perfect; everyone says so. Daddy says she's the most wonderful person in the world.'

Marion was surprised to feel a powerful twinge of jealousy.

In the afternoon, also as usual, everyone put on their gardening clothes and took up their billhooks. Marion was almost glad to take part today. Relief seemed to have brought with it a new capacity for appreciation. The fresh air was delicious and the soft warmth of the afternoon sublime. Above the lawns, flower beds and shrubberies rose a blue dome of sky into which curled billows from the duke's ever-larger pyre of burning rubbish. She breathed it in, the smell and the crackle, the bright flash of fire, the sparks whirling up with the smoke. Perhaps the duchess was right about Eau de Bonfire.

Next to her, Ivy grumbled as she yanked out her namesake from the wall to which it clung.

Marion pulled up a dandelion with a long, thick yellow root. 'Look at it!' she cried in triumph. 'It's the size of a parsnip!'

Ivy aimed a kick at the passing Dookie, who was eyeing up her ankles. 'Bugger off, you bloody animal.'

Marion had to agree. Even in her new rapturous mood she could not love Dookie. While a dog had been her idea, he was the very last she would have chosen. The corgi was an arrant snob, drawing blood from those below stairs while crawling shamelessly to their masters. 'With any luck,' she said to Ivy, 'they'll soon get tired of him.'

Ivy snorted. 'They're saying the same thing about the Prince of Wales an' Mrs Simpson.'

'Who?'

The housemaid gave her a wise look. 'You mean you 'aven't 'eard?'

"Eard, I mean heard, what?'

Marion sat on her heels in the grass and listened as an entire unsuspected world was revealed. The royal family seemed rather like the moon; you saw only the shining parts while the rest was unknowable darkness. Within these mysterious shadows, Marion learned, the Prince of Wales had been having sex every afternoon for fifteen years with Mrs Dudley Ward, the wife of a Labour MP. More recently, he had added to his harem Lady Thelma Furness, the titled wife of a shipping magnate. But both of these had now been dispensed with in favour of Mrs Simpson.

She stared at the grass. She had thought the royal family had no idea of what was going on in the world outside. But the world outside had no idea of what went on within the palace. 'It's unbelievable,' she said eventually. By which she meant that she, personally, didn't believe it.

Ivy's next words made her think again. 'It's doin' all their crusts in. 'Is Majesty's especially. They've drawn up this big list of princesses for 'im to choose off, but 'e won't even look at it.'

Marion stared at her. Could it be true? She had heard the prince mention the list with her own ears.

'He could 'ave anyone, the Prince o' Wales could. An 'e chooses 'er. A skinny old foreign bag with two 'usbands.'

'Two 'usbands? *Husbands?* That's impossible.' And definitely not true.

A golden period now began. Marion sought, and was granted, permission to resume Operation Normal. The duke and duchess gave little resistance; they themselves seemed busier these days. Even the playclothes had been accepted in the nursery. Marion felt that Fortune was smiling on her at last.

The trip to Woolworths was the first triumph. They returned to Piccadilly with a great many small pottery horses, which Lilibet promptly rushed with to her mother's boudoir.

'Mummie, look! What we got from Woolies!'

'*Too* sweet, darling,' said the duchess, with a slight shudder.

Next, determined that Lilibet learn the value of money, Marion took her by bus to the Bank of England. 'Where's the old lady?' the princess asked, looking round as she hopped off.

'What old lady?'

'You said we were going to see the old lady in Threadneedle Street.'

'A figure of speech.' Smiling, Marion waved at the pillared edifice. 'It's what people call this place.'

Inside, the frock-coated chairman conveyed them through a sequence of neoclassical chambers to the vaults below. They entered through a succession of iron gates and were shown a bewildering number of curiously shaped keys. In the bullion room, Lilibet's childish features glowed in the reflection of the masses of gold bars. 'If you can pick one up, you can keep it,' the chairman told her. Marion laughed to watch her red-faced charge struggle, unsuccessfully but with typical determination, to raise one of the heavy ingots.

They went to the tiny police station hidden high up in the Wellington Arch, just across the road from Piccadilly. 'We could see Grandpapa's soldiers passing underneath on their horses!' Lilibet excitedly told the duchess later. 'And the view was all over London, it was wonderful.' The exhilaration of freedom shone from her every pore. 'And oh, Mummie, the best thing of all!' Lilibet was hopping up and down with excitement. 'It had a *cat*! A real cat! It's called Sherlock and it lives in the arch and *solves crimes*!' She pointed across the road, where the great white monument was visible through the trees.

The duke looked astonished. 'S-solves *crimes*?'

'Absolutely, sir. That's what the sergeant in charge told us.' Marion met the duke's eyes seriously. She had no intention of abandoning the amusing pretence for the sake of mere adult dignity.

'Well, it all sounds too delightful,' the duchess cooed to her daughter. 'But you'll have to say goodbye to your sleuthing felines for now. Balmoral awaits!'

Chapter Twenty

Marion was frustrated. The interruptions were over, or so she had thought. The dancing classes and singing lessons were much fewer and farther between these days. But this was the biggest interruption of all. There would be no scope at all for Operation Normal, not in the middle of a country estate.

'What am I supposed to do with Lilibet there?' she grumbled to Ivy. 'From the pictures I've seen, it's all towers and tartan.'

Ivy grinned. 'And the rest.'

'Please explain!'

They were at 145 Piccadilly, sitting on Marion's bed. Ivy drew up her knees and clasped them with her hands. Her shoes hovered above the bedclothes, carefully not touching them. 'Where shall I start? Queen Victoria's favourite chair what no one's allowed to sit in? Even though she's been dead thirty years?'

'You're joking!'

'The pipers what march round the dinin' table every night? Noise blows yer bleedin' 'ead off, and one of 'em's always drunk.'

Marion shook her head. 'I don't believe it.'

'Or the 'ead butler what wears a shepherd cloak to serve dinner in 'cos some 'ead butler to Queen Victoria stood in for Prince Albert when 'e were bein' painted as a shepherd?'

'Say that again?'

'Or the picnics by the lochside with silver, tablecloths an' footmen?'

Marion had clasped her head and was shaking it from side to side. 'No!' she moaned. 'No!'

'Yeah!' countered Ivy with wicked relish. 'They 'ave their own special tartan too. Only the royals can wear it. Only they'd want to, if you ask me. It's 'orrible. Oh, and 'Is Majesty takes his own personal parrot with 'im.'

Marion flopped back on her pillow and stared at the ceiling. She had no idea if any of this was true, but experience told her it could be. She would, she resolved, find something normal even at Balmoral. It would be a challenge.

In the meantime, there were preparations to make. Sartorial ones in particular. Ivy warned that visitors to the king's Scottish holiday home were expected to change three times a day, and while different clothes for lunch, tea and dinner would not be expected of a governess, there was clearly a high degree of formality. Marion wrote to her mother to tacitly enquire after the new outfits that had been promised her.

Balmoral would also be a good opportunity to get Margaret out of the pram. Rumours were starting to spread. She and Lilibet had overheard some women on the bus discussing the fact that, as they put it, 'all wasn't quite right' with the youngest York. Lilibet had looked at Marion gleefully.

'If only they knew! Bud is so *naughty*!'

And so clever, Marion thought. The littlest princess was barely three, but she could already pick out tunes by ear on the piano.

Margaret would need playclothes too. Otherwise she would be plodding through the heather, satin shoes soaked with bog water, frills dragging on the gorse spikes. Marion sought out the duchess. This would be a difficult one.

'Really, Crawfie, I think that's a decision for Alah, don't you?'

Marion felt exasperated. 'Perhaps a hint from you, ma'am? Margaret is obviously feeling restricted.'

The duchess smiled. 'Bud never feels restricted! She has her ways. She has large blue eyes and a will of iron. Which is all the equipment a lady needs!'

Marion said nothing. A lady needed considerably more equipment, in her view. But arguing would be unwise. The blue-eyed duchess also had her ways, and those who overstepped the mark felt the will of iron. Sudden, capricious displays of power were not unknown.

The duchess leaned forward with a conspiratorial grin. 'But if she disguises her will and uses her eyes, all will be well!'

Marion smiled and bobbed a curtsey, preparing to leave.

But the duchess was looking at her. 'There's something different about you. Is it your hair?'

'Possibly my clothes, ma'am.' The new outfits had arrived, one an exact copy of a Jaeger suit that Marion had seen in the fashion pages. It was blue, with a jazzy, modernist print. Lilibet had loved it. 'Crawfie! What lovely patterns!'

'That's a very striking outfit.'

Marion smoothed down the blue jersey, reddening with pride on her mother's behalf. 'Thank you, ma'am.'

'But I think brown is more your colour,' the duchess went on, brightly.

Marion blinked. '*Brown*, ma'am?' She hated brown. It made her look sallow.

'We all have our colours, the ones that suit us best. I always feel blue is mine. I rather wonder if two of us can wear it in the same house.' The duchess put her head persuasively on one side. 'Don't you agree?'

The royal train rolled up the country, its gleaming length sneaking unnoticed through the sooty outskirts of industrial towns with their dank canals, dirty tenements and factories with black chimneys. Looking out, Marion glimpsed sooty washing strung in the narrow gaps between houses. Seeing the gaunt young women pushing prams, wearing men's caps against the rain, she felt horribly uncomfortable.

She was used, by now, to the Yorks' privileged existence. But even that had not prepared her for the pomp and circumstance of the monarch departing on holiday. There was a private platform at King's Cross, and a train whose luxurious carriages – one for each royal family member – were furnished not only with silver-framed beds, but baths encased in gleaming mahogany. There were sitting rooms with lampshades, carpets and curtains. Armchairs and gold-framed paintings. A chef in a white hat, with a full kitchen brigade.

Looking at it all, as she went in search of her own much simpler berth, Marion was swept once again by feelings of defeat. In the face of all this, her efforts to normalise Lilibet stood as much chance of success as a matchstick in the sand stood to hold back the tide.

'Come on, Maz,' said Ivy, who had the bunk above hers. 'Balmoral's not going to be that bad.'

Marion was indignant. 'You made it sound awful.'

'Well, there *are* compensations,' Ivy said, mysteriously. 'The servants' quarters are pretty close. Men's and women's, I mean. Corridor creeping isn't unknown.'

'You mean Alf's coming, I suppose.'

From the bunk above came giggling.

'Well, lucky you,' said Marion. She turned over again, but the bunk was uncomfortable – tiny and narrow and hard – and the unheated carriage was cold. Yet the real discomfort, she knew, was inside her. Mixed with her guilt and sense of futility was an aching longing. She envied Ivy her simple happiness. If only she had someone to creep down corridors to as well.

But footmen, with their breeches and powdered hair, did not appeal. Yet Ivy was right – men outside the royal circle were now out of bounds. Tom and his camera had almost ruined her. That he had not appeared on any of the recent outings was a huge relief. He had, she heard, also left Mr Adams' studio. Hopefully she would never see him again.

She sighed, long and heavily, but tried to turn it into a yawn.

Ivy obviously wasn't fooled, because now she struck up again. 'You'll enjoy the ghillies' ball, Maz. Their Majesties dance with the estate staff.'

'Very gracious of them,' said Marion, sourly. She shifted onto her back and lay staring into the darkness, breathing in the musty air.

'It's a larf,' insisted Ivy. 'None of the men wear anything beneath their kilts. Prince Henry sits with his legs wide apart so you get a good butcher's at his crown jewels.'

Marion turned over. 'Ivy, you're really selling it to me.'

A silence followed and she was almost asleep when Ivy spoke again.

'Heard the latest about Mrs Simpson?'

'No.' Marion still wasn't sure this fascinating personality actually existed. She had scoured the papers for news of her, but there was never a word, not even in the social columns.

'They say she can fire ping-pong balls out of her you-know-what.'

Marion was suddenly wide awake. '*What?*'

'Well, that's what they're saying.'

The Prince of Wales was on board, she knew. If Mrs Simpson was joining him, Balmoral might be bearable after all.

Marion opened her eyes. It took some seconds to recognise where she was – in the train. Mixed in with Ivy's deafening snores from the bunk above was the sound of bagpipes from outside. 'Scotland the Brave' was being played at full blast.

Blinking, she twitched back her window curtain. A red-faced piper in a kilt was marching up and down the platform. His eyes were bulging and his scarlet cheeks inflated to an improbable size. The platform sign said 'Ballater'. The nearest town to Balmoral.

'Ivy! We're here!'

There was as yet no sign of the royal family besides plenty of their luggage. The little platform was heaped with travelling wardrobes, hatboxes and vast heaps of shoes, all polished to a mirror finish and tied together with their laces. There were trunks of plates and silverware. But no parrot, from what she could see.

Ivy had been joking about that at least.

Or had she?

Two footmen in red-coated uniforms now descended, the powder in their hair dissolving in the drizzle. Marion recognised Alf. He carried a huge gold cage containing something large and grey. Alarmed by the bagpipes, it started to squawk indignantly.

Alf raised the cage and muttered something that did not sound especially polite.

'CHARLOTTE, M'DEAR!!'a great roar echoed down the platform. The king was emerging from his monogrammed carriage. 'HAD A GOOD NIGHT, HAVE YE?'

He wore a kilt, a short tweed cape and a tam-o'-shanter with pompom and feather. Below astonishingly knobbly knees were thick socks complete with silver dagger and a pair of Scottish brogues, elaborately laced up the calf. The look was completed by an immense sporran with tails so long they touched the ground.

The Duke of York, sporting similar knees, kilt, brogues and dagger, followed his father. The Prince of Wales followed, and after him Prince Henry and Prince George, the king's younger sons. All seemed nervous as the king looked them critically up and down, as if inspecting a parade ground.

'NOTHING LIKE THE GARB OF OLD GAUL, EH?' His quarterdeck boom echoed round the platform.

The Prince of Wales slapped some insects from his bare knees. 'Hello, Midge Heaven,' Marion heard him mutter.

Queen Mary came out next. She too was wearing the garb of old Gaul, but as a long Edwardian skirt. Her customary toque was firmly in position, and she clutched a tartan parasol. 'Ah, ze gut loyal Highlanders!' she remarked, watching various station personnel stagger past under her luggage.

'So blissful!' exclaimed the Duchess of York as the piper blasted past again, his cheeks like red footballs.

'Crawfie! Crawfie!!' Lilibet leaped out onto the platform and grabbed Marion's hand. At her touch, a world that had seemed surreal and ridiculous suddenly righted itself again. She would cope with all this. Somehow.

The procession of cars drove through the lush and ferny valley. The Prince of Wales sat in the front of Marion's, next to the chauffeur. In the rear, facing forward as ever, was Mrs Knight. On her dark-uniformed lap, also as ever, squirmed Margaret.

Marion looked out of the window. There was little to see. The drizzle at Ballater had become a full-blown downpour. Sheets of water hammered on the car roof.

'Good old Deeside,' the Prince of Wales remarked ironically. 'Lowest rainfall in Scotland, they say.'

The grey wall running along the roadside now gave way to an imposing entrance. Two tall black-and-gold gates, with 'VR' in wrought ironwork, stood open. A crowd of people stood just inside: housemaids, gardeners, cooks and footmen, Marion realised in astonishment. They were all sodden. The rain had detached well-combed hair from its moorings and rendered well-ironed aprons transparent with wet. Soaked shoes, thoroughly polished, were planted doughtily into muddy grass bubbling with moisture.

All bowed and curtsied as the royal entourage swept past. Marion slid a look at Lilibet, who was waving regally, and felt her spirits slump again. What did her recent triumphs mean beside this level of accrued entitlement?

The castle came into view, much bigger than Marion had expected. It sent her thoughts flying to the little fort near Royal Lodge. This too looked improbable, but in a different way. If that was Arthurian, this was the Brothers Grimm. It was spiky and spiry, a great tower with pepper-pot turrets rising from a roofline of domes. Behind were huge mountains covered in cloud and before it stretched a wide green lawn. It looked as if hordes of midges lived in it.

The inside was breathtaking – wall-to-wall tartan, as Ivy had said. Every square inch was decorated, and heavily at that. A slightly stunned Marion followed the royal group through rooms that lurched wildly from fan-vaulted cathedral Gothic to gilded Baroque with moulded ceilings. The walls of the passages repeated endlessly Queen Victoria's initials. Even the fire buckets bore her monogram.

Tartan was not the only emphatic reference to Scotland. That the actual place was visible through the windows had clearly not been enough for Victoria's husband Albert, who had apparently designed everything. Antlers sprouted from walls like the branches of invisible trees. The wallpaper in the passages bristled with thistles.

Prince Albert himself was the other leitmotif. Standing in the hall was his white marble statue in a white marble kilt; a first in Marion's experience. He featured in endless paintings, mostly violent and gory. She walked past them: Albert on a mountain astride a recently slaughtered stag. Albert before the deer larder with piles of dead animals, his wife looking on in ballgown and tiara.

Having briefly mustered in a huge dark drawing room, the royal party disappeared in different directions. A bewhiskered and very wet gamekeeper had taken off the king and dukes. A housekeeper who seemed somehow to have sidestepped the soggy reception line had borne away Lilibet, the queen and the duchess. Mrs Knight, firmly clasping a struggling Margaret Rose, had ostentatiously gone off to rekindle some below-stairs acquaintance. Ivy, of course, had long since disappeared.

In the gloomy, silent drawing room with its view of dark hills, Marion felt as though she were in a mausoleum. What a place for a child to spend a summer holiday!

Tiredness dragged at her eyelids. A small chair – covered in plaid, naturally – was positioned nearby. She was lowering herself down when someone cried out. In the silence it was like a brick smashing the window.

'Crawfie! *Stop!*'

Marion shot to her feet. 'What's the matter?' Her nerves were jangling painfully.

The Duchess of York stood in the doorway. 'You can't sit there! It's Queen Victoria's favourite chair. No one's ever allowed to sit there, *ever!*'

From this unpromising start, things went from bad to worse. Ivy, Marion discovered, had not been joking about any of it. At dinner, in the vast panelled dining room, six ear-splitting pipers really did circle the table, one of them, as advertised, clearly drunk. The wizened creature who preceded them, wrapped in what looked like a huge brown rug, really was the head butler whose predecessor had stood in for Prince Albert when he was being painted as a Highland shepherd by Landseer.

Marion's disbelief had been suspended so often she had decided just to leave it hanging. Her neighbours were an elderly man called Canon Dalton, and Sister Agnes, an old woman in an orange wig. Neither spoke a word to her.

Few people spoke at all; the royal circle seemed to be a small one, which was perhaps why she had been asked to the meal, to swell numbers. The diners huddled in the middle of the long table. After the deafening pipes, the silence was profound. Fork clattered against plate. An expression of agonised boredom transfixed the Prince of Wales' face.

'DINNER AT BALMORAL DOESN'T COST MUCH!' boomed the king suddenly as he helped himself to salmon from the shepherd-butler's silver platter. 'SALMON FROM THE RIVER! VENISON FROM THE HILL! RASPBERRIES FROM THE GARDEN! ALL MOST ECONOMICAL!' His voice ricocheted off the panelled walls

'Quite so, sire,' said Canon Dalton hurriedly.

Marion stared at her plate, which, along with the cutlery and glassware, bore Queen Victoria's monogram. It depended on what was meant by economical, she thought. If you didn't count the astronomical fixed costs of estate and servants, perhaps it was.

The Prince of Wales sighed loudly. His father rounded on him immediately. 'WILL YOU GO OUT WITH THE GUNS TOMORROW?'

Reluctance rippled the delicate features. 'If you don't mind, Papa, I'd rather stay here and work on my needlepoint.'

'NEEDLEPOINT?' the king almost screamed. 'NOT GO OUT AND SHOOT THE GROUSE, THE GREATEST SPORTING BIRD IN THE WORLD!'

The prince rose, evidently wearied of the turn the conversation had taken. The monarch continued to glare at him. Now that he was standing it could be seen that the prince had changed from the kilt of earlier. His new outfit was as strikingly fashionable as his previous had been quaint: a suit of exuberant check over a jersey of peacock blue. His colourful striped silk tie was fastened with an unusually broad knot. His trousers were baggy and had wide, modish turnups, American style.

'IS IT RAINING IN HERE?' his father yelled.

The prince was lighting a cigarette. He jumped, and it dropped from his mouth. 'Raining, Papa?'

'WHY TURN UP ONE'S TROUSERS EXCEPT TO CROSS PUDDLES? TWEED SUITS ARE ONLY SUITABLE FOR RAT CATCHERS!'

Marion glanced at Queen Mary. Surely she would intervene? She sat expressionless and unmoving apart from the glitter of her diamonds in the candlelight.

The king resumed his attack. 'YOU'RE THE WORST-DRESSED MAN IN LONDON! NOT A SINGLE ONE OF YOUR FRIENDS IS A GENTLEMAN!'

With this damning indictment ringing through the air, the king turned back to his dinner. He shoved some lettuce through his beard with a force bordering on savagery. 'Papa – ' began the Prince of Wales. He had found another cigarette and was lighting that one now. His hand shook.

'KEEP QUIET!' The infuriated monarch rammed in more salad.

The Prince of Wales took a drag of his cigarette, sending a plume of smoke high into the air. 'It's too late now.'

'YOU'RE DAMNED RIGHT IT IS! MORE'S THE PITY!'

'You misunderstand me, Papa. I was just trying to tell you that there was a caterpillar on your lettuce. But you've eaten it.'

Chapter Twenty-One

It was obvious, given this state of hostility between the king and his heir, that Mrs Simpson was unlikely to make an appearance. Any fun that was to be had they would have to make themselves. As the atmosphere in the castle could be cut with a ceremonial sword, it seemed wisest to look outside it.

Marion scoured the surroundings in the hope of finding ordinary distraction for Lilibet. But if this was tough in the London of 1932, the Balmoral estate, where everything had ground to a halt in 1851, made it almost impossible. There was, for a start, a lot of blood to avoid. Ivy had warned her about the daily return of wagons heaped with the corpses of the greatest sporting bird in the world, the ponies bearing huge dead stags, their flanks running with blood and their eyes rolling upward. Marion took Lilibet's shoulders and deftly steered her away.

At night, in her chilly, cheerless room at the end of the nursery corridor, Marion listened to the rain beat on the roof.

'Let's have a golden-syrup-bread-eating competition!'

Lilibet stared. 'A what?'

Marion feigned amazement. 'You mean you've never tried to eat so many slices of bread and syrup that you've almost burst? Just to beat another person?'

The golden curls shook in a negative.

'Think you can beat me?'

The princess's eyes gleamed. 'Yes!'

In the middle of a nearby stream was an island that proved to be the perfect spot. Lilibet proved a champion syrup-eater. Her unbeaten record was twelve.

'I don't know what's happened to her appetite,' Mrs Knight huffed, when it was time for nursery tea. Marion avoided Lilibet's laughing eye and felt slightly guilty. Mrs Knight, of late, was showing dangerous signs of reasonableness. Contrary to expectation, she had accepted the playclothes without murmur. Perhaps she was just sick of all the washing, or had left her goffering irons in London.

Down by the railway line, they waited, breathless with anticipation, for the Aberdeen Fish Express. As it was heard in the distance, Lilibet stared excitedly at the coins on the rails. Marion had shown her how to place them so that the train's weight would flatten them out as it passed. After the locomotive roared through with its load of North Sea cod, they scrambled down the bank. 'It *worked*!' shrieked Lilibet, holding out a palm on which a squashed penny, shiny with the impact, reposed. 'And just *look* what it's done to Grandpapa's face!'

They went up into the hills. The princess was a good walker, willing to go out in all weathers, which they often encountered in a single day. It was while looking for shelter that they first discovered the bothies – small stone houses hidden in remote wood clearings or alongside high-secret lochs. While some retained their original appearance, of simple shelters for hunters and shepherds, some had been considerably enlarged and aggrandised, for excursionists from the castle, presumably. One such, the highest and remotest of all, even had a piano in it, and a chaise longue.

It was their favourite and they often visited it. They made toast before the fire, Lilibet holding it on the fork in the flames until it was practically black before tipping it on to VR-monogrammed plates.

They would eat on the bench outside the door and watch the wildlife, which up here was especially magnificent. Wide-wing-spanned birds swooped over the lonely lochs, and the ptarmigan – the snow grouse – rose silently up the sheer, dark cliff face of Lochnagar.

One day their route up took them past the cairns: eleven enormous piles of grey stone in a variety of shapes, from tall triangles to stubby circular towers. Set dramatically among enormous bright green ferns, they looked incongruously exotic, like some lost Incan village or other relic of a once-mighty civilisation. In actual fact, the civilisation they dated from was the no-means-unmighty mid-nineteenth century. Mainly, they commemorated the marriages of Queen Victoria's children, but the biggest was a memorial to a death.

It was a vast grey pyramid dedicated to 'The Beloved Memory Of Prince Albert, The Great and Good Prince Consort' by 'His Broken-Hearted Widow, VICTORIA RI'. They stood before it; Lilibet's kilt and red jersey glowing against the bracken.

'Do hearts literally get *broken*?' she asked, frowning. 'Do they actually smash in pieces?'

'It means she was upset because she loved him very much.'

The princess looked at her curiously. 'When people fall in love, Crawfie, do they actually fall, on the floor?'

Marion swallowed. 'Of course not,' she said, her voice muffled. 'It just means it can be very sudden.'

Lilibet continued to fix her with questioning blue eyes. 'Has that happened to you, Crawfie?'

Marion forced a smile. 'That's a very personal question.'

'Will it happen to me?'

'Probably.'

The little brow knotted. 'How will I know?'

Marion felt a sudden rush in her chest. 'Oh, you'll know.'

One day after lessons she took Lilibet into Ballater. It wasn't an especially down-to-earth place, with great lions and unicorns over every other frontage proclaiming the establishment to be By Royal Appointment. But it did have a sweetshop, which was something.

Lilibet was thrilled. She gasped at the array on offer. Rows of glass jars on shelves at the back glowed yellow with lemon drops, green with limes, red with aniseed balls and black-and-white with bull's-eyes. On the counter in front were glistening heaps of toffees in shiny wrappers, chocolate bars, liquorice bootlaces, many-coloured lollipops and gobstoppers plain white on the outside but a rainbow of succeeding shades within. 'I don't know what to choose, Crawfie!' Lilibet gasped, clutching in her hot little hand the shilling that Marion had given her.

As befitted a proper sweetshop visit, they had stood outside for several minutes, discussing the jars in the window. 'Do you think they'll do the weighing-scale thing, Crawfie?' Lilibet asked.

She knew from their London adventures that the sign of a really good sweetshop was if the proprietor popped an extra one on top after weighing them out. But the Ballater sweetshop had something even better in store.

'Would you like to try any before you buy them, Your Royal Highness?' the shopkeeper said with a smile.

'Ooh! May I?'

Half turning away to let the princess handle the transaction independently, Marion spotted a figure at the rear, ostensibly consulting the newspapers spread out for sale. He was tall and broad-shouldered, with wavy fair hair.

Her surprise was so great it was like being hit by a train. He seemed to sense it, and turned. Walking up to her, the camera winking round his neck, he smiled. 'Hello, Marion,' he said lightly.

She stared at him, then at Lilibet, who, thankfully, was completely absorbed in watching the shopkeeper weighing out Jelly Babies. She grabbed his tweed-jacketed arm and dragged him towards the back of the shop. 'What are you doing here?'

How had he found them? Now he no longer had his private source of information.

He raised a laconic eyebrow. 'How about the Court Circular?'

Of course. News of the royal family's exodus to Scotland would be reported in the official gazette, which went to every newspaper. Anyone with a map could work out where they were likely to be. And Tom, aware of her habits with Lilibet, would immediately spot the potential of the sweetshop.

'Go. Or I'll tell the detective.' Marion's heart was thundering. She could see Cameron from here, peering suspiciously from beneath his hat brim up and down the near-empty street, yet seemingly unaware of the presence of a man within the shop.

'The royal Sherlock Holmes, you mean.' Tom knew about Cameron too, of course. His grin was unpleasant; she hadn't seen it before. She could see that something had changed in him, but now was not the time to wonder about that.

'You have to go!' she hissed.

Lilibet, meanwhile, watched with satisfaction as the shopkeeper popped one extra Jelly Baby on the pile.

'Please!' she begged, feeling suddenly helpless and desperate. Around his neck, the camera looked back, like a malevolent third eye. 'Please don't do this to me, Tom.'

He sighed. 'Marion, I'm sorry.' His wide eyes now held something of their old expression. She felt a leap of hope.

'Can't we talk?' she asked. Purchase completed, the little figure in red wool and tartan was now fumbling in her purse. But she would turn round any minute. He must go. Now.

His lips twisted. 'What is there to talk about? I'm not here to chat. I'm here to take pictures.'

Panic raced through her. 'But you'll lose me my job.'

'Well, you lost me mine,' he flipped back.

'What?'

'Mr Adams sacked me.' His face was hard, accusing.

Marion's heart thundered. So the duchess had known after all? 'Why? Because of the photographs?'

'He never said so. Said it was time for me to move on, that was all. But someone must have said something.'

She felt sick. 'Not me. I never said a word.'

He snorted. 'Can I believe that?'

'I *swear*, Tom.'

He looked at her for a few moments, his fingers playing on the camera. 'Okay,' he said. 'But we obviously can't talk here. So where?'

Her mind went blank for a moment with sheer relief. When everything reloaded, she realised she knew the perfect place. She gave him the directions.

*

It was a calm evening, full of birdsong. The way up the hillside zigzagged through scented heather and between grey boulders. Above the dark trees, a huge yellow moon lit up a landscape that widened as she climbed. Crags and gullies appeared, then sweeping glens in which lochs glinted.

At the top of the hill, the bothy showed between the tree trunks. Marion paused, heart thudding in her chest. She wasn't entirely sure what she was going to say. Seeing him again had released something in her, a longing, that she had kept shut up since their last, angry encounter. Despite all he had done, she still felt for him, she realised, and that was not exactly going to help matters.

She was in the clearing before the building now. It was shadowy inside, but the chaise longue was visible, the white-painted fireplace.

The door opened almost before she knocked. His mouth was on hers. Need ignited within her, and blazed, but she pushed him away. 'Not now. We have to talk.'

'Afterward.' He pulled her back to him fervently. 'I've missed you, Marion.'

And I you, she almost said, feeling herself almost surrendering. She steeled herself, however, and glared at him. 'How could you? Betray my trust like that? Take pictures of Lilibet.'

When he said nothing, she added, furiously, 'What about your photojournalism? You were going to record all that was wrong with the world!'

He gave her a satirical smile. 'The three million out of work. Mosley and his racist thugs. The Thousands of policemen, some mounted, beating up the hunger marchers in Hyde Park.'

'Exactly.'

'Read about that at the Balmoral breakfast table, did you?'

In fact, she had. As the king's parrot picked its way through the silver flatware, pecked off the top of His Majesty's egg and laid a large grey turd next to the royal butterpat, Marion had read, hot-eyed, about how Ramsay MacDonald's national government had used force against its own people. 'The most extensive public order precaution since 1848,' *The Times* had said.

He gave her a rueful smile. 'Actually, a picture of Princess

Elizabeth playing is worth more than a picture of policemen bashing miners.'

'You've sold out,' she accused, contemptuously. He laughed.

'What about you? You're a fine one to talk! What happened to the slums? To Grassmarket?' His tone was taunting.

She felt a hot, defensive fury. 'How dare you?' she snarled. 'I'll be going back to Grassmarket . . . eventually.'

'Really?' His smile was wry – mocking, even. His wide, broad shoulders filled her with a brief, powerful longing but she forced it furiously away. How could she hate him and desire him at the same time?

'Who are you to judge me?' she demanded.

'I might ask the same of you. As for the pictures, I'm the thin end of the wedge, Marion, believe me. One day the royal family won't be able to move for people like me recording their every move.'

The thought was too horrible to contemplate. 'And you think that's justified?'

'What about the way they live?' he shot back. 'Is *that* justified?'

There was no easy answer to this, of course. She sidestepped it. 'What's absolutely not justified,' she snarled, 'is what you did to me. You *used* me.'

He sat down, heavily on the chaise longue. It wasn't just that he had hardened, she could see now. Something within him had broken. She saw for the first time how tired he looked. His formerly clear grey eyes were bloodshot, and there were dark shadows beneath them. She felt the self-righteous fury drain out of her and concern take its place. She dropped to her knees beside him and looked into his face. He seemed on the brink of tears.

'What's the matter?' she asked, softly, feeling, at that moment, that she could forgive him anything. 'Is it Kate?' She had forgotten about his sister.

He screwed his eyes up; nodded.

Horror bowled through Marion. 'She's not . . .'

The fair head shook. 'No, but she's very ill. That's why I did it, Marion.' His eyes opened and locked on hers, as if willing her to understand. 'To pay for her care. A good hospital, where she could be comfortable.'

164

Marion hung her head. He was a villain to her and the duchess, but a hero to his family. It all depended on your point of view. Life was complicated; people were contradictory. They were not absolutes; either one thing or the other. Look at her, an egalitarian feminist, working for the most patriarchal and conservative of institutions.

He must have misinterpreted her musing silence for a critical one, because he suddenly added, 'I had to do something after Mr Adams got rid of me.'

Her sympathy, despite everything, must have showed in her eyes because now he reached for her hand and squeezed it. 'Stay with me? Just for tonight? I'll go in the morning, I promise.' There was a smile in his voice. 'Without taking a single picture.'

She looked away. Outside the window, it had grown dark. She imagined the castle, lit up in the valley below. Dinner would have started now, drunken pipers and all. Lilibet would be in bed. If she stayed here, no one would miss her. She looked at the rug and the hearth, imagining a leaping fire, bright flames in the dark warming their naked limbs. Desire twisted in her belly.

But then she remembered Mr Adams, and something cold slithered down her spine. If she had been spared this time, it probably would not happen again. Any relationships from now on – in the unlikely event she felt like forming one – would have to be with insiders. No one else could be trusted.

Something had switched within her; a realisation. The world in general might be ambiguous, nuanced and contradictory, but not the royal world. That had no middle ground, no shades of grey. You were entirely in or entirely out. You had to choose.

Chapter Twenty-Two

The year 1932 ended, and 1933 got off to an inauspicious start. The unemployment figures continued to rise, and as austerity continued, the government refusing to reverse the benefit cuts introduced two years before, even the previously prosperous were now being pulled into poverty's pitiless net. The situation abroad was no less concerning. In January, Adolf Hitler became Chancellor of Germany.

'He used to be a house painter, apparently,' the duchess said dismissively. 'He looks quite ridiculous, with that moustache.'

Marion felt Hitler was far more sinister than laughable. Horrible things were happening in Germany. A huge fire at the Reichstag, the German Parliament, was instantly declared a Communist plot by the Führer, as Hitler called himself. The evidence was that a half-blind Dutch Communist with learning difficulties had been found nearby with a few household firelighters; experts, meanwhile, testified that the Reichstag blaze had been started with petrol and chemicals.

Seeing the newspaper pictures of the bewildered young man, head hung in the dock in his prison clothes, Marion felt sick with pity. She had no doubt that it was a set-up. She shuddered every time she passed Carlton House Terrace, where a huge red, white and black swastika hung from the flagpole of the German Embassy.

Operation Normal continued, Marion always glancing over her shoulder in case of following photographers. A twisted neck, as well as a bruised heart, was the legacy of her relationship with Tom.

But Lilibet's company, her capacity for simple happiness, was the perfect antidote to the complex miseries adults inflicted on one another. They went to visit the pelicans in St. James's Park, the princess having no previous idea that these huge, exotic birds lived so close to her grandparents' palace. They went to the new cinema in Victoria Station, which specialised in cartoons. It had an elegant modern facade in the style of an ocean liner, and Lilibet loved sitting in the small, cave-like interior with its curved roof and rows of seats. Her favourite spot was right in the centre of the front row.

The fact that the cartoons were preceded by newsreels had almost blown their cover at first. Marion had not anticipated the effect that seeing film of her relatives going about their official business would have on Lilibet. 'Look!' she shouted as, before the *Three Little Pigs* began, images of Queen Mary launching an ocean liner flickered over the screen. 'It's – '

But Marion had gently pressed a hand across her mouth. The crowd around tittered, assuming an ultra-patriotic child. No one tittered, however, when Queen Mary was followed by Joseph Goebbels addressing the youth of Berlin before a pile of burning books.

'Why are they setting books on fire?' Lilibet's whisper was puzzled.

Marion sighed. There was no easy way of explaining this. 'The Nazis are getting rid of the ones they don't approve of. The ones that they don't agree with, and that don't agree with them.'

'But, Crawfie, you always say that it's important to consider other points of view.'

'It is. But Hitler wants to control what people think.' It was a relief when the Silly Symphonies music started and the trio of porkers appeared on the screen.

But whatever storm clouds were gathering abroad, life at Piccadilly and Royal Lodge continued unchanged. As a sparkling winter gave way to a beautiful spring and the evenings warmed and lengthened, Marion walked in the Great Park in the early evenings. The size of it, rolling away in every direction, gave her a sense of freedom, and the ancient, timeless feel of the landcape was reassuring. There was an unexpected wildness to it, and a great variety of flowers. Their colours were intense: campions both pink and white, deep blue cornflower, creamy yellow scabious, sprinkles of sky-coloured speed-well, rich scarlet poppies.

She liked in particular to go to the great silver lake, Virginia Water. There was an intriguing little fort at the other side. Its turrets poked over the treetops, romantic and chivalric. She would stand there, wondering whom it belonged to.

Tonight, adding to the medieval effect, a herd of deer had gathered under an oak tree. With their soft brown backs stippled with white, pale legs almost invisible in the brightness, they looked like creatures from a medieval illuminated manuscript. Marion looked from them to the cluster of towers above the treeline across the lake. She found that she was holding her breath, almost expecting a slim white arm to appear from the shining water, holding a jewelled sword.

Whosoever pulls this sword from this stone is rightfully king of all England.

It did look like the fortress of a fairy prince: small, decorative, its battlements and castellations heaped with merry abandon. Against the blue sky, a jolly flag rippled. It was now or never, Marion thought. She just *had* to find out who lived there.

She reached the end of its drive and heard music, laughter and loud talking. The owners were having a party.

She knew the tune, and started to hum. It seemed to invite her in, up the drive. The gardens were similar to Royal Lodge's: rhododendrons, azaleas, cedars. A smooth green lawn was edged by a semicircle of battlements, to match the little castle. They had real little cannons in them, with tiny cannonballs neatly stacked alongside. The whole place was like a life-sized toy. All that was required for the full effect was a regiment of little redcoats.

An arched door, white-painted, was open in the centre of the little fort. But the laughter and music were coming from round the back. She could hear shrieks now, and splashing. She could see a pale stone terrace and the edge of a blue swimming pool. The shining horn of a gramophone. Waiters with champagne bottles.

'Can I help you?' The voice came from behind her. It was low, female and warmly American. Marion froze.

Slowly, she turned. The woman behind her looked like someone from a black-and-white photograph, with large black circular sunglasses and intensely black hair that shone like lacquer. Her face was pale and smooth, like the inside of a shell. She wore a white blouse and black skirt with bold zigzag patterns. The only colour was her lipstick: a loud, bright red.

'Are you press?' she asked.

'Press?' Marion was confused. In her yellow summer frock, did she look like a journalist? Surely they wore mackintoshes and carried notepads. Cameras.

There was another burst of laughter from the pool. Perhaps the woman was just being careful. Some of her guests might be well-known.

'I'm staying nearby,' Marion explained. 'I was out for a walk and saw, well, this.' She waved an awkward hand at the castellated building. 'I was interested. I'm sorry.'

The woman seemed to relax at this. Her red lips stretched in a surprisingly warm smile. 'So whaddya think? You like it?'

'It's beautiful.'

'I tell David he's got turrets syndrome. All these towers.'

Marion laughed. She wondered who David was. The owner of this place, presumably.

'That's better. You're real pretty when you smile, honey.'

The woman had very thin white arms, with broad jewelled bangles flashing on each wrist. More jewels flashed on her fingers. She was holding a bunch of mint.

'For the juleps,' she explained. 'Always get the mint myself. Damn butler never can find a decent leaf in the whole damn garden. You like cocktails?'

'I've never had one.' Nor had she ever heard of juleps.

'Never had a cocktail? Honey, where you *from*?'

'Scotland.'

A well-shaped eyebrow rose quizzically. 'I mean where around here. You're staying nearby, you say?'

'I work at Royal Lodge,' Marion told her.

This seemed to surprise the woman for some reason. 'With the Yorks?'

Marion nodded. 'I'm Princess Elizabeth's governess.'

She braced herself for warm interest. Who wasn't fascinated by the Little Princesses? But the woman just looked at her. 'Well, honey,' she drawled, eventually, 'looks like you just walked right into the enemy camp.' She flashed a final red-lipsticked smile and was gone, mint and all.

Marion thought about the encounter all week, but mentioned it to no one, not even Ivy. The woman had been friendly and charming, but the words 'enemy camp' were ominous. She was taking no chances. She kept it to herself.

All the same, the next weekend, she decided to take Lilibet boating. There was every reason to do so; it was a skill the child had yet to master. And if she knew who lived at the little fort, and the sight of it prompted her to reveal it, then so much the better.

Ringed by trees and banked by bulrushes, Virginia Water lay under a warm blue sky. It was all very quiet. Birds could be heard, and the drone of the bee. Otherwise just the wet-wood slap of oars in water and the occasional grunt of the child who pulled them.

Lilibet had begged to row the moment she boarded. Having applied her usual concentration and application, she was soon cutting through the water with clean, swift strokes.

Trailing a hand in the rippling lake, Marion kept her gaze on the treetops and the cluster of towers. But Lilibet, grappling with the rowlocks, kept her attention on the workings of the boat.

Time drifted by, slow like the floating leaves. Insects danced in the shafts of thick light. Across the silver water surface, the shadows lengthened. They would have to go soon.

'What's that, Lilibet?' Marion pointed to the miniature turrets.

Lilibet twisted round, glanced briefly, then twisted back again. 'Oh, that's the fort.'

Marion smiled. 'I can see it's a fort,' she said gently. 'But whose fort?'

'Uncle David's.'

'I didn't know you had an Uncle David.'

Lilibet stared. 'Of course you do. Everyone does.'

Marion shook her head.

'But you must!' the child insisted. 'He's going to be the next king!' 'Isn't his name Edward?'

'Yes. Edward Albert Christian George Andrew Patrick *David*.' Lilibet rattled off the names matter-of-factly. 'But everybody in our family calls him David.' The princess looked at Marion. 'You'll probably just call him Your Royal Highness, though,' she suggested helpfully.

Marion did not reply. Her mind was spinning. *I tell David he's got turrets syndrome.* An American accent. A witty sophistication. Had it been, could it be, the famous Mrs Simpson?

'Duck down, Crawfie!' yelled Lilibet. Seconds later, they were clasped in the tangled embrace of a weeping willow.

Marion was glad of the leaves concealing her face. Her thoughts whirled. Was she right? The woman had been nothing like the vulgar schemer, the predatory bigamist of Ivy's stories. Perhaps she was someone else.

Once they were out on the lake again, Marion returned to the subject. 'Don't you ever visit him?'

'Who?'

'Uncle David.'

'No.'

Something in the child's tone made Marion hesitate. She sensed she was on the verge of something. Something connected to the woman she had met. Something that perhaps she should not know. Yet she could not resist. 'Why not?'

Lilibet pulled back on her oars. 'Because of the bad lady.'

Marion's insides jumped. 'The bad lady?'

'Mrs Simpson.' Lilibet carefully replaced an oar in the rowlocks.

Marion swallowed. So there it was. Now she knew. She felt excited, but also wished that she had not asked the question. Mrs Simpson was not a subject for a seven-year-old.

But something in the child seemed released. After casting a cautious eye round the lake's deserted shores, Lilibet leaned eagerly forward. 'It's a secret,' she hissed, her blue eyes huge. 'I'm not supposed to know about her but I do. I've heard them talking. The bad lady is an evil witch, but Uncle David doesn't think so.'

Marion looked into the water. She agreed with Uncle David, but now was not the time to say so. She glanced about for a change of subject. 'Look at those moorhens. Lilibet!'

The boat was rocking wildly. 'The oars, Lilibet!' Marion cried, as both threatened to slip into the water. She leaned forward and grabbed them just in time.

Chapter Twenty-Three

Lilibet did not mention Mrs Simpson again. Marion listened and watched carefully, but there was nothing. Gradually, she forgot her concerns. There were lessons to plan – Lilibet was starting French now – and outings. At the zoo, Lilibet admired the elephant, thrilled to the tigers and clapped her hands at the chimps' tea party. She seemed perfectly happy.

Mrs Simpson, too, was having fun, it seemed. Ivy had heard that she had been back at Fort Belvedere and danced all night with the Prince of Wales in a Mayfair club.

'But what about the two other mistresses?' Marion asked.

'Lady Furness and Mrs Dudley Ward? They're still around,' said the all-knowing Ivy.

'So it can't be that serious,' Marion concluded.

Other things were, though. At Oxford, the Union debating society had sensationally supported the motion that 'This House Would Not Fight For King And Country.' Marion read the story, chewing her lip. If the Oxford Union, the university institution regarded as the epitome of the Establishment, was taking an anti-monarchical, anti-patriotic stance, what did it mean for everyone else? What did it mean for the royal family? For Lilibet?

Summer became autumn, and they returned to Balmoral. That the Prince of Wales was present seemed to imply that the royal engine was still running as usual. The king was certainly running as usual: as irascible as ever with his son. 'STOP THAT INFERNAL ROW!'

he yelled out of the window onto the terrace where the prince, in the rain, was playing the bagpipes.

'I pray to God,' Marion overheard him saying to Canon Dalton, in an uncharacteristic whisper, 'that David doesn't have children and nothing stands between Bertie and Lilibet and the throne.'

Marion, raising a spoon of Brown Windsor soup to her lips, lowered it again, shocked. Lilibet and the throne! The idea was astonishing, frightening, horrible. But, thankfully, it was only the expression of an old man's jealousy of his charismatic son. Later, though, thinking it over in bed, an echo of a distant conversation came back to her. The Prince of Wales to his sister-in-law: *You know, I've just had the darndest idea. You and Bertie should be king and queen.*

And the duchess's reply: *Not even in jest.*

No, thought Marion. Not even in jest.

She spent Christmas with her mother in Edinburgh. She had not been home for many months, and the house, never large but always adequate, now seemed quite unbelievably small and dark. Her elbows seemed to bang against the passage walls. She had got used to huge spaces, she realised. To high ceilings and long, light windows. To breakfast trays being deposited at her door, lavish with butter and milk from the royal farms, each silver knife and monogrammed plate shining and placed just so.

A line had been crossed. She had always thought she could come back, resume things, live as before. Now she realised she could not.

Her mother was touchingly glad to see her, but full of questions Marion now dared not answer. Discretion was everything. Parrying the good-natured queries was difficult; her mother was puzzled, she could see. It made a division between them, invisible but there, like a glass wall.

She tried to divert the flow with queries of her own. 'How's Annie?'

As her mother sighed, she froze. 'They went away,' Mrs Crawford said.

'*Away?*' Marion blinked. 'Away where?'

'Moved on. I don't know.'

Marion sank down onto a hard chair. She felt winded, as if someone had punched her. Slum people were itinerant, she knew. To be poor meant to be constantly on the move. She had meant to do so much for Annie, but she had so far done little, and now she could do nothing at all. Guilt broke over her in a huge wave, but in its slipstream, unacknowledged, came a ripple of what might have been relief.

Nor was that her mother's only piece of news. 'Peter's home,' she said.

Marion felt a little spike of embarrassment – but her main emotion was joy. It would be a relief to see someone from the old days, especially kind, reliable, clever Peter.

They met at Jenners again. Of the awkwardness of their last meeting there was no hint. 'You look beautiful, Marion.' His pale eyes were admiring. 'London's agreeing with you, clearly.'

She wondered if it was, really. Sometimes she felt that she was under a great strain, one she could not talk of even to Ivy. Even to her mother; especially to her mother. A wild urge possessed her to tell him exactly what it was like, the feeling of trying to fit two different, conflicting sides of herself together; of being a mother and not being one; of being part of a family yet outside it; of coming home and not being able to relax. Of the guilt and responsibility; above all, of the loneliness. She gave Peter a bright smile. 'Yes,' she said. 'It's marvellous.'

She asked him about his job. He had moved schools and was now at one in Leicestershire, as head of the classics department. That he loved it was clear; his pale eyes shone as he spoke about his pupils, decent strapping chaps to a man. She answered his questions about her own pupil briefly and reluctantly, giving as little away as possible. 'You can trust me, you know,' he said at one point, clearly hurt. 'I can keep a secret.'

'But, Peter' – from the other side of the glass wall, she met his gaze unblinkingly – 'there are no secrets to keep.'

He smiled in an accepting sort of way and opened another flank of enquiry. 'Are you married?'

She laughed. 'They don't do marriage in the Royal Household. Unless you're actually royal, you have to leave their service.' But even this, once it was out, felt like a confession too far. Although it had done the job, made it clear she was unavailable.

She cut into her cake with a fork. 'How about you?'

He shook his head, which was almost hairless these days. 'Married to my job, I suppose.' He smiled again.

Afterward, they hugged and went on their separate ways. She envied him his straightforwardness, the uncomplicated nature of his work. Hers, increasingly, seemed the exact opposite.

Nineteen thirty-three turned to 1934. 'I've got some news,' Ivy said.

Cold horror went through Marion. 'You're not leaving!'

Ivy cackled. 'Only to Buckingham Palace.'

To be with Alf, obviously. She looked so happy and radiant that Marion felt a sickening rush of envy. Ivy was so lucky to have found someone to love. And on the inside as well. Within the glass wall. It was not a fate she looked likely to share.

'Don't look like that, Maz. I'll get the hottest Prince of Wales gossip. The Buck House lot know all there is to know.'

'But I'll miss you.' The gossip was nothing beside the companionship. 'Who'll I have a mother's ruin with in the rub-a-dub?' Or a gin in the pub, in Ivy's East End argot. They had sometimes gone, in the evenings, when Alf was on duty.

Ivy squealed. 'Blimey, Maz. You've got the rhyming slang off now, aintcha?'

With Ivy gone, and no one to laugh with, things that already seemed serious now seemed utterly dire. In Germany, Jewish shops were being boycotted. Hitler, claiming that they were plotting to overthrow him, had murdered Röhm, his former best friend, and Schleicher, the former Chancellor. Hundreds of others had died in this 'purge'. Most shockingly of all, Nazis had broken into the Chancellery in Vienna and shot dead Dr Dollfuss, the Austrian leader. Meanwhile, in the House of Commons, Chancellor of the Exchequer Neville Chamberlain ordered MPs to be of good cheer. Things, he insisted, were about to improve. 'We have now finished the story of *Bleak House* and are sitting down to enjoy the first chapter of *Great Expectations.*' Marion threw the paper across the room. She tipped her head back and massaged the tight muscles at the back. Pain beat at her temples. How long was it all going to hold together?

She did her best to look interested when Ivy's Buckingham Palace contacts did, as promised, produce the very latest news on the Fort Belvedere front. Lady Furness, one of the Prince of Wales' mistresses, had gone to America. She had asked Wallis Simpson to look after her royal lover while she was away.

'Talk about puttin' the bleedin' fox in charge of the henhouse!' chortled Ivy.

Marion still could not believe that the good-natured woman she had met at the Fort was so ruthless. However, when Thelma Furness returned, the scene Ivy reported suggested that she was.

'They was all at dinner together, and Wallis was next to the prince. Jokin' and slappin' 'is 'and.'

'Slapping his *hand*?'

Ivy nodded. 'So they say. And Lady Furness gives 'er such a look, but she gives 'er another look back and the next mornin' Lady F flounces out. 'Asn't been back since.'

'But there's still Mrs Dudley Ward,' Marion pointed out. 'Mrs Simpson hasn't got the field to herself quite yet.'

But a few weeks later Ivy reported Mrs Dudley Ward had been blocked on the palace switchboard. 'Sixteen years of devotion!' Ivy shook her head in wonderment. 'Snuffed out with an order to an operator!'

That night, Marion lay awake, worrying. She could hear, down the nursery landing, the rasping snores of Mrs Knight. In and out, like the crashing of great waves. But also something else. Marion sat up, listened and swung her legs out of bed.

There was a light under the door of Lilibet's room. Marion pushed it open. 'What are you doing?'

The princess was not in bed, but crouching by it in her rose-printed nightgown. In the candlelight, her alarmed eyes shone through the rumpled gold of her hair. 'I'm straightening my shoes.'

'Straightening your *shoes*? But it's the middle of the night!'

'They weren't quite straight.'

Marion's heart sank. The compulsive behaviour was back with a vengeance.

She lowered herself down and pulled the child to her, inhaling the warm scent of soap. 'Don't worry,' she murmured.

Lilibet stiffened in her arms. She jerked backward and stared wildly at Marion. The reflected candle burned in her eyes. 'But I *am* worried! He's going to marry her!'

'Who?' Marion held the child's shaking shoulders. 'Who's going to marry who?'

'Uncle David and the wicked witch!'

'*What?* That can't possibly be true.' Even Ivy had never mentioned that, and she mentioned everything.

'It is! I've heard Mummie and Papa talking!'

But where is Mummie now? Marion couldn't help thinking. It wasn't her comforting Lilibet, was it?

'Your uncle Edward is the Prince of Wales,' she said soothingly. 'He could marry any woman in the country; anyone in the world!'

'Yes, but he only wants her! The wicked witch! I'm so worried about it. What's going to happen?' She began to sob, gulping for breath. She had been upset before, but this was different.

Marion rubbed her back and held her close. It felt intimate, such a motherly embrace. Feeling the stiff little body relax, she felt a rush of protective love. 'Don't worry,' she muttered into the warm, silky hair. 'Nothing's going to happen. Everything will be fine.'

Lilibet did not reply. Her breathing, formerly fast and shallow, became slow and deep. *She's going to sleep*, Marion thought.

'What's an adventuress?' Lilibet murmured.

'What?' Marion, almost asleep now herself, woke up sharply. The blue eyes were looking at her with quite their old interest. The flames had gone. 'Is it someone who goes on adventures?' Lilibet pressed.

'Er . . . it sounds like it, doesn't it? Why do you ask?'

'I heard Grandmama say it.'

Marion could not think of a reply to this, although it was easy to imagine on whom the unflattering epithet had been bestowed. She looked at the brogues gleaming in the candlelight, placed precisely together, their laces exactly equal lengths. 'Well your shoes look very neat now. I think you can go back to bed, Lilibet.'

The princess looked at the shoes. 'Yes, Crawfie. I think I can.'

Marion waited for the small figure to hop back between the sheets before returning to her room, where sleep evaded her the rest of the night. This could not go on. She had to do something.

Chapter Twenty-Four

'A *public swimming* baths?' The duchess was doubtful.

'Yes, ma'am. It will do the girls good to mix with those their own age. Margaret can come too.'

'But princesses should never disrobe in public!'

Marion took a deep breath. 'It's not possible to swim without doing so, ma'am.'

The chosen mixing and disrobing venue was the exclusive Bath Club in nearby Dover Street. But Miss Daly, the club's fresh-faced young swimming teacher, was doubtful too. 'Do I have to curtsey at the end of every length they swim?'

'Really not necessary.' Marion smiled. 'We're all the same in the water.'

The lesson quickly became the highlight of the children's week. Marion would sit on the wrought-iron viewing balcony while, below, Lilibet happily trod water and Margaret, plump in her dark blue swimming costume, stood on the edge, gripping the stone flags with her toes, obviously reluctant to jump in.

'Come on, Margaret! Don't be a limpet!' Lilibet stuck out a hand and grabbed her sister's ankle. Margaret squealed in horror.

Ker-splash. Margaret was finally in now, and screaming hysterically. Lilibet was laughing. It was good to see, and even better to hear.

The warm, chlorinated air made her feel tired, suddenly. The last few weeks especially had been very strained. Marion bent forward and rested her forehead on the rail.

'Miss Crawford?' Miss Daly suddenly sat down beside her.

"Can I have a word?" She flicked a meaningful gaze over the balcony.

Marion peered over to look. 'Not *again!*'

Miss Daly's smile was as white and reassuring as her crisp sportswear. 'I've tried to tell her to stay in the changing room but it might be better coming from you.'

'Oh, much,' Marion agreed ironically as she followed Miss Daly down to the poolside, where Mrs Knight, not for the first time, had camped out beside the water with a pile of towels, hairbrushes, talcum powder and even boxes of chocolates. 'There's enough to equip an expedition,' Marion muttered, as the two of them walked across the tiles. 'I can't think why she hasn't included a lifeboat.'

Summer came. This year the Prince of Wales was conspicuous by his absence at Balmoral. He was cruising the Caribbean with a party including Mrs Simpson. Ivy had a story about her making the prince beg like a dog. 'You're making it up,' Marion said, irritably.

Ivy gave her a wise look. 'Am I, Maz? You'll be telling me next that Prince George don't like to dress up as a woman, didn't used to be a drug addict and ain't being blackmailed by one of his ex-boyfriends in Paris.'

Marion snorted disbelievingly. Prince George, the youngest of the king's four sons, was tall and gloriously handsome. A less sordid sight was hard to imagine.

'And who ain't bein' teed up to marry this Greek princess as quick as yer like.'

Marion shook her head. 'Your problem, Ivy, is that you don't know where to stop.'

A day or two later, the duchess swept into the Piccadilly dining room. 'Exciting news, Lilibet! Uncle George is getting married! To a beautiful princess from Greece, called Marina.'

Marion looked at the white tablecloth, hard. She must on no account catch the eye of Ivy. Her friend was standing against the wall waiting to begin the service, looking as if butter, especially that stamped with the royal crest, wouldn't melt in her mouth.

'You are to be a bridesmaid at the wedding, and wear a special frock,' the duchess went on.

Lilibet looked uncharacteristically mutinous. 'I don't like special frocks,' she muttered. 'You can't climb trees in them.' She looked down at her kilt and jersey. 'I like these clothes best.'

Marion hid a smile. Her charge had come a long way since the days of frills and ribbons.

The duchess was still smiling brightly, but Marion detected irritation. 'You can't wear them in Westminster Abbey though, darling sweet. Crawfie will take you to the fitting tomorrow morning.'

It was Marion's turn to be dismayed. 'Tomorrow morning?' Tomorrow morning was supposed to be spent in the schoolroom. She had thought the days of interruption were over.

The duchess's gaze was glassy blue. 'With Mr Hartnell in Bruton Street. I've ordered the car.'

'No thank you,' Marion said firmly.

The duchess looked astonished. 'What?'

'Bruton Street is only round the corner, ma'am. We can walk.'

Lilibet went dressed to the nines in quite the old way, with a white coat and fussy frills. 'Don't touch those dirty railings with your gloves, Lilibet!' Mrs Knight warned.

Marion scowled as she hustled the princess out of the door. There was no need for gloves at all in her view, let alone snow-white ones with pearl buttons at the wrists. There was no need for this whole outing, especially not during her teaching time.

But a small part of her, even so, could not help being interested. Norman Hartnell was an up-and-coming couturier. She had seen his clothes in magazines; they were beautiful.

Lilibet was skipping at her side. 'Mr Hartnell's a what?'

'Couturier. Dressmaker.'

'Isn't that a funny job for a man? That's what Alah says.'

'She would.'

'What?'

'I said good, we're here.' Marion pressed the shining brass bell to the side of the imposing double doors.

She had not known what to expect of a designer's studio – perhaps a small room with scissors and bits of material everywhere. But Hartnell's atelier was a very grand Georgian house. The large hallway rose to a tremendous height, a great chandelier filling the space below. There were huge, gold-framed mirrors, tall white doors, long windows to let in natural light and an elegant staircase with wrought-iron balustrade.

A man appeared, moving quickly towards them, heels clicking on the black-and-white marble floor. 'Good morning,' he said briskly. 'I'm Norman Hartnell.'

Marion had anticipated someone tall, thin and aesthetic. The man before her had the build of a sailor with a broad, tanned face and light brown wavy hair. His burly body was encased in a grey double-breasted suit of perfect fit and his shoes were polished to a brilliant shine.

'We're here to get my frock for Uncle Prince George's wedding,' Lilibet announced grandly.

'Yes, isn't it exciting.' Norman Hartnell's hazel eyes gleamed with amusement. 'Would you like to see Aunt Princess Marina's wedding gown?'

Liilbet's red mouth opened in an O of amazed delight. 'Yes please.'

He nodded at a pair of closed doors behind him. 'It's in there. Off you pop, then.'

Lilibet popped off. The doors crashed noisily behind her. Marion shot an apologetic look at Hartnell. 'Sorry.'

The hazel eyes gleamed. 'Never mind. I don't expect she's used to opening her own doors. And, my dear, what *is* she wearing? The skirt of her mother's dressing table? Why do all royal women dress so badly? I've seen sacks of potatoes with more style than the Duchess of York.'

Marion stared. She had never heard anyone criticise the duchess before. It felt like heresy. It felt naughty and delightful. 'Her nanny put her in it.'

'Oh, so you're not the nanny, then.'

'I'm the governess.'

'*Governess?* My dear, how *antiquated*. I didn't realise they still existed!'

She stared back, affronted. She was a young and modern woman, didn't he realise?

He had folded his arms and was looking her up and down. 'Mmm. I can see it now though.'

'See what?'

'The governess thing.' He cocked his head to the side. 'Frumpy. Mousy.'

She felt a flash of fury. How dare he? '*You* try looking gorgeous on what the Yorks pay!'

He raised a weary eyebrow. 'Believe me, dear, I do. They don't pay me much either.'

Marion was hurt. She had always kept pace with fashion. But possibly not lately. The days of flippy pink frocks and Eton crops were far behind her.

There was a full-length mirror on the wall close by. She studied her reflection, as now she rarely did. Looking back at her was someone she barely recognised: a tall woman without make-up and with hair in a practical bob. Her suit, of a stout, hard-wearing material in a serviceable colour, was in a style that would not date but would never be fashionable either. Her shoes, again for practical reasons, were cheap, clumpy and flat. Pure horror seized Marion. Had she turned into Mrs Knight without realising it?

Hartnell was standing behind her. He was picking at the worn shoulder seams of her jacket, inspecting them. 'But there's no excuse for *this*. Just what *is* this colour? Less *eau de Nil*, more *eau de* sludge. Make it yourself, did you?'

'No, my mother did,' Marion snapped.

She watched, in the mirror, as Hartnell let go. His eyes were full of apology. 'I do beg your pardon. That was very rude of me.'

'Yes,' she said. 'It was.' He deserved it being rubbed in, odious man.

'Perhaps I can help. This is quite good material, really.' He pulled at the jacket again, bringing it in on either side of her. 'I could nip in the waist, shape the skirt, raise the hem.' He came round to the front and winced. 'And recut those lapels. It's sharp and narrow at the moment. New buttons would make a difference too.'

No thank you was on the tip of Marion's tongue. She bit it back. Hartnell was a famous couturier. The suit had seen better days. If he wanted to make amends by entirely transforming it, then let him.

He stood back, arms folded, smiling. 'You've got a marvellous figure, you know, dear. Wonderful height. Shame not to show it off, really. You'll look like one of my house models once I've finished with you!'

She felt her liking for him return.

'Crawfie!' yelled Lilibet excitedly. She was behind them, in the open doorway. 'Come and look at Aunt Princess Marina's dress!'

'Do you think,' Hartnell murmured, as they walked off together, 'that poor Aunt Marina has the faintest idea what's in store for her?'

Marion looked at him. How on earth did he know?

'Dear George has a very chequered history,' Hartnell continued. 'But they say he's put his bad old ways behind him. So Kiki Preston, the Girl with the Silver Syringe, is unlikely to be on the abbey guest list. On the other hand, some *very* surprising people are.'

Marion glanced at Lilibet. She was through the doors and in the next room, sliding in her stockinged feet on the polished floor.

The next room was high-ceilinged and filled with light. A mannequin took centre stage. It wore a column of shimmering silver brocade.

'How beautiful,' Marion breathed.

'How almost impossible, you mean. Twelve feet of fragile family lace lined with French silver lamé that would break if you looked at it. *And* made by Russian refugees.'

'Russian refugees?'

'Don't get me started. Our Marina's half Russian. She wanted displaced persons from the mother country involved. Which is all very well for her to say, but guess who had to find Russian refugees at a moment's notice. Ones who could sew, as well.' He closed his eyes, shook his head and groaned, as if to dispel a nightmare.

'Well, it was worth it. It's the perfect royal wedding gown.'

'Which isn't saying much,' Hartnell retorted. 'The last one was the Duchess of York's, which was the ugliest in the entire history of the world. Madame Handley-Seymour should have been shot.'

Marion was still laughing when Lilibet slid up. 'Why do you always have your hand on your hip?' she asked Hartnell.

'So I know where to find it,' the couturier flipped back.

They left an hour later, Lilibet clutching sketches of a white knee-length frock with puffed sleeves and a wide tulle skirt, worn with a headdress of roses. Marion was amused. Hartnell had more in common with the duchess's dressing table than he thought.

Chapter Twenty-Five

Norman had been even better than his word. The reworked suit was utter perfection. With effortless elegance it drew attention to her straight shoulders and slender waist. It stopped bang on the knee, to show off her long legs. He had swapped the worn leather buttons for flat shiny black ones and taken the lapels off and replaced them with contrasting black velvet. 'I look like a completely different person,' Marion breathed, looking in Hartnell's mirror.

'It's better than that,' exulted Norman. He was clearly delighted with the success of it. 'You look like the person you're supposed to be. Glamorous, forward-looking, woman of the world.'

It was true. Norman had negotiated a discount at a Bond Street salon, where a flamboyant stylist had snipped away to reveal what he called her swan neck. Her cheekbones, lately hidden under curly clumps, reappeared as well.

Now, when she looked in the mirror, the bold girl who had cropped her hair and swirled her skirt smiled back. Dowdy Marion had gone.

'You're a genius,' she told Norman.

'It has been said. Now off you go to the ball, Cinderella!'

'You mean the wedding. The ball's the night before, and I haven't been asked to that.' The king and queen were giving a dance at Buckingham Palace, which promised to be extremely grand. The duchess had been auditioning tiaras all week.

'No, but you know who has?' The hazel eyes gleamed with excitement. 'I hear on the grapevine that a certain very flashy frock has been made for a certain very flashy lady.'

He meant Mrs Simpson, obviously. 'She's not flashy,' Marion said. It was a source of deep frustration to Norman that she had met Wallis and he hadn't. Even more frustrating was the fact that he had not been asked to design for her. She wore Chanel, whom Norman hated. 'Anyone can do that minimalist stuff! It takes real genius to be maximalist, like me!'

She doubted Norman's information about the ball. It would be a highly formal occasion. The Prince of Wales would surely not invite his mistress, a woman Queen Mary had called an adventuress. Lady Furness; the devoted Freda Dudley Ward; they had never made such public appearances. Norman had to be exaggerating.

Marion hoped so, fervently. She liked Wallis, but any increased ascendancy in the Prince of Wales' affections spelled trouble – for Lilibet, and therefore for her.

On the day of the wedding, she sat in the abbey transept. There was a buzz of anticipation as those gathered waited to see the beautiful Greek princess.

'Marinamania' had gripped the capital. It loved everything about her, from her romantic name to her hats. Two types were in circulation: a droop-brimmed one with a high crown and pompom, and a perky pillbox with an upstanding side feather. Both had been much in evidence in the vast crowds cheering the princess in her coach every inch of the route from the palace to the abbey.

Norman, of course, preferred to believe that the real excitement was his dress. 'They're all desperate to see it!' he had crowed earlier, in the abbey foyer. 'Not bad for the son of a pubkeeper from Streatham Hill!'

Marion stared. 'You told me your father was in the wine and spirits trade.'

'And so he is,' the irrepressible Hartnell returned.

Sitting behind Marion was a gossipy collection of elderly peeresses. In front, across the aisle, she could see the Prince of Wales. As Prince George's best man, in his naval officer's outfit, he looked astonishingly handsome. But, as always, astonishingly bored. She watched him beckon a passing clergyman and light a cigarette on his processional candle.

There was a gasp from behind. 'Did you see that? And to think he's to be Defender of the Faith!'

The prince, perhaps aware of such remarks, possibly even keen to encourage them, blew a fat plume of smoke upward.

Another whisper from behind. 'He took *her* with him to the palace ball last night.'

In her new suit, Marion stiffened.

'Appalling woman. Foxtrotting about like the cat who'd got the cream.'

'The servants at the Fort saw him coming out of her room in the morning. Covered in lipstick.'

'No!'

'Apparently she has complete power over him. Not to mention delusions of grandeur. I hear that in Biarritz she was complaining because she wasn't introduced to all the local aristocracy.'

'She'd complain more if she had been.'

Marion swallowed nervously. She could still hardly believe that the good-natured woman she remembered was also the brazen creature of these stories. But all the stories were like this. How could everyone be wrong, and she be right?

She tried to concentrate on the abbey's splendour and beauty, the carving and gilding, the glowing stained glass. She looked at the Greek royal family, sitting in the nave. Apparently they didn't actually have a throne and were currently living in exile. But they certainly compensated with looks.

They had gathered in the palace beforehand, among them a blond boy of startling handsomeness. His name was Philip and he was a cousin of Marina's. Lilibet, from across the room, had gazed at him shyly. He had not seemed to notice her.

The mighty abbey organ now announced the advent of the bride. People strained to see Marina as she came slowly up the nave, the shafts of coloured light from the ancient windows making her diamonds flash and glitter.

Marion slid a glance at the Duchess of York. Sitting in the nave dressed in palest pink, she wore a look of bright, unruffled serenity. Marion was not fooled, however. Elizabeth of York loathed Marina. It was said that the Greek princess considered the Scottish earl's daughter beneath her. The earl's daughter had repaid in kind.

But she was possibly not feeling quite so triumphant now, Marion thought, watching Marina approach. Shimmering beneath the powerful lights, Hartnell's gown looked magnificent and set off to perfection the princess's dark and delicate beauty. She was fashionably etiolated in a way the Duchess of York never would be, and her popularity was almost as great.

Lilibet now appeared in her tulle frock, walking slowly down the aisle behind Marina. She looked adorably serious beneath the flowers in her hair. But like Marina, she had her detractors. At her mother's feet, Margaret crouched on a velvet stool looking furious. She passionately resented not being a bridesmaid too, and had none of her mother's skill at concealing it. From under her little white bonnet she blazed with all the red-hot fury a four-year-old could summon.

Behind Marion, the old peeresses were still on Mrs Simpson. 'They say she demands endless money and jewels.'

'Snaps off the ends of pencils to make more work for the servants.'

'Reduced the gardener to tears by demanding all his peach blossom!'

'No!'

Marina reached her husband-to-be at the altar. To mark his marriage, Prince George now had an extra title, Duke of Kent. With his height and slick dark hair he had a film-star glamour. Perhaps that was appropriate. According to Norman, the prince had once, under a pseudonym, won a dancing competition in Cannes.

The Prince of Wales now stood up, the braid on his uniform flashing under the chandeliers. He took another long drag on his cigarette, which he then tossed to the floor. He glanced about with his quick, darting gaze. He seemed to be looking for someone.

'Oh, and she's here, of course,' came from behind Marion. 'He gave her the best seats, naturally.'

'*Seats?* Is the husband here?'

'Yes. Have you heard? They're calling him "The Unimportance of Being Ernest".'

'How very amusing.'

A hat moved several rows in front of Marion, and shock barrelled through her as, quite suddenly, she realised she was looking at Wallis.

She was seated in the choir in a fitted dark jacket that made an elegant contrast to the gold all around. She was hatless, her black hair gleaming above her pearly face. Did she look hard, scheming and ruthless? Marion wondered. Or exactly the same as before? Her red lipstick was bright as blood and her big dark eyes, while not looking in Marion's direction, had the amused glitter she remembered.

'*There!*' hissed the trouts. '*Look!* His face!'

The prince was staring at Wallis as if she were the only woman in the world. It was a private moment, played out in public. Only an idiot would doubt what was going on now.

Marion glanced at Lilibet, poised and patient behind the glittering Marina. There was something touching and vulnerable about the small white figure amid the ancient and vast surroundings.

She felt a sudden, fierce resolve. Whatever happened, she had but one priority. She must protect her little princess.

Chapter Twenty-Six

The king's Silver Jubilee was approaching. It seemed singularly ill-timed to Marion. Marking it with lavish celebrations seemed a positive risk.

The Kents' wedding had been lavish, but it had had at its centre Princess Marina, a glamorous young woman. Moreover, it was confined to London. This would be nationwide, and would be centred on an irascible old man.

Marion was nervous. If there was to be a revolution, then surely it would be now. The country, riven by poverty and unemployment, could hardly be expected to praise a man who had everything. And his subjects, of course, only knew the half of it. They hadn't the first idea about the tensions in the family, and how an American divorcée threatened to blow the lot sky-high. What if they found out?

Surprisingly, however, the nation seemed to view the anniversary as a welcome distraction. An opportunity to put aside their woes.

The authorities, it had to be said, provided a magnificent setting in which to do this. The Mall was lined with huge flagpoles topped with gold imperial crowns. An eighty-foot statue of Britannia, flanked by golden lions, stood on top of Selfridges in Oxford Street. Floodlighting, appearing for the first time, made a sensational nightly spectacle of the royal palaces, Westminster Abbey, County Hall and the fronts of the Tate and National Galleries.

The king's four sons had been all over the kingdom, Gloucester to Ireland, York to Scotland and Wales of course to the principality. They had received rapturous welcomes in each. The king himself, along with Queen Mary, had gone on four great carriage drives through London – north, south, east and west. His Majesty had told Lilibet, who had passed it on to Marion, that the East End streets had been the gayest of all, with bunting, paper flowers, flags and streamers disguising the mean brick terraces and the sun bouncing off the brass helmets of the local fire brigades. There had been pianos in the roads, groups having sing-songs, neighbours lending tea urns and trestle tables.

'Grandpapa said he had no idea they felt like that about him,' Lilibet excitedly reported. 'He said that, after all, he's only a very ordinary sort of fellow.'

The centrepiece for the ordinary sort of fellow was a thanksgiving service at St. Paul's. The princesses were to drive in procession from Buckingham Palace with their parents and grandparents. Marion had promised Lilibet she would stand in the crowd and wave. 'I'll wave back to you, Crawfie,' Lilibet assured her.

It was still only mid-morning, but the heat was already powerful. Against the simmering blue sky, the gold crowns atop the flagpoles blazed. She had planned to walk to the cathedral, taking the route down the Mall, but it was immediately evident how hopeless this was. There were far too many people; the Mall's pavements were tight-packed. Even the smallest progress involved twisting, sidling, ducking and squeezing between the pressing masses.

Marion looked at them. Battered shoes, patched elbows and pinched features were much in evidence. These were the unemployed, the means-tested, the angry citizens. What if they suddenly realised the unfairness of it all and rose up against their oppressors, as Valentine always put it?

Fear tightened within her. It had been a long time since she had been in a crowd. Even when she was out with Lilibet, Cameron was always close by. But now she was on her own.

A great shout now erupted, followed by a silence. She stiffened. Was this it? The moment when everything turned? She glanced about her apprehensively, trying to read the stiff faces. She thought of Lilibet and Margaret in their open carriage. Against a rampaging mob they would have no chance. She looked at the bright red line of Grenadier Guards. Would they turn and start firing into the crowds?

The silence dinned in her ears. Into it came a clatter of hooves and a jingling of harness. Above the shoulders and between the hats, Marion caught flashes of red and gold, the tossing head of a horse, the wave of a gloved hand. Queen Mary's meringue-like toque appeared, its feather swaying with the movement of the carriage. Marion saw part of the king's beard, an explosion of braid and medals and then the bored, contemptuous profile of his son and heir. Would people see him for what he was?

'God Bless the Prince of Wales!' screamed the mob.

Lilibet now came into view, smiling and waving with her little white gloves. The crowd went wild with delight. 'God bless the little princesses! God bless Princess Elizabeth!'

Marion felt that she would burst with pride. This child that they were all cheering – she was her work. Lilibet's natural manner, her ease with this great mass of people, must have something to do with all the trips they had taken together, out into the city. Operation Normal had been a success. The sacrifice had been worth it. Happy tears blurred her vision and she rummaged in her pocket for her handkerchief.

It was then, as she glanced about, that she saw him. He was a few yards away, his face turned towards the carriages. There was no doubt it was him. He looked exactly the same, even though three years had passed since last she saw him. A pair of wide dark eyes with a shining wave of black hair above. A red scarf dancing like a flame.

Alarm juddered through her, mixed with warning. This man had hurt her terribly. She should avoid him, and nothing would be easier than to duck away in such a vast crowd. On the other hand, his treatment of her had led to Lilibet, whom she so loved and who loved her back, and to an important job at which she had been successful, as the events now unfolding showed. Perhaps they were even, after all.

But as she sidled her way towards him through the roaring masses, she was aware of another motive. She was curious. What was he doing here, an avowed revolutionary, in a crowd cheering the monarchy? Had he changed his mind?

'Valentine!'

He turned. She had half wondered if he would even remember her, and was gratified to see his face light up. 'Marion. You look *fantastic*.'

Norman's early work on the suit had since been augmented by work on dresses and skirts. Today she was wearing a yellow frock bought for a song in a sale, but transformed by Hartnell's clever needle and accessorised with bold red buttons.

'And you,' she said, smiling back, 'look exactly the same. But why are you here?'

Valentine had accessorised too, she saw. Wth a placard, which he now raised in the air. It read 'Nobody Voted For The Monarchy.'

Her eyes widened. 'Are you mad?'

'No, unlike everyone else in this deluded crowd.' He grinned, the same flashing grin she remembered. 'This is Decca, by the way.'

A toothy girl with thin, arched eyebrows and shining blonde hair popped her head round Valentine's shoulder. 'Hellair!' Decca's accent was jauntily upper-class. She too was waving a placard. Marion stared, confused.

'Oh, it's not what you think.' Valentine grinned. 'Decca's with Esmond.'

Marion glared at him, annoyed by his casual assumption that she gave a hoot about his romances. She also now remembered, with a speed that amazed her, the schoolboy editor, japester and iconoclast whom Valentine had hero-worshipped. Here he was, in the flesh. His solid, rather square head had appeared beside Decca's. He waved his placard. 'Hellair.'

'And I'm Philip.' A gaunt young man with glasses and bad skin, as well as the inevitable placard, popped his head round the other side.

Marion nodded. 'Hellair. I mean, *hello*.'

She felt suddenly confused, as if what had been certain a minute ago no longer was. Here she was in a crowd of London's poorest who were cheering London's richest. And in the middle of that, a pocket of privileged upper-class youth disguised as left-wing egalitarians – one of whom had betrayed her in the past. It felt too much to cope with. 'I'd better go.' She turned to head into the crowd.

'No, stay!' insisted Valentine. 'Or let me take you for a cup of tea.'

'No,' she muttered, pulling away from his hand which held her shoulder in a way her body seemed to remember fondly.

She expected him to pull her back, but instead he began to sing, raising his fist in the air. 'Arise, ye workers from your slumbers! Arise ye prisoners of want . . .'

People in the crowd were looking at him suspiciously. She twisted back. '*Stop* it!'

He was still singing. There was a teasing look in his eye. 'So comrades come rally/And the last fight let us face . . .'

Around him eyes were narrowing. She pictured dirty fists curling, toes flexing in steel-toed boots, ready to kick. The narrow Edinburgh passage of long ago flashed into her memory, Valentine slumped on the ground.

He shook his placard. 'Workers of the world unite! Join the revolution!'

'Stop it,' Marion pleaded. Two thuggish men had exchanged glances before looking back meaningfully at Valentine.

She grasped his wrist in terror. 'They'll . . .'

'Tear me limb from limb?'

'Something like that.'

'And you'd care?' A dark flame danced in the back of his eyes. She felt the old rush of longing, and pushed it back, fiercely.

'No. Of course not.' But as he raised his placard yet again, she grabbed his wrist.

He shook his head. A hank of hair flopped into one eye, quite in the old way, and made her melt, quite in the old way. 'If you want me to stop,' he warned, 'you'll have to come for a cuppa.'

She groaned. 'Just one.'

Because everyone was watching the procession, the nearest Lyons Corner House was practically empty. They sat by the bow window. 'Are you married?' It was his first question. Men always asked her that, she thought. Although for different reasons. Peter had asked it to discover if he yet had a chance of being her husband, while Valentine, she had no doubt, was asking it to see if there was a husband in the way.

'None of your business,' she told him.

He had left Edinburgh, he told her, soon after she had gone. 'It was no fun without you.' He pulled a mock-mournful face.

She eyed him disbelievingly. 'And that was really the reason, was it?'

'Well, that and the university throwing me out for failing my exams. So now I'm down here, fomenting international proletarian revolution and the end of imperialism.'

'And it's going really well, I can see,' Marion snorted, gesturing towards the windows, where passing crowds were waving pictures of the king-emperor.

He spoke through a mouthful of Victoria sandwich. 'They just need their consciousness raised. The triumph of the workers over the ruling classes is historically inevitable.' He waved the cake in his hand. 'On the glorious day, this will be Stalin sandwich.'

She shook her head. She was surprised how little rancour she felt. Now she had come to terms with what he had done, weighed it against her gains, she could appreciate once again his stupid jokes, his ridiculous Communist rhetoric. 'And just where in London are you plotting the defeat of capitalism?'

'Rotherhithe. By the river. It's a blast. Our house belongs to a friend of Esmond and Decca's.'

'They live there too?'

Cake bulged in his cheek as he nodded. 'She's run away from her family. Her father's an earl,' he added proudly.

'How strange,' said Marion. It sounded complicated and intriguing, but she was resolved not to seem over-interested in Decca.

'"Strange" is the word,' Valentine enthusiastically agreed. 'Her sisters are all completely different. Ideologically, I mean. Diana's a Fascist, Unity's a Hitler fan and Debo just wants to be a duchess.' He spoke as if he knew them all intimately.

'Hitler? Fascist?' Marion gasped, her resolve vanished.

'And Decca is a Communist, obviously. Crazy mixed-up bunch,' Valentine concluded fondly.

Marion stared at him. 'I don't believe you. No one has a family as mad as that.'

He laughed. 'What about the one *you* work for?'

She scowled at him. He took an unrepentant swig of tea. 'Why don't you come round? We have amazing parties. We're having one tomorrow, as a matter of fact.' He shoved in the last of the cake. 'You should swing by.'

Chapter Twenty-Seven

Later, at the Jubilee lunch, in the Palace State Dining Room under an ornate gold and white ceiling, Marion sat at a long table. It was draped in white, heaped with silver and lined with facing rows of royals and eminences. Her seat right at the end meant she was so close to the red-jacketed military band she could see the title on their music sheets. They were performing 'The Departure of the Troopship' – a royal favourite.

Her neighbour was the king's new private secretary, Alan Lascelles. She had not met him before. He was a tall, lean, upright man with chiselled, aristocratic features and sharp dark eyes set deeply under a craggy brow. His centre-parted hair was thick and black and his manner almost ridiculously grand.

They discussed the success of the Jubilee, Marion attempting to conceal her surprise. It was no surprise to Lascelles. 'Any human system demands a visible figure of God's majesty,' he declared pompously. 'In offering a connection to the past and the future, kings and queens belong to the world of poetry.'

Marion suppressed a snort. She did not think George V belonged to the world of poetry. Or of art in general. She had once heard him yelling that he could 'MAKE BETTER MUSIC THAN WAGNER BY SLAMMING MY BEDROOM DOOR!'

'Kings are like a church spire you see across a river valley,' Lascelles went on. 'The expression of age-old beliefs.'

Marion did not answer. She was watching Margaret across the table, who was staring hard at a particular footman. Her intent surveillance was clearly making him nervous. His tray was shaking, and now, as a fork plunged from a tray to the carpet, Margaret bounced in her chair triumphantly and gave a little gurgle of delight.

Marion leaned forward. '*Margaret!*'

A pair of wicked violet eyes met hers. 'Yes, Crawfie?'

'You did that on purpose!'

A pair of long lashes batted innocently. 'I don't know what you mean, Crawfie. It wasn't me, it was Cousin Halifax.' This imaginary figure was behind most of Margaret's transgressions.

She sighed and turned back to Lascelles, who was still pontificating on the monarchy. It was obviously his favourite subject. 'The phenomenon can be explained in secular ways too. One man is king only because other men stand in the relation of subjects to him.'

Marion knew the quote. 'They, on the other hand, imagine they are subjects because he is king,' she finished. 'Karl Marx.'

Lascelles now seemed to look at her properly for the first time. 'You are acquainted with the works of Karl Marx, Miss Crawley?'

She remembered Dr Stone, who had also called her this, and felt her dislike of this man harden. 'Craw*ford*. And yes, I am interested in Marx, as all intelligent people should be. Communism is a powerful force in the world.' It felt rather daring to be talking of such things in Buckingham Palace.

In the recesses of the craggy brows, the black eyes glinted. 'Indeed. But not a force that will ever find favour here. We Britons are a free people, detesting violence and hysteria. It is only slaves who go in for bloody uprisings.'

While Marion felt this a good thing, she kept her face neutral. 'And Britons never never never shall be slaves.'

A wintry smile lit the gaunt features. 'Never never never. You know what King Farouk said, of course.'

'Actually, I think I missed that.'

'By the end of the twentieth century there will only be five monarchies left in the world. The kings of hearts, diamonds, clubs, spades – and England.'

The Prince of Wales now stumbled in, late and apparently unrepentant. The table fell silent and his father cast him a glance of loathing. Unable to resist a tease, Marion leant towards Lascelles. 'I wonder if His Majesty shares your confidence in the monarchy's future. In the person of his son and heir, I mean.'

'Yes to the former, but almost certainly not to the latter. And I have to say I share his views.'

'You don't like the Prince of Wales?'

'I left his service some years ago,' was the unexpected response. 'The circumstances were slightly difficult.'

Marion was riveted. 'Difficult?'

'Forgive me if I don't go into the details. Suffice to say I always felt that I was working, not for the son of the King of England, but for the son of the latest American millionaire.'

Marion was amazed. 'But the prince is very popular.'

'He has magic,' Lascelles agreed. 'He's one of the most attractive men I have ever met. No one else in the family comes near to him for glamour. But are magic and glamour what the Throne requires?'

'I don't know,' said Marion. 'Are they?'

Her neighbour sipped his wine. 'A certain middle-class ordinariness is now an important element of what the British people demand in their monarchs.'

She felt she had never met anyone quite so pompous. She wanted to say something to rattle him. 'Really? How does Mrs Simpson fit into that?'

Her neighbour, not rattled in the least, merely dabbed his lips with his napkin. 'There are certain things,' he remarked, 'that the nation expects their Royal Family to do, and certain things which it expects them not to do. That includes marrying a certain type of woman. The British people will not tolerate their monarch taking as his wife and their queen a shop-soiled American with two living husbands and a voice like a rusty saw.'

Marion sat back. It was a harsh description of the woman she had met, but it also seemed to settle the question once and for all: Lilibet really did have nothing to worry about. She now had it on the highest, most official authority that when the Prince of Wales became king, marriage to Mrs Simpson was out of the question.

The table drank to the king's health. 'You think he's healthy?' Marion asked her neighbour. They both looked at the monarch, now haranguing the conductor for a repeat of 'Troopship'.

Lascelles gave a lofty smile. 'I was assured when I took this job that His Majesty was in excellent health with several more years ahead of him.'

She had said no to Valentine's party and meant to stick to it. But perhaps it was the lingering memory of pompous Alan Lascelles that sent her, the next evening, walking down the street he had named, to the address he had given her.

Why not? It wasn't just rebellion against a supercilious courtier. She was lonely. Without Ivy, the evenings at 145 Piccadilly dragged terribly. She could walk around the streets, staring into the windows of the local art galleries, but this only made her feel more isolated as laughing couples, arm in arm, hurried by on their way to the West End's pubs, clubs and restaurants.

A party, with other young people – she was still a young person, just, at twenty-six – would be something. And, after the first shock, it had been fun to see Valentine again. They had both moved on; they could at least be friends. They were both grown-ups now. Well, thought Marion, with a wry twist of the lips, she was, in any case.

The river smell was close and dank and hung in the foggy, cobbled streets. Dim figures went past in the gloom. It was a poor neighbourhood, evidently, but it had an energy about it, a spirit. She could hear people laughing and shouting in nearby streets.

As she dithered outside the battered door with its peeling paint, a wraithlike young man with a cadaverous face came drifting out of the fog. 'Can I help you?'

'You're Philip,' she said.

Behind the round glasses, his eyes widened. 'Gosh, yes, and you're . . .'

'Marion.'

'Come to the bottle party?'

She nodded.

'Brought a bottle?'

She rummaged under her coat and produced one. It had been one of several on the dining room sideboard. The duke would not miss it, she felt. After all, he had plenty more.

Philip took it and whistled. 'Pol Roger 1927. Cripes. That's going to raise the tone a bit.'

She followed him into a hallway crowded with rusted bicycles. Laughter and music could be heard from upstairs. She felt a swell of excitement. It felt like a long time since she had been with people her own age.

Philip's heels crashed on the uncarpeted stairs. He went up, waving the bottle. 'Look, everyone! We really are champagne socialists now!'

Marion followed shyly. The landing was full of people: young men in turtlenecks and women with bobs and cigarettes. They were all laughing. Decca, head thrown back, was laughing the loudest.

'You came!' Suddenly, Valentine was beside her, hair flopping in his eyes. 'You look wonderful.'

Her frock was black and fitted. It had been ordinary enough but now had the indefinable something Norman brought to everything he touched.

She felt sophisticated, but not grand. Just right, in fact. Suddenly, everything felt just right. Her heart seemed to swell and flower and pulse a warm happiness right to the ends of her fingers.

'Have a drink.' He pushed something into her hand. It was a jam jar, half full of red wine.

She looked at it, then back at him. 'But I brought champagne!'

'Oh!' He looked round. 'Philip! Over here with that bottle!'

One hand now clutching a jam jar half full of Pol Roger, Marion allowed herself to be pulled round with the other.

'Marion!' Decca was dipping by. She was wearing a yellow print dress and red lipstick and looked exquisitely pretty. 'This is my sister Debo.'

Debo was a smaller, younger version of Decca and was wearing jodhpurs and a tweed jacket. She was perched on an open window-sill. 'Here,' said Valentine, sloshing champagne into her jam jar.

Debo looked glumly at the dancing bubbles. 'I hate champagne. Makes your breath smell.'

'Oh, do shut up, Debo,' Decca responded robustly. 'No one made you come.'

'Actually, Muv did. After that story about you this morning. And straight from my riding lesson, too.' Debo gestured down at the jodhpurs. 'Really, Decca,' she added peevishly. 'You might be more considerate. I'm trying to marry a duke but it's a bit tricky if your sisters are in the papers all the time. Muv says that whenever she sees the headline "Peer's Daughter blah blah blah" her heart sinks because she knows it's one of us.' She swung out a polished riding boot. 'Sometimes I really *hate* being a Mitford.' She got up and disappeared into the throng, thrusting angrily through the crowd with her narrow tweed-jacketed shoulders. Marion sipped her champagne from her jam jar. The bubbles danced on her tongue and went straight to her head.

The house was a mess, she thought, but she liked it. On the walls were unframed canvases rendered in thickly daubed oils. The furniture seemed entirely composed of *Daily Workers*, in piles serving as seats and tables. The light came from candles stuck in bottles. The effect was chaotic, but romantic.

'Let me introduce you to some people.' Valentine had reappeared again and was pulling her up from the window seat. 'Meet Eric, he's a writer. Back in a sec.'

Eric was gaunt and lugubrious. In the dim candlelight, he looked worn, as if he had had a hard life. 'What are you writing about?' she asked, politely.

Eric pulled hard on his roll-up. 'It's called *The Road To Wigan Pier*.'

'It's about the seaside?'

He looked at her scornfully. 'Not exactly.'

Decca sidled up, smiling her toothy smile. 'Actually,' she said in her cut-glass accent, 'it's about the working classes in the north struggling with the Means Test. It's a right ripping read, isn't it, Eric?'

'Bugger off, Decca,' growled Eric, not unaffectionately.

'Working on a sequel?' Decca prodded.

'Of a sort. Matter of fact, you can tell me what you think. How's this for a first line? *It was a bright cold day in April and all the clocks were striking thirteen.*'

'*Thirteen*! But no clock strikes thirteen!'

Within his deeply recessed brows, Eric's eyes rolled. 'Precisely. That's the point.'

Marion liked these intense, laughing people. They interacted so easily, and so equally. Everyone talked to everyone else. She realised that she wasn't used to that any more.

She could see Esmond at the other side of the room, an admiring crowd about him. His rather square face was alight with conviction and he was talking with big, gesticulating movements. It wasn't just Valentine who hero-worshipped him, it seemed. They were an argumentative lot, but excitingly so, she thought. Opinions flew from every direction. Unemployment. Mussolini's invasion of Abyssinia. German rearmament. Stanley Baldwin, widely expected to replace Ramsay MacDonald as prime minister. People seemed to have strong views about all of them.

Slowly at first, then more and more confidently, she found herself joining in, saying what she thought too. The freedom of being able to express herself was exhilarating, extraordinary. She realised how repressed she had been, how lonely, just reading the papers in her room and feeling she was the only one who cared.

Someone, somewhere, was singing 'The Red Flag' to the accompaniment of a ukulele. She smiled. This was fun. Really fun.

The ukulele stopped and someone put a record on: '*Night and Day.*' She felt the music flow through her, along with the wine. She wanted to dance, suddenly. It was ages since she had done so. It was ages since she had done anything a normal girl in her twenties did. God, she was twenty-six now. Where had the time gone? Panic seized her. She took another mouthful of champagne, a big one, closed her eyes, and began to sway gently to the music.

She felt someone take her hand. She gasped, opened her eyes and found herself looking into Valentine's. He pulled her into him and kissed her. They swayed gently together. Candle shadows flickered on the walls. She felt that, even though she had seen gilded ballrooms and glittering crowns, these peeling walls and dusty floorboards were more glamorous still.

'Shall we?' he muttered into her hair.

His bed was just a mattress on the floor. She stared at it. He was behind her and had slid his arms through hers, clasping her breasts. Her breath caught in her throat. Desire beat within her, like a drum. It had been so long. She wanted him so much. Desire whirled in her head, spinning her downward, to the floor.

'No,' she said, as he planted his mouth on hers. She pushed him away. 'No!'

She scrambled to her feet. What was she thinking of? She couldn't hang around in shabby riverside houses talking freely about politics with young left-wingers. She worked for the royal family. And Valentine was not only behind the glass wall, he was a Communist into the bargain. If anyone found out – and they would find out, the Tom business had made that clear – this would be the end.

She remembered with horror the conversation with Lascelles about Karl Marx. She had thought herself so clever, but it had been a stupid thing to do. She had learned through bitter experience that she could not be two things at once. She had made her choice, and she must stick to it. 'I've got to go,' she said, her voice sharp, panicked.

He lay on the mattress, annoyed. 'God, Marion. You're such a prick-tease.'

She hurried down the stairs.

In the kitchen, Decca was having an intense conversation with a bearded young man. 'They sent me to finishing school in Paris, which almost did finish me off, actually.'

'Didn't you like Paris?' The bearded young man was gazing at her admiringly.

'What was there to like? We learned bridge, did a cathedral a week and went to the opera. But we had to leave before the last act of *Faust* because the ending was considered immoral.' Decca giggled.

'Then I came back and got threatened with the London season. That was the last straw, the idea that I was supposed to find someone to marry among all those chinless wonders!'

Marion slipped past, down the stairs. The battered door stuck briefly before it wobbled open. Outside, the fog rolled up the cobbled street. The gables of warehouses loomed in the mist; boats hooted on the river. She hurried towards the Underground station, feeling like Cinderella in reverse. Cinderella had to leave the palace. But she had to get back to it. Before the clock struck and everything disappeared.

It was hard, even so, to turn her back on all that fun. Most nights, as she sat in her silent room, she thought of the cheerful arguments, the candlelight, the scruffy camaraderie of the Rotherhithe house. She pictured Valentine's mattress and groaned. Must she live like a nun? Sometimes it seemed that in trying to bring normal life to Lilibet, she had cut herself off from it.

Given all this, the annual long trip to Scotland that autumn was almost a relief. But the new Duchess of Kent, visiting with her husband, evidently felt the opposite.

'AND HOW ARE YOU FINDING BALMORAL, MY DEAR MARINA?' the king's voice boomed like a volley from a warship.

Princess Marina, doubtfully poking her haggis, started at the shattering noise. 'There are many insects.' She gave a rueful glance at the red bumps on her slender, lily-white arms.

'YOU SHOULD SMOKE NAVY CUT! KEEPS THE BUGGERS AT BAY!' instructed her father-in-law.

Marina's beautiful dark eyes widened in amazement. The Duchess of York, no fonder of her sister-in-law, tittered. Prince George leaned forward. 'She doesn't smoke, Papa.'

There was a short interlude as the king was served from a silver tray of venison borne by the man in the brown plaid rug. 'MY OWN DEAR PARADISE IN THE HIGHLANDS,' he boomed, as the rug moved on. 'THAT'S WHAT QUEEN VICTORIA CALLED BALMORAL!'

'It's very . . . historical,' said Marina.

'CHARMING, DON'T YOU THINK?' the king roared on,

making the crossed swords rattle on the panelled walls. 'KEEPING EVERYTHING THE WAY SHE HAD IT? THE CHILDREN LOVE THE FACT IT NEVER CHANGES.'

Prince George and his brothers exchanged incredulous glances. Marina dabbed her red lips with her napkin and squinted through the flickering gloom. 'What is happening there?' She gestured at a large painting hanging opposite her seat.

Her husband shot his father an apprehensive look. 'It's Prince Albert gralloching the stag, Marina.'

'What?'

'Gutting it,' Prince George sighed, as Marina looked nauseous.

His York sister-in-law now leaned forward. 'You really must go out shooting with His Majesty, Marina. He is an *extraordinary* shot! He *never* misses! His birds are *dead* in the air before they even reach the *ground*!'

The Greek princess raised a glittering hand to her mouth.

After dinner, Marion was dismissed. Queen Mary, her tartan skirts sweeping the tartan carpet, progressed to the drawing room with her newest daughter-in-law. 'Your nails are very red, my dear. My Chorge doesn't like painted nails.'

'Well, my George does,' was the Greek princess's spirited reply.

Marion mounted the plaid-swathed staircase. A loud cry reached her ears, coming from the direction of the drawing room.

'Marina! You can't sit there! It was Queen Victoria's favourite chair!' The voice was the Duchess of York's and held a definite note of triumph.

Chapter Twenty-Eight

That Christmas, Marion returned to Edinburgh to find her mother had suddenly aged. Her formerly bright eyes now seemed wavering and dim. Dusty shelves and grubby cupboards pointed at a steady loss of sight – her mother, who had been so house-proud! It tugged at Marion's heartstrings, as did the sight of her hands, eternally knitting or sewing as always as she sat in her armchair, but shaking as they never had before.

Marion thought about London, and returning there after Christmas. As always, distance enabled a more detached view. Could she really go back and leave her mother? She had mothered Lilibet for long enough, at the cost of considerable personal sacrifice. She was almost twenty-seven now. She had missed the boat with Annie, but she could still return to teaching. And perhaps it was time now for some little girls of her own.

Her mother, whom she had half expected to object, agreed that she had done her duty. As the Jubilee had shown, the monarchy rested on the firmest of foundations. And she had Lascelles' assurance that the prince would not marry Mrs Simpson, whose existence her mother knew clearly nothing about. The newspapers were still ignoring her as well. Perhaps, after all, she really wasn't very important.

The idea of now finally having a life of her own gathered more momentum with a letter from Ivy.

From Sandringham, where she had gone as part of the palace household, Ivy wrote, in her unexpectedly beautiful handwriting, to say that she and Alf were to wed in the spring. *So we'll be leaving! Alf's dad's got a costermonger business, he'll be joining that.*

Marion had no idea what a costermonger was.

She thought of Sandringham. It was her least favourite of all the royal residences, a great sprawl of Victorian red brick, like a golfing hotel. Royal peculiarity seemed at its most intense here, with the king's obsession with punctuality given full expression. He had even created his own time zone there: Sandringham Time, where all the clocks were half an hour fast. Ivy described the paternal greeting received by Prince Henry, two minutes delayed to dinner after an absence of six months: 'LATE AS USUAL, HENRY!'

Ivy's letter offered highlights of the royal Yuletide. The Prince of Wales had given offence by going to play golf during his father's Christmas broadcast. Extravagantly bored throughout the festivities, he had subsequently gone skiing in Switzerland with Mrs Simpson.

Lilibet, in painstaking pencil, offered a sunnier account. 'Everyone loved their presents from Woolworths! Grandmama was very pleased with her china mouse and Uncle David loved his handkerchief.'

Marion smiled as she remembered the shopping trip. Margaret had come too. The little girls had excitedly bought calendars and pencils for their relatives. A bottle of brilliant pink bath salts for Mrs Knight had been an especially inspired purchase. The image of her chief adversary dyed a bright shade of magenta had added considerable cheer to Marion's festive season.

She had tactfully pretended not to see them buying the little bead necklace she eventually unwrapped on Christmas morning. Mrs Crawford was delighted with the little elephant on a pin the princesses had sent to her. 'They've left the price on the box though, bless them.'

They were in her mother's tiny sitting room, cosily battened against a winter storm, when the news came over the radio that the king was confined to bed with a cold. 'Poor chap,' said Mrs Crawford, over her knitting.

A few days later, the king's weak heart was reported. Marion, clearing the dinner plates, paused and frowned. But the king had not been ailing. On the contrary. She had it on the best authority that he had many, many years in him yet.

Alan Lascelles had been wrong, it now seemed. 'The king's life,' said the radio announcer, a few days later, 'is moving peacefully towards its close.'

Marion looked out at the snow, whipped by violent winds, whirling past the windows in thick flakes. It mimicked the panicked thoughts swirling about her brain. What was happening to the girls in this time of trouble?

Chapter Twenty-Nine

'Death came peacefully to the king at 11:55 p.m.,' announced the radio on 21 January. Dutiful to the end, he had held a Privy Council in his Sandringham bedroom and attached a wavering signature to a parchment.

Marion saw the pictures in the newspapers. Crowds at the entrance to Sandringham, huddled in winter coats, to read and reread the framed bulletin. It felt strange seeing from outside what she knew so well from within.

The decorative wrought iron of the Norwich Gates, through which she had passed so many times. The distant factotum coming down the snowy drive from the Big House, his gloved hand holding the cardboard envelope. Did she know him? She could almost hear the eager, questioning Norfolk voices in the crowd, an accent that had once been new to her but was now familiar.

She wondered about Lilibet and Margaret. How were they coping? The duke and duchess were sure to be swept up in procedure and protocol. Who was with the princesses? Alah, presumably. Marion could hardly bear to think of the flint-faced old stoneheart being their only source of comfort.

'I should go to them,' she said to her mother.

'No you shouldn't; it's your holiday,' Mrs Crawford pointed out. 'And you've just said you're leaving them.'

But then the telegram arrived. Marion read it, walking slowly back from the front door. 'The duchess wants me to go back,' she told her mother.

'What?' Mrs Crawford looked up from her sewing. 'Cable her and say you can't.'

But the lines were down, the telegraph boy had said. It was the snow. There was no way of getting in touch.

'See it as an opportunity,' said her mother. 'Now is a good time to break with them. A new king, a new start.'

'Yes, but I can't get in touch,' Marion fretted. 'They'll think I'm ignoring them.'

'They'll understand. Wait until the snow clears, and then tell them.'

'They won't, Mother. I'll have to go down and do it in person.'

The journey was endless and freezing. It was like the first time, but a hundred times worse. The first thing she heard on entering Royal Lodge was sobbing. It was a dreadful keening, expressing a world of terrible agony. It echoed round the green-panelled entrance hall. The girls? Horror clutched Marion's heart.

Dumping her suitcases in the hall, she dashed up to the nurseries. In the gloom of the upstairs passage, two small figures were visible. Neither seemed to be crying.

'Crawfie!' yelled the taller child, hurtling across the lino. 'We've been waiting for you to come!' Margaret rushed after her sister. Laughing and gasping at the force of the assault, she held them tightly, her nose buried in their silky hair, breathing in their soapy, little-girl scent, hugging one and then the other.

The howl of anguish sounded again. 'It's Alah,' Lilibet said.

'But we don't know why,' Margaret added scornfully. 'She didn't really know Grandpapa.'

'But everyone's sad about His Majesty,' Marion pointed out. 'And most people didn't know him.'

'I didn't know about the rabbit,' Margaret conceded.

'What rabbit?'

George V had, it seemed, once bought a half share in a rabbit. The animal had been the joint property of a small sister and brother. Discovering that, to the dismay of his sister, the brother intended to sell his half, the king had bought the boy out for ten shillings and presented the share to the little girl. 'Wasn't that sweet of him?' Lilibet asked.

'He never bought *me* a rabbit,' Margaret grumbled. 'He didn't like me. Only Lilibet. She said goodbye to Grandpapa. But not me.'

Lilibet described how they had learned about the king in the Sandringham gardens. Her account was simple yet vivid and Marion could see the dark berberis, the rhododendrons thick with snow, the flower beds hidden, the lawns wide, white and empty apart from two excited little figures sticking a carrot nose on a snowman. The carrot nose glowed, a brave dash of bright orange in the sombrely monochrome scene.

Then, out of the great red-brick house with its gables, chimneys and pepper-pot turrets had issued a tall, forbidding figure. Gliding towards them over the snow had come Queen Mary in her long Edwardian skirts. It was time for Lilibet to say goodbye. 'Just Lilibet,' Margaret repeated. 'Not me.'

Lilibet looked agonised. 'I'm sure Grandmama didn't mean anything – '

'She did. She doesn't like me.' The littlest princess paused and assumed a familiar frown and heavy German accent, 'You are so *small*, Margaret! *Venn* are you goink to *grow?*'

Now that Alah had stopped yowling, Royal Lodge seemed very quiet. 'Are Mummie and Papa here?' Marion asked.

'They went to London. But Mummie left you a note.'

In her familiar, leisured, looping handwriting on thick cream crested paper the duchess had written two sentences: *Don't let all this depress them more than is absolutely necessary, Crawfie. They are so young.*

Not a word of thanks, Marion thought. She had moved heaven and earth to get here. Had she done the right thing after all?

Lilibet wanted to tell her every detail. Grandpapa's bedroom, she reported, had lots of words in frames hanging on the walls. One said 'There Is Nothing the Navy Cannot Do' and another 'Teach Me to Be Obedient to the Rules of the Game.'

'But what rules does Grandpapa mean, Crawfie?' Lilibet looked puzzled.

'Noughts and crosses,' Margaret declared authoritatively. 'Tell Crawfie about the deathbed, Lilibet. The doctor had a funny name.'

'Oh yes.' Lilibet grinned. 'Sir Farquhar Buzzard.'

'Hee hee. And what was that sign about the beast?'

'If I am called upon to suffer, then let me be like a well-bred beast that goes away to suffer in silence.'

'But Grandpapa never suffered in silence,' Margaret pointed out. 'He was always shouting.'

Mrs Knight's sobs struck up again.

'Why not play with your farm set?' Marion suggested to Lilibet.

A pair of doubtful blue eyes met hers. 'But, Crawfie – *ought* we to play?'

'Of course you should. Grandpapa wouldn't want you to be unhappy.'

Margaret was certainly not unhappy. She was dancing around the landing.

'Uncle David's going to be king now,' she declared. 'He's Edward the Eighth. I'm the niece of the king! Hooray!'

Marion looked from one to the other: the sober elder princess, the cock-a-hoop younger. That she was in charge of the king's nieces had not occurred to her before. From a position on the sidelines, she was now right at the centre of the national drama. She could not, like Margaret, help feeling excited too. Perhaps, for the moment, she would stay. Until everything calmed down. Then she would go.

Chapter Thirty

They remained at Royal Lodge while the duke and duchess dashed back and forth. Strange stories reached them about the new king. At his father's bedside, once the old king had died, Edward the Eighth had sobbed for a full hour on his mother's bosom. Marion found this hard to believe. Queen Mary's bosom was invariably stiff with diamonds. It would have been like weeping on a gravel drive.

It was much easier to believe that the new monarch's first act as king had been to adjust the Sandringham clocks to the right time. Marion imagined him wearing enormous trouser turn-ups when he issued the order, surrounded by all his ungentlemanly friends. Mrs Simpson would no doubt be among them. Servant gossip had her dancing round Fort Belvedere in delight, planning her coronation robes and refusing to wear mourning dress. 'I haven't worn black stockings since I gave up dancing the cancan,' she was supposed to have said. Was this true? It sounded unlikely, but Marion wasn't sure what to believe any more.

The old king was mourned, grievously. The newspapers showed the carpets of flowers that sorrowing subjects had left at Windsor and outside the Sandringham gates. The lawns around St George's chapel were completely hidden with blooms.

Pale-faced in her black coat, wearing her black velvet tam-o'-shanter, Lilibet went with her parents to the lying-in-state in Westminster Hall. Queues of every class, creed and colour stretched back two miles late into the freezing January nights in order to file past the royal coffin.

'But we came in through a special door at the back,' Lilibet said excitedly on her return. She spoke breathlessly of the silent crowds, the scent of the great piles of flowers, the huge, glowing candles. But what had really caught her imagination was her father and uncles standing guard in military uniform, one at each corner of the purple-draped catafalque. 'Uncle David was there and he never moved *at all*. Not even *an eyelid*. And everyone was so *quiet*. As if Grandpapa were asleep!'

The funeral was to be a festival of gloomy ceremonial, featuring a lengthy procession through the streets of London. The coffin would go to Paddington, and from there by train to the burial at Windsor. There would be massed bands, muffled drums, carriages galore and what crowned heads of Europe remained after the last war. The princesses were required to attend.

Marion went to see the duchess. 'I think they would find it very long and difficult, ma'am. And the crowds would be enormous.'

Elizabeth of York was at her desk, gaily signing cards with black edges. She rattled her fountain pen between her teeth. 'Oh, very well, Crawfie. Perhaps they could just wave him off at Paddington.'

They drove to Paddington through a strangely silent city. Businesses were closed as a mark of respect. Neon signs had been extinguished. London was as grey as the sky above it. The streets were black with the crowds waiting to witness the king's last journey.

The great terminus was heaving; the atmosphere was charged. If they were spotted, anything could happen. They must go somewhere for shelter, but where? The lavatories were obviously out of the question, although would have the advantage of separating them from Cameron. But they could hardly spend an hour and a half there.

'The waiting room,' was the royal detective's less-than-brilliant suggestion. Marion did not dignify it with a response. Fighting through the crowd to get to it, wherever it was, would mean being trampled underfoot.

'The buffet,' suggested greedy Margaret.

Marion spotted a sign and felt a rush of relief. 'The station master's office!'

The station master of the Great Western Railway snatched his cap from his pink bald head, sent for tea and gave up his desk and chair. Over the hour and a half wait, his entire supply of notepaper was sacrificed to games of noughts and crosses.

At the large, plain solid desk under the Bakelite clock, Lilibet marked a firm 'X' next to two previous ones. 'You've won *again*!' exclaimed Margaret, outraged.

Her sister grinned her monkey grin. But almost immediately her smile faded. Above the crowds outside, other sounds could be heard. Drums, a band playing, the clatter of horses' hooves.

Lilibet stood up. Her small face was very pale and, just for a second, seemed to quiver. But then she raised her chin, put her shoulders back in their ink-black jacket and met Marion's eye steadily. 'We must go, Crawfie. Grandpapa is here.'

Pulled by sailors with ropes before and aft, the king on his gun carriage came slowly down the ramp. The diamonds in the Imperial State Crown reflected the lights of the terminus. Spread beneath it, over the coffin, were the lavish folds of the Royal Standard. Its scarlet and gold provided a splash of brilliant colour amid the greys and blacks of the waiting crowd.

Lilibet gasped. 'There's Uncle David! And Papa!'

'Look at their funny hats!' giggled Margaret.

'Who are all those men behind them?'

'Kings, I think.'

'The one in the white uniform looks very handsome. But the one in all those feathers looks silly!' Margaret giggled again. 'Who's the fat man in the shiny cap?'

A shiver went down Marion's spine. She knew from the newspapers that General Goering, Hitler's right-hand man, had wanted to represent the regime at the funeral. He had been discouraged, but someone had come, all the same.

'What's that funny sign on his arm?' Margaret wanted to know.

The band played on with muffled drums. Above the station's glass canopy, the daylight was fading. The last rays caught the crown on top of the coffin, which gave a final, brilliant glitter. As the cortège transferred from ramp to platform, the carriage wheels jolted on the rails. The gun carriage jerked, the coffin and crown with it. The diamond cross detached and clattered to the floor.

'*Christ*,' the new king exclaimed impatiently. 'What's going to happen *next?*'

The funeral was over, but a thick pall of gloom still hung over the York family.

The duchess laughed much less these days. A muscle ticked continuously in the duke's fleshless jaw, and his stammering had worsened considerably. Margaret, whose high spirits alone remained undimmed, had dubbed his displays of sudden rage 'Papa's gnashes'.

What lay behind the gnashes was not discussed. But that it was the new king was obvious. There was a tension in the air, as if everyone was waiting for something to happen.

Something was certainly happening in Spain. The former governor of the Canary Islands, a short, strutty man called Franco, had led a rebellion against the republican government. Marion read the newspapers avidly. Some commentators believed the Iberian conflict was the front line in what would became a war against Fascism. *No Pasaran* – the Republican slogan, They Shall Not Pass – was frequently mentioned.

Marion longed to be at Rotherhithe, discussing it with Valentine and his friends. She could imagine the candlelit arguments, the lively discussions, lubricated by rough wine from jam jars while, outside, the brackish Thames lapped the house wall.

It would be something just to attend a public meeting, where Spain would be discussed. She dared not, however. If it became known that she went to political gatherings, there could be trouble. She began to frequent Speakers' Corner at the north end of Hyde Park, a place where anyone could make a speech, on any subject, and did so, on weekend afternoons in particular. She would stand, eagerly drinking in what was said, envying the orators their freedom of expression. Hers was beginning to feel rather crushed and compromised.

The king, however, was all the Piccadilly household seemed concerned about. Devoid of explanation, but sensing something afoot, people had started listening at doors. It became normal to cross the Piccadilly hall and see a servant spring back from a keyhole. She had not intended to stoop like this herself. Until, that was, she had been passing the drawing room where the duchess was taking tea with the Archbishop of Canterbury.

'You've heard about the ministerial boxes?' The high, breathy voice came floating out the door.

Marion stopped and slowly retraced her steps. The ministerial boxes were sent from government departments to the king. They were covered in black leather, stamped with the crown and royal initials and contained confidential state papers to be read and signed.

'Some of the papers are sent back covered in drinks rings.'

'Good heavens,' said the archbishop.

'But at least it shows he reads those.' There was an agitated rattle of a cup in a saucer. 'Others are sent back weeks late with no initials. He obviously hasn't so much as glanced at them.'

'How dreadful.'

'Mr Baldwin's started to take out the sensitive things because apparently my brother-in-law leaves Cabinet documents lying about the Fort. In full view of *that woman* and her questionable friends.'

'That sounds rather a security risk.'

'Indeed it is, Archbishop. You know the Foreign Office are watching her? Bertie's terribly worried.' Marion had never heard her employer sound like this before. Distressed, serious, close to tears, even. 'David won't tell him *anything*. Bertie's not in his confidence *at all*. He has no idea what's happening.'

'Well, thankfully the British people have even less. The press blackout is holding.'

Press blackout? Marion frowned. Was this why there was never a reference to Mrs Simpson in the newspapers?

'Yes, Lord Rothermere and Lord Beaverbrook are keeping their word. For the moment.'

Marion pressed her back against the wall and looked up at the chandeliered ceiling. Press censorship was undemocratic. It was what they did in the Fascist countries Valentine's friends were so concerned about. She should be outraged, she knew. But somehow it was different when you were on the other side, the side that knew. The chandelier above her glittered and tinkled. She felt a dark excitement. This was what it felt like to be at the centre of things.

The duchess was speaking again. 'But there were pictures in the American press of that wretched Nahlin cruise. They're calling it the greatest story since the Resurrection.'

'Outrageous!' gasped the archbishop, as well he might.

'Thought you'd appreciate that.' The old impish humour gleamed through for a second. 'She's getting divorced now, you know,' the duchess added, more gloomily. 'If she gets the decree absolute, David could marry her before the coronation in May.'

'*Surely* he won't do that!'

'Brandy, Archbishop?'

'Yes please.'

Amid a clinking of cut glass, the duchess went on. 'Bertie's been told that it could end in abdication.'

'*Abdication?*' spluttered her interlocutor.

Abdication? The hallway seemed to spin around Marion.

Chapter Thirty-One

Things were worsening in Spain. The radio news, every night, related the melodious, unfamiliar names of towns falling to the right-wing rebel forces. Young British men in their droves were joining the International Brigades, the Communist-organised forces supporting the republic. It was easy to imagine Valentine joining them too, especially after spotting, in one newspaper, a 'Special Dispatch from the Front Line' written by Esmond Romilly.

Marion read it with shaking hands. It described a violent battle outside Madrid. Had Valentine been there? He probably didn't know one end of a rifle from the other. He'd been a pacifist at school. But it seemed that the brigades were made up of idealists and amateurs: shopkeepers, university lecturers, waiters. What chance did they have against Franco's professional soldiers?

Meanwhile, at Piccadilly, Edward VIII continued to be the only topic. A stream of statesmen, legislators and experts now daily arrived at the house to see the Duke of York. From the circular gallery at the top of the residence, Marion observed a succession of important-looking people cross the hall below and disappear into the drawing room.

Prime Minister Stanley Baldwin, harassed and clutching his trade-mark pipe. In glamorous, loping, unhurried contrast, the pinstriped Foreign Secretary Anthony Eden. Queen Mary's distinctive toque was another that came and went, and Marion had even seen Alan Lascelles once or twice, stalking across the hall and quite unaware of her watching from above.

As the tension mounted, she felt relieved she had not left royal

222

service after all. In these strained circumstances, distracting the girls was all-important. They swam, they shopped, they visited museums, to which they rode on buses. At weekends, at the Little House, they cleaned intensely. Even Margaret, who hated housework.

They were working on the crockery from the miniature oak dresser when there came the sound of a large automobile passing. Lilibet paused, up to the elbows in soapsuds. 'What's that?'

'It's Uncle David!' yelled Margaret, who stood at the window, arms dripping. They ran to join her. The car shot through the Royal Lodge gates and made a complete, sharp swing around the circular driveway. A spray of gravel scattered like gunfire across the stone steps.

'He's got someone with him!' Margaret gasped. 'A lady!'

Marion frowned at Lilibet before she could say anything. Thanks in no small part to her efforts, the smallest princess had no idea about the existence of Mrs Simpson. On her own behalf she felt a tremor of disquiet. Would Wallis remember their meeting in the driveway of the Fort? It might be awkward if so.

But it was years ago now. Surely not. And there was, anyway, an outside chance that the woman in the car was someone other than Mrs Simpson.

They hurried to the Lodge to find the duke and duchess, in their gardening clothes, standing by the car. A woman in white-rimmed sunglasses sat in the passenger seat. From a white headscarf of some floaty material peeped a front of glossy, centre-parted black hair. Her face was pale, the only colour her lipstick: blood red.

Marion felt a swell of dread.

'We've just driven over from the Fort!' King Edward, resplendent in checked tweed and goggles, sat with his gloved hands on the polished steering wheel. His gold hair glinted in the sun and he was grinning through the clamped teeth holding his cigarette in place. 'Thought you'd like to see my American station wagon!' he called to his brother.

'But not his American woman,' the duchess muttered darkly into her husband's boiler-suited shoulder. She looked uncomfortably aware of the contrast with the immaculate newcomer presented by her scruffy gumboots and string-tied coat.

'Who is it, Mummie?' Margaret was pulling on her mother's fingers. The duchess affected to ignore her.

'Come and try it out, Bertie!' the king invited. He seemed full of rakish bonhomie.

The duke looked doubtfully at his wife, then longingly back at the gleaming car. The magnificent cream roadster was long and roofless, with running boards, shining spokes, big glass-fronted headlamps, ribbed leather seats and glittering chrome fittings. Margaret was dancing excitedly round it. 'Poop poop!' she was shouting, pointing at the big brass horn. 'Poop poop!'

They had recently read *The Wind in the Willows*.

'You can honk it if you like.' His Majesty demonstrated the device's mighty blast.

Mrs Simpson laughed as Margaret squeezed the great black rubber bulb and squealed with delight at the noise it made. The duke and duchess looked silently on, Lilibet obedient at their side.

'Come and try it out, Bertie!' urged his brother again, gaily.

The duchess's plump hand pressed into her husband's blue-boiler-suited back. 'Go on,' she hissed. 'Get it over with. I'll show *her* round the garden.'

Mrs Simpson now rose gracefully from the passenger seat. Her clinging dark jersey suit, trimmed with white in Chanel's signature style, perfectly displayed her flat stomach and non-existent hips. A great jewel-studded cuff flashed in the sun.

The duke climbed in the front where Mrs Simpson had sat. They drove off in a spin of wheels and a splatter of gravel.

Wallis walked confidently towards the duchess, high heels crunching through the gravel, red lips stretched in a broad, friendly smile.

'A walk in the woods before tea, Crawfie?' the duchess murmured over her shoulder.

'But who *is* it?' Margaret demanded loudly as Marion grasped her hand and pulled her away.

She glared accusingly at her sister, whose air of superior knowledge was unmistakable. '*Lilibet* knows! Don't you? Why can she know and not me? It's *not fair*!'

Later, they returned for tea. They entered the mint-green-panelled hall and crossed to the door of the drawing room. The servants gathered around it scattered guiltily.

The garden tour, and the car ride, were evidently over. The duke, duchess and their visitors sat in a group round the central fireplace. As Marion and her charges paused in the doorway, the conversation floated over to them. Mrs Simpson, dark and at ease in one of the padded armchairs, was happily giving the duchess her opinion of the garden.

'It's pretty. But I wonder if it could be improved by moving some trees. And taking away part of that hill, maybe?'

The duchess stuffed her cake into her mouth, apparently to stop herself from saying anything. Her eyes were blazing. Under her seat, her foot waggled furiously. She had shed the gumboots for a pair of heels, but an unravelled air hung about her still.

The king sat next to Wallis, his blue eyes adoring. 'Isn't she *wonderful*? Her eye for design is absolutely unparalleled. You should see her flat.'

'I'd love to,' said the duchess drily.

Wallis flashed her a dazzling red beam. 'Drop by anytime for one of our potluck suppers!'

The duchess began to cough.

'They're quite wonderful,' the king said. 'Wallis does all her own shopping!' He spoke, Marion thought, as if this were a rare and amazing feat – which to him it possibly was.

The duchess, red-faced and now almost choking, groped for a glass of water.

'I ask for trout all the same size,' Mrs Simpson went on. 'And if the butcher doesn't cut the steak the way I want, I get out my cookbook and show him the diagram!'

The king's eyes were sparkling. 'Isn't she wonderful?'

'Astonishing,' said the now-recovered duchess, which was of course not at all the same thing.

Edward continued to gaze at his companion. As in the abbey, Marion had the powerful impression of complete and utter devotion. 'Wallis is just the most extraordinary person I've ever met. The only woman who's ever been interested in my job.'

'Really?' The duchess's smile was stiff. Her tone conveyed doubt at the idea that only a truly exceptional woman would be interested in the head of the British Empire.

The king seemed oblivious to any irony, however. 'Oh yes. She loves hearing about my visits to housing associations, the unemployed of the Welsh valleys, whoever.'

The duchess now caught sight of her daughters in the doorway and stretched out her hands as to a saviour. 'Margaret! Lilibet!'

Marion felt her insides contract. Would Wallis recognise her? Acknowledge her? As they approached, the big black eyes looked into hers for a second. Then they passed on.

That night, Marion woke suddenly. She had heard something. Was it Lilibet again? Straightening her shoes?

She took a deep, disappointed breath. She had hoped to jolly the princess out of any return to her obsessive, worried ways. But perhaps, especially after this afternoon's visit, it wasn't possible.

She got out of bed, wincing as her warm soles hit the ever-freezing floor. She opened the door and put her head out into the corridor. The sound seemed to be coming from Mrs Knight's room, a few doors down.

Marion went to her door and listened. It sounded . . . although, surely not. She listened again. Yes, definitely. No doubt about it now. Mrs Knight the indomitable, Mrs Knight the flint-faced, Mrs Knight, of all people, was crying.

Chapter Thirty-Two

Marion knocked. There was a creak, a grunt and the sound of two large bare feet making contact with the lino.

Marion had never seen Mrs Knight at bedtime, and she made for a peculiar sight. Over her voluminous white flannel nightgown, she wore her heavy black outdoor coat. It looked crumpled, as if she had been sleeping in it.

'Are you all right?' Marion asked. It was a stupid question. The woman's square face glistened with tears.

The nanny now turned away. Her hair was down from its habitual bun. A long grey plait, never before seen, hung thinly down the length of the broad back.

'What's the matter?'

'*Him!*' was the strangled reply.

The extraordinary possibility of some thwarted romance, some secret, treacherous lover, flashed across Marion's mind. She blinked. 'Him?'

Mrs Knight whirled round, her gimlet eyes blazing. 'He'll do exactly as he likes, no matter what it means for everybody else.'

She was talking about the king, Marion realised. 'You mean you think he'll marry Mrs Simpson?'

Mrs Knight's big white hand was clamped over her mouth. She nodded, eyes brimming. The hand came away. 'And what will that mean for Lilibet?' she burst out.

Something shifted in Marion's mind. So used was she to seeing Mrs Knight as an obstacle, the idea that she might love the little princess had never occurred to her.

She stared at the coat again, obviously worn against the cold, and at the thin grey plait. It could have been thick, black and glossy once. Mrs Knight had been young, and might even have been beautiful. But her youth and beauty had faded in the service of the family. As had her chances of marriage – her title was only a courtesy one – and children. Likely there had never been a lover, secret or otherwise. She had sacrificed everything.

Marion put her hand on the rough coat sleeve. All her resentment and dislike had gone. To understand was to forgive, and she could understand now. See the threat she must have appeared: a bumptious young woman taking charge of beloved Lilibet. The duchess would have explained little of what was happening, if anything.

'You really think he'll marry her? But she's foreign, a divorcée . . .' But even as she spoke the words she recognised their irrelevance. She had seen with her own eyes the depth of the king's devotion. She remembered the overheard conversation with the archbishop. 'But what if he has to abdicate?'

Mrs Knight looked weary. 'He'll do exactly as he likes, Miss Crawford. He always has done. And it's the likes of you and me that will have to clear up the mess.'

She made a possible national crisis sound like a nursery spillage. Marion squeezed the coat sleeve. 'Oh, Mrs Knight.'

'Call me Alah,' the other said gruffly. 'It's about time you did. We might just have a big job ahead of us. Looking after the heir to the throne.'

She went round to Rotherhithe the next day. She felt she didn't care who knew it. If even Mrs Knight could give way and reveal her inmost feelings, then surely she could go round and find out about Valentine.

She wore the suit Norman had altered for the Kents' wedding and made herself up carefully. Her hair, recently cut, revealed her neck and cheekbones. She hurried down the foggy street, her heels hammering on the cobbles.

'He's not here,' Philip said, opening the battered front door.

She caught her breath sharply in her throat. 'He's gone to Spain?' Philip sighed. 'You'd better come in.'

She sat in the kitchen. Thick evening light streamed richly through the dirty window, irradiating unwashed pans stacked in unsteady towers. She thought of the crowded party, and all the laughter.

Philip explained the route. As she had suspected, Valentine had gone with Esmond. The first stop was Marseille in the hope of boarding a cargo ship. After that they had sailed to Valencia and were sent to a training camp at Albacete. 'He's fine, I'm sure,' Philip insisted, when it was established there had not been any news for a while.

When Marion left the house, she leaned briefly against it, as if saying goodbye to something. She knew, however, that she had said goodbye to Valentine long ago, if indeed he had been hers in the first place. Their romance was an illusion; the reality had been betrayal and hurt. Why was she behaving like this?

Because, she knew, she had a big ball of love inside her, with no one to give it to and nowhere to put it. Apart from one place, of course. As she descended into the Underground, the little girl's face glowed in her head. She had Lilibet, after all. Lilibet, to whom she now felt as close as a mother.

For this year's Scottish holiday, the Yorks had eschewed the castle for Birkhall, a nearby house on the Balmoral estate. The official reason was that they needed the extra space. But as rumour had it that Mrs Simpson was a guest of the king, the real motive was not hard to guess.

Birkhall was quite different from the castle. It was a large, rambling, white-painted building formed of several houses knocked together, some of which were clearly very old. It was a romantic-looking place, fitting the Valley of the Dee's landscape much more naturally than did its somewhat incongruous neighbour.

Inside was also easier on the eye: pine panelling and framed cartoons of long-defunct Victorian politicians rather than endless tartan, stags and Prince Albert. Marion's bedroom here was less bleak than at the bigger houses, with an actual carpet, and a dressing table.

She was sitting at it now, sweeping the little brush through the cake of mascara. That was better. She blinked and widened her big brown eyes. Was that a new line on her forehead?

A droop at the sides of her mouth? Hurriedly she slicked on red lipstick, raised her chin, smiled at herself, got up and went outside

The Birkhall gardens were pretty and bright with thick lawns and a stream that plunged merrily between fringes of rhododendron and laburnum.

The many trees, their leaves detached by the near-constant Scottish breeze, meant optimum conditions for Happy Days, a game Marion had taught Lilibet. You had to catch leaves before they reached the ground, and each captured leaf represented a 'happy day' for the future. Lilibet was adept at it, laughing and leaping at the twirling forms tossed by the peaty Scottish breezes.

Hair tumbling over her face as she jumped, the princess was the picture of merry abandon. Seeing Dookie at Lilibet's heels, trying to snap at some happy dog days of his own, Marion felt affection even for him.

'I'm going to have a *very* happy life,' the princess announced with satisfaction, proffering a skirtful of leaves. She peered at Marion's haul. 'Oh, dear Crawfie.' She bit her red lip. 'It doesn't look like you are!'

Marion smiled. 'Only because I let you catch most of the leaves. I sacrificed my happy days for you, you see.'

A short distance away the Yorks were sitting on the lawns, reading; the duchess was cackling at P. G. Wodehouse. 'So amusing!' she was saying to her husband. The duke did not look amused. He was frowning over *The Times*, which reported more rising unemployment figures and accompanying unrest and demonstrations.

'Oh really, Bertie,' said the duchess, impatiently. 'Those men are being exploited for political ends. Everyone says so. Marching from one end of the country to the other is hardly the best way of dealing with their problems.'

'P-perhaps,' the duke conceded. 'But it is the only way they know.' He laid aside the paper and sighed. 'They're d-d-desperate, Elizabeth. I wish there was something we c-c-could do to h-help.'

'Bertie, we already help.'

'Yes, b-but opening the odd f-fete. W-what difference does that m-make?'

His wife sat up in her deckchair. 'It's a lot more than that. We distract them from themselves and their poor miserable lives. Give them something to believe in. National allegiance. Continuity.' The duchess paused and took a swig of champagne. 'Always remember, Bertie – when it comes to royalty, nothing succeeds like succession.'

Marion, catching leaves with Lilibet, envied the duchess her robust, uncomplicated view of the world. She had always known there was steel beneath the floating misty blue, and it seemed to be coming ever more to the fore.

Ainslie appeared, gliding across the lawn. 'Cometh the hour, cometh the man!' The duchess gaily waved her empty champagne glass.

The butler had no bottle in his hand, however. Marion watched as he hurried to the duke's side and murmured something in his ear. The duke gasped in horror and leaped to his feet.

'Bertie! What is it?'

'Aberdeen H-hospital! D-David! We must go . . .'

They hurried off towards the house.

Lilibet stared at Marion. 'What's the matter? Is Uncle David ill?'

'In a manner of speaking, quite possibly,' Ainslie murmured as he returned to the house.

The evening paper arrived at Birkhall in the mid-afternoon, before the duke and duchess returned. Marion, in the house to fetch tennis racquets, saw it lying on the hall table.

She picked it up. The front page had two photographs, both taken that afternoon. One showed the Yorks stepping in for the king, who had become indisposed at the last minute and unable to open Aberdeen Hospital's new wing.

The other was of the king himself, in obvious good health, wearing driving goggles and a gay smile at Aberdeen railway station.

'Mrs Simpson's train was late,' Ainslie remarked as he crossed the hall. 'His Majesty had to hang around waiting. Seemed to think his goggles would stop people from recognising him. But everyone did, of course. Apart from one policeman who told him to move his car.'

'So she's here,' Marion said slowly. And in what seemed absolutely farcical circumstances.

'Aberdeen, I fear, will never forgive him,' was Ainslie's verdict. 'Nor the rest of Scotland, now the story's out.'

That evening, Marion went for a walk. She had a headache. There had been many of late. Her own inner struggles seemed one likely reason; her employers' another.

On her return to Birkhall, the duchess had blazed through the door like an avenging angel, face taut with fury. She had picked up the newspaper, seen the headline and hurled it across the hall. 'So *absurd* for him to go in person to meet *that woman*! You and I have been made to look absolute idiots, Bertie!'

That woman seemed to hang over the estate like a great black Chanel-suited cloud. Marion decided to go up to the cairns, above it all, in the high, fresh air.

She climbed up the hill, feeling better with every step. With the curlew calling, the water rushing and the grouse in the blooming heather, Birkhall and its problems soon seemed far away. After a while, the great pointed piles loomed through the trees.

Here was the Purchase Cairn, the very first, built to commemorate the acquisition of the estate. Marion and Lilibet agreed that it looked exactly like the prow of a rowing boat that had fallen from the sky and sunk halfway into the ground.

And here was the great, flat-sided pyramid dedicated to 'The Great And Good Prince Consort By His Broken-Hearted Widow'. She stood before it, recalling the conversation with Lilibet about love. *Do people really fall down, on the floor?*

Her heart twisted within her. Lilibet was growing up. Soon, in not so many years, she would herself embark on the perilous high seas of romantic affection. Hopefully, she would have better luck. As for herself, it increasingly seemed as if love had passed her by altogether.

She leaned against the cairn and let the tears slide down her face.

'Whatever's the matter?' asked a curious voice behind her. Marion gasped, and whirled round.

A woman was standing there, a woman in a long, elegant coat of houndstooth check. Her gleaming black high heels showed no sign of the walk they must have made up from the valley, and her jet-black, centre-parted hair was immaculate. Her pale face, with its pearly sheen, showed no sign of exertion, but there was concern in the large dark eyes and the red-lipsticked mouth was stretched in sympathy.

'You can tell me all about your troubles, honey,' said Wallis Simpson, with a weary smile. 'And then I can tell you all about mine.'

Chapter Thirty-Three

The shock was absolute. All of a sudden, from out of the wooded twilight, the wicked witch of Lilibet's nightmares was upon her. The scheming seducer, the brazen disturber of royal peace. She was so surprised she could not speak.

Mrs Simpson, however, seemed perfectly at ease. 'I know you, don't I?' she said in the warm Baltimore drawl Marion remembered. 'You're the girl who came to the Fort that time.'

'Yes. But I thought you'd forgotten. When you came to Royal Lodge.'

A wry, red-lipsticked smile. 'It seemed safer for you that way, honey.'

It took a few seconds for realisation to land. Wallis had been protecting her. 'Thank you.'

An amused glance. 'You're welcome, honey.'

Marion's mind was racing. Her initial impression had been the right one after all. Mrs Simpson was not the selfish social-climbing monster of popular legend. She was sympathetic and sensitive to other people. Even humble governesses. She could so easily have betrayed their earlier meeting, if only to score a petty point and annoy the Duchess of York. Yet she had not.

She felt a sudden, keen sense of the unfairness of it all. Wallis seemed to be a good person, but those she worked for regarded her as *that woman*, a creature too horrible even to deserve naming. A threat to not only their happiness but their whole way of life.

Marion longed, somehow, to bring the two sides together. There was so much misunderstanding. But as soon as the idea struck, she dismissed it. It was out of the question. Things had gone too far. The only connection between the two sides was her, for all the good that was.

For all the good that was. She pulled the thought back and considered it. And yet, might it not be? She had thought she had no power at all. But might she, Marion Crawford, humble governess, be able to influence the great?

The idea gathered pace in her head. Mrs Simpson was sympathetic towards her. Could she really succeed? But crazy things happened. In this family more than most. There was hope, definitely.

She felt breathless. The possibility was dizzying. Dazzling. If it worked, she would have saved the Yorks. Saved the monarchy too, possibly. How grateful they would all be! They might put up a cairn to her as well.

These thoughts had taken mere seconds. Wallis, meanwhile, was tucking her beautiful coat underneath her. 'Shall we sit?'

This woman who loomed so large in everyone's imagination was so tiny in real life. And so, so thin. She lived on black coffee and grapefruit, people said. She weighed herself every day and starved if the scale was a fraction over seven and a half stone.

Marion perched on the boulder next to her, gathering her courage. Her heart thundered and nausea swirled in her belly. An intense autumn sunset spilled gold over the grass. She bent and picked a piece of heather, a particularly rich and purple one.

'C'mon, honey.' Wallis softly touched her hand with a gloved one of her own. The gloves were exquisite: bright red and skin-tight. 'Tell me what's on your mind.'

The word crouched on Marion's tongue, ready to spring. She thought of Margaret on the diving board. Lilibet's cheerful voice. *Come on, Margaret! Jump in!*

Dare she jump in? She braced herself. 'You,' she said, in a rushed breath.

Wallis, who had been leaning forward, jerked back in surprise. 'Me?'

Marion looked pleadingly into the black eyes. 'They're all so frightened. The little girls especially. They're terrified of what will happen if you marry the king.'

Wallis's brow, less smooth up close than it appeared from afar, scrunched. 'They want me to leave him alone?' She spoke slowly, her tone neutral.

A still silence followed, so still that it seemed that even the birds were holding their breath. The cairns behind them, now sunk in shadow, seemed to be listening too. Testaments to many a royal event of the past, they awaited developments on the latest.

Wallis's perfectly groomed brows had drawn together. The little hands in the red gloves had clenched.

Marion waited, but for what she could not guess. A howl of fury? A hiss of rage? A cold fear swept her. This woman was all-powerful, the mistress of the king. What had she been thinking?

A sound now split the still air, sharp and shocking. 'They want *me* to leave *him* alone!' Wallis bent over. She was shaking, but with laughter. Loud, disbelieving peals of mirth now shattered the evening calm.

Marion's heart plummeted. She had completely misread the situation. Mrs Simpson had no intention of renouncing her royal lover. Why on earth would she?

After a while, Wallis raised her head. She dabbed at her streaming eyes with a scarlet finger. Marion waited to hear she was an impertinent fool. She stared down at the gilded grass.

'I would give him up, believe me,' she heard Wallis say. 'There is nothing I would like more.'

Marion jerked her head up, frowning. Had she imagined it?

'Especially if it helps those little girls,' the other woman went on. 'They're sweet. I'd have liked to get to know them better. I never had any children of my own.' For a moment, she looked sad.

From absolute despair, tremendous hope now gripped Marion. 'So give him up, then. It would solve everything. Everyone would be so grateful. They'd . . .'

She was talking fast, excitedly. Triumph blazed within her. She had done the impossible, made the breakthrough.

She saw now that Wallis was gesturing at her, smiling. 'Honey, it's just not possible.'

The world, which had been whirling, now slowed down and stopped. 'But why not?' Marion practically wailed.

'Because *he* won't give *me* up,' Wallis replied, simply. 'And you try saying no to someone who rules an entire empire and who has never been said no to in his life.'

Marion remembered the besotted king at Royal Lodge. His adoring gaze in the abbey. Everyone had thought it was Wallis who had the power. But not everyone had heard the spoiled, imperious creature in the Piccadilly hallway. *God, how I hate being Prince of Wales.*

She took a deep breath. This all rang true. She could believe it, absolutely.

'That's why it's so useless, everyone being against us.' The Baltimore drawl had a weary tone. 'It just makes him all the more determined to get his own way.'

He'll do exactly as he likes, Miss Crawford. He always has done.

Wallis frowned at her red gloves. 'They're doing everything to stop it. Lying about me, spying on me, trying to scupper my divorce . . .'

Marion remembered the press blackout.

'I'm surprised I haven't had a motor accident by now.'

The sprig of heather Marion had picked now rolled in her palm, thin and bare. She had rubbed away the blooms. All the luck had gone. She stared at it numbly. There was nothing to be done here. She could not save the Yorks after all.

Nor could she save Wallis. Lilibet, it turned out, was not the only one in a gilded cage. But the difference was that no one cared about the king's mistress, or wanted to help her. The exact opposite was true.

'Oh, I know what they say about me.' Her tone was low, musing, as if she were talking to herself. 'I'm a witch, I'm a dominatrix, I'm a sadomasochist, I'm a man. David has a mother fixation, a nanny fixation, a mental imbalance. Oh, and I'm a close friend of von Ribbentrop's. You're aware of that, no doubt? He sends me seventeen red carnations a day, one for each time we've made love?' She gave Marion a sharp look, which she answered with a reluctant nod. Mrs Simpson's supposed closeness to Hitler's ambassador had shot like wildfire round the servant gossip circuit. 'Von Brickendrop' was the duchess's name for him because of his oafish manners.

'Not true. I saw Ribbentrop only twice, both times at Emerald Cunard's, at a lunch. Such lies they tell.' She gazed into the darkening distance. 'And, for the record, I *don't* want to be Queen of England. Why would anyone? I can't think of anything worse. For one thing, I'd have to come to *this* place every year. Insects. Rain. Bagpipes at dawn. The worst decor in the world. Hunting McPuke everywhere you look.'

Marion chuckled. The American was a woman after her own heart. Wallis flashed her a grin. 'And the food is *beyond* disgusting. Haven't seen a green vegetable since I got here. And they've never even *heard* of a club sandwich.' She shook her sleek head.

Against the deepening gold of sunset, her tailored shoulders were sharply outlined. Marion saw them rise in a sigh. 'I didn't want to come to Balmoral, believe me. And how was I to know about that darned hospital? David never told me he was supposed to be opening a ward. I never asked him to come meet me. I'd have been perfectly happy getting a cab from the station. But he insisted on coming and now it's all my fault. The wicked witch strikes again.'

She looked suddenly weary and old. Marion wondered abruptly how old, exactly. A good twenty years more than her; as, for that matter, was the king. They were middle-aged people, really.

Wallis glanced at her watch, stood up and brushed down her clothes. 'Gotta go. There's a dinner tonight at the castle – God only knows what the menu will be. And those Yorks of yours are coming. I'm supposed to be hosting. Better get back and polish my P's and Q's.'

Marion scrambled to her feet too. Wallis had already set off down the path. Her hands were in her pockets, her head down, concentrating on the darkening way.

'I'm so sorry about it all,' she offered, hurrying after the other figure. It was an accurate summation of her feelings. The situation was a mess, and worse than she had thought. Worst of all was the obvious fact that there was clearly no way out of it. They were hurtling towards some dramatic denouement whose outcome would damage everyone – the monarchy included. For what would the country say, when finally it found out?

'Mr Baldwin says I should leave Britain,' Wallis said over her shoulder, as if hearing her thoughts. 'I have a friend with a villa in Cannes. But it would do no good. David would only follow me.'

'I can see that,' Marion said, picking her way over the tree roots. 'It's really difficult. Actually, it must be terrifying.' To be so alone, against the world. She could hardly imagine it.

'It can be,' Wallis admitted. 'People shout at me. They write nasty things on my house walls and throw bricks through my windows.'

Marion frowned. 'But I thought the only people who knew were the newspaper proprietors.'

'Yes,' Wallis placidly agreed. 'It's them that do it. They pay people. Poor Mr Loo is terrified.'

'Your . . . butler?' She imagined an Asian factotum of some sort.

Wallis, ducking under a branch, laughed loudly. 'Actually, he's my dog. David gave him to me.'

How brave she was, Marion thought. How courageous, tactful, intelligent and witty as well. How generous and perfectly groomed. It was so ironic. She would make a perfect queen.

Wallis stopped, turned, smiled her red flashing smile and put out her little red glove to squeeze Marion's hand for a moment. 'Don't look so worried, honey. I can cope. I'm a tough girl. And if a tough girl can't cope with tough times, what's the point of a tough girl?'

They were near the castle now, at the point where the paths divided, one to Balmoral, the other to Birkhall. The sun had now set and all was in shadow. But she could see, even so, that Mrs Simpson was regarding her closely. 'You need to be a tough girl too, honey.'

'Yes.'

'You love someone in that family as well.'

Understanding dawned. 'Lilibet?'

The last of the light caught the nodding, glossy black head. 'And if you don't get out, it'll end badly for you too.' A hand suddenly grasped Marion's once more. 'Look, I can't have children. That ship has sailed for me. But not for you; not yet.' The hand squeezed. 'Get out in time. Promise me?'

Chapter Thirty-Four

Christmas was coming, and it had a strong Wallis Simpson flavour. Taking the girls to Woolworths as usual meant running the gamut of topical variations on the old carols. 'Hark the herald angels sing/ Mrs Simpson's pinched our king' was a popular variant. Jokes like 'Edward the Eighth and Mrs Simpson the Seven Eighths' had people laughing the length and breadth of the land.

Wallis's actual position seemed anything but amusing. Marion had overheard several versions, to different people, of what had proved a disastrous dinner party at Balmoral. 'She came towards me, smiling that triumphant smile,' the duchess declared in disgust. 'I walked straight past her and said, "I have come to dine with the king!"'

Their talk together now had the quality of a dream. But had her plea had an effect? The press blackout had now been lifted, the unlikely catalyst being the Bishop of Bradford's criticism of the king – for irregular church attendance – at a diocesan conference. All the newspapers now piled in, and the headlines claimed that Wallis had, after all, renounced her royal lover and fled to her friend in France.

People snorted at the idea, doubting the truth of it. Mrs Simpson didn't really mean it. She was treating the king mean in order to keep him keen. Why would she end the relationship? She had the king where she wanted him. Her claws were well and truly in. She was having the time of her life on the Riviera, treating the king like a servant and counting the jewels, money and days before she ascended the throne.

From Fort Belvedere came gossip about the agonised calls to Cannes. The connections were so bad that you could hear His Majesty screaming, weeping and begging from one end of the building to the other. 'It doesn't matter where you go, I'll follow you to the ends of the earth,' he had yelled down the line to France. Wallis had been entirely correct in her predictions. Her situation was not triumphant, but desperate.

Knowing the real story, as Marion did, was a source of great secret satisfaction. She had the sense of being the one true witness to history in the making.

But had Wallis really taken her for a fool? Marion had almost begun to question herself when, one afternoon, hands dangling with Christmas parcels, she returned to the Piccadilly house. She quickly mounted the wide grey stone front steps and knocked at the big double doors. Stamping her frozen heels, she thought with relief of the warm interior, the fires in the marble hearths, the fat iron radiators.

'It's 'er! Look!' The shout came from behind her, someone on the street.

'Mrs Simpson!'

Surprise jangled through Marion. But the Ritz Hotel was only just across the road, a few hundred yards in the other direction. Perhaps Wallis had been spotted going in.

A small crowd had gathered on the other side of the railings. 'It's 'er, innit?'

One of them shook a skinny fist. 'Bleedin' American whore!'

Marion's jaw dropped. Her suit, while expertly tweaked by Norman, bore no resemblance to the Chanel creations in which Wallis habitually dressed. Her brown fur cape was fake. Moreover, and most importantly, she was twenty years younger. 'It's not me!' Marion called back.

One of the women shoved to the front. Her eyes glinted angrily in her dirty face. 'Keep yer stinkin' 'ands orf 'Is Majesty!'

'Go home, you whore! Leave our king alone!' Something whistled past Marion's ear and smashed against the grey stone lintel. She stared at the yellow yolk flecked with shell, the transparent white running downward. Some of it had splashed on her fur.

Her teeth were chattering with terror. She banged on the front door with both fists, but it remained unyieldingly closed. She pressed her finger hard on the bell. 'Please, Ainslie,' she begged. 'Please open the door.'

When, after what seemed like years, Ainslie did, Marion threw herself across the threshold, her fingertips clawing the carpet as she landed on the floor. There was no question now that Wallis had been telling the truth.

But even that was not the worst of it. There had been a photographer at the back of the mob; presumably he too had thought she was Wallis. Initially, at least. Once she had turned and confronted them he had melted away. But not before their eyes had met and she had recognised Tom.

He had not helped her or defended her, as one might expect of someone to whom one once had been close. The door in her heart marked 'Tom', which had only been ajar anyway, slammed shut forever.

The festive season edged nearer. The Yorks should have been going to Sandringham and Marion to Scotland. But no one, for the moment, was going anywhere. Everyone was waiting. The storm was about to break.

The duke and duchess were rarely visible. The duke was constantly in meetings, the duchess in bed with a string of migraines. Marion, by now accustomed to keeping things normal in abnormal circumstances, set the girls to work on Christmas decorations. Whole heaps were made and Royal Lodge was liberally festooned with the results. In strange contrast to the gloomy atmosphere, the house was gay with handmade paper chains. Stockings shakily hand-knitted by small fingers lay stuffed with presents beneath the big, thick-needled Christmas tree. As usual, Alah was in for some powerfully coloured Woolies' bath salts.

The bathroom romps of old took place no longer, but the evening violent card games continued. What she had once deplored as too much excitement before bed now seemed to Marion useful in dissipating tension. Cries of 'Brute!' and 'Beast!' filled the woodsmoke-scented air as Lilibet and Margaret fought over Racing Demon. The leaping flames in the marble fireplace lit up the green Gothic panelling and brightened the gilt edges of the many pictures. At the high, arched windows, thick curtains were drawn cosily against the darkness. It was as happy and domesticated a scene as one could wish for, Marion would think, looking round. Under the circumstances, she was doing a good job. A great job.

One evening the flames in the fireplace flickered, as they rarely did, on the worn features of the Duke of York. His thin hand, a cigarette streaming between its fingers, dealt out *vingt-et-un* on the hearthrug. The duchess, as usual, was shut in her room.

'Everybody ready?' The duke looked around with a credible effort at a smile.

'Yes, Papa.'

Her father looked enquiringly at Lilibet. 'T-twist or stick?'

'Stick.'

The duke turned to Marion. 'Crawfie?'

'Twist,' she said, and was disappointed. Her five-card trick was not going to happen.

Now it was Margaret's turn. With typical recklessness the youngest princess twisted, then twisted again, then threw her cards exasperatedly in the air. 'Bust,' she groaned. The duke shook his head at her rashness. 'You sh-sh-should be more careful, Meg.'

'It was Cousin Halifax,' Margaret said, predictably.

'Then Cousin Halifax should be more careful.' Lilibet turned up her cards as the duke, as bank, went bust as well. 'Look,' she said delightedly. 'A royal pontoon!'

The telephone rang in the hall. The duke's expression, which had become warm and pliant in the firelight, now stiffened and froze. Ainslie came in. 'Your Highness, it is Fort Belvedere on the line. His Majesty wishes to speak to you.'

The duchess appeared in the doorway in a long white nightdress. Free of make-up, her hair in a long black plait, she looked about sixteen. The girls looked up in surprise. 'Mummie! You're better!'

The duchess did not look better. She hurried to her husband's side and took his hand. They left the room together.

Lilibet had won again, and her sister gone bust again, by the time a car started up outside. Over the cries of triumph and disaster, neither girl heard it. It crunched on the gravel drive, then faded into the distance. The vehicle had still not returned by the time Marion went to bed.

Chapter Thirty-Five

Next morning, she stood outside the duchess's white bedroom door. She had been sent for, but the door remained shut. Voices were coming from inside, low and urgent. She decided to wait, not to knock.

The bedroom door suddenly opened and Queen Mary appeared on the landing. She seemed to have shrunk and aged even beyond her considerable years. Normally ramrod-erect, she was stooped. Even her bust looked smaller.

As Marion rose from her curtsey, the old queen surveyed her gloomily. 'Vell, Miss Crawfort. Zis is a pretty kettle of fish, *nein?*' She stomped away, leaning heavily on her parasol.

From the threshold of the bedroom, the figure in the blue and yellow bed looked tiny. It lay propped up with pillows, dark hair in a plait flowing over a lace bedjacket. A white hand raised. A faint voice spoke. 'Do come in, Crawfie.'

Marion crossed the pale blue carpet. To her surprise, the hand extended; it seemed she was to come right up to the bedside and take it. The duchess rarely engaged in physical contact, but now the small white fingers lightly held hers. The great blue-violet eyes turned towards her.

'I'm afraid,' she said murmurously, 'that there are going to be great changes in our lives, Crawfie.'

A clang went through Marion. So it had happened. The crown had passed from one brother to the other, and the woman lying in this bed was no longer the Duchess of York.

'Your Majesty.' For the second time in almost as many minutes,

Marion curtsied to a queen. Her thoughts were rolling over one another. Tumbling together were relief and regret. And surprise that, after so much waiting and wondering, it had happened so fast.

'The move to Buckingham Palace is bound to be a painful one,' the queen continued in her voice of soft regret. She seemed to be alluding to something.

Understanding passed through Marion like a swordblade. So sharp was it that it made her gasp. She was being dismissed, just like that. It made sense, of course. The palace would be full of staff to look after the little girls.

All the same, it was rather sudden. She had expected more . . . what was the word? Gratitude?

She gathered herself. This was what she had wanted. On and off, anyway. It was probably a good thing. It was not too late to start life behind the glass wall. She would go home, look after her mother.

'Yes ma'am.' Her throat felt hard and blocked. 'And may I wish you the very best of luck.'

The queen sat bolt upright, her voice high and shrill. 'You surely are not saying that you are going to leave us?'

Marion almost wept with relief. So they still wanted her! Then she thought of her mother. The life outside. She hesitated.

The blue stare drilled into hers. 'Because, as you must surely see, Crawfie, that would not be at all convenient just now.' The queen's voice became soft, persuasive. 'We need you. Margaret and Lilibet need you.'

That did it. She was needed by the king and queen. And the heir to the throne. The thought blazed in her mind, brilliant, shining, wildly flattering. Her mother would understand. And life outside could wait. 'Yes, Your Majesty,' she heard herself saying.

'Oh, and Crawfie,' came the voice from the bed. 'Tell the girls, would you?'

Marion gasped. *Tell them?* That you are king and queen?'

She was used to being a parent substitute, of course. But surely news this tremendous should not come from a governess. Informing two small children that their mother and father now headed the world's most famous royal dynasty?

The queen blinked wide blue eyes at her. 'Is that a problem, Crawfie?'

'Of course not, ma'am. Your Majesty.'

Marion curtsied and walked to the door. With her shock now mixed a sense of awe. The other people who needed her, the other plans that she might have had, faded into the background as a glorious sense of being part of history came to the fore. Up until now, she had only been in the wings. But now she had a walk-on part in the greatest show on earth.

Later, Marion took the girls into the boudoir and closed the door. Excitement plunged and reared within her. She had been given a great responsibility. The girls, especially Lilibet, would always remember this moment. She would be framed in it forever and was determined to play her part well. She had thought carefully about what to say.

The girls stood before her in their matching jerseys and kilts. They looked vaguely indignant. 'But we've already done our lessons,' Margaret pointed out.

'This isn't about lessons,' Marion said gently. 'This is about moving.' She had decided to approach it from that angle.

Margaret's violet eyes widened. 'Moving? What sort of moving?'

'Well, house.'

Margaret frowned. 'I don't want to leave our nice house!'

'Not even if it's for an even nicer one? A bigger one?'

The littlest princess brightened. 'Oh, a bigger one. That's all right, then.'

Marion glanced at Lilibet. She had said nothing so far and her expression was hard to read. Her ability to conceal her feelings had become more marked of late. Margaret, on the other hand, wore her heart on her sleeve and her thoughts on her face.

'You're going to change your names,' Marion went on. 'You won't be Princess Elizabeth and Princess Margaret of York from now on.'

Margaret gasped. 'We won't be *princesses* any more?'

'Not of York.' Marion took a deep breath. This was not going as planned. She had meant to handle it sensitively, but the littlest girl was clearly devastated. The violet eyes were brimming with tears.

'But I've only just learned to write "York"!' Margaret howled.

She was going to have to come straight out with it. All her careful phrasing would have to be abandoned. 'You are moving to Buckingham Palace,' Marion blurted.

Finally, Lilibet reacted. 'What?' she said sharply. 'You mean forever?'

'Yes. You are the daughters of the King and Queen of England now.'

Margaret's brimming eyes immediately blazed with joy. 'Papa is the king! I'm the king's daughter!' She began to caper around the gilded room. 'Hooray!'

Lilibet remained still, her impression inscrutable. She was processing the news in her own way, Marion guessed. Perhaps some of its possible consequences were occurring to her.

Margaret now stopped capering and turned to her sister, her round face full of awe. 'Does that mean you'll be queen next, Lilibet?'

'Yes,' Lilibet said, matter-of-factly. 'It does.'

Chapter Thirty-Six

'But you're writing the wrong name, Papa,' pointed out Margaret. 'Your name is Albert, not George.'

They were with their father in his study. Marion had taken the girls to say good night and found the king – as she must now think of him – sitting solemnly at his desk. He had been practising his new signature on a sheet of writing paper.

'My n-name is still Albert in private. But G-G-George in public.'

'King George,' Lilibet said. 'Like Grandpapa.'

'Precisely.'

And as if normal service had now been resumed after an unfortunate aberration. The ex-king had not been mentioned by anyone.

Above stairs, that was. Below stairs, gossip bubbled and seethed. The abdication scene at Fort Belvedere sounded extraordinary. 'There's no ink in the damn pot!' Edward VIII had exclaimed, waving the royal quill in the air over the fateful document. Someone had handed him a fountain pen.

The ex-king would soon be leaving the country, sailing from Portsmouth in a Navy destroyer, ultimately to join his mistress, date of return unknown. Not one of his personal servants had agreed to go with him. He, who had abandoned the throne, was being abandoned in his turn.

'What's the matter, Lilibet?' the new king asked. She was staring at the desktop in awe.

Lilibet pointed at an envelope. It was addressed to *Her Majesty the Queen*. 'That's Mummie now, isn't it?'

The former Edward VIII had, however, one public act still to perform. He was to broadcast a farewell speech to the nation, and this had precipitated the first crisis of the new reign.

The director-general of the BBC, John Reith, had planned to introduce the ex-king as plain Mr Edward Windsor. The new king had stepped in and, in his first monarchical act, had created his brother His Royal Highness the Duke of Windsor.

'Would you like to come and listen to it with me, Miss Crawford?' Alah asked, gruffly. Such shows of friendliness, while rare, were not unknown these days.

And so, later, with the girls safely in bed, Marion sat with the nanny in the nursery sitting room. They, who Edward VIII's actions had affected more than most, would listen to his final address together.

Alah sat by the big wood-encased wireless, in charge of the operation. Despite the cheerful firelight, the room seemed sombre. The outside fog pressed against the windows; the books huddled in the cupboards. Even the teddies on the shelves had a serious air.

There was a click as Alah joined the Piccadilly nursery to the rest of the Empire. Marion imagined the vast world beyond the royal walls. People were listening from India to Islington, from the wilds of Canada to villages in the Cotswolds. All would be wondering about the drama that she had been at the centre of. The players in it were just photographs to them. But to her, they were people. She was part of their company. An important part. *We need you. Lilibet and Margaret need you.*

She wondered if Alah felt the same. Nothing about her suggested it. She had taken up her knitting and was clicking her needles calmly. 'So,' she said in her soft Hertfordshire voice. 'Let's see what he has to say, then.'

The voice from Windsor Castle came floating out of the radio. 'A few hours ago, I discharged my last duty as king and emperor . . .'

To her surprise, Marion felt tears prick at the corners of her eyes. It had all been an illusion, of course. He had never wanted the job and was almost entirely unsuited to it. But in other ways it was a tragedy and a loss. He had, as no one else in the family had, true star quality. He had been one of the most popular figures on earth. That it had come to this was unbelievable.

The weary, wistful voice went on. 'I have found it impossible to carry the heavy burden of responsibility without the help and support of the woman I love . . .'

Marion thought of Wallis, listening in her villa in Cannes. Her worst fears had been realised.

The ex-king was now talking about his brother. 'He has one matchless blessing, enjoyed by so many of you and not bestowed on me, a happy home with his wife and children . . .'

Alah's needles were silent. She groped in her pocket for a handkerchief.

'And now we all have a new king. I wish him and you, his people, happiness and prosperity with all my heart. God save the king.'

Marion pictured the lonely figure leaving the ancient fortress and heading through the fog to Portsmouth and an uncertain future. Edward VIII's reign had lasted less than a year – just 325 days.

There was a creak, a rustle, a suppressed grunt. Alah was getting to her feet. Her eyes were glistening, Marion saw as she scrambled up too. The young woman and the old stood together. 'God save the king,' they said.

Next day, the king appeared mid-morning, his pale, haggard face offset by the splendid blue, white and gold of his naval uniform.

'I know that one – it's Admiral of the Feet,' Margaret proclaimed proudly.

'Fleet,' corrected Lilibet.

A wintry smile briefly irradiated the new monarch's wasted features. He turned to Marion. He was going to St James's Palace to meet the Accession Council. The queen was still in bed.

'That means,' Marion told the girls after the door had closed, 'that when Papa comes home for lunch, he will be properly king of England. You will have to curtsey to him.'

Margaret looked astonished. 'Curtsey to *Papa?*'

'And Mummie too. I know, it does seem odd, doesn't it? Let's get some practice in, shall we, before he comes back. We can't have you toppling over.'

They spent the rest of the morning sweeping a series of ever-more-unlikely obeisances. Margaret's were particularly theatrical and exaggerated. There was much laughter.

The king arrived back to find two perfect curtseys awaiting him in the hallway. He stood stock-still, his face blank with shock.

'What's the matter, Papa?' Lilibet asked after a few uneasy moments. 'Are we doing them wrong?'

George VI shook his head. His throat was working; he was having far more than the usual difficulty speaking.

Marion guessed that for him too, the moment of revelation had come. Here was the proof that the impossible had really happened. He really was the King of England.

He stared at his daughters, the glassy blue eyes brimming, the thin hands twisting his gold-braided admiral's hat. Then he stooped, drew them to him, and hugged them hard.

PART THREE

BUCKINGHAM PALACE

Chapter Thirty-Seven

It was a mouse. It was sitting on the towel in her bathroom, staring boldly back. It didn't seem scared in the least. On the contrary, it seemed to think it owned the place.

Beyond the gilded public rooms, Buckingham Palace was riddled with vermin and generally falling apart. That very morning, the curtains in her room had collapsed. The entire edifice – pelmet, curtains and heavy brass pole – had smashed to the floor only inches from where she stood.

And it was cold, so cold. The fire in the small fireplace did nothing to address the bone-piercing chill. The wind had moaned in the chimney like a thousand tragic ghosts. Given the parlous state of the monarchy, it was difficult not to see it all as a metaphor.

The drama of the abdication might be over, but the extent of the damage to the monarchy was becoming clear. The new occupant of the throne was not popular. George VI's stammer and shyness fuelled rumours that he was frail and weak. According to malicious gossip, he would not even survive the coronation in May, let alone the burden of monarchy.

But he had Debo's support, at least. Marion had bumped into her near the palace, soon after moving in. She wore a fur coat against the freezing February chill. 'How are you?' Marion had asked.

Debo rolled her wide green eyes. 'As well as can be expected. Considering all I have to put up with.'

That morning's front pages had been full of the fighting in Spain. Madrid, held by the government, was under heavy attack from

Franco's forces. Hundreds of international volunteers had been killed. Did Debo have any news?

'Esmond's back. He got dysentery. He works in advertising now.'

'And Valentine?'

'Don't know, sorry.' An elegant eyebrow raised. 'Didn't realise you still cared. It was years ago, wasn't it? You and him?'

Marion looked down. She realised how she must look to this rich and beautiful child: old, worn, subordinate. Pitiable, really.

Debo changed the subject. 'You've heard about Unity? In Germany with the Führer. They have lunch every day – they're like *that*.' Debo crossed her first and second fingers and held them up.

'How *horrible*.'

'It gets worse. My sister Diana has fallen in love with Oswald Mosley. She's left her husband and he's left his wife. Frankly,' Debo added, 'my only hope now is your lot.'

'My lot?'

'The king and queen. They're bringing back debutantes. I'll be spotted by the dear old Duke of Right and live happily ever after in some vast pile in the country.' She looked at her watch. 'Cripes, I'll be late for the hairdresser.'

Standing in her bathroom, Marion looked at the mouse. It looked back with wide, wicked black eyes. A Communist rodent, she had no doubt.

She went outside. Her bathroom was across a wide corridor, floored with the inevitable lino. Something moved at the passage's far end. She recognised the palace postman, an individual whose existence had amazed her at first. That the palace was actually a village, and its corridors effectively streets, had taken some getting used to. The vastness was beyond anything she had expected. Her visits before had not scratched the surface of the size of it.

The postman ambled steadily towards her, whistling, a rasping, tuneless whistle. 'There's a mouse on my bath towel,' she told him.

The postman was plump, with a round pink face. He put a finger to his lips and leaned conspiratorially forward. 'Not so loud. Or they'll all want one.'

'Ha ha.' Marion folded her arms. 'But I want to get rid of it.'

'You'll need to send for the vermin man. Does all the rats and mice. You'll find him in the green book. Cheerio, dear.' With that, the postman went whistling off.

She returned to her room and stepped over the shattered corpse of the collapsed curtains. The holes in the wall above gaped like wounds. On her plain desk was the volume the postman had recommended. It was an inch thick, stamped with the crown and entitled: *Offices And Addresses Of Their Majesties' Households and Officers of State and Other Royal Households.*

On her first night in the palace, Marion had read it in disbelief. The rotting palace had more than four hundred staff, mostly with bizarre and arcane titles. There were Yeomen not only of Gold and Silver Pantries but Glass and China ones as well. There was a Hereditary Grand Falconer and a Raven Master; a Bargemaster, a Keeper of the Swans, a Historiographer Royal and a Silver Stick in Waiting. There were Aides de Camp, First, Flag and Principal Naval and literally hundreds of Equerries, Extra Equerries and Gentleman Ushers.

Turning the pages, she had shaken her head. Was this extraordinary list romantic or ridiculous? She knew what she would have thought once. But now she was here and part of this household, it was becoming increasingly difficult to tell.

There were other things to get used to as well, like the vast distances that getting to different parts of the building involved. From her bedroom in Piccadilly to the boudoir took two minutes. From her Palace room to the schoolroom was ten.

It was large, light and overlooked the garden. The first choice of schoolroom had been on the top floor, where the king himself had been schooled as a boy. But showing her the cramped, dark space with the bars over the windows, he had closed the door hurriedly. 'No. That won't do at all.'

Lunch with the family was also a thing of the past. Now she ate with the Household. This was a more confusing journey even than to the schoolroom, down endless corridors and round corners that all looked the same. She had arrived late and flustered for her first few lunches. The Household Dining Room was as grand as a state dining room; a big table full of people with silver cutlery spreading like wings on either side of crested plates. There were flowers in silver vases, silver cruet sets, huge napkins. There were clusters of crystal glasses and footmen in red and gold braid. Servants to wait on servants.

Not that the Household members were especially servant-like. The ladies of the bedchamber all had thick, shiny hair and rangy racehorse figures. The equerries had the sorts of noble features associated with ancient lineages and coats of arms. Marion had felt like the new girl at a very exclusive school. One she was not at all certain she was going to like.

However, she had quickly got used to it, and now recognised most of the regulars. Her neighbour today was new, however. Dark and lean with chiselled features, he had a craggy brow and his hair was thick and black. She felt a leap of recognition. 'Mr Lascelles!'

A blush swept her cheeks. Had she sounded overexcited?

He raised an eyebrow and gave a hint of a smile. 'How are you finding the palace, Miss Crawford?'

She had rallied now. She eyed him confidently. 'Shall I be honest, Mr Lascelles? My room is falling to pieces and there was a mouse in my bathroom this morning.'

An equerry a few places away leaned forward. 'Just the one?' he called cheerfully. 'I've had three in mine.'

Laughter ran round the table. Lascelles dabbed his mouth with his napkin. 'The refurbishment programme is somewhat behind schedule, certainly.'

This provoked more laughter, followed by the murmur of general conversation. Marion picked up her fork and prepared to address her smoked salmon. Her gloomy mood of earlier had lifted; she felt almost skittish. Was it Lascelles? She wanted his attention, she realised. 'Actually,' she murmured, leaning close to him, 'the mouse is not my only complaint. The last time we met you misinformed me.'

Beneath the craggy brows, the dark eyes narrowed. 'Indeed, Miss Crawford? About what?'

The corner of her mouth tugged sideways. 'You said, Mr Lascelles, that the king had many years in him yet, and that the Prince of Wales would not marry Mrs Simpson.'

Lascelles stared at her. She met his gaze. He was the first to drop his, and gave a rueful smile. 'You are quite right, Miss Crawford. That was my information in the first instance, and my assumption in the second. But as you say, I was wrong.'

Marion guessed there were few people the lofty Lascelles ever admitted that to. She felt triumphant, and rather excited.

'I wish I could see Papa,' Margaret started to say.

'You can't. He's busy kinging,' her sister would reply. It was true that the king was almost constantly occupied. He was learning the craft of monarchy on the job and from the bottom up. There was no spending the afternoon gardening any more, or games of cards before bed. Touchingly, he had placed the girls' rocking horses outside his study, so he could hear the thump of them riding and feel them nearby.

'He spends more time with Mr Lascelles than with us,' Margaret complained. 'I don't like Mr Lascelles. Do you?' She looked hard and suddenly at Marion, who, to her annoyance, felt her cheeks begin to burn.

'Ha!' crowed the youngest princess, triumphantly. 'Crawfie is in love with Mr Lascelles!'

'Don't be *ridiculous*!' Marion spluttered, furious. But the truth was, she liked Lascelles very much. He was an amusing and erudite conversationalist, albeit slightly pompous at times. She looked forward to seeing him at lunch and was disappointed if, out with the king on an engagement, he did not appear.

He never came into the schoolroom. So it was a surprise, one afternoon, to look up and see his tall, dark and evidently annoyed form in the doorway. She took a deep breath to still the sudden flutter in her chest. 'Mr Lascelles!'

His hooded eyes rolled suspiciously round the room. The girls, at their desks, looked up at their unexpected visitor. Margaret looked particularly angelic.

'I'm being constantly summoned to see His Majesty,' Lascelles ground out from under his moustache.

A high voice piped up. 'But isn't that your job, Mr Lascelles?' It was Margaret who had spoken.

Lascelles gave her a flinty look. 'Not necessarily. Especially when His Majesty is not expecting me.' He glanced at Marion. 'According to the palace switchboard, the summonses were coming from the schoolroom telephone.'

The telephone was newly installed. Margaret especially loved playing on it. Marion stared at her, eyebrow raised. The youngest princess looked innocently back, batting her long black lashes.

Lascelles cast a final glance at Margaret, in which warning and suspicion seemed entwined. As he left, he caught Marion's eye too. The wry friendliness of the lunch table was gone. His expression was all icy disdain. It seemed to convey his contempt not only for her poor control of her pupils but for herself as well. A kind of despair filled her, along with fury at Margaret, who had obviously done this on purpose, to embarrass her.

The door hadn't quite closed before the royal culprit collapsed loudly into raucous giggles.

'Margaret!' thundered Marion.

The violet eyes blinked innocently. 'It was Cousin Halifax!'

'Oh, Crawfie!' Lilibet looked at Marion in despair. 'What are we going to do about her?'

Never mind that, Marion thought. What was she going to do about Alan Lascelles? He would make a dangerous enemy.

Chapter Thirty-Eight

It was the spring of 1936. As the blossoms appeared on the trees, Hitler's troops reappeared in the Rhineland, goose-stepping through Essen, Dusseldorf and Cologne in direct contravention of the Treaty of Versailles. A furious France demanded action. But in the House of Commons, foreign secretary Anthony Eden promised to help France only if it was attacked; Britain would otherwise pursue a policy of negotiation. Marion, following all these events, uneasily remembered the Rotherhithe Street assessment of Hitler: that he was unappeasable.

This view was not the majority one. Many in the Household Dining Room felt that anything was better than another war. There was even some sympathy for the German position. 'Can't say I blame Jerry really,' said one equerry. 'He took a licking in the last show, after all.'

The coronation was now a year away. This was to give the Earl Marshal of England, the Duke of Norfolk, sufficient time to organise it, Marion gathered. She saw him occasionally, coming for meetings with her employers. For someone entrusted with such a vast feat of co-ordination he looked to her surprisingly badly put together himself; almost scruffy, in fact.

The ceremony was to be on 12 May, 1937, which had been set for Edward VIII. 'Same date, different king,' said the Marquess of Cholmondeley, whose magnificent name, Marion learned with amazement, was pronounced 'Chumley'. As Lord Chamberlain he was assisting the Earl Marshal with his duties and Marion knew from her studies with the girls that his role in former times had been to bring the monarch his shirt on coronation morning, and put on his spurs – for rendering these services he had been allowed to keep the king's night attire. 'But surely not now,' Lilibet said. 'Papa wears ordinary flannel pyjamas. Whoever would want those?'

The new king, try as he might to hide it, was obviously dreading the crowning ceremony. The queen was just as obviously enjoying her fittings for her gown and train. She was often found pacing the palace corridors with a sheet pinned to her shoulders and a crown on her head. 'To get used to the weight, you see, darlings,' she trilled to her awed daughters.

As the weather improved, Marion returned to the practice of outdoor lessons. Their favourite place in the palace gardens was not by the pristine borders, nor on the spotless terraces, but on the little hill by the wall alongside the road which offered a view over the street.

'I'd like to have a coat like that!' exclaimed Margaret, who loved commenting on clothes worn by passing children. She was developing a marked interest in fashion.

'Look, look! There's Mummie!' Lilibet pointed at a polished black car sailing past, silver fittings gleaming, a familiar profile in the rear window.

'We hardly see her any more,' Margaret sighed. The queen's workload had quadrupled since coming to the palace. Every day there were ribbons to be cut and foundation stones to be laid.

Before a gloomy silence could take hold, Marion beamed at them both. 'Let's play If.'

'Ooh, yes!' Margaret, gloom forgotten, leaped up and began to prance about, chanting, 'If I could be anything I liked, do you know what I would be?'

Marion, grinning, gave the customary reply. 'A good girl!'

'I would be . . .' And Margaret paused, thought and then let forth a stream of fantastic professions. 'Pirate! Film star! Dancer! Aviator!' She had been much impressed by the exploits of lady flyers such as Amy Johnson and Amelia Earhart, as reported in *The Children's Newspaper*.

Marion turned to Lilibet. 'And you?'

The elder princess tended to take this game much more seriously and tried to connect it to the real world outside the palace walls. 'A butcher's boy,' she said, as one now rolled past on a bicycle, basket full of meat.

Margaret was appalled. 'A *butcher's boy*! But you'd be *poor!*'

'But I'd have a bicycle,' Lilibet pointed out. 'And that would be useful. I could cycle along the corridors with our dinner. That way it wouldn't be cold when it reaches our dining room.' It wasn't just the staff that the Palace's size inconvenienced. The distance between the kitchen and the royal table was immense.

Marion rose to her feet. 'Time to get back to our lessons.'

But someone dressed in black was now crossing the green lawn towards them. The stout figure marched up and took Margaret's hand. 'You're wanted by Mr Birley,' Alah announced.

Marion groaned. Mr Birley was one of the artists, currently working on a portrait of the new royal family. He was very charming, but also very inconvenient.

Margaret was jumping up and down excitedly. She loved to be admired and looked at, so getting dressed up and having her picture painted was a wonderful new game to her.

Lilibet was less keen, but submitted to it obediently, as she did to everything. 'Rather you than me,' she muttered, wandering off towards the lake.

A huge silver mirror in the midst of all the green, the lake was lined with graceful, full-skirted weeping willows. In the middle was an island, on which ducks built their nests. Lilibet was intensely interested in them, as she was in all animals.

Alah, who had interrupted, was complaining about the many interruptions. 'They *say* it'll all calm down after the coronation.' She was complaining now about Norman Hartnell, who was making the girls' outfits for the ceremony. 'A man *like that* in the palace!'

'Like what?' challenged Marion, even though Norman himself made a joke of Alah's homophobia. He exaggerated his movements even more than usual when she was about.

He cared little for what she thought anyway. His star was rising. He was also making gowns for the queen's maids of honour. 'Quite the education,' he said. 'I've had to find sarcenet and miniver. And learn how to make a tunicle, would you believe.'

'A what?'

'Type of tunic, dearie.' His green eyes twinkled. 'They're going to be the next big thing. We'll all be wearing one soon.'

The only fly in the Hartnell ointment was that the ultimate honour, that of making Her Majesty's coronation gown, had gone to the same Madame Handley-Seymour, who had, in Norman's phrase, 'committed' the queen's wedding dress in 1923.

As Alah, still grumbling, went back inside, Marion hurried to the lake. Lilibet needed to be herded back to her studies.

The bank looked empty, no white-socked child in a kilt at the water's edge staring at the ducks. Perhaps Lilibet, dutiful to a fault, had gone back to the classroom by herself.

Something, though, was in the water. Something that was surging, and splashing. 'Crawfie! I wanted to see the duck nests and I fell in!'

Marion groaned. Lilibet had taken her lifesaving certificate at the Bath Club. Her being in the water was safe enough. But Alah would have plenty to say about this. She hurried to the lake edge.

Something dark flashed past her, followed by a violent splash. Someone else had got there first.

Alan Lascelles looked completely different when he was soaked in water and covered in weeds.

'But I can swim!' the soaking-wet Lilibet was telling him indignantly. 'I did my lifesaving certificate!'

'She did,' Marion confirmed. Part of her was horrified, part trying not to laugh. The horrified part imagined that, after the telephone incident, this would be the final straw. The other part noted that the aristocratic face now wore a sheepish expression, as well as a good deal of green slime.

'I saw her from my room,' the private secretary gasped. 'I didn't realise anyone else was there.'

She saw, suddenly, how his shoulders looked broad and lean in the clinging wet shirt, and when, suddenly, he took it off, screwing it up to squeeze out the water and wipe his face, how his chest was slim, but muscled. He was rubbing himself down, his wet flesh gleaming in the sunshine. Her eyes widened. Her heart rate quickened.

She forced herself to concentrate on the matter at hand. Lilibet was wet and Alah would no doubt go straight to the queen. 'I've got to get her back inside before . . .' She stopped, reluctant to reveal the situation. He would hardly be sympathetic. Especially if he was still smarting about the telephone incident.

'Before that old dragon of a nanny finds out?' The water had soaked his hair to a liquid black. The ruler-straight side-parting had gone; it was rumpled and wild and made him look about fifteen.

'Something like that.'

'We can put her in my coat.' Lascelles indicated the jacket he had ripped off before diving into the water. 'We'll smuggle her in through my rooms. They lead straight into the garden. She can use my bath, and you can fetch her some dry things. The dragon would be none the wiser.'

She stared. Why was he being so helpful? He had no reason to; the opposite, if anything. Perhaps he had forgotten about the telephone; it was some weeks ago now, after all. 'Thank you,' she said, grateful. Charmed.

Lascelles' quarters were much more luxurious than her own. As Lilibet took a hot bath, Marion looked about her. There were carpets, sofas, silver cigarette boxes, polished wood, mirrors. Through an open door, she saw the end of a double bed, draped in blue. Something inside her turned over.

'You have good rooms, Mr Lascelles.'

'Call me Tommy; everyone else does.' He was rubbing his head with a towel.

'And I'm Marion.'

On the marble mantelpiece was an imperious-looking blonde in a frame. 'My wife,' he said. 'Her father is the viceroy of India.'

She was disconcerted to feel a sudden, hot stab of jealousy. An awareness swelled within her grass-stained skirt, and she felt dismayed to think that her lipstick, applied this morning, no doubt had now worn away.

He was watching her, she saw. 'What's her name?' she asked boldly, aiming to sound unimpressed even as the heat rose up her neck.

'Joan.' He was standing close. His silk paisley dressing gown was loosely belted and hung off his lean frame. The scent of his bare skin rose in her nostrils. He was naked beneath the robe, she thought.

'She lives in the country.' His breath was warm on her ear.

Her nervous gaze now met his. The deep-set dark eyes seemed full of a warm, suggestive intent and quite suddenly she felt a great thrum of desire. It shot to her every nerve ending and set her head spinning. She tore her gaze away and looked hard out of the window, across the lawns, trying to regain control.

What was wrong with her? She had lost her head. An affair, especially with a married man, especially with *this* married man, was out of the question. Why was she even thinking about such a thing? 'You have a fine view,' she said, not seeing it at all.

He seemed to step back at that and resume his former light, distant tone. 'It is a good view. Less so on garden party days, of course. Palace garden parties are like the Day of Resurrection. One sees so many people one had thought dead.'

She snorted with laughter. But at the same time she was wondering whether she had imagined the deep, dark, warm look, and he had never meant anything at all.

Chapter Thirty-Nine

Summer ended. Autumn saw Oswald Mosley and his Fascist following tried to march through the East End; a pitched battle with police ensued. The morning after the battle of Cable Street, as it became known, a group of unemployed shipbuilders set off from their hometown, Jarrow. Unlike the many other such marches that had taken place, this one had caught the popular imagination. It was being led by the fierily determined Ellen Wilkinson, the diminutive redheaded MP for Jarrow. The progress of the march was reported nightly on the BBC, and daily bulletins appeared in the papers.

Christmas approached. Back in Edinburgh, Marion was shocked at the change in her mother. The shakes were worse, and she had lost a lot of weight. 'I'll come back,' Marion promised, as she dusted and cleaned and ironed. Her mother hardly seemed to do any housework now. 'Just as soon as the coronation is over.'

'Of course you will,' Mrs Crawford said placidly from her armchair, which no longer had a sewing box beside it.

Marion shot her a sharp look. 'Mother, I mean it.'

'Of course you do. By the way,' Mrs Crawford said, adroitly changing the subject, 'Peter's moved school again. He's gone to one in the south, near London. I forget which.'

Nineteen thirty-seven began. Lessons, especially history ones, were now bent towards the coronation, in which both princesses would take part. At eleven and seven respectively, they were considered old enough.

For a lover of history like Marion, the coronation was a fascinating subject. The ceremony of crowning was as complex as it was colourful. Much of it dated back to medieval times. Past coronation processions had included the King's Herb-Woman, who strew flowers before His Majesty. There had also been until recently a King's Champion, who rode into Westminster Hall in full armour and flung down his gauntlet. They at least had been expunged from the list of offices. The process of modernising royalty may be slow, but it wasn't entirely non-existent.

Margaret seemed determined not to take any of it seriously. She laughed heartily at ancient heraldic offices such as 'Blue Pursuivant', and her sister's new title of 'Heiress Presumptive'.

'I've looked it up,' Margaret said triumphantly. 'It means "impertinently bold".'

'That's "presumptuous",' said Marion, smiling at the dismayed Lilibet. 'You've looked up the wrong word.'

Margaret was jealous, she knew. 'It's not fair,' she sulked. 'Lilibet is now third lady in the whole land, after Grandmama and Mummie.'

Perhaps in reaction to all this, as May approached, Marion found herself following the news more closely. As the preoccupations of those around her went back to the twelfth century, it seemed crucial that someone at least was keeping an eye on the here and now.

The daily paper made, as ever, uncomfortable reading. Popular support for the Jarrow Crusade had not persuaded the government to help the unemployed. Rather, on their return the marchers had had their dole money docked for being unavailable for work. But on 27 April, a mere fortnight before the coronation ceremony, something happened in Spain that, briefly at least, superseded all other concerns. The small Basque town of Guernica was almost completely destroyed by bombs dropped by German and Italian planes.

Shocked and sickened, Marion read George Steer's account of the atrocity in *The Times*. Four thousand bombs had dropped out of a clear blue sky. Innocent civilians – women and children – had died in their homes, in the hundreds. In the thousands, possibly. Were they looking at the future? Everyone knew how massive Hitler's rearmament programme had been; still was. What were his intentions? Did they include Britain?

Between lessons, back and forth from lunch, she paced the palace corridors, fretting. The fact that no one else seemed to be discussing it, or even thinking about it, was more worrying still.

'Oh! Crawfie!'

Marion jumped back. She had rounded a corner to find the queen, sheet pinned to her shoulders, crown on her head, walking towards her over the red carpet. She held an open book before her; to help her balance, presumably.

Marion dropped to a dutiful curtsey but felt exasperation. Had the queen not heard about Guernica? Was she not concerned about Hitler?

'Have you read this, Crawfie?' Marion rose to find the queen waving the book at her. Its cover bore two words in black Gothic lettering: *Mein Kampf*.

'Even a skip through gives one a good idea of his mentality and ignorance,' the queen said in her high, clear voice. 'And, worst of all, his obvious sincerity. Did you know that every newly married couple in Germany is being given it? What a wedding present.'

She swept off, the sheet slithering over the red carpet behind her. Marion looked after her. She felt, if not cheered exactly, then somehow relieved.

Finally, the great day dawned. No one had slept very much. The night had been noisy with the testing of loudspeakers and crowds singing and cheering. At five in the morning a regimental band had struck up, all drums and brass, rehearsing for the procession later.

The girls stood before Marion in their first long dresses − white lace trimmed with silver bows − and the special coronets that had been made for them.

'Do you like my slippers?' Lilibet lifted her glittering hem to show a pair of sparkling silver feet. Above her snow-white socks were a couple of brown knees scratched from tree-climbing. The sight made Marion smile.

'Do you like my train?' Margaret swished around importantly. A length of ermine-trimmed purple velvet slid across the lino bedroom floor.

There had been ructions when the younger princess discovered her sister's outfit would have a train and hers wouldn't. A second had been produced on the double. The velvet was so soft you hardly realised you were touching it.

Margaret raised a little hand to check the silver-gilt circlet on her shining dark gold curls. She was passionately looking forward to it all.

But her orderly sister fretted about the vast, uncontrollable ceremony. It would be a huge event, broadcast worldwide on the radio. Stands had been built all along the processional route, and viewing galleries had been constructed in the abbey as high as the roof. It was easy to see why Lilibet was worried.

Determined to head off a return of the old obsessive behaviour, Marion suggested she write a diary. The idea was seized on immediately. An exercise book carefully trimmed with pink ribbon now stood ready to receive the account. The title was written in red crayon on the cover. *The Coronation, 12 May 1937, to Mummie and Papa, in memory of their Coronation, from Lilibet by Herself.*

'Look at Crawfie's make-up!' said Margaret, staring hard. 'Hasn't she got a lot on?' There was mockery in her tone. 'I wonder if she's hoping to impress someone!'

'It's a special occasion,' Marion returned, determined not to appear rattled. But, as ever, Margaret had put her merciless little finger on it, and pressed it hard.

She had done her make-up more boldly than usual, after the fashion the salesgirl at Harrods' Elizabeth Arden concession had shown her. A touch more eyeshadow, another layer of pressed powder, a darker shade of lipstick. The shade was Carmencita, and one of Miss Arden's new 'wardrobe of lipsticks'. The persuasive salesgirl had succeeded in selling her Miss Arden's newly launched perfume, Blue Grass, into the bargain.

Having delivered her blow to her satisfaction, Margaret swished across to the window. 'Just look at the crowds!' she crowed. 'All come to see us!'

Marion took the girls down to the reception. The ornate room was full of excited people holding coffee cups carefully distant from ceremonial robes. Hanging in the air was the faint but unmistakable scent of mothballs.

She gratefully accepted a cup of coffee from a footman. She would need gallons of it. The procession would leave the palace at eleven, but none of them would return before five.

Lilibet was scanning the room. Her eleven-year-old face wore an expression Marion had seen once before. But Prince Philip, the handsome boy she had met at the Kent wedding, was not present, although his cousin Marina was, exquisite in tiara and silver lace. The Duchess of Kent was smiling gamely, but what was she thinking? Her sister-in-law of York, once looked down on, had now gained unimaginable eminence.

A tall, familiar figure glided into the room and she felt her chest tighten. Tommy looked splendid in army dress uniform, his Military Cross glinting and his imperious blonde at his side. Joan Lascelles was far more beautiful in the flesh than she'd appeared in her photograph, and evidently very grand, greeting the assembled peers like the old friends they obviously were.

Marion raised her chin and refused to meet, across the room, a certain naughty, knowing, violet eye.

'Marion.' He was looking at her wryly. 'You look splendid.'

'Thank you, Tommy. So do you.'

Was Miss Arden's scent working? He seemed to be lingering, but that might be just wishful thinking.

'Tommy!' Joan was calling her husband.

She met the dark, deep-set eyes. 'You'd better go.'

'I had.' He held her gaze a second longer, then turned. She watched his back recede in the braided coat and remembered the skin beneath, slicked wet from the lake.

'I would!' The whisper came in her right ear. Hartnell's wide-set mischievous eyes smiled into hers. His wavy hair was impeccably combed, and his small, powerful body, more a stevedore's than a designer's, was encased in a grey double-breasted suit of perfect cut.

'Norman!'

'Your fairy godmother. In every sense of the word. Love the slap. Very fetching.' He touched her cheek lightly.

She smiled at him warmly. 'I'm so pleased you're here.'

'On hand should anyone burst out of their sequins. Mentioning no names, but some of them are sewn up like sausages in their casings.'

She giggled. In the corner of her eye someone tall and dark moved towards the door. She glanced, involuntarily.

'You're smitten!' cackled Norman.

'Rubbish. It's completely out of the question. He's married.'

He cocked his head on one side. 'Your point?'

The room was emptying. Peers and peeresses were called to the coaches lined nose to tail downstairs in the palace courtyard. The princesses' carriage awaited them in the Grand Entrance.

Norman gave her a little push. 'Off you go, Cinders. Enjoy the ball.'

Chapter Forty

'The arches and beams at the top of the abbey were covered with a sort of haze of wonder as Papa was crowned,' Marion read out from Lilibet's little ribbon-trimmed exercise book. She looked up. 'What a beautiful description.'

They were sitting in the glossy grass in the shade of an oak in the palace garden. Having just completed her diary of the great day, Lilibet was busy on a daisy chain. 'Do you really think Papa and Mummie will like it?' she asked shyly.

'They'll absolutely love it. I can't imagine any official historian doing a better job.' Not even the Historiographer Royal. This august-sounding figure remained a mystery, having not yet made an appearance in the Household Dining Room.

Lilibet flopped back on the grass. 'Oh, Crawfie! It really was such a *wonderful* day. Wasn't it?'

'It really was.'

Several days had passed since the coronation and she still felt suspended in a glamorous dream. The horses and carriages had all been put away now, the panjandrums and crown princes all returned overseas. But, in the words of the song, the memory lingered on and no one was talking about anything else.

'Let's play Did You See,' Lilibet suggested excitedly. It was her favourite game, and one in which she had the advantage. Not only had she walked in procession up the abbey nave, but her view from the royal box just behind the queen's throne had been vastly superior to Marion's up in the roof. But the privilege had not been wasted; Lilibet had missed nothing. The game produced new details every time.

'Did you see Mrs Ronnie?' Lilibet began, giggling. 'She was wearing the biggest diamonds ever. Even bigger than Granny's.'

It was true that the diamonds were enormous, visible even from an eyrie in the vaulting. But it was no more than one would expect of Mrs Ronnie Greville. 'She told me she was a beeress, not a peeress,' Lilibet chuckled.

The daughter of an extremely rich Scottish brewer, Mrs Ronnie was a social lioness and collector of celebrities. She had become a close friend of Queen Mary's through the simple but brilliant ruse of promising to leave her magnificent Surrey mansion to the king in her will. She now had a permanent place right at the centre of the royal circle.

'And did you see the maharajah and princes with their turbans covered with diamonds?' Lilibet especially loved to talk about them. 'The horses pulling their carriages had the most gorgeous tack on.'

Marion remembered the miles of jewel-encrusted potentates, escorted by high-stepping horses. They had looked like something from a fairy tale. The colours had glowed, the silk had shone, the gold had glittered, the feathers had nodded. At the ends of arms solid with bracelets, jewelled hands had waved.

'Our soldiers looked so handsome,' Lilibet said, a little wistfully. She liked a uniform.

'And walked in such straight lines,' Marion added, recalling the rigid box formations in which they had marched. Not a man had been out of place. You could have laid a ruler under the feet of the regiment in front of the palace.

Carriage after carriage had passed up a Mall hung with long banners bearing the royal arms and flanked with specially built viewing stands. Among them had been Queen Mary, magnificent in gold behind bevelled glass, with her sister-in-law the Queen of Norway. Behind her, the princesses, peering excitedly from the carriage of the Princess Royal.

'Margaret waved so much that her coronet fell off.' Lilibet shook her head indulgently. 'And, Crawfie, the noise was simply *deafening*. People were screaming more than cheering.'

The crowds, packed into every inch of park and pavement, even climbing the Victoria Memorial, had seemed to exceed even those of the Jubilee.

'People were in the trees, and in their best clothes too.' Lilibet's voice was full of wonder.

But as the king's gold state coach swung into view, there had been the briefest beat of silence, perhaps in awe at the fantastically theatrical conveyance, covered in gold leaf and carved with plumes and tritons, topped with a crown and pulled by eight white horses, each with its own gold-braided groom. Following it were beefeaters in Tudor red, mounted cavalry with flashing helmets and all manner of other uniformed magnificences. Gentle sounds had filled the air: the jingle of harness, the trot of hooves, the rumble of carriage wheels.

Then came the noise, cracking like thunder, the fanfares and drum rolls, the thunderous cheering, wave after roaring wave of it. On and on the cavalcade went: Highland pipers, Canadian Mounties, Sikhs on foot, prime ministers from all over the Dominions; each new appearance a new sensation.

Marion's own journey to the abbey was in a staff car, not a carriage. The route had been via the back streets, away from the procession. But she had seen coaches, albeit ones gone astray. Family carriages from stately homes in the provinces were accompanied by staff with little knowledge of London. Thunderous peers were to be seen sticking their heads out and shouting, 'Go right at Piccadilly Circus!' Owen had several times to stop and offer his assistance.

'What did you see in the abbey?' Lilibet asked. 'Could you see us?'

'I did, and you both looked splendid.' The two small but composed figures in their furred and braided cloaks walking up the aisle had been impressive. But what had stirred her emotions was the warning look Lilibet had given her sister as they settled into their seats in the royal box. Margaret, about to fidget and swing her legs as she did in the schoolroom, sat up instantly.

'Did Margaret behave nicely?'

'She was wonderful,' the elder sister said loyally. 'I only had to nudge her once or twice when she was playing with the prayer books too loudly. Tell me what else you remember.'

'Let me think.' Marion shut her eyes. Pictures rolled through her mind. The blaze of gold plate on the altar, hung with embroidered silk. The balconies of the abbey hung with red and gold brocade. The Coronation Chair in its sea of golden carpet, so plain amid all the pomp and panoply, and yet so much more important. The peeresses, all curtseying as one to Queen Mary, swaying like a field of graceful reeds. The bended knees, the oaths and fealties, the swords, orbs and sceptres. The glitter of tiaras and necklaces under powerful lights. abbey bells mingling with the blare of trumpets and the boom of cannonfire. From all these dazzling sights and sounds it was difficult to select just one.

'Did you see the peers?' The princess's fingers were busy with the daisies. 'They kept their sandwiches under their coronets!'

'I loved "Crown Imperial",' said Marion. The rousing march, by the rising young composer William Walton, had been especially written for the event.

The organ was directly below where she was sitting and she had felt the notes through her feet. A small group of choirboys had been on a balcony nearby. She had watched them, immaculate in their snowy robes and smooth, side-parted hair, pinching each other during particularly long parts of the service.

'Which procession did you like best? Mummy's or Papa's?'

She thought. The king's, while impressive, had featured two rows of rather doddery old churchmen. A single splendid page had held the thick fur end of his train. Holding the queen's even more sumptuous embroidered cloak had been six aristocratic beauties whose gowns Norman had designed. He had particularly liked the small one with the widow's peak, Lady Ursula Manners, whom he said was 'larky'. He had been less keen on the 'terrifying old bat' otherwise known as the Duchess of Norfolk, Mistress of the Robes, who followed immediately behind the train in a furred gown, the epitome of magnificent hauteur.

Norman's dresses had looked stunning: fitted white satin with puffed sleeves and embroideries of corn sheaves down the front. 'Not embroideries, dearie, those are for tray cloths,' she could hear him saying. 'These are *paillettes*.'

They were interrupted now as Margaret came running over the lawn, released from her portrait sitting. She flopped herself down.

'I liked the queen's procession best, I think,' Marion said to Lilibet.

Margaret looked up. 'Oh, you're playing Did You See. Can I join in? Did you see Dr Lang lose the thread?'

This had become something of a *cause célèbre*; the archbishop, worried about putting the crown on the wrong way round, had tied a coloured thread at the right end. But at the crucial moment the scrap of scarlet cotton had disappeared. The archbishop had been seen fumbling frantically with the heavy jewelled object, trying to spot it.

Lilibet frowned at her sister. 'You know Papa doesn't like that being talked about. The moment he was crowned was very serious.'

'And it was beautiful,' Marion assured her, flashing a warning look at Margaret, who was drumming the heels of her sandals on the grass to release some of her pent-up energy.

'Papa looked like a medieval knight,' Lilibet agreed, mollified. 'In his lovely long gold mantle.'

'I thought it looked like a dressing gown,' giggled her sister.

'It looked wonderful,' Marion said firmly. And it had been. The moment of crowning had been the point at which every other detail faded away to nothing and everyone's entire attention was on the slim, pale figure on the throne.

Lilibet took back the exercise book now and began reading. 'And when Mummie was crowned all the white-gloved peeresses put on their coronets simultaneously, it looked wonderful to see arms and coronets hovering in the air, and then the arms disappear as if by magic.'

Margaret had abandoned her efforts at a daisy chain. Dying flower heads lay strewn around her dress hem. 'Lilibet and I got more cheers than anyone else,' she announced. 'When we came back from the abbey in Grandmama's carriage. There was a machine on a roof somewhere, a special one that measured noise. Our noise was louder than even Mummie and Papa's.'

There had been people on roofs everywhere, Marion knew. Window views along the route had been rented for unbelievable amounts of money.

'And then we had to go out on the balcony with our crowns on, so many times. Hundreds and hundreds and *hundreds* of times. All those people looking at us and cheering wildly.' Margaret's violet eyes gleamed at the memory.

'People singing the national anthem in the dark and rain,' said Lilibet, softly.

Margaret scrambled to her feet. 'Give me the daisy chain,' she said to her sister. 'I'm going to crown you. Because next time all this happens, it will be you. And then I'll be the second lady in the land!'

Chapter Forty-One

'You've heard, I take it?' Tommy leaned closer and murmured to Marion at lunch.

'Heard what?' She was instantly on high alert. It was a month since the coronation, which now felt like a huge party after which everyone had come down to earth with a bump.

'The wedding.'

The Duke and Duchess of Windsor, Marion now learned, had married at the Château de Candé, in the Loire Valley. 'On George V's birthday, which was questionable timing,' Tommy commented. 'No member of the family and only seven English friends. Not even Louis Mountbatten went, and he and the ex-king were inseparable at one stage. But Louis' main loyalty is to himself, so no surprise there.'

Marion thought of Wallis. What was she feeling? After all the sound and fury, she had married her prince in obscurity. It now looked as if they would live in exile. Perhaps she preferred it that way. But it seemed a sorry ending to a momentous story.

'They've flatly refused to give her a royal title,' Tommy murmured from beneath his moustache.

'So she won't be HRH?' Marion frowned. 'Why ever not?' The king had left his throne; they both had left the country. What harm could it do?

Tommy raised a dark eyebrow. 'Someone up there doesn't like her, shall we say.'

He meant the queen, Marion knew. Wallis's implacable enemy. The scene in the Piccadilly hall came back to her: the duchess kissing her brother-in-law so fondly. How he must hate her now.

'He's incandescent, of course.' Tommy seemed to read her thoughts. 'She really wanted the title, apparently. But he's going to have to make it up to her in other ways.'

Marion doubted the wanting bit. But perhaps the *other ways* bit was true.

Soon after came the shocking news that the duke and duchess had gone to Germany and met Hitler. Newspaper pictures showed the two of them looking charmed. 'Though one may be in the lion's den it is possible to eat with the lions if one is on good terms with them,' the duke was quoted as saying.

Marion studied the images of the beaming Wallis. She remembered her denials about being friendly with Ribbentrop. They seemed less believable now. That same dazzling smile turned on Hitler in the photograph had been turned on her. The thought was sickening. The ex-king, consorting with an evil dictator who was now in a position to attack Western Europe. But would he?

Apart from a maverick middle-aged Tory called Winston Churchill, no one seemed to seriously think so. Germany had, even so, signed agreements with Italy and Japan and actively backed the Fascist side in the increasingly bloody Spanish civil war.

Marion wrote of her worries to her mother. But the letter was not answered or even opened. By the time it arrived, Mrs Crawford was dead.

Marion hurried to Scotland in a shell-shocked daze.

She tried to rationalise the guilt and grief that threatened to overwhelm her. It wasn't that she hadn't wanted to come back – it was that she couldn't. She had been steering the princesses through the coronation. Returning home had been out of the question. Now there was no home to which to return. The thought was heartbreaking, but also, she was aware, liberating. Her mother was free from illness and she herself had no other loyalties. The girls, especially Lilibet, could be the focus of everything.

Back at the palace, she threw herself into her job. For all its rot and labyrinthine passages, Buckingham Palace had extraordinary resources with which to teach. Chief among these was the royal art collection. Kenneth Clark, Surveyor of the King's Pictures, was the man to ask for access.

Far from the dusty, naysaying fuddy-duddy she had anticipated, Clark proved to be an energetic young man whose wit was as sharp as his suits and who was keenly enthusiastic. Every week, two brown-overalled, white-gloved men appeared in the schoolroom staggering under the weight of a Rembrandt or Canaletto. Marion couldn't bring herself to tell Clark, who hated Landseer, that the painting most preferred by the girls was one of dogs entitled *Dignity and Impudence*.

'I'm Dignity and Lilibet's Impudence,' Margaret would claim, in a blatant reversal of the truth.

But, actually, both girls were Impudence these days. Having discovered that the palace guards had to salute her whenever she passed them, Margaret passed them at every opportunity, often running back once she'd passed in order to pass them all over again. Whenever she could not be found she was usually out in the palace courtyard, torturing whatever unfortunate regiment happened to be on duty that day.

Even Lilibet, formerly the most unspoilt of children, was getting above herself. She was, for the first time ever, misbehaving in the classroom, and had recently upset an inkpot on her head to express frustration with a French lesson. The dark blue liquid, cascading down her golden curls, had dripped on her clothes and pooled on the school-room floor. Marion had been, as she rarely was, angry with Lilibet. She made her fetch a bucket and mop and clean the mess up herself.

It did not seem to have had the required effect, however. A few days later the princess returned to the palace from a carriage ride with her grandmother.

The footman extended a red-liveried arm. 'Down you come, young lady.'

From the open carriage door, Lilibet glared. 'I am not,' she said haughtily, 'a young lady. I am a princess.'

From the carriage, Queen Mary harrumphed. 'And one day,' she said sharply, 'we hope you will be a lady too.'

Only the king and queen ignored or failed to notice the recent deterioration in their daughters' behaviour. 'Lilibet is my pride,' the king would blithely say, 'and Margaret my joy.'

This seemed to be the case even when, bored at a tea with her mother and a friend, his pride rang for a footman and announced, 'Kindly call a taxi. Our guest is leaving.'

Something had to be done. The abdication was over, the coronation had happened. The new reign was settling down. It was time to return to first principles. The princesses must meet the normal world again.

But taking them out and doing ordinary things was not an option now that they were the daughters of the king. They could no longer travel about incognito. Security concerns meant that the ordinary things would have to come to them. But what things?

It was a breathless summer. The heat pressed down on London like a lid. In the parks, the grass wilted and turned brown. On the streets, the pavements burned into the soles of her shoes. The sun glared off plate-glass windows right into her eyes. Waiting one afternoon to cross the road, Marion felt she might faint.

During one such wait, she saw a girl in blue uniform on the opposite side of the road. She stood next to an old lady, whose arm she gently held, obviously intending to help her across the road when opportunity allowed. A Girl Guide, Marion realised. Waiting to do her good deed for the day.

She felt something click in her brain. Here was the answer. The Girl Guides, whose motto was to be prepared for anything, whose mission was to empower young women, whose outlook was international and whose practice was to mix all classes in pursuit of mutual benefit and understanding. From a practical point of view, an organisation that could be established anywhere, even within the walls of palaces. Most importantly of all, it would be fun.

Miss Violet Synge, Chief Commissioner of the Girl Guides, clearly felt otherwise. Walled in behind her desk, a solid figure in uniform, she stared at Marion disapprovingly through stern wire spectacles. 'The princesses can never be Guides,' she said in an emphatic

Manchester accent. 'It would never work. Guides must all treat one another like sisters.'

'But they *are* sisters.'

Miss Synge leaned forward, her meaty hands folded, her expression baleful. 'Indeed, Miss Crawford. But they're *princesses.*' She rolled her mouth round the word as if it was something distasteful.

'But they only want to be treated like any other girls of their own age.' Marion tried not to think about Lilibet and the footman and Margaret and the guardsmen.

The broad Mancunian features radiated disbelief. 'Miss Crawford. The Guide movement is intended to create opportunities for those rather lower down the social ladder. Many Guides come from the working classes. Princesses,' she went on, 'surely have plenty of opportunities of their own.'

'Not necessarily,' Marion began, then paused. This was not the place to reveal intimate details about restricted royal lives. Miss Synge's lack of sympathy seemed almost inverted snobbery.

Then something caught her eye and her spirits rose. She met the commissioner's skeptical gaze with a steady one of her own. 'Am I to understand, Miss Synge, that you feel royalty has no place in the Guide movement?'

A pair of solid arms folded. The spectacles glinted suspiciously.

She pointed at the framed photograph on the wall behind Miss Synge's desk. It was of Princess Mary, the Princess Royal, sister of the king and the Guides' patroness and benefactor. Miss Synge twisted round to look, the corsets beneath her uniform audibly creaking.

Marion hastened to press her advantage. 'I understand that when the Princess Royal got married, "The Marys of the Empire" – the British subjects who shared her name – all contributed to a fund. The princess presented it in its entirety to the Guides.'

When Miss Synge creaked back round, her spectacles had lost some of their fierceness.

'Come and meet them.' It was a gamble. Few were the people who could resist an invitation to Buckingham Palace. But Miss Violet Synge might well be one of them.

In the event, she was not. Lilibet rose to the occasion, overseeing every aspect of the tea. She was completely determined that Miss Synge would be persuaded. The chief commissioner arrived, magnificent in her blue uniform, to find both ham and egg sandwiches as well as a cake and the jam pennies no royal tea was complete without.

Miss Synge piled her plate high and munched through the lot while listening to a breathless running commentary from Lilibet and Margaret about how keen they were to join the Guide movement. No one, surely, could either doubt their sincerity or fail to be charmed.

No one except Miss Synge, that was. Eventually, apparently replete, the commissioner wiped her bewhiskered mouth with a monogrammed napkin. Her three hostesses sat up expectantly. The audition was over; the verdict was at hand. But surely, after such hospitality, a refusal was out of the question.

Miss Synge drew breath. Her navy-jacketed bosom inflated alarmingly. 'I'm afraid,' she said in her flat Mancunian tones, 'that it's not possible.'

'What?' gasped Lilibet, as Margaret's eyes began to swim and her lower lip to wobble.

Marion wanted to strangle the woman. Everything at the palace was beautifully ready. She and the girls had even cleared out George V's old summer house to serve as a headquarters. She forced herself to sound calm. 'May I ask why not?'

Miss Synge eyed her beadily through the spectacles. 'Because Princess Margaret is too young to be a Guide.'

For someone heading an organisation aimed at female empowerment, Miss Synge was one of the most contrary women she had ever met. It seemed that the females to be empowered were working-class only and preferably northern. Perhaps she should just give up.

Lilibet still had some fight left in her though. 'You don't think we can get her in somehow?' Her blue eyes were turned persuasively on the recalcitrant commissioner.

Miss Synge shook her head. 'It's out of the question. She is too young.'

As two pairs of blue eyes now turned despairingly in her direction, Marion prepared to come to the rescue. 'Forgive me, Commissioner, but don't girls not old enough to be Guides join a Brownie pack instead?'

Lilibet gasped. 'Margaret could be a Brownie!'

Miss Synge replaced her teacup heavily. 'I came here to discuss a Guide Pack.'

But having spotted the flaw in the argument, Lilibet was now like a dog with a bone. 'Margaret would make a wonderful Brownie. She's very strong, you know,' she went on in a salesman-like patter recalling the days of the bread deliveries. She looked at her sister. 'Pull up your skirt, Margaret, and show Miss Synge.'

The younger princess yanked up her kilt, revealing her chubby knees.

'You can't say those aren't a very fine pair of hiking legs, Miss Synge! And she loves getting dirty, don't you, Margaret? And she would love to cook sausages on sticks!'

Marion hid a smile. Lilibet's charm at full wattage had an irresistible power and there wasn't a person on earth who could withstand it. Even the commissioner was visibly melting now. 'Can't there be a Brownie group for the smaller children?' pleaded Lilibet.

'Pack,' interrupted Miss Synge. 'Not group.' But her tone had lost its sternness.

'. . . attached to the older one for the Guides?' Lilibet finished.

The commissioner looked at her, raised an eyebrow and reached for another jam penny. They held their breath as she bit on it and swilled it down with tea. Eventually she put down her napkin . . . 'After due consideration . . .' she began, weightily.

They all gasped softly.

'. . . I don't see why not.'

Marion and the two princesses looked at one another and cheered.

Chapter Forty-Two

Nineteen thirty-eight began with the resignation of Anthony Eden. The dapper Old Etonian Foreign Secretary's attempt to appease Hitler over the Rhineland had rebounded when his Prime Minister, Neville Chamberlain, adopted the same approach to Mussolini over his invasion of Abyssinia. And appeasing Hitler had not worked anyway. Once again the Führer marked the coming of spring by sending his troops into another country. This time it was Austria. A month later, his possible intentions towards the industrially depressed Sudetenland, the border with Czechoslovakia, began to emerge.

The equerry who had praised Hitler at the Household dining table was silent on the matter this time.

The debutante season began, a surreal counterpoint to all these events. The girls hung excitedly over the balustrade, watching the girls in white arrive. 'We have a fly's-eye view!' hissed Lilibet.

A military band was playing popular hits. Beneath the huge chandeliers, the debutantes, graceful in white gowns, looked like a gaggle of exotic birds, ostrich plumes nodding, lace tails gathered up over arms in long white gloves. All the same, they seemed anachronistic to Marion. Advertising the fact that you wanted a rich man – how demeaning. She had not said so to the girls, though. To do so would undermine their parents, who were clearly hoping this old-fashioned ceremony would restore old-fashioned security to their beleaguered reign.

'Tea for two,' sang Margaret, waltzing about the balcony in her dressing gown.

'There's Grandmama,' said Lilibet, leaning dangerously over the balustrade. 'And the beeress.'

Directly beneath them, Queen Mary stood with Mrs Ronnie. In accordance with her belief that jewels were a competitive sport, the latter was wearing so many diamonds she looked like a chandelier herself. Queen Mary, not to be outdone, was wearing pearls the size of new potatoes.

'There's Aunt Marina!' breathed Margaret in awe. The Duchess of Kent looked dazzlingly lovely in white brocade embossed with pink and silver flowers.

The white-gowned procession made its slow way towards the red and gold thrones. The king's torso was ablaze with more stars than the Milky Way, and the queen's gown sparkled almost as brightly. Each debutante paused before Their Majesties, heard her name announced, stepped back and swept a low curtsey. Behind them, ushers with long rods picked up the endless lace trains of the debs and threw them skilfully over the arms of their owners as each curtsey finished. Relatives, sponsors and suitors crowded round to watch the debs' big moment.

'Is that it?' Lilibet asked, suddenly.

Marion blinked. 'It?'

'They get all dressed up and sit in the traffic just to curtsey to Mummie and Papa?'

'Exactly.'

'How silly. When I'm queen I won't have any of *that*.'

A triumphant smile tugged at Marion's mouth. She would make a feminist of Lilibet yet.

Later, having handed the girls over to Alah, Marion headed for her own room. Her way back led her through the picture gallery, whose curved glass ceiling flooded the room with light during the day. She paused, as always, to admire the painting of the Old Masters, which glowed like jewels on the pink brocade walls.

'Marion!' said someone. The voice – light, disdainful – was familiar. On one of the gold and white sofas that stretched beneath the paintings was a blonde girl in a white satin gown. White feathers rose from her golden hair.

'Debo!'

She looked stunning, Marion thought. She had the type of perfect skin all aristocratic women had, seemingly specially bred to show family diamonds at their best advantage. They winked round her neck and on the band round her perfect Marcel wave.

'It's rather full-on in there.' Debo waved a careless, white-gloved hand towards the ballroom entrance. 'I'm taking a breather. Met some lovely dukes though. One in particular.'

'Good,' said Marion, intending to continue on her way.

'I'm so sorry,' Debo added, with rare sympathy.

'Thank you.' She was surprised that news of her mother had come this far.

'He was so young. Such a waste.'

Marion felt suddenly as if she were looking at herself. She watched herself gasp, stumble, grip the arm of a chair. Her enquiry, to her own ears, came from very far away. 'Who are you talking about?'

'You don't know about Valentine?' Beneath the nodding feathers, the green eyes were wide.

The music from the ballroom swelled in Marion's ears. 'Know what?' she muttered, but she had already surmised what Debo would say.

She could not sleep that night. She lay, tossing from one side to the other, listening to the wind lamenting in the chimney. She felt a heavy sadness, but knew she was mourning more than just Valentine. Rather, she was lamenting her own loneliness and everything she knew she had denied herself. The tragedy of her first real love – her only one, really – wasn't just that the bright gleam of romantic happiness had faded so quickly. It was that it had never been repeated, and while she worked for the king and queen, it never could be.

Chapter Forty-Three

'Nine children! Can you imagine?' Alah was buttoning Lilibet into her frilly frock.

'Like the old woman who lived in a shoe,' said Margaret, who was admiring herself in the mirror.

'Well, this one lives in the American Embassy. Mrs Kennedy is the American ambassador's wife.'

'Perhaps she got all her babies from a shop,' suggested Margaret. 'That's how babies come, isn't it?' She slid Alah a naughty glance.

Lilibet, now securely buttoned, looked up from pulling up her socks. 'Of course not. People are like horses, their babies come from between their legs.' She had been spending a lot of time in the Windsor stables recently.

Margaret stared at her sister in disgust. 'I don't believe you!'

'That's enough.' Wearily, Marion took both girls' hands. 'Time for church.'

The Kennedys, who had arrived in London the year before, were spending the weekend at Windsor. Last night there had been a dinner, and today the princesses were to meet them and their children.

An air of unusual importance surrounded the encounter. The king and queen had started to throw their weight behind the diplomatic effort. The Munich peace agreement, struck by Chamberlain amid much fanfare the previous September, was still holding. But while Hitler had been ceded the Sudetenland, which he had anyway invaded six months before, there was widespread suspicion of his intentions towards the rest of Czechoslovakia.

Should appeasement fail, which Churchill continued to insist it would, America would be a powerful ally in the event of a war. The question was whether the neutral President Roosevelt could be got on their side.

As Marion ushered the girls into the cool and coloured gloom of St George's Chapel, she saw that Roosevelt's representative and his family were already present and correct.

He was a strange-looking man, with a high forehead, thick round spectacles and a huge white manic grin. Mrs Kennedy, also smiling excitedly, was as slim and young-looking as advertised. The children, who filled the pew, were the picture of American healthiness, all thick hair, tanned complexions, and their father's big white teeth. Ranging in age from something close to Margaret to late teens, they stared openly at the princesses as they filed in behind their parents. Lilibet kept her gaze demurely on the floor, but Marion could see Margaret staring boldly back at the visitors. One of the older boys, a handsome brown-haired youth, winked at her.

Afterward, at morning coffee, Margaret hastened to sit near the winking boy. For all their difference in age – he must be twenty at least – they were soon deep in conversation. They seemed to be laughing a lot, although about what Marion could not hear. Hopefully not Lilibet's earlier bombshell.

She sat near the back of the room, ostensibly in charge of the girls. The nearby window had a view of the castle's moat garden and the much-adored dahlias of Lord Wigram, the castle warden.

The queen was in sparkling form. She sat next to the rather silent king on a sofa whose frame was carved with golden neptunes and chatted merrily to her rapt American audience.

'The crew of our ship did Maori hakas and Marquesan pig dances,' trilled the queen. This was about their trip to Australia some ten years before.

'A what dance?' asked Mrs Kennedy.

The queen looked at her with mock surprise. 'You've never seen a Marquesan pig dance? My dear, it is just too delightful!'

The ambassador slapped his knee, cackling with laughter. 'Your Majesty, as we say in the States, you're quite a dame.'

The queen turned on him her most radiant smile 'Thank you, Ambassador. You're quite a man, too. We'll need men like you on our side, should things turn nasty with Mr Hitler.'

From the back of the room, Marion blinked. The queen had moved like lightning. Under the flag of small talk, she had been awaiting her opportunity, and seized it.

Kennedy saw this, and moved to block it. 'The American people don't want a war,' he said, quoting the official line as he picked up his coffee cup.

'Not even to defend democracy?' twinkled the queen, her voice so light and teasing it was impossible to tell whether she was serious.

Now Kennedy's smile was tight. 'We went into the last war to make the world safe for democracy. And look what happens – a whole crop of dictatorships.'

The queen beamed. 'But if we had the United States actively on our side, working with us, think how that would strengthen our position with the dictators!'

Marion held her breath. The queen was taking no prisoners. The steel below the swirling misty blue could now be seen. As the dark clouds of conflict gathered above her country, Her Majesty had risen to the challenge. The caprice and self-indulgence had been put aside to reveal a bold and skilful diplomatic negotiator. But would it work?

There was a silence for a moment. Mrs Kennedy cleared her throat and straightened her skirt. The king looked at the ceiling. Kennedy replaced his coffee cup, bending his head to hide his face. When he raised it again, he too was beaming.

'Your Majesty, you know, you should visit America.'

'A royal tour!' The queen clasped her hands in delight. 'I'd absolutely *love* to. I only know three Americans. Fred Astaire, J. P. Morgan – and *you*!'

Everyone was laughing now. The difficult moment was past. What was more, a diplomatic coup had been pulled off. At the back of the room, Marion felt a warm wave of admiration. The king obviously felt the same, looking at his wife in undisguised amazement.

The queen was back on the subject of Hitler, voice bubbling with amusement. 'My mother-in-law Queen Mary can't abide him, you know. She says he speaks the most *abominable* German!'

Later, Margaret revealed her conversation with the Kennedy boy. 'His name is John, but everyone calls him Jack. He once exploded a toilet seat with a firecracker.'

'What?' said Lilibet.

'For a joke at school,' Margaret continued with an admiring tone. 'He got into awful trouble though. The headmaster took the toilet seat into chapel assembly and *brandished* it.'

'His poor parents,' Alah sniffed. 'A young man like that will never amount to anything.'

Nineteen thirty-nine arrived. In March, Hitler marched into Prague. As had been widely feared, Czechoslovakia had ceased to exist. The Munich Agreement was in ruins, the German ambassador was expelled from London and an unconditional guarantee was given to Poland that Britain would come to its aid in the event of invasion. Should a European war erupt, a strong relationship with America would be more than useful – it would be vital.

The tour of Canada and the United States was fixed for May. There was no doubt of its importance now, although the queen still affected to see it as a delightful adventure. The world stage on to which she had stepped with such confidence seemed to suit her, as did her new role as national figurehead and chief morale-raiser.

Her special genius was her lightness of touch and unflagging sense of humour. 'Tinkety-tonk, old fruit,' she would say to friends on the telephone. 'And down with the Nazis!' After a rocky first few years, the monarchy had found its purpose.

The tour preparations included a vast new wardrobe for the queen. Norman, to his delight, was back at the palace. Marion bumped into him one morning, bowling down the red-carpeted corridor with the urgency of the White Rabbit.

'Can't stop! I'm making the frills to frustrate the Führer! The gowns to bring down Goering! The Himmler-repelling hemlines! The frocks that will save the free world!'

'Yes, all right, Norman,' Marion said, laughing.

He gestured at the small woman behind him, almost buried under bolts of silk, tulle and lace in sugared-almond colours. 'This is Gladys. She's here to do the measuring, pass the tape over the royal bosom and so forth. It's not done to see one's royal client in their underwear. Isn't that right, Glad?'

"S right, Mr 'Artnell,' Glad confirmed in a curiously low, gruff voice.

'I love the colours,' Marion said. 'And the material. It looks so romantic.'

'Beyond romantic! We're going totally Winterhalter!'

His portraits hung in many places in the palace: large-eyed, tiny-waisted princesses and empresses in huge gauzy crinolines. They presented a sugary Victorian ideal of womanhood, but there was no doubt this was a brilliant idea, a style that would flatter the queen's plump figure and suit her sweetly old-fashioned air. 'Clever of you.'

'It was the king's idea, would you believe. Frogmarched me from picture to picture and said, "I want her to look like that!"'

Marion thought, and not for the first time, that the king could be a surprising man.

The royal schedule sounded exhausting. The princesses followed it closely in the newspapers. But when the queen rang her daughters in the evenings, she sounded as bright as if she had just woken up.

'Mummie's eaten a hot dog!' Margaret reported after one such conversation.

'Don't listen, Jane.' Lilibet bent to put her hands over the ears of the nearest, newest corgi.

Their eventual return, at the end of June, was much anticipated, not just by the girls but by the whole country. There was no doubt in the support for the monarchy now. Alah, Marion and the princesses arrived at Southampton to find great cheering crowds massed on the quayside.

'Do we have to sail out to meet them?' Lilibet was dismayed at the prospect.

She disliked the sea, for its unpredictability. Supremely composed as she mostly was these days, there remained about Lilibet some aspects of the former anxious child.

It was windy on deck, and loud with vibrations from the engine. Alah immediately disappeared below. Margaret went to inspect the captain's cabin and returned with the news that it was amazingly plain and bleak. 'His mirror's the size of a postcard!'

'That would never do for you,' Lilibet teased.

The princesses were given some cherries, a rare treat. 'But what shall we do with the pips?' asked the orderly Lilibet.

'Shove 'em down the shafts,' said Margaret, tipping hers with a rattle down a nearby pipe.

As her parents' liner, the *Empress of Britain*, neared, both girls became excited in their different ways. Margaret jigged about waving wildly, while Lilibet stood still at the rail, her delight contained.

The reunion was joyful. 'Mummie, Mummie! Look how thin I've got!' Margaret was leaping up and down. The queen, looking considerably slimmer too, hugged her daughters close. 'You'll never guess what I've brought back for you! A totem pole!'

A riotous celebration ensued. Champagne cocktails of an unfeasible strength were served and drunk. Marion did her best to disguise the fact that her eyes were tying themselves in knots, but the queen, as ever, missed nothing. 'Oh, Crawfie! I should have told you. They make them very strong on board!'

Perhaps everyone was feeling the effects, because the king started pushing balloons out of the portholes while one of his equerries tried to pop them with cigarettes. There was riotous dancing on deck. The king stood apart, watching his eldest daughter whirling round.

Marion taking a breather, went to the ship's rail to join him. The cocktails had made her bold. 'Are you all right, sir?' His thin face wore a puzzled expression.

'Something's changed about Lilibet. But I can't put my finger on exactly what it is.'

Marion looked at the laughing, dancing princess, with her sparkling eyes and bouncing hair. As ever, she was dressed identically to her sister, but beneath her childish printed frock a notably womanly figure was visible, with hips and generous breasts. She felt a pang as she saw what the king could not. Lilibet was growing up.

Chapter Forty-Four

Some weeks later, to Lilibet's dismay, another sea voyage was mooted, in the royal yacht *Victoria and Albert* to Dartmouth College, the naval academy in Devon the king had attended himself as a boy.

'And Grandpapa before me,' he told his eldest daughter in an effort to raise her spirits. 'His nickname was S-sprat.'

'What was yours, Papa?'

The king sighed. 'Bat Lugs.'

Margaret squealed. 'Because of your ears, Papa?'

'I assume s-so.'

The way up to the college, a vast red-brick building on a cliff overlooking the river, was via a flight of very long and steep steps. Lilibet, in a larger version of the same pink coat as her sister, planted one white-sandalled foot in front of the other, as she plodded patiently up.

'It's so boring,' puffed Margaret, beside her. 'Why can't Papa inspect this stupid college on his own? Why do we have to come?' She stared up at the skies. 'Please, God, make something happen to stop it.'

Lilibet was shocked. 'You can't ask God to do things like that.'

'Why not?'

'You're supposed to save him for big things.'

'This might be a big thing,' said the irrepressible Margaret.

God answered her prayers. They reached the top of the stairs to find that two cadets had come down with mumps. It was decided to whisk the girls out of harm's way, to the Captain's House. Some brothers called the Dalrymple-Hamiltons lived here, and Margaret, who loved boys but was rarely exposed to them, was delighted. 'Thank you, God!'

The Dalrymple-Hamiltons were a disappointment, however. They were less interested in flirting than in showing the princesses their train set. As her sister huffed and pouted, Lilibet looked at the neat little locomotives and the model details that set the scene; the tiny trees and bridges; the cars waiting at the level crossing; the animals in the fields. 'Look at this man on the platform. You can even see his newspaper.' She bent over to squint at it, her glossy dark hair falling on the tiny tracks. 'I think it's *The Times*.'

'You're obsessed with *The Times*,' groaned Margaret. The king had recently started reading it with his elder daughter, pointing out articles he thought might interest her. Margaret, still confined to *The Children's Newspaper*, was jealous, as ever.

Lilibet, as ever, ignored her. 'Here's a lady in a headscarf with dogs,' she observed placidly. 'I wonder if they're her horses in that field she's walking past.' She sat back on her heels and looked dreamy, suddenly. 'When I'm married, I'd love to be a lady in the country with lots of horses and dogs.'

Margaret, her hackles up, seized on this. 'You can't though,' she reminded her sister, spitefully. 'You're going to be queen. You have to marry a king.'

Lilibet's strong brows drew together, giving her an uncharacteristically rebellious look. 'I'll marry who I like,' she said.

'You can't,' repeated Margaret, tauntingly. 'Uncle David tried that and look what happened to him!'

The door of the playroom now opened and someone came in. Lilibet, still absorbed in the train set, did not look up immediately. But Margaret did. Marion saw her violet eyes dilate and her lips part slightly. She turned to see who it was.

A tall boy of astonishing beauty lounged nonchalantly in the doorway. About eighteen, he had clean-cut Nordic features and hair so blond it was almost white. He looked vaguely familiar, but Marion could not place him. The room, which had been still, now felt charged.

Lilibet, sensing something, looked up. Her eyes met his, and the toy train dropped from her grasp.

'You're to come to lunch,' he said abruptly.

The Dalrymple-Hamiltons had scrambled to their feet. 'Philip!'

Now she remembered. This exquisite youth was the cousin of Princess Marina, Prince Philip of Greece.

Lunch was on the gold-and-white *Victoria and Albert* with its cretonne curtains and painted coats of arms. Lilibet, who had complained throughout the journey from London of the pitching and rolling, was not complaining any longer.

She gazed fixedly at Philip of Greece, hardly touching anything on her plate. He, conversely, ignored her completely and ate a huge pile of prawns. Lilibet watched his long fingers rip them apart with expert ease. A pile of pink shells rose beside his monogrammed plate.

Mrs Ronnie, who with her usual ingenuity had managed to secure herself a place in the royal party, leaned towards Marion, powdered jowls wobbling. 'I do so love *youth*!' she whispered, her egg-like eyes darting meaningfully between the Greek prince and the English princess.

Conversation, somewhat inevitably, turned to Hitler. 'I wonder what he's like as a person,' someone mused.

The king, who could be puckish, darted a wicked glance at Marion's neighbour. 'Ask Mrs R-Ronnie. She's met him.'

'It was years and years ago. Before he became what he is now,' blustered the collector of social lions, whose collecting in that particular case had been wide of the mark. The powdered jowls were purple with embarrassment.

Afterward, Marion went with the princesses and Philip back up the long steep steps from the harbour. At the college tennis courts, he leaped over the nets in an obvious attempt to impress them. Lilibet was transfixed. 'Look how high he can jump, Crawfie! Isn't he good?'

Marion wondered how high Philip might want to jump in quite another direction. There was something focused about his nonchalance, as if he knew that the way to impress Lilibet was to treat her in an offhand manner while making a big fuss of her sister.

Later, when the *Victoria and Albert*'s engines started up, its departure was accompanied by a flotilla of Dartmouth cadets in any craft they could lay their hands on. Lilibet and Margaret stood on deck, watching them in delight and waving back quite as madly as their cheering young escorts, who, undeterred by weather and a strong sea, insisted on a grand patriotic send-off.

The heavy yacht cut effortlessly through the choppy waters. As it approached the entrance to the Channel, the accompanying scatter of rowboats, motorboats and excited boys was still with it. The wind on the deck was getting up, blowing hair about, teasing scarves and carrying conversations from one end of the ship to the other. The king, his lunchtime gaiety quite gone now that London and officialdom beckoned, was barking at the captain about the boys. 'It's ridiculous, and very unsafe! You must signal them to go back.'

Margaret and Marion watched the sailor run to the flag deck and fetch the appropriate colours. The message, in that mysterious naval language, was run up the mast in minutes. Lilibet, who had grasped the railing and stared out to sea all this while, seemed to be in another, separate world. As the boys began to fall back, turn round, and return to Dartmouth, her eyes remained fixed on the one boat that still followed, a rowboat manned by a Viking god, sculling with all his might over the muscles of the sea.

'The young f-fool!' expostulated the king, standing behind his daughter with his binoculars rammed to his eyes. 'He m-must go back! Or we'll have to h-h-heave to and send him back!'

Lilibet said nothing, just turned and removed the glasses from her father's hand. She put them to her own eyes and looked at Philip for a long time. Meanwhile, around her, there was shouting through the megaphone at the audacious prince in the boat, until even he got the message and turned round to row back.

Only when he was a very small speck in the distance did Lilibet take the binoculars from her eyes and sigh.

'Lilibet loves Philip!' said Margaret mockingly.

The queen looked at her eldest daughter. 'You can't fall in love with the first boy you meet, darling. Love at first sight is just a myth.'

Lilibet did not reply.

Chapter Forty-Five

'Do you really think there will be a war, Crawfie?' Lilibet asked. The three of them were sitting on the little hill in the Buckingham Palace garden. The September sun was warm on their faces, and above them, in the blue sky, birds wheeled and swooped.

Almost certainly, Marion thought. You could feel it in the air – a grim expectation. You could see it all around. Across the road, in Hyde Park, trenches had been dug. Sandbags had been put outside Whitehall offices where arrangements were being made to send London children to the countryside.

She looked at Lilibet. Thanks to her newspaper reading, she was well-informed. She would not be fobbed off. Honesty was usually the best policy. 'Depends on Russia,' she said. 'Stalin hasn't joined the Axis yet.'

'But if he comes down on Hitler's side, the Nazis will take Poland,' Lilibet pointed out. 'And you know what will happen then.'

'Horrid Hitler!' Margaret was tearing daisies from the grass. 'Spoiling our trip to Balmoral!'

Lilibet looked at her sister. 'Well, at least we're not going to Canada.'

There had initially been suggestions that the royal family leave the country. The queen had firmly refused. 'The children would never leave without me. I would never leave without the king. And the king would never leave' had been her much-quoted response.

Her transformation from socialite to state figurehead continued apace. When she discovered that Hitler had called her 'the most dangerous woman in Europe', she had been thrilled. 'What can the most dangerous woman in Europe do for you, Crawfie?' she would crow whenever Marion went to consult her. 'The most dangerous woman in Europe calling!' she would cackle when she rang up her friends.

But she had been careful never to do this in earshot of her daughters, who, she believed, had remained largely ignorant both of the war and who had caused it. She was wrong, of course, especially about Lilibet, who was currently trying to explain Hitler to her sister.

'He's the leader of Germany,' she began. 'They call him the chancellor.'

'We've got one of those,' Margaret put in, confidently. 'He's in charge of all the money.'

'Not that sort of chancellor. Hitler is like a prime minister and a president rolled into one. He is all-powerful and has no legal opposition.'

'So king of absolutely everything?' Margaret looked impressed.

'It's called a dictator.'

'I've seen pictures of him.' Margaret clasped her arms round her legs. 'He never takes his coat off. Not even when it's hot. I bet it's smelly.' She ruffled the nearest corgi. 'I wonder if Hitler has any pets.'

'He has a cat called Schnitzel, I believe.'

Marion stared at Lilibet. Her memory for details was astonishing. Wherever had she picked this one up?

'How did he become so powerful?' Margaret wanted to know. This, of course, was the difficult bit. Lilibet looked at Marion, stumped.

She took a deep breath. 'He's very good at speeches. People believe what he says.'

'But what does he say?'

Marion hesitated. 'He tells the Germans that they were born to rule over other people.'

'Papa was born to rule over other people!' exclaimed Margaret.

'Yes, but not that way.'

Four challenging blue eyes were turned on her. 'Why not?'

'Well, because we are a democracy. Our monarchy is constitutional and derives its power by permission of Parliament and people. It can't act alone.'

The princesses looked puzzled.

'Hitler also tells the Germans that he'll give them all jobs. A lot of Germans lost their jobs and were unhappy about it.'

Lilibet was alarmed. 'But people here don't have jobs and are unhappy.'

'Well, yes. But it's not quite the same.'

'But why not?' demanded logical Lilibet. Her mind was clearly bounding ahead, linking things together. 'What if we get a dictator here? What will happen to Mummie and Papa and Margaret and I?' She glanced at the dogs chasing each other through the heather. 'And Dookie and Susan?'

Margaret shook her fist. 'Don't worry, Lilibet! We're going to give those beastly Germans absolute hell!'

'Our last lessons in peace,' chanted Margaret on the morning of 3 September. Hitler had, as expected, invaded Poland, and the Germans, also as expected, had ignored the British request for a withdrawal of troops. Unless they did so by 11 a.m., Britain would declare war.

'Shut up,' said Lilibet, throwing an exercise book at her.

'Beast!'

'Brute!'

'It doesn't look much like peace to me,' said Marion.

Both girls kept looking at the clock on the wall above her desk. 'Half past ten!' exclaimed Margaret. Then, fifteen minutes later, 'A quarter to eleven!'

While she fought to seem unruffled, Marion found that her knees, under the table, were shaking.

'Eleven!' shouted Margaret. She started dancing around the classroom.

'Stop it! Stop it!' yelled Lilibet. 'Tell her to stop, Crawfie!'

Marion switched on the schoolroom radio. The sad, quiet voice of the prime minister floated into the room. 'I'm afraid I have to tell you,' the former champion of appeasement was saying, 'that no such undertaking has been received and as a consequence this country is at war with Germany.'

Margaret stopped shouting. She turned to Marion, her violet eyes full of fear. 'Crawfie! What's going to happen now?'

Chapter Forty-Six

As the car slid into the ancient stone maw of Windsor Castle's Henry VIII Gate, it felt like entering a prison.

'It's so dark,' Margaret whimpered, looking round the lightless courtyard. 'I don't like it.'

'You mustn't complain,' Alah said severely. 'You're very fortunate. Think of all those little evacuees who are having to leave their families and go goodness knows where. They might never see their mummies and daddies again.'

This had the inevitable result. The smallest princess burst into floods of tears.

'How long will we be at Windsor?' Lilibet asked. She was sitting quietly next to Marion in the car.

'Only for the rest of the week,' Alah said firmly.

While these had been the queen's instructions when she called Royal Lodge earlier that day, something in her voice had stirred Marion's suspicions. She had immediately packed everything she had.

What people called the Phony War had been going on for months. But things were now beginning to change. Reports from Europe were universally depressing, with Norway and the Netherlands falling to the Nazis and the Allies being pushed back towards the Normandy coast. Would France be next? The Dutch queen, Wilhelmina, had only days ago arrived at Buckingham Palace with nothing but the clothes she stood in. Marion had heard the story from Norman, who had been summoned to supply the refugee royal with an outfit. 'We showed her any number of hats,' he reported, rolling his eyes. 'But Her Majesty didn't like any of them, oh no. Then she saw Gladys's hat – my assistant, you remember . . .'

Marion recalled the little old woman overburdened with silk and tulle who had come with Norman for the American tour fittings.

'. . . and pointed at it and said, "I want that one!"'

Chamberlain had been forced to resign as Prime Minister, and the Hitler-hating Churchill, for so long the maverick out on a limb, had now replaced him. Marion admired what he had said to Parliament when he had taken up the job. 'Blood, toil, tears and sweat'; 'victory at all costs'; and vowing to 'wage war against a monstrous tyranny never surpassed in the dark, lamentable catalogue of human crime'. She liked his stirring language, his air of indefatigable resolve and, especially, his growling, contemptuous pronunciation of Hitler's followers as 'Naarzis' – English-style, without the Germanic 't'.

'Why do Mummie and Papa have to stay in London?' Margaret piped up. 'Do you think the Germans will come and get them?'

'Not a chance,' Marion asserted, before Alah could make one of her doomy predictions.

'I hope Hitler won't come over here,' Lilibet said nervously.

'Well, if he does, he'll be dealt with,' said Alah, as if she was going to put him over her knee and spank him with a hairbrush.

The great medieval gates of Windsor slammed behind them.

The Master of the Household was waiting to receive them and walked them down passages whose panelling looked black in the shadows.

'We dress for dinner,' the Master announced in his plummy tones. His name, Sir Hill Child, was as improbable as this instruction. Apart from anything else there were hardly any lights; all chandeliers had been dismantled and all bright bulbs swapped for dim ones.

'*We* dine in the nursery with Their Royal Highnesses,' Alah announced back. She was employing the royal plural, talking about herself.

'But *we* don't,' Marion put in, hurriedly. Whatever the circumstances, dinner with grown-ups was not to be sniffed at.

'Eight o'clock in the Octagon Room,' Sir Hill instructed, before disappearing into the gloom. It was, Marion realised, a good job she had brought her evening gown, crushed in her hastily packed luggage. But was it brave or crazy that in a medieval castle in wartime people were acting as if they were at a country house party? Of course, in one sense they were. A paragraph had gone to all British and American papers saying that the princesses had been evacuated to 'a house in the country'.

Lilibet, Margaret and Alah were in the Lancaster Tower, in the comfortable pink and fawn nursery suite with its roaring fire that they usually stayed in when visiting Windsor. But for reasons unknown Marion had been billeted in a distant corner of the fortress, alone at the top of a tower and reached by a winding stair. The stone steps were worn down in the centre by centuries of feet. The walls, rough elsewhere, were marble-smooth at elbow level from centuries of passing arms.

Her bedroom was dark red, huge and as cold as the grave. It smelled musty, as if no one had occupied it for some time. There was a big, gloomy, dark green sitting room hung with small, dim oils. Both rooms had tiny fireplaces, and though fires had been lit, the warmth made little impression. What limited light might creep in through the pointed medieval lancet window was firmly repelled by a blackout curtain. Her bathroom, such as it was, was in a hut out on the roof. 'But you do have it all to yourself, madam,' said the footman who had shown her there.

Marion forced a smile as she examined it. It was freezing, and lacked even the comforts of the one at Buckingham Palace. There wasn't even a mouse. Just a tiny bar of soap, strips of newspaper on a nail by the lavatory and a black line painted round the inside of the bath, indicating the level above which water was not to rise. About three inches, it seemed. The king, keen not to waste resources, had introduced the initiative. A small animal might manage a good soak. But not a full-sized person, particularly a tall one like her.

The tower, the winding stair, the castle of darkness; it was like being in a frightening fairy tale. Rapunzel perhaps, except that her hair was too short. Jack and the Beanstalk, then – but no, all the bold young men were far away at the moment. There was an ogre, though, and everyone knew who he was.

Later, Marion's heart thumped as she hurried through rooms full of furniture in dust covers. Glass-fronted cabinets were turned ominously to the walls. The castle had so many windows to black out, she had been told, that by the time they finished for the night, it was morning again.

Down the unlit passages, the castle's thousand-year history seemed to press close. She listened hard; was that a footstep? A distant wail from long ago? Her every turn seemed to lead her farther away from the possible location of the Octagon Room.

Her footsteps were closely followed by the eerie slither of velvet on stone; once or twice she had turned, expecting a terrifying phantom. But there had been only gaping darkness. She realised it was her own dress she was hearing. Her mother had sewn the gown from blue tapestry curtain material once intended for her bedroom. It had a low-cut front which Mrs Crawford had had doubts about; they had argued about it, Marion remembered, with a stab of regret.

Suddenly, round a corner, came the sign that she had arrived. A half-open door revealed a dark cavern of a room with a carved Gothic ceiling and a fire roaring in a black marble fireplace. It was indeed, she saw as she hesitated on the threshold, octagon-shaped.

Beneath the light of a single dim bulb, three men in immaculate black tie sat around a table set with silver and crystal. It looked like dinner in the underworld.

The surreal tableau broke up as Sir Hill rose to his feet. 'Miss Crawford. May I introduce Sir Dudley Colles. And Mr Gerald Kelly, whom I believe you have met before.'

Marion nodded at the small, ebullient Irishman. Kerald Jelly, as the princesses called him, was a familiar sight around the palace. He had, for the past few years, been painting coronation portraits of the king and queen, neither of which ever seemed to be finished. It was said that he enjoyed life in the royal circle so much he scrubbed out part of what he had painted every day to prolong his employment.

Footsteps could be heard coming up the stone passage. The table was set for five, she now noticed. The one next to her was empty, but the last guest was about to appear. She felt a stir in the air, a sudden tightening of her muscles. The hair on the back of her neck stood on end.

'Tommy! Good to see you, old chap.' A scrape of chair as Sir Hill stood up again, extending a long white hand.

And there he suddenly was, dashing in his dinner jacket, the candlelight gleaming on his thick black hair. She felt the familiar shooting longing but composedly shook his hand. His touch seemed to scald her skin, and from the depths of his brows, his dark gaze flicked across her breasts like a riding crop. She felt it and her blood raced.

As they sat down, he looked at her briefly, expressionlessly, but placed his leg hard against hers. Shock barrelled through her. It was, she sensed, no accident; he was asking an unspoken question.

It was as if a switch had been flicked, one long untouched. She felt suddenly, thrummingly alive. She did not move. His thigh pressed against her once more, as if in confirmation, then edged away. He settled into his seat.

Her stomach swooped and swirled which, was just as well, given the food now borne in with due ceremony by two footmen. She eyed a brown crust of potatoes with some sort of mince underneath.

Tommy leaned towards her. 'Shepherd's pie,' he said in a low voice. 'Probably made with actual shepherd.'

Wizened chops were laid to rest on a thin bed of grey mashed potato. Any hope that Windsor would be somehow exempt from the rationing that gripped everywhere else was unfounded. But she did not care. She was full of a barely contained excitement. This dark, confined wartime world suddenly seemed full of thrilling possibility.

Tommy was keeping the table amused with a laconic ease that amazed her, given the circumstances. He described how the king, giggling helplessly, had knighted him on a train during the tour of North America.

'And how is Lady Lascelles?' Dudley asked, suddenly. 'Is she here at Windsor too?'

Marion held her breath. She felt as if she were a glass vase, about to fall off a shelf.

'In the country,' Tommy said smoothly, and she felt her whole body relax.

A conversation began about the queen. 'The mere sight of Her Majesty raises morale,' Sir Dudley said of her visits to Women's Royal Voluntary Service, Air Raid Precaution and Red Cross units the length and breadth of London.

'But she never wears a uniform,' Sir Hill pointed out. 'There's the brilliance of it. Her Majesty is always dressed as a civilian while the king is always in uniform. So, while he stands for all the fighting men, she represents every British housewife rolled into one.'

'The most dangerous woman in Europe,' Sir Dudley said with a smile, struggling with his chop.

It was agreed that the king was finding the war much more difficult. 'Without the queen, he would collapse under the strain' was the general view.

'Those big blue eyes of hers,' Kelly remarked dreamily, helping himself liberally to more port. 'But she's as tough as old boots underneath.'

Blue eyes and a will of iron, Marion remembered. *That is all the equipment a lady needs!* Pudding came: a grey jelly. 'Reminds me of Dead Man's Leg at school,' remarked Sir Hill, peering at it.

'We used to call it Nun's Toenails,' said Sir Gerald, in his Irish accent.

When, at long, endless last, the final glass was emptied and they all stood up, Tommy turned to Marion. 'Perhaps, this being the blackout, you might allow me to escort you to your door, Miss Crawford.' His tone, so deceptively formal and distant, sent a delicious shiver down her spine. A powerful desire filled her. This was the moment!

They filed out. Polite good nights were exchanged with the others. The heels of handmade shoes crunched off down stone-floored passages. They were left alone.

She waited. He was hard to see in the dark. Just the tip of his cigarette, marking the location of his mouth. She swallowed.

She jumped as his fingers touched her elbow. 'This way, Miss Crawford.'

'Marion, *please*,' she said, giggling. Perhaps the wine had gone to her head slightly.

He steered her along, talking about gardening. 'Last weekend Joan and I were carting potatoes, of which we have a fine crop. I was continually struck by the resemblance that General de Gaulle has to the average potato, although the potato is the more malleable of the two.'

'What?' He was making the smallest of small talk, and mentioning his wife into the bargain. And yet he had stared at her breasts, pressed his leg against her. She was sure of it. Or was she? Had she, once again, misinterpreted the situation?

He left her at the entrance door to her tower. She stood, watching him walk into the shadows. 'Good night, Miss Crawford.'

Chapter Forty-Seven

The girls had taken to wartime with surprising ease. They seemed to part with their past, pampered life with never a backward glance, and certain aspects of the new one they positively enjoyed. The official recommendations, in Lilibet's case. They satisified her strong desire for order. Poring over maps, she quickly established the positions of all the first-aid posts, fire stations, telephone boxes and police stations in the surrounding areas.

'If you know where they are, you may be able to save someone a few precious moments in an air raid,' she would solemnly inform Marion, who nodded just as solemnly, although the likelihood of the princess having to tell anyone anything was remote. It was a shame, in a way. Lilibet would have made a formidable Air Raid Precaution warden.

She took the strictures on saving energy just as seriously. She watched Alah like a hawk to make sure the bath was not run over the requisite five inches and made cardboard rings to slip under the light switch covers. They were in the shape of a face; the knob forming the nose. 'Please Turn Me Off,' in the princess's distinctive hand, was written round the edge.

'Is this from food groups one to four?' she would enquire at mealtimes, consulting her ration book and staring at the butter with the royal monogram supplied by the Windsor farms. 'Remember,' she would add soberly, quoting the slogan on the posters, 'you can use every bit of a pig except its squeal!'

Margaret was more taken with the idea of fifth columnists, of dastardly enemy agents disguised as nuns or mothers with babies.

'Bet you anything there's a machine gun under that bedding,' she would hiss whenever they passed a woman pushing a pram in Windsor Great Park. From time to time Marion and the girls would come across little bands of Local Defence Volunteers drilling with whatever equipment they had been able to find: kitchen knives lashed to broom handles, pitchforks, garden spades. An elderly sergeant major strode up and down in front of them, shouting, in a strong cockney accent, 'What we want is not to shoot the Boche but bayonet 'im! That's what the Germans don't like, cold steel. They don't like it up 'em! You stick it in the throat, in the lungs or in the stomach, giving it a twist as you pull it out.'

They would straighten up proudly and salute on seeing the princesses. 'Gosh,' Margaret would mercilessly remark as they walked on from the motley collection of old men and young boys. 'Hitler's not going to have a very hard time if he gets here, is he?'

'Margaret!' exclaimed Lilibet. 'Don't be so mean!'

Scorching day followed scorching day. They dug for victory in the castle gardens, using the gardening skills honed at Royal Lodge. Later, after hearing the teatime news reports, Lilibet moved flags about on a big map, following the movements of the various armies. The reports were not encouraging. Hitler had taken the Netherlands and Belgium. He was advancing through France.

One day, the sound of shattering explosions and gunfire, and endless RAF coming over, made the princesses pause their game of Hide and Seek. 'Crawfie, whatever is it?'

The answer came later as they listened to *Children's Hour* on the radio. A new voice came on, a man speaking in a firm, calm but urgent way.

'What's going on?' Margaret demanded indignantly from the corner of the nursery where she was playing with her Spitfire pilot. 'What's happened to Larry the Lamb?'

'Shhh!' said Lilibet, frowning. She was listening hard.

'Something about boats?' demanded her sister. She was listening herself now, repeating the words. 'If you have a boat capable of crossing the Channel, take it now to the coast of France and bring home some British soldiers.' She stared at the others, dumbfounded. 'But why? What for?'

Lilibet was quicker on the uptake. Her face, as she looked at Marion's, was drained of all colour. 'Because the Nazis have driven us back.'

Marion's throat was blocked. Tears pricked at her eyes. She blinked them back determinedly and tried to smile reassuringly at Lilibet.

But the princess was ashen. 'That means,' she said slowly, 'that Hitler now occupies the entire seaboard from Iceland down to Spain. Oh, Crawfie!' Her blue eyes filled with tears. 'That's absolutely terrifying. What's going to happen to us?'

Margaret, behind her, had got up. She stood there in her summer frock, brows drawn and eyes flashing. 'We're fighting with our backs to the wall. Death or glory!' she declared in resounding tones. They were currently reading *Swallows and Amazons*, and Margaret had immediately seized on bold Nancy Blackett as a literary soulmate. 'Any invader who sets foot on British soil is for it! No mercy! We will be shooting parachutists down and throwing hand grenades about!'

Lilibet's white, scared look had gone. She grinned her trademark broad grin and assumed a familiar cockney accent. 'What we want is not to shoot the Boche but bayonet 'im! That's what the Germans don't like, cold steel. They don't like it up 'em! I know where to stick it, too.'

She beamed at her sister as they chorused 'In the throat, in the lungs or in the stomach! Giving it a twist as you pull it out!'

The girls' fighting spirit reflected that of the rest of the country, in particular Prime Minister Churchill, whose speech to the Commons in the wake of Dunkirk was quoted on the radio news. 'We shall go on to the end . . . we shall defend our island whatever the cost may be. We shall fight on the beaches, we shall fight on the landing grounds, we shall fight in the fields and in the streets, we shall fight in the hills, we shall never surrender.'

'Never!' agreed Margaret, waving her pencil. She was drawing a Squander Bug copied from government posters that urged people to save for the war effort and not waste their money on consumer goods. The bug had teeth and the Führer's face, with swastikas all over its belly.

Even so, it was looking increasingly as if Britain might be fighting on alone. France's surrender to the Germans had been a shock, and the Americans, despite the queen's efforts and Norman's hostess dresses, were still pursuing a policy of neutrality. When would, as Churchill's speech had continued, the New World, with all its power and might, come to the aid of the old?

Chapter Forty-Eight

The princesses stared at the round metal container in amazement.

'A biscuit tin!' said Lilibet. 'Papa wants you to bury the Crown Jewels *in a biscuit tin?*' Her manner was sufficiently Lady Bracknell to make Marion smile. A smile was also twitching the thin, scholarly face of Sir Owen Morshead, Librarian of Windsor Castle and the man chosen to put the king's most recent orders into action.

'It's the perfect size, Your Royal Highness,' he explained as the footman holding the container descended into the cellar that had been specially dug into the castle's chalk foundations and secured with two double metal doors.

'I think it's a good idea,' said Margaret stoutly. 'Hitler will never think of looking for the Black Prince's Ruby in a biscuit tin.' She paused and looked thoughtful. 'Unless he likes biscuits, of course.'

Margaret herself was extremely fond of biscuits, to which rationing had severely restricted her access. Marion let her continue to wonder aloud about what kind of biscuits the Führer preferred. Far better that than having her realise that the need to bury the jewels was tacit acknowledgement that an invasion could be imminent. Photographs of Hitler in St Edward's Crown were not even to be thought of.

Hitler, of course, had not bargained for any of this. His expectation that Britain would roll over and surrender after the fall of France had proved something of a misjudgement. Churchill had once again swung into action with stirring oratory about this being Britain's finest hour. His determined hope exasperated many who felt the fight was over. Even the king and queen had their doubts.

'He's just told me that success consists of going from failure to failure without any loss of enthusiasm,' the king told his wife after one prime ministerial meeting.

'He told me that if you're going through hell, keep going,' replied the queen, with a shake of the head. 'But he's right, Bertie. What else can we do but Keep Buggering On?'

Meanwhile, in the skies above southern England, the Battle of Britain had begun. Vicious dogfights between the Luftwaffe and the Royal Air Force became part of everyday life. 'Hitler wants to destroy the RAF so he can invade,' said Lilibet. 'But he's chosen the wrong country!'

Her favourite plane was the Lancaster bomber. Margaret, meanwhile, became obsessed with Spitfires. 'Is it true,' she demanded, 'that they were named after someone's bad-tempered little daughter?' The king had told her this and she was obviously envious of the child concerned. She was determined to contribute to the Spitfire fund launched by Lord Beaverbrook, the Minister of Aircraft Production. Housewives were being asked for saucepans and kettles, zinc baths, anything that could be melted down to make an airplane.

'What have you got under your frock, Margaret?' the queen asked one lunchtime as her youngest daughter left the table, walking in a strangely careful fashion and clanking gently. After a determined but fruitless resistance, Margaret lifted her dress to reveal a quantity of silver cutlery pushed down the sides of her knickers.

'Wh-what – ?' began the king.

'The Spitfire Fund!' Lilibet squealed, pressing both hands to her mouth in delight. Margaret shot her a cross look. She did not enjoy having her thunder stolen.

'Margaret?' The queen spoke gently, but there was a definite twitch about the corners of her mouth.

The child fixed on her parents a pair of defiant violet eyes. 'A whole Spitfire costs five thousand pounds,' she announced.

'More like twelve and a half,' muttered the king, but he looked amused.

'But twenty-five hundred pounds would buy the fuselage and eighteen hundred pounds the wings, so this' – she held up two fistfuls of knives and forks – 'will buy some screws and rivets and maybe a roller blind for night flying. They cost seven and six,' she added, emphatically.

The summer went on. From attacking the Channel, the Luftwaffe came inland. Vapour trails and the rattle of gunfire became commonplace as German bombers with their guardian fighters struggled to get through the Spitfires and Hurricanes sent up to intercept them.

Both girls became experts in identifying, by shape, the planes that screamed and soared overhead. Sometimes aircraft flew so low that fuselage markings were visible. 'Ours!' the girls exclaimed in delight as a plane with the red, white and blue target came over. 'Theirs,' they would snarl in disgust at a swastika.

One sunny afternoon in September they heard a vague but ominous thrumming, growing louder. It was the sound of airplane engines. Lilibet stopped, one foot up the trunk of a tree. 'Listen.'

'Ours,' said Margaret confidently, from higher up in the branches. 'Going out on a bombing raid.'

Muffled, distant explosions followed. Lilibet gasped. 'Theirs. That's London.'

Dookie had grasped the situation before anybody. He hared off across the lawns and back into the castle. Scrambling down and racing after him, the girls and Marion found the dog in the nursery bathroom huddling behind the lavatory. He refused to come out, even when the air-raid bell rang. 'Come on,' Marion said, seizing the fat ginger body and yanking it out. 'Let's get to the shelters.'

Windsor's air-raid shelters had been set up in the castle dungeons. They were rudimentary: a few hasty and unfinished reinforcements and a few recently imported little beds for the girls. Around them, in the shadows, iron rings were set into solid stone and arched chambers ended in unfathomable darkness. The atmosphere seemed heavy, not just with damp, but with the terror of those who had, over the centuries, been imprisoned here.

Determined as ever to distract the girls, Marion handed out copies of *A Midsummer Night's Dream* and they all took parts. The Nazis were soon forgotten in the rude mechanicals' hilarious efforts to put on a play. They emerged to find that, in the direction of London, the sky was glowing red. 'Don't worry,' Margaret, with Dookie in her arms, valiantly assured him. 'We're going to beat the bloody hell out of those Germans.'

And so the Blitz began. The mournful sound of Wailing Willie, as the air-raid sirens were known, and the clatter of the ack-ack anti-aircraft guns became part of everyone's lives.

One night, Marion was woken by a loud bell; the wardens on the castle roof were sounding the alarm. Wriggling out of her nightdress she reached for her thick green velvet siren suit, grabbed her gas mask, and ran.

The way to the dungeons was through a trapdoor beyond the castle's vast kitchen. A steep staircase, much frequented by beetles and spiders, led down to the bowels of the earth. Hurrying down it, Marion would close her eyes.

In the shelter, Sir Hill Child was still in his dinner black tie. His gas mask box hung around his neck, slightly askew. He held a flashlight, and his distended shadow jerked ghoulishly over the rough stone walls. 'Where are Their Royal Highnesses?' Sir Hill demanded.

'With Alah,' Marion replied. During a night-time raid, Alah was in charge of bringing the princesses to the shelters.

Sir Hill groaned. 'Where is the woman? Didn't she hear the bell?'

'This is impossible.' Lord Wigram, Governor of the Castle, stepped forward. He too was in his black tie. 'This is a red warning, Miss Crawford. Bombing is expected. The princesses simply must come to the shelter *now*.'

Marion plunged out of the dungeon entrance and ran back up the passage, expecting, any minute, to encounter three hurrying figures, one big and two small, accompanied by nannyish admonitions to be careful and not slip. But no one materialised in the gloom.

Up and up the stone stairs, slippery with wet and ghastly with insects. Surely they were coming? Heart hurting with the effort, legs heavy in the thick green velvet, she clattered through dark stone chambers and shoved open foot-thick, iron-studded doors. The alarm bell screamed on.

Finally, the Lancaster Tower was reached. She stumbled up to the nurseries. As she approached she could hear high girlish voices, mixed with Alah's low rumble. They were all still here!

'Alah!' Marion was right outside the nursery door now. She rattled the handle. 'It's Crawfie! Lord Wigram and Sir Hill and everyone else are waiting in the shelter and you must come down. What are you *doing?*'

The door opened to reveal the tall figure of Alah, her uniform pristine, her cap slightly askew. She had evidently been in the process of pinning it precisely into place. Her gas mask was nowhere to be seen and her expression, when she saw Marion, was predictably outraged.

Lilibet's voice floated over. 'We're dressing, Crawfie,' she called. 'Alah says we must dress.'

Peering round the nanny's bulky side, Marion's incredulous eye caught the end of a frilly frock and a pair of white socks, laid out neatly on the bed. Something snapped within her. 'Come with me!' she yelled. 'Now!'

A minute later, the girls, coats over their nightdresses, holding their Mickey Mouse gas masks with the red rubber noses, hurried down the stone passages. Alah followed, grumbling, at a distance.

The shelter was fuller than before. Other residents of the castle had arrived. Sir Hill was a nervous wreck, while Lord Wigram was pacing up and down. Their relief, as the little party filed in, was palpable.

Soon afterward, Margaret was asleep on Marion's lap, while Lilibet lay calmly on one of the beds, reading. Sir Hill did *The Times* crossword in the lamplight while Lord Wigram sat close by absorbedly perusing a dahlia catalogue.

Gerald Kelly, in the shadows at the back, was chatting quietly. A slight clink of glassware, as of port bottle against cut crystal, occasionally emanated from his direction. Alah, as always, was knitting. She was making seaboot stockings for sailors, and seemed intent on supplying the entire Royal Navy.

There was, Marion thought, a strange peace to this wartime scene. It was convivial; even cosy. She shifted the warm weight of the sleeping child against her, and heard the occasional slide of paper as the absorbed Lilibet turned a page. She buried her nose in Margaret's soft hair, breathing in the soapy clean scent, and sent up a silent prayer that everyone would be safe, that they would all survive.

It was two in the morning before the all-clear sounded. Hideous though it was, it struck the ear like beautiful music. Sir Hill bowed ceremoniously to Lilibet. 'You may now go to bed, ma'am.'

Next morning, Lilibet was full of defiant fury. 'I want to join the army!'

'You already have,' Margaret pointed out. 'You're colonel-in-chief of the Grenadier Guards.'

Marion hid a smile. Lilibet had recently been elevated to the honour and took her inspection duties typically seriously. After one parade when she had, in her high-pitched voice, taken several soldiers to task about their boots, the commanding officer had drawn Marion aside. 'Miss Crawford. You might mention to Her Royal Highness that the first requisite of a really good officer is the ability to temper justice with mercy.'

Lilibet was as yet too young to join up properly, but the idea lingered in Marion's mind. Incarceration in Windsor seemed increasingly stifling. No one seemed to know – or if they did, they were not saying – how long the war would go on.

Her unsettled feelings were further rattled by the sudden arrival at the castle of Antoinette de Bellaigue, an elegant young aristocrat who had escaped from her homeland just before the German invasion. As usual, nothing was directly explained, but Marion gathered, in piecemeal, imprecise fashion, that it had been decided that her own command of French had reached its limits and lessons from a native speaker were required.

While it was a secret relief to hand this particular instruction over, the lack of consulation was hurtful. Even if, as Marion reminded herself, the king and queen had the defence of an entire nation to think about.

It wasn't long before 'Toni' was the name constantly on the princesses' lips. Margaret in particular was in ecstasies about Mademoiselle de Bellaigue's perfect clothes and shiny dark hair. She had escaped, Marion noted gloomly, with her French sense of style intact at least. And Toni, for her part, seemed instantly at home with the girls. 'Lilibet is *tres naturelle*,' she exclaimed to Marion in her charming accent. 'Such a sense of duty! And yet *quelle joie de vivre!*'

Soon came another unexpected innovation; drawing lessons in the company of Alathea Fitzalan-Howard, a child of the nobility slightly older than the girls who had moved to the Great Park for the duration of the war. Then Lilibet began learning to ride side-saddle. It was starting to seem to Marion as if all the efforts she had made to keep the girls in the real world now counted for nothing.

Even the Buckingham Palace Guides and Brownies, once so important, no longer seemed to interest them. Admittedly, the venture had not quite worked out as planned.

Success had seemed certain after the facing down of the formidable chief commissioner. The venue chosen for meetings was a little summer house in the palace gardens, where once George V had worked when the weather was fine. The desk had been just as he left it, pens and paper still in position. The girls and Marion had cleared it out themselves. At the inaugural meeting, dressed up in their new uniforms, they were beside themselves with excitement. The king, too, had taken a keen interest in their appearance. 'No black stockings,' he said. 'They remind me of my childhood. Let's have beige ones instead.' When Princess Mary came to officiate, he stood behind his sister, muttering things to try and make her laugh. It was a side of the king Marion hadn't glimpsed since the old days at Piccadilly.

The problem, an unforeseen one, were the other recruits; the daughters of court officials and friends of the family. At the first meeting, Lilibet turned in horror to Marion. 'Why have they all brought their nannies?' she hissed.

They had, all lined up behind and fussing over their charges. In the breezy, bright little summer house, they made a black gaggle of hats and dark coats.

'Some of them aren't even in uniform,' Margaret snarled. 'They're in party clothes!'

'Let's get started,' said Marion, picturing the whole thing fizzling out before it had even begun. She hadn't gone through Miss Violet Synge for that to happen.

They started with a game designed to break the ice. Everyone had to take off their shoes and put them in a heap in the centre of the floor. Then, at a signal, they would run for their shoes, put them on and return to their original place. The first to complete this exercise would be the winner.

'Go!' cried Marion as the girls all hurtled towards the heap. The happy anticipation drained from her face as it quickly became apparent, from the blank expressions, the puzzled rummaging and even, in some cases, the tears, that most of the Guides had no idea which shoes belonged to them. Or, even if they did, no idea how to put them on. Girls in party dresses were hopping on one half-shod foot to Nanny, dangling the other shoe in one hand.

The frustration Marion had felt had only increased since. The exclusive nature of the recruits had become, if anything, worse since the onset of war and the move to Windsor, where the pack was supplemented by the offspring of military top brass. The original idea, to mix the princesses with children from other backgrounds, seemed farther away than ever. Perhaps, now, it really was impossible. Perhaps she was fighting a losing battle.

So perhaps she should fight another one. The one everyone else was fighting. Plenty of young women like her were in the services. She had seen the posters in Windsor High Street. 'Join The Wrens! It is Far Better to Face the Bullets Than be Killed at Home by a Bomb!'

Marion agreed. She didn't seem to be needed by the family any more. And surely it was more important to defend freedom and democracy than show life outside the palace to two young princesses. So why not join up and do her bit? Fight for king and country? In her case, of course, she would have to leave the king to fight for the country. But she doubted that would be difficult. They would hardly miss her.

*

But as ever, when a truly big question presented itself, the queen proved elusive. And Windsor Castle was a vast place to look for someone; moreover, Her Majesty spent weekdays at Buckingham Palace. Marion took advantage of Toni's presence to hurry to Windsor and Eton station and board the mid-morning London train. It was full of servicemen, all cracking jokes and chaffing each other. Morale, despite everything, seemed to be high. Marion felt a swell of pride. Their Majesties had something to do with this.

The statue of Eros had gone from Piccadilly Circus. But it still seemed to be a popular place to meet; soldiers and their sweethearts milled cheerfully around.

She hurried down Piccadilly, noting the denuded shop displays. Fortnum's was making a brave effort, but was a shadow of its former luxurious self. How could it be otherwise when, as official posters everywhere declared, 'Extravagance in Wartime is Bad Form and Unpatriotic'?

She cut through Green Park. There were trenches where once there had been deckchairs, and much of it was planted with vegetables. Even here, people were Digging for Victory.

The palace loomed in front of her, grey front gleaming in the September sunshine. As Marion hurried towards it, something swelled in her ears. The thrumming drone of something huge and heavy.

She looked up. The plane was coming from the east. She could barely register its presence before it was up the Mall and above her, blocking out the sun, German markings clearly visible on its fuselage. There came then the roar of aircraft. As Marion herself hit the ground she heard the unmistakable screaming noise of a falling bomb, then a deafening explosion. Then, only horrible silence.

Marion lay, face pressed in the mud for a few seconds. She could not breathe. It had all happened so fast it was difficult to believe. She raised her head. People were gathering, talking in shocked tones. She scrambled to her feet and ran.

The palace frontage was mainly intact, except for the windows. Not a single one remained. Marion stared at them. The day was warm, but she felt cold all over. Despite all that had happened already, she wondered if she had really believed in the war until now.

She hurried through the anxious knots of people before the railings. 'Is His Majesty all right? The queen?' The policemen were doing their best to answer the questions, but Marion could see from their faces that they had no idea, and wondered the same thing.

'Sorry, miss, you can't go through there . . . oh, Miss Crawford, it's you. Carry on.'

It was with a sense of unreality that she carried on, picking her way over the broken glass in the forecourt. People had started to emerge, white with shock, some clinging to one another, but none, it seemed, actually injured.

Beyond the central arch, in the quadrangle, she could see piles of earth and thickly billowing black smoke. Heaps of broken stone surrounded a huge and gaping hole from which, it seemed, some monster had recently emerged. It was the other way round, of course; it was here that the monster had gone in, and here that the damage was worst.

She crept closer, her heels crunching on the debris. It was hard to see properly in the swirling smoke, but part of the left-hand side of the building seemed missing, torn away like the open front of a doll's house. Inside was wrecked magnificence: spars of gilded wood; torn, charred fabric; broken vases; smashed statues. A child-sized marble hand lay on the ground – some cherub's. Marion's eyes blurred; thank God the girls were at Windsor.

'Miss Crawford.'

Even in these dire circumstances, his voice held its tone of light irony. She could see, through the rags of smoke, that he looked as impeccable as ever. His cuffs were snowy, his glossy moustache immaculate, and even his bow tie was straight. She thought of the front of her suit, covered in the mud of Green Park.

'Mr Lascelles! How . . . how *are* you?'

'Well, it blew my bath out,' he said drily, 'but on the plus side it got rid of that excrescence to the left of my window.'

She remembered, uncomfortably, his window and tried to picture what had been to the left of it. 'You mean the swimming pool building?'

He inclined his head, not a single strand of thick, dark hair out of place. 'Precisely.'

She felt herself warming to him again. He was a strange man, but an admirable one. His *sangfroid* was extraordinary. And uniquely British, like his understatement. Emblematic of the national fighting spirit. She should follow his example.

She raised her chin. 'The king?' she asked. 'The queen?'

He raised his eyebrows. 'Ah.'

The fighting spirit was hard to maintain as she imagined them lying in the ruins, the queen's famous misty blue spattered with blood. 'Ah?'

Lascelles spoke into her panic. 'They are perfectly well.'

Though weak with relief, she tried to sound businesslike. 'I need to see Her Majesty. Do you know where she is?'

'You will find her in the garden with His Majesty. By the way, Miss Crawford,' Lascelles added lightly, as she unsteadily walked off.

She turned, glass grinding beneath her heel. 'Yes, Mr Lascelles?'

'Better not use the garden entrance. It no longer exists, as a matter of fact. My tip is to use one of the side doors.'

She stared at him. 'Thank you, Mr Lascelles.'

The glass in the door was shattered and the handle blown off. She had to tie her handkerchief round her hand to feel for the handle inside. The passage was full of thick, stinking smoke, the red carpet spattered with mud and dust. Marion glanced at it, remembering how the middle had once been reserved for members of the family only. It had been well and truly trodden on now.

In the distance, she could hear people coughing, and the shouting of the palace ARP wardens. She needed to find the queen before these notoriously officious personnel stopped her and sent her back.

A figure loomed. It wore pale clothing, and something tall and white on its head. Her heart contracted and for a second she wondered if she were seeing a freshly minted ghost. Then she realised the hat was a rather bent toque and this was the palace head chef.

'Monsieur.' Marion summoned up her best accent. It was a decent one, as even Toni acknowledged. '*Ça va?*' she asked, even though it was a ridiculous question.

The chef, whose whites were distinctly blackened, managed a nod. He was still clutching a wooden spoon. '*Ça va, mademoiselle,*' he said. '*Un petit quelque chose dans le coin, c'est tout. Un petit bruit.*'

A little something or other in the corner, that's all Marion translated to herself. *A little noise.*

Tears pricked her eyes. How brave. She had been wrong about Lascelles. The stiff upper lip was not confined to the British, nor was understatement. The French had courage too. She thought of Toni, not resentfully now, but sympathetically. Did her giggly manner disguise misery at the humiliation of her homeland?

She smiled at the chef and placed a hand across her breast.

'*Vive la France!*'

His head shot up. His shoulders went back. Even his toque looked straighter. '*Vive la France!*'

Lascelles was quite right; the garden entrance was now somewhere under a pile of debris. As the route onto the lawns was through a hole in a broken wall, there was no need to seek out a side door. Holding her breath so as not to inhale the thick dust, Marion made her way carefully through, glancing about constantly for falling masonry, timbers that might suddenly give way, a pane of glass that might decide to fall.

She went out to the lawn. If you did not look behind you, there was no indication that a bomb had just dropped. The grass stretched glossily away, the flower beds glowed with bright autumn colour: frothing blue and white hydrangeas; dahlias from fuchsia to rust; the occasional late rose in pink or apricot. The big, blousy trees were turning, with glints of gold, copper and red amid the green. A lazy bee buzzed past.

The air here was fresh and clear and Marion could finally breathe deeply. She wondered where the king and queen were. That they were out here at all seemed odd, considering what had just happened. They were surely not gardening. That would be taking the bulldog spirit a little too far.

She headed towards the lake, looking about her for a familiar smudge of misty blue. There was no sign of her employers, however.

They could be anywhere, and the palace gardens were huge. She decided to call for them. 'Ma'am? Sir?' Nothing.

Then, out of nowhere, the sharp crack of a single gunshot. It echoed in the air. A bird squawked and flew off. Then, silence again. From one of the nearby trees, two golden leaves detached and twirled gently down to the grass.

Marion realised both her hands were pressed hard against her mouth. They must have flown there instinctively, to stop a scream of terror. Her heart was hammering in her chest and she was shaking. She looked back towards the ruined palace; should she go there? Get help? But for what?

She pressed on in the direction from which the shot had come. Horrid imaginings crowded in, which she tried in vain to force away. The king and queen of England dead on the grass and a Nazi officer, in full uniform, standing over them. Anything, at this moment, seemed possible.

A great rhododendron bush reared up before her. She must be close to where the gun had been fired now. She forced herself forward, almost whimpering with fright.

'That's it, d-d-darling,' she heard the king say.

In her rush of relief, Marion ran round the corner to find, to her horror, the queen standing directly in front of her, pointing a gun straight at her heart.

'Crawfie!' There was a blast, and Marion dropped to the ground.

'Goodness, Crawfie,' said the queen. 'I almost shot you.'

'It was,' agreed the king, 'a d-d-damned c-c-close r-r-run thing.' The war had brought his stammer back with a vengeance.

Marion was sitting on a bench by the lake, her employers on either side of her, trying to absorb her own close encounter with mortality, and the news that the queen was taking shooting lessons. 'Just in case I meet Mr Hitler or one of his friends,' she said, turning her pearl-handled revolver in her hands.

'I w-wouldn't w-w-want to b-be him if you d-did,' said the king. 'You're a c-crack shot, Elizabeth.'

The queen looked pleased.

'I'm so sorry about the palace,' Marion offered.

The queen looked at her with cool blue eyes. 'Well, I'm glad. It means we can look the East End in the face.'

Her insouciance was reminiscent of Lascelles', and the bravery of the chef. It impressed on Marion that the home front was just as important as the fighting one, and just as brave. They were one and the same. You faced bullets and the bombs in both places. Perhaps she didn't need to join the Wrens after all. She felt glad, now, that she had not mentioned it to anyone. Perhaps she had said something to Toni, but that was hardly likely to go any further. Toni seemed largely uninterested in her.

The powerfully sweet song of a blackbird started up somewhere in the bush. 'Listen to that,' said the queen, smiling. 'We'll win this war. It'll be all right, you'll see. Blackbirds are never wrong.'

Marion swallowed. She felt the powerful urge to cry. The afternoon had been such a shock; a series of shocks.

The queen was looking at her, bright-eyed. 'Oh, Crawfie. We little guessed what was coming our way, did we?'

Her throat too full to speak, Marion twisted her head.

The queen patted her hand. 'The king and I are so fortunate in those who work for us. You especially. The king and I could not carry on if you weren't here.' Tears were now openly coursing down Marion's cheeks. How could she ever have thought of leaving? They also served who took charge of the children. And not just any children; the children of the country's leaders. Who couldn't carry on without her. They needed her after all. She felt a fierce, hot pride.

'Anyway, Crawfie.' The queen's blue gaze was roguish. 'Even if you did join the Wrens, you'd only be cooking some old admiral's breakfast.'

Chapter Forty-Nine

'Lessons in *constitutional history?*' Lilibet echoed in horror. 'But I wanted to learn how a gun works.'

It had been the king's idea. Marion was far from happy about it too, especially after the Toni business. Her French might be shaky but as was not history her best and favourite subject? Yet, again, the decision had been taken over her head and without any consultation. It was as if the interview with the queen in the garden had never been and she was back to square one.

Sir Henry Marten, vice provost of Eton College, was to be Lilibet's instructor in the mysteries of government and the monarchy. The school was close to the castle. They walked down the street towards the gates, Marion battling to overcome her resentment in order to reassure her apprehensive pupil.

They stood outside the porter's lodge. Groups of boys passed wearing top hats with dark coat-tails. They looked, Marion thought, like a convention of teenage undertakers.

Lilibet stared. 'Some of their hats are dusty,' she whispered. 'And some are polished and shiny.'

A long-faced man in a bowler hat appeared. 'This is Her Royal Highness the Princess Elizabeth,' Marion told him.

The porter seemed unimpressed. He stopped a passing boy. 'Douglas-'Ome. Visiters fer Sir 'Enry.'

'Visiters!' sniggered Lilibet, amused. Marion looked at her in surprise. She was considerably less afraid than expected.

Douglas-Home's topper was one of the shiny ones. He removed it politely, exposing a sleek side-parted head that sent Marion's thoughts flying back to her own Eton crop. How long ago that seemed now!

Douglas-Home set off rapidly on his long pinstriped legs. They hurried after him over a large cobbled courtyard. Surrounding it on all sides were low, mellow buildings with mullioned windows and castellated rooflines. A clock tower with turrets formed the centre-piece and to the right rose the side of the famous college chapel. Marion took in the height of its windows, its delicate spires and carvings, its grace and ambition, its astonishing age.

'What a pretty chapel,' she remarked to the unforthcoming boy.

Douglas-Home shrugged his frock-coated shoulders. 'You don't really notice it after a while.'

'Is Sir Henry a nice teacher?' Marion persevered.

She received a scornful look. 'At Eton we call them beaks.'

'Beaks?' Lilibet giggled. 'How funny.'

In the medieval enclave, among the top hats and accreted jargon, it was easy to forget there was a war on. And yet now came a roaring in the skies. The crowd of boys looked up. 'Junkers 87,' shouted one, boisterously.

'Junkers *88*,' Lilibet corrected in her clear tones. 'It's got two engines, look.'

Sir Henry's study was empty – of Sir Henry, that was. Otherwise it was crammed, especially with books. They were everywhere, spilling from shelves, rising from tables, stacked on the floor like stalagmites.

'Do you think he's read them all?' Lilibet was staring at the jumble of volumes next to her. They had titles like *The Law and Custom of the Constitution* by William Anson, *English Social History* by G. M. Trevelyan and *Imperial Commonwealth* by Lord Elton.

Marion tapped the fat spine of *The Groundwork of British History* by Sir Henry Marten. 'I expect he's read this one.'

Douglas-Home bowed deeply to Lilibet and gave a cursory nod to Marion. He knew exactly who they were after all. He clattered off down the stone steps.

Another door opened and in came a short, round-faced man with something dark and glossy hunched on his shoulder. It took a couple of beats for Marion to realise what it was. Lilibet got there first. 'A raven!' she exclaimed. 'Is that why you're called beaks?'

Sir Henry looked surprised. 'Perhaps,' he said. 'As a matter of fact, no one's ever asked me that before.'

'Princess Elizabeth,' Marion smiled, 'has a very original turn of mind. She is a delightful pupil to teach.'

Sir Henry didn't seem to hear her. Perhaps he was a little deaf. She rummaged in her handbag for the notes she had prepared about Lilibet's progress so far. She approached Sir Henry, holding them out.

The raven, which had hopped on top of a lampshade on the chaotic desk, cocked its head to stare at her.

'Shall we begin, gentlemen?' Sir Henry asked Lilibet. He had even looked at Marion, standing there with her papers in her hand.

'Gentlemen!' giggled Lilibet. 'I'm a girl, Sir Henry.'

'But a very special girl,' Marion put in swiftly, before she could stop herself. The words seemed to hang in the room. She reddened. She sounded, she realised, just like Alah, when she had first arrived at Royal Lodge.

Sir Henry did not seem to hear her anyway. 'Do you know what a palimpsest is?' he went on, addressing Lilibet.

'Is it like a pimple?'

'It's a parchment that's been written and overwritten on many times. That, in a nutshell, is the British constitution.'

The lesson had started, Marion realised in surprise, and without involving or consulting her in any way. It was as if she didn't exist. Dismayed, disbelieving, she cleared her throat in what she hoped was an assertive fashion.

A pair of pleasant, mild eyes turned towards her, and seemed to see her for the first time. 'Oh. Miss . . . er?'

'Crawford. Marion Crawford. I'm the princess's governess. I've been teaching her for several years and – '

'Like something to read?' Sir Henry interrupted. He rose to his feet, revealing the fact he still had bicycle clips on. He went to his desk, picked something up and passed it to her. 'His latest, I believe.'

Marion stared at the cover of *Uncle Fred in the Springtime*. With careful fury, she put the book down. Unobserved by Sir Henry or his pupil, she headed for the door. As she left, the raven made a cawing sound, as if it was mocking her.

Outside, in the courtyard, next to the magnificent medieval chapel you ceased to notice after a while, Marion walked angrily to and fro, glaring at the cobbles. She felt insulted and patronised.

'Marion? Is it really you?'

'Peter!'

Under a tasselled mortar board, within the folds of a black gown, there he was. He was older now – still slight, but more impressive, somehow. He seemed to have gained an air of authority.

So this was the school in the south he had gone to. The one his sights had been set on, right from the start. 'You got here at last!' she crowed.

'I wouldn't take it too seriously,' Peter counselled, after hearing her account. 'Sir Henry's not a bad chap really.'

They were in his rooms, which were small but meticulously clean. Books lined the walls and two battered leather chairs stood on either side of a small fireplace. There was a rich smell of wax polish in the air, and the diamond-pane windows sparkled. The view they offered was of the wide cobbled courtyard and of knots of boys, hands in pockets, slouching across it. 'They're a good lot,' Peter said, noticing her cross expression. 'And a joy to teach, some of them.'

'Sir Henry treated me like a servant,' she complained. 'A rather dim one, at that.'

Peter smiled. 'He comes from a generation when women were either servants or wives. He's probably never met a female teacher before, let alone a young one.'

'Or a female pupil. He called Lilibet "gentlemen".'

Peter shook his head indulgently. 'Strictly speaking, he's not really part of the twentieth century.'

'Is anything, in this place?' Marion took another bite of bun. All the sugar was having a calming effect.

'Possibly not,' Peter admitted. 'But given how the twentieth century's turning out, I'm not sure that's a bad thing.'

He had already explained that he had been deemed unfit for active service. 'It's dreadful, though, seeing the older boys joining up. Who knows if they'll ever come back.'

They talked on. He was sad to hear about her mother. 'Such a good woman. And so proud of you.'

Marion nodded. She tried not to dwell on what her mother would have thought of the humiliating scene with Sir Henry.

'Will you stay with them?' Peter asked. 'If you don't mind me saying, it sounds a little frustrating.'

She looked at him indignantly. 'It's an important job, Peter. She's the daughter of the head of state and this is war.'

He toyed with a teaspoon. She sensed he was trying to decide whether to say something. Eventually, he raised his head. His tone was gentle, puzzled. 'It's just not what I imagined you doing. You were always so passionate about the slums, about the education of the poor.'

I still am leaped onto her tongue. It did not leap off, though. She urged it to, but it would not.

Peter stirred his tea, smiling a little. 'You used to make me feel so terrible, wanting to work at a public school. All those speeches you used to make about equal educational opportunities.'

Those speeches felt far away to Marion. They seemed to press down on her now, rather than lift her up.

'Still not married?' Peter enquired next. She felt exasperated. He seemed to be going out of his way to ask the most uncomfortable questions.

'No. I'm married to my job now,' she assured him, brightly. 'Like you.'

He raised his eyebrows. 'I've been having second thoughts about that, actually. Time's moving on, and I'd quite like some children of my own.'

As his pale eyes lingered on her, she looked away. 'Surely there are some smart rich widows at your school?' It was a joke, but admittedly not a very good one. There was irritation on Peter's good-tempered face.

'It's not *Decline and Fall*, Marion.' He was referring to the Waugh novel, which she had recently read, about a hapless master at a hopeless public school.

She blushed. 'Of course not. I didn't mean – '

He cut in. 'I don't want to marry Lady Tangent, or whatever her name was. As you suggest, I see quite a lot of them. My idea of a wife is someone completely normal, with her feet firmly on the ground.'

She left soon after that. The farewells were awkward. 'It was wonderful to see you, Marion,' Peter said, not entirely convincingly. 'Come whenever you like.'

To her relief, the lesson was still going on. She could hear the vice provost's distinctive tones as she hurried up the stairs. 'The sovereign has to sign all laws passed by Parliament.'

'But what if they don't want to?' Lilibet's voice was clear and high.

'The concept of a veto is unthinkable, but the possibility remains.'

'Sir Henry, it seems to me that being a monarch is more about what one doesn't do, than what one actually does.'

'I think, ma'am, if I may use the phrase, that you have hit the nail on the head.'

Chapter Fifty

For fifty-seven consecutive nights now, the Heinkel bombers had pounded London. Thousands were dead. The East End lay in ruins. Now the Luftwaffe were extending their campaign to other cities and ports. There were great crashes in the sky and explosions even shook the chalk hill on which the castle stood. One night, stepping shiveringly outside to her bathroom, Marion caught sight of two unmistakable figures on an adjacent roof. They stood together, the man with his arm around the woman, both their faces turned towards the red glow in the east where the capital burned. The woman raised a hand to her face, as if brushing away tears. It was a rare view of the indomitable queen in despair.

Margaret's initial enthusiasm for the war had turned into boredom. 'You know,' she said glumly one breakfast time, 'I can hardly remember when there wasn't a war.'

Marion knew what she meant. It was hard to recall a time when food wasn't scarce, when night didn't drop like a thick black blanket and when one wasn't constantly awaiting the dreaded drone of the bombers. But plenty of people had it much worse than they did at Windsor Castle.

Not Margaret though, in her own estimation at least. She was ten now, and restless. Being confined in one place was taking its toll, as was the unchanging social scene.

'Lilibet gets to go out to a boys' school,' she complained. 'Why can't I?'

'Because I'm older than you,' her sister explained. 'I'm fourteen.'

Margaret pushed out her lower lip. 'It's not *fair.* What about *me?* What fun do *I* have?'

'It's not fun,' Lilibet rather piously pointed out. 'I'm learning about constitutional history.'

'Because you'll be queen one day, I suppose,' fumed Margaret. 'But what about me? What will I do?'

In the short term, she set about making a nuisance of herself. Fir cones were put into wellington boots and sticky sweets into coat pockets. The gardener, briefly turning his back, would find his broom had been stolen. Things came to a head when someone – it was never quite established who – pressed the castle alarm bell, obliging all the inhabitants to evacuate. Fortunately the king and queen were in London, but that something had to be done about Margaret was obvious.

Marion pondered on the problem as she walked into Windsor town. Her way led her past St George's Chapel, whose stained-glass windows had been taped and boarded and much of whose statuary had been removed for safekeeping. But there was still no disguising the exuberance of the springing buttresses, the beauty of the carving and the soaring confidence of the gold-topped pinnacles. A blackbird sang from the top of one of them and Marion remembered what the queen had said. *It will be all right. Blackbirds are never wrong.*

She walked on, out of the Henry VIII gate and down the cobbled drive, past the statue of Queen Victoria, who had known wars, but never one like this. Marion paused to examine her, plump and proud with her orb and sceptre. She, too, seemed to radiate an indefatigable confidence.

On the town's meandering main street, the ancient walls of the castle showed between rustling, richly coloured trees. The low autumn sun picked out decorative details in the quirky old buildings. Low-beamed pubs smelling of leather, beer and tobacco jostled for space alongside shops with bow fronts and bull's-eye glass. The clip-clop of hooves could be heard, as they had been for centuries. Only the tape across some windows and the occasional sandbag hinted that a world war was raging.

She paused outside the toy shop. Margaret claimed to be too old for toys now, and these had a decidedly military tone anyway. The toy howitzer that fired lead shells at three ranges might interest Lilibet, but not her sister. But Margaret was still a Spitfire fan and might appreciate the scale model Hawker Hurricane. Even Snakes and Ladders had had a wartime makeover, Marion saw. It was now being marketed as ARP, a Blitz-themed take on the old favourite. There was also an Evacuee card game, where children were matched with appropriate families.

Marion looked at the card game. Something about it resonated with her. There were many evacuees in the Windsor area, children whom the Luftwaffe had driven to the relative safety of the countryside. Many were from the London slums; relatives, in terms of situation, of the Grassmarket children she had once known and whom she had once been determined to help. A faint echo of her old zeal came back to her. She remembered Peter's words, in his Eton study. *You were always so passionate about the slums, about the education of the poor.*

But that was then, she told herself. As she had told Peter, these days she had another crucial job. She was safeguarding the children of the king and queen as they rallied the nation in its darkest hour. What could be more important?

As she stared into the shop window she had noticed, in its reflection, a woman walking to and fro behind her, glancing at her curiously. Now she stopped and spoke. Her tone was cockney, and disbelieving. 'Maz? It is you, ain't it?'

Marion whirled round. Under the bright autumn sun the sharp little face looked much older. The dark hair had streaks of grey. But there was no doubt who it was.

'Ivy!'

A pair of slight, yet strong arms gripped her. 'You're skin and bone, girl!' Ivy exclaimed.

'And you're just bone!' Beneath her dark frock, Ivy hardly existed.

'What are you doing here?' Ivy glanced at the castle behind them. Her smile wavered. 'Maz! You're *surely* not still workin' for the royals?'

'Well . . . yes. Yes.' She smiled into her friend's astonished face. 'And what are you doing here?'

'On 'oliday.' Ivy glanced upward. 'Courtesy of a Mr Goering.'

'You've been evacuated?' Marion looked at the playing cards. How strange. No wonder she had felt something. They were a premonition.

'With me school. We're 'avin' a right old time of it, I can tell yer. Sheltering from the Blitz in the Underground. People were even sleeping on the bleedin' escalators.'

But only one word had resonated with Marion. 'Your *school*?'

'Teaching, ain't I? That's right,' Ivy added, laughing at Marion's dumbstruck expression. 'I took a leaf out o' your book, Maz. I went to college once I'd left. The first in our family to get an ology,' Ivy added, proudly.

'Ology?' Marion was still reeling at the news.

'Qualification!'

She had recovered slightly now. 'That's amazing, Ivy! Congratulations! Got time for a cup of tea?'

'Always got time for one o' them.'

In the nearest café, Ivy tore into a Bath bun in a way that reminded Marion that not everyone, like her, benefited from the royal farms and dairies. War or no war there was milk, cream and butter, which made living on rations a good deal easier.

'Funny, ain't it,' Ivy said. 'I escaped the royals and trained as a teacher. You did the opposite, Maz.'

Marion put her cup down. The joy of reunion had dimmed a little. Tact had never been Ivy's strongest point. 'Not at all,' she said brightly.

But Ivy, hand on her chin, was surveying her with sharp eyes. 'You don't have to pretend with me, Maz. I've been there. I know what it's like. Bleedin' medieval. Like the twentieth century don't exist.'

The implication that Ivy had swapped an old-fashioned institution for a modern career while she had done the opposite stung. As in Peter's study, she felt defensive.

'As it happens,' Marion said, with some heat, 'I've done a lot to take the girls out into the world and show them how people live.'

Ivy was staring at her. 'Blimey, Maz, calm down. I'm only teasing.

You used to think it was all hilarious, remember? That time I told you about Balmoral?'

Marion's smile was forced. It had been a long time since anything about Balmoral had seemed odd, so used to it had she grown. These days she was almost fond of it. She decided to change the subject. 'How's Alf, anyway? He had a business as a fruit-seller, is that right?'

To her horror, Ivy's eyes filled up. 'Not any more.'

'He's not . . . ?'

But Ivy was nodding, hard. 'In a Lancaster bomber.'

Lilibet's favourite plane, Marion thought.

'He wanted to be a pilot but there were more vacancies for rear gunners.' Ivy paused. 'I should have realised why but I didn't. They don't last more than six missions, and if they're shot at they have a life expectancy of twenty-two seconds. So it were quick, at least.'

On a sudden impulse, Marion reached over the chequered table-cloth for her hand. 'I know what it's like,' she said gently. 'It happened to me, too.'

She felt disingenuous. But as a device, a distraction, it had worked. Ivy's face, formerly accusing, was full of sympathetic horror. 'Oh, Maz! I had no idea! And there was me, thinking you'd given up men for that lot. Sacrificed everything.'

Marion looked down. Why on earth had she said that? She felt ashamed, but it was too late to retract it now. She hoped Ivy would not probe further. Revealing that she had split with Valentine long before his death and he had been with someone else anyway hardly compared to what Ivy had suffered.

Ivy delicately moved on, however. 'And now I've just got my schoolkids.'

Unable to stop herself, Marion nodded her bent head. 'Me too.'

'Alf and me, we never had any of our own. We didn't 'ave time.' A tear brimmed. She blinked hard. 'I guess you didn't either.'

The bent head shook.

Ivy sniffed. 'Still, no use cryin' over spilled milk.'

'No.' Marion raised her head. 'What's your school like, Ivy?'

The sharp black eyes rolled. 'An effing nightmare, if you'll pardon my French. We're using a church as a classroom but the vicar's very sniffy about it and it's almost too dark to see. No running water or lavs, just buckets. The children kneel on the floor and use the pews as desks. There aren't enough pencils or paper. They 'ave to take turns to write things down. All the age groups are together.' Ivy shook her head at the impossibility of it all and took a fortifying swig of tea.

Marion half-wondered if there were any empty properties on the Windsor estate. There were lots of buildings about. Perhaps she could ask. It would feel like recompense. While she had not quite deceived Ivy, she had misled her.

'But I'd rather 'ave that,' Ivy continued, 'than be walled up at Windsor. Must be a bleedin' nightmare. Them girls must be bored out o' their 'eads.'

'They are, a bit,' Marion admitted, thinking of Margaret and that it would be politic to admit something. Ivy knew too much, after all.

'We should get them together,' Ivy joked. 'Princesses and evacuees. An eye-opener for both of them.'

Marion was about to laugh, when the smile faded from her face. Had not Ivy hit on something here?

Peter's voice came back to her. *You were always so passionate about the slums, about the education of the poor.*

And here was an opportunity to show her commitment to the poor, as well as to bring the princesses together with a new range of companions. Ordinary children, as Marion had originally intended.

'We definitely should,' she said.

Chapter Fifty-One

It was a little white-painted cottage, near the lake at Frogmore. The princesses hung back as they approached it. 'Come on,' Marion urged them. 'They won't eat you, you know. They're children, just like you.'

'Not *quite* like us,' Margaret said in her most princessy voice. And indeed, in their matching blue coats, berets and pristine white socks, there seemed little to link the king's children with those of some of his poorest subjects. 'Alah says they sleep on chairs.'

'Yes, but not because they want to.' She knew from Ivy that a number of the evacuees from the poorest homes, with insufficient beds, had had to be taught to lie down.

Ivy had been delighted at the king's generous offer of the cottage by the lake. He, for his part, had been relaxed at the idea of his daughters mixing with evacuees. The new egalitarianism of war extended even to royal circles. When visiting troops, the king had made a point of seeking out the lowliest ranks, not just their superiors. His equerries, to Tommy's horror, were no longer aristocrats exclusively.

While not purpose-built as a school, the building had enough space and light to work as one. Moreover it had a lavatory and running water and lacked a disapproving vicar. Plenty of desks and chairs had been found, although writing materials remained a problem; the Royal Household was as rationed as any other, and more than most, given the king's zeal in enforcing the rules.

'You must put them at ease,' Marion told the girls as they approached the worn little front door. 'They're away from their families and a lot of them have had their homes bombed.'

Ivy opened the door and smiled broadly at the girls. 'Come in, come in.' They passed her haughtily and Ivy looked put out.

'Didn't I curtsey deep enough? I'm a bit out of practice. Wasn't much call for it in Bermondsey.'

'They're just nervous,' Marion muttered, more crossly than she meant.

Ivy looked at her, eyebrows raised.

'Good morning, Your Royal Highnesses,' chorused the class as the girls entered. They may have sounded respectful, but the forty or more East End eyes now seizing on Margaret and Lilibet had a distinctly irreverent gleam. Lilibet cast Marion a rather desperate look.

Ivy, whom neither girl seemed to recognise as a former royal servant, hastily began making introductions. 'This is Reg,' she said, indicating a freckled boy of about thirteen whose hair stuck up in all directions, despite obvious efforts to plaster it down. He had long green eyes and a pointed chin and looked like a naughty pixie.

Reg stood up and stuck out his hand to Lilibet. ''Ow d'ye do mam-as-in-spam-not-marm-as-in-smarm.'

'What?' asked Lilibet, while Margaret giggled.

Reg looked from Lilibet to Ivy indignantly. 'That's what you said I was to call 'er, Miss. Mam-as-in-spam-not-marm-as-in-smarm.'

'Yes, but not the whole thing, Reg,' exclaimed Ivy, while the rest of the class cackled behind their hands and nudged each other. 'Just the first word. Ma'am.'

The laughter got louder and more abandoned. Reg, having been offended, became delighted. As official breaker of the ice he was the hero of the hour. Margaret settled next to him. 'What's it like to be bombed?' she asked.

Marion gasped at such tactlessness, but Reg was keen to explain. 'Well it's not very nice to 'ave bricks fall on you,' he began. 'But it's quite exciting. First there's 'ordes and 'ordes of 'Einkels coming over. Like great 'orrible black beetles, all protected by their fighters. With our fighters trying to get between them and shoot 'em down. *Ratatatatat. Ratatatatatat!*' He made some startlingly lifelike machine-gun noises.

'How do you do that?' Margaret asked.

"S easy. Just press your tongue against your teeth. Like this. *Ratatatatatat!*'

Lilibet, meanwhile, had gone to the back. Ivy followed her. 'This is Susan,' she said, of a redheaded girl about the princess's age. The two of them looked at each other uncomfortably.

'How are you enjoying the countryside?' Lilibet asked stiffly.

'Quiet, ain't it?' said Susan.

'I suppose it is, rather.'

Susan suddenly grinned, widely. 'Never mind though, eh. It's near Slough and that's where the Mars Bar factory is. They're rationed at 'ome.'

The boy in front of her turned. 'Everything's bloomin' rationed,' he pronounced gloomily, then grinned. 'Includin' soap!'

In the front, Reg continued to hold Margaret spellbound with bombing stories. 'I had me shoes and socks on in bed,' he announced, of the direct hit on his house. This to him was obviously the great drama of the occasion. 'I was blown from one side of me room to me brother's bed opposite. Then I ran to the shelter with me mum 'olding a dustbin lid over me 'ead.'

Margaret's eyes were wide. 'What's a dustbin lid?'

Marion and Ivy looked at each other, eyebrows raised.

Several rows behind, Lilibet and Susan had found common ground in animals. 'I 'ad a kitten,' the girl said sadly. 'A little stray black one. Ever so sweet, 'e was. I called 'im Winston, after the prime minister. Don't know where 'e is now, though. 'E got blowed up, I reckon.'

Lilibet's eyes filled with tears. She could not bear anything bad to happen to animals. 'That's so awful. You must come and see my dogs. They're adorable.'

'Not quite the description I'd use,' muttered Ivy, glancing at her ankles. 'I've still got the scars.'

'Dookie's much better behaved these days,' Marion heard herself saying.

Ivy stared at her for a second, as if about to say something. She seemed to bite it back, and looked around. 'All we need now is a few textbooks and something to write with. Are you sure 'Is Majesty doesn't have a few spare pencils?'

Marion nodded. 'I've asked, I promise you. But everything's needed for the Household, apparently.'

Ivy knitted her brows. 'There must be somewhere we can get them. Someone you could ask?'

Marion was about to shake her head when Peter slid into it. Eton seemed to have a super abundance of everything. She felt again the need to compensate Ivy for something. Surely the most privileged school in the country could provide some materials for one of its most deprived?

'But it might be awkward,' she warned, having explained the plan. She could not imagine how Peter would react to such a request, or even how she would request it.

'Not as awkward as snapping pencils in half and tearing paper into bits to go round!'

The impressive pillared gates of Eton loomed up before them. Marion hastened to get in front of Ivy. 'You can't just walk in. Let me handle it.'

Ivy walked in anyway. She stared round the quadrangle, with its magnificent chapel and the lovely, mellow buildings in which future leaders were educated. 'Blimey,' she said. 'Good job I smartened meself up.'

Ivy had done more than smarten herself up, Marion thought. Her best suit, snugly fitting, made her frame look both curvy and delicate. Lavishly applied mascara and bright red lipstick gave her pale, sharp face the smouldering air of a Spanish señorita. On her narrow shoulders, her black hair shone and curled.

'Marion! What are you doing here? It's not your day, is it?' Peter, with impeccable timing, emerged from the porter's lodge. He looked, in the golden evening sunshine, both youthful and smart in a well-cut suit instead of his usual black and flapping gown.

'We were just passing,' Marion began, uncertainly.

'We want you to 'elp us,' stated Ivy, in her throaty cockney.

344

'Perhaps we could have tea,' Marion added. But she could see Peter was not listening. He was staring at Ivy like someone on whom a great and glorious truth had dawned.

'Yes,' he said, in a slightly mesmerised voice. 'Absolutely. Of course. Won't you both come this way?'

Ivy got her materials. The writing paper was edged in purple and stamped with the school's distinctive coat of arms, lilies on a shield with 'FLOREAT ETONA' underneath. 'Christ only knows what their parents will think,' she said, handing it out so the children could finally write letters home.

Lilibet and Margaret, now keen visitors to the school by the lake, volunteered to help with the correspondence, supplying sentences to describe the strange new rural sights.

Apples grow on trees, Mum, wrote Susan. *Not in boxes in shops. Just fancy!*

PS I have not been hit by a bomb yet! wrote Reg. *PPS I have not been gassed yet! PPPS I have not come into contact with an air gun yet!*

Margaret helped address the envelopes, with more enthusiasm than tact. *Reg's Mum,* she wrote on one. *The Slums, London.* Marion whisked it away before Reg could see.

Ivy also got a new member of staff. Peter volunteered to spend his lunchtimes teaching classics at the school by the lake. The children, suspicious at first, quickly grew fond of him. 'Of arms and the man I sing!' Reg would roar when the familiar conical head with its wispy suggestion of fair hair could be glimpsed through the classroom window. Peter, for his part, regarded Reg as potential scholarship material. 'His brain is like lightning,' he told Ivy, who looked delighted.

Marion had noticed that Ivy was looking delighted quite a lot lately, as was Peter. She felt a stir of envy. Love had gone from her life but left its shape behind. Thank goodness she had two little girls, one in particular, to fill it. They were everything to her now.

Chapter Fifty-Two

One afternoon, Marion and the princesses accompanied their parents into the East End. Cheering cockneys waving Union Jacks stood on smashed pavements scattered with broken glass. Behind them rose battered heaps of bricks that had once been houses. Huge holes gaped in the earth and hideous burned-out shells of buildings stood like blackened and broken teeth. Blasted heaps of rubble were topped with smashed pieces of furniture, broken pub signs, and children, combing them for treasure.

The girls were pale with shock. But the queen had given them strict instructions not to stop smiling under any circumstances. It was, she said, crucial for morale. Obediently, Margaret and Lilibet managed shaky beams through the car's plate-glass window.

They watched from the car as, surrounded on all sides by people eager to have a brief ray of royal sunshine in their broken lives and hearts, the king and queen clambered about the wreckage. 'Thank God for a good king!' shouted one man.

The king smiled and touched his gold-braided cap brim. 'Thank God for a good people.'

Marion's eyes were so full of tears she could hardly see. Beside her, Margaret giggled suddenly. 'Did you hear what that lady said?' She pointed at a bent and ancient woman, talking to the queen over what remained of her gate. Her house lay in ruins behind her.

'No, what?' asked Lilibet.

Margaret assumed her best cockney accent. 'We're not going to get beat by that there 'itler!'

*

The likelihood, admittedly, had receded slightly. After fifteen months of solitary fighting, Britain was no longer alone. The long-sought help from the New World had finally come.

Nineteen forty-two had been a terrible year. At times it had seemed nothing but defeats, with the U-boats destroying the Arctic convoys, Stalingrad under siege and the sickening truth about Hitler's Polish death camps slowly emerging, like blood under a door. Closer to home, the death of the Duke of Kent in an air crash had been a body blow to the royal family. The king and queen had been devastated, and Princess Marina, now left to bring up three children alone, was almost crazed with grief. A long, sad way, Marion thought, from that triumphant girl in the abbey, sailing up the aisle in Norman's gown.

But following the Japanese bombing of Pearl Harbour, Hawaii, where the US Pacific Fleet was at anchor, the United States was now in the war, 'up to the neck and to the death', as Margaret put it, with bloodthirsty relish. 'Got any gum, chum?' she kept asking Lilibet.

'What?'

'Got any gum, chum. It's how you're supposed to greet an American,' Margaret spoke with great authority.

The newly arrived GIs, part of Roosevelt's 'Europe First' strategy, sent electric excitement through princesses and evacuees alike. Reg, predictably, positively haunted the nearby camp, making friends with the Snowflakes, as the white-helmeted military police were called. They would send him on errands, for which he was paid in the only currency that mattered. Whenever Margaret and Lilibet visited, he would proudly display his haul of chocolate Hershey bars, Baby Ruths and Life Savers as well as the 'funnies', American comics featuring Superman, Captain Marvel, Looney Tunes and Bugs Bunny.

'Let me have that!' Margaret would insist, imperiously snatching Bugs Bunny.

'Oi!' Reg would reply, snatching it back. From time to time the two of them would disappear and return with a suspicious odour hanging about them.

Ivy would eye the irrepressible boy. 'You wouldn't happen to have any cigarettes about you, would you, Reg?'

'Why d'you ask, Miss?' came the cheeky reply. 'You want one?'

Susan's interest in the Americans was of a different order. 'Overpaid, oversexed and over 'ere,' she giggled to Lilibet.

'What?'

There was an elder girl evacuee living in Susan's house who had found her way onto the 'passion wagon' that took girls from the town centre out to the American base for dances. Susan conveyed, wide-eyed, her second-hand account of the splendour of the dance hall. 'It's hung with Stars and Stripes and Union Jacks together! The music's wonderful.' She began to hum 'Moonlight Serenade'. 'And they know all the new dances.' She taught Lilibet the jitterbug and styled her hair into a roll.

Marion watched all this and wondered why she didn't feel more pleased about it. Combining princesses with East Enders should have been the culmination of all her ambitions. Instead, she found herself wishing that she had not introduced them.

She had not anticipated how sharing the girls with other people would make her feel. It was much harder than expected. She had become accustomed to being their constant companion, their all in all. Others came and went – Toni, Sir Henry, the king and queen, needed in London most days. Even Alah presided over what was mostly hours of sleep. But she, Marion, ordered their days.

Their near-prison conditions, with the ever-present dangers, had brought an added intensity to things. She had relished the girls' dependence on her, and by extension the dependence of their parents. The feeling that, in some way, the fate of the nation depended on her had been powerfully seductive. But more seductive and powerful even than that was the idea that the girls were, to all intents and purposes, her daughters; she their mother.

And now she had surrendered that power.

Months had passed since she had seen Tommy Lascelles. As private secretary to the king, he was based at Buckingham Palace. Their paths, these days, rarely crossed. Yet here he was, all of a sudden, striding towards her under a late-autumn sun in Windsor's cobbled courtyard. He greeted her cheerily. 'Miss Crawford! Marion, if I may.'

'You may,' Marion said shortly. She was determined not to waste any time on him. He still made something jump within her, but nothing would ever come of it.

She could not help noticing, even so, that he was as attractive as ever. War had made little impact on his looks, but they had been austere to start with. His hair was still thick and black and his figure tall, spare and elegant. From beneath the recesses of his brow, he fixed her with his wry gaze. She felt the familiar surge of longing, and glanced away.

'So how are you finding Windsor? Still sheltering from the Heinkels in the dungeons?'

The sardonic nod she gave him in return did not reveal how fundamental even this had become. It was crazy, she knew, to almost relish air raids, but she had grown to derive enjoyment from the intimate darkness of the old prisons, the closeness of the young girls and the triumphant knowledge that she, not their parents, was protecting them in this time of mortal danger. She kept her tone matter-of-fact. 'It's hard to imagine it being any other way.'

He shot her a dark gleam of a look. 'Oh, it will be. It's no longer whether or when we shall beat them, but how we shall dispose of them once they are beaten. America is with us now, don't forget. Everything has changed.'

He began to talk about the forthcoming visit of Eleanor Roosevelt. 'The Lord Mayor of London's being rather difficult. Insists on meeting Mrs Roosevelt on the steps of St Paul's.'

'What's wrong with that?'

Tommy's expression was one of mild exasperation. 'Because the main object of her coming is to take home to the USA the impression that we are devoting ourselves exclusively to the defeat of Hitler. For her visit to begin with a piece of medieval ceremony would be unfortunate.'

He had a point, she thought admiringly. 'You think of everything.'

'It's my job.' He looked at her intently. She glanced away. She had made a fool of herself twice, but it would not happen a third time. 'Your job too,' he said. 'No one else understands.'

'Understands what?' She battled to resist, but there was a dark fire in his eyes that mesmerised her.

'What we do. You and I.'

She swallowed. 'You and I?'

'How they need us, the king and queen, and no one outside possibly could understand what that is like. How intense it is, how it never switches off, how it requires absolute commitment. No one knows, apart from us two.'

She looked down, overwhelmed with the truth of what he had said and how passionately she agreed. He was right. No one else understood. Ivy certainly didn't; Peter didn't; perhaps even the king and queen themselves didn't. And if the princesses didn't either – and how could they, at their age? – she could forgive them that. It was all for them anyway.

Tommy's voice was gentle. 'Shall we sit down?'

They found a bench in the garden against a sun-warmed tower wall. The sweet scent of late roses ebbed about them and they gazed upon the green and rolling Berkshire landscape. 'Glorious, isn't it?' Tommy murmured, but his gaze was fixed on her.

The world around slowed and went silent. *No one outside. Us two.* He was leaning towards her, breathing rapidly. His peppery cologne filled her nostrils. He was, she realised, about to kiss her. Finally.

She closed her eyes. Nothing happened. She heard him shift in his seat and clear his throat. He had moved away, she sensed.

'I'm reading a most interesting book,' he said, lightly. 'The collected letters of one Ponsonby, a former private secretary to Queen Victoria.'

Marion stared out at the landscape, only half listening, face entirely burning. Had she imagined it, yet again?

'Queen Mary objected to its publication very strongly. But surely, if those behind the scenes were never to put pen to paper, history would lose some of its most informative documents. I don't see how history can arrive at the truth if contemporaries aren't allowed to write it.'

Chapter Fifty-Three

In the Windsor Castle sitting room, the American First Lady looked moved. Deeply ensconced in a green brocade armchair, Mrs Roosevelt held that most English of symbols, a cup of tea, along with a slice of that most American of confections, a pumpkin pie. 'I'm touched beyond words,' she said, her large eyes glassy with emotion. 'What a wonderful idea!'

'The girls thought of it,' beamed the queen. 'They hoped you would like it.' She sat opposite her guest on a green silk sofa. Immaculately coiffed, high-heeled, blue-dressed and legs crossed at the ankles, she was the picture of the relaxed hostess. No one would think she was the queen of a threatened country entertaining its most powerful ally.

Marion, sitting at the back by the window, felt it was probably petty to want the credit for what had actually been her pumpkin pie idea. As the king kept telling the nation on the radio, these days they were all in it together.

The fragrance of cinnamon and nutmeg wafted into the air as Lilibet shot her governess a guilty glance. 'Crawfie's been teaching us about America and the Pilgrims,' she said in her diplomatic way.

Mrs Roosevelt looked at Marion with friendly interest. 'Is that so? Well done, Crawfie.'

'So we thought we might celebrate Thanksgiving, while you were here,' the queen put in, smoothly. 'A little early, I know.'

Mrs Roosevelt raised her silver fork, took a bite and looked enchanted. 'The early bird catches the best pumpkin pie!' Everyone laughed politely. The rest of the group comprised Mrs Roosevelt's secretary, a lady-in-waiting and a dark-haired male figure next to Marion that she was trying her level best not to look at.

The queen gaily clapped her glittering little white hands. 'Well done, Margaret and Lilibet!'

The group obediently clapped, and the activity gave the dark-haired figure the opportunity to shift towards her. The familiar cologne ebbed at her nostrils. She kept her head facing front. She would show no interest; none at all.

'I'm guessing that it's actually well done, Miss Crawford.' His low voice was warm with amusement.

'The girls did help,' she said stiffly. 'They collected everyone's sugar rations.'

Lascelles snorted. 'I imagine that went down a treat.'

Marion kept her eyes facing front. 'But I hear *you're* the one who should be congratulated, Mr Lascelles. Mrs Roosevelt's visit has been a huge success.'

Tommy had indeed done his work well. The lord mayor and his entourage had been nowhere to be seen. From the moment she arrived, Mrs Roosevelt's experience had been of a Britain battered by its enemies but standing firm. From Paddington she was whisked straight to Buckingham Palace, where she saw the boarded-up windows and the black line painted round every bath. From here to the East End, with its glass-crunching streets and heaps of smoking broken brick, and St Paul's with its nave open to the sky.

'I can't take all the credit,' Lascelles muttered. 'The cupboards were Her Majesty's idea.'

Cecil Beaton, an up-and-coming photographer, had been summoned to the palace to take pictures of Mrs Roosevelt in front of miles of empty kitchen cupboards. The king, reluctant to show his nation in quite such an abject light, had not been keen. But his wife, her PR touch as sure as ever, had prevailed.

Nor had she stopped there, making sure Mrs Roosevelt slept in her own bedroom with a one-bar electric fire and boarded-up windows. She had eaten off gold plates, but the menus, hand-written on monogrammed cards, had been utility ones. The first lady had enjoyed, if that was the word, 'mock goose' – layers of potatoes and apples baked with cheese and pickled onions, with beetroot pudding for dessert. No wonder she was so pleased to see the pumpkin pie.

The Windsor tea was her last engagement before leaving. And perhaps this was the queen's greatest coup de théâtre of all, because above the green brocade chair in which Mrs Roosevelt sat were holes in the ceiling where glass chandeliers, now removed for safety, had once sparkled. Wires hung down like black roots. Antique cabinets and tables, their carving and gilding shrouded under sheets, were turned to the tapestry-covered walls

Beside Marion, Tommy spoke again. 'I am,' he murmured, 'in possession of some very interesting information.'

Excitement shot through her, despite herself. Reports from intelligence agents the world over passed daily over his desk. Was she about to hear some incredible secret? Something was happening in Egypt, she knew. The king was like a cat on bricks almost as hot as the Western Desert, where Montgomery and his Eighth Army currently were. Now, finally, she turned to look at him. The dark eyes were glinting mischievously.

'I hear,' he said, 'that you are organising a pantomime.'

'*That's* your interesting information?'

'Isn't it true?'

'Well, yes. As it happens. We're doing *Cinderella*.'

It had begun as a casual suggestion in the air-raid shelter, born out of the *A Midsummer Night's Dream* acting sessions. Margaret and Lilibet had taken the idea up eagerly, and so she had floated it with Ivy and Peter, both of whom thought it the ideal distraction for their pupils.

The latter, with his knowledge of classical drama, had even offered to write it. 'Don't make it too miserable,' Ivy warned.

Peter gave her an indulgent look. 'The ancients invented comedy as well as tragedy.'

'If you say so.' Ivy shrugged, but fondly.

'I hear Princess Margaret has the lead role,' Tommy said.

'Who else?'

'Always one of my favourite fairy tales,' he went on. 'The humble girl elevated to great and glorious heights.'

There was a crash now, as of doors bursting open. A woman stood in the doorway, a dark-haired woman in a neat navy suit with a tight waist and a widely flared skirt. She had toweringly high heels, bright red lipstick and quick, sparkling, dark eyes that danced assessingly about the room. Her swift, sharp survey struck Marion as being at odds with her attitude of cartoonish apology. 'Excuse me, ma'am, ma'ams,' she gasped, waving her hands helplessly and curtseying wildly to all and sundry.

An out-of-breath footman in the battledress issued for the war's duration had now caught up. He was evidently anguished. 'Your Majesty, I apologise, this lady insisted you were expecting her.'

The queen remained composed on her sofa, legs still crossed at the ankle. Her face evinced nothing but mild surprise. Beside her Margaret and Lilibet were agog. Marion slid a glance at Tommy. His aristocratic ease gone, he looked frankly horrified. Lady Delia Peel, the lady-in-waiting, was scarlet. Confusion, meanwhile, was written all over Mrs Roosevelt's large, jowly features.

Entirely unabashed, the newcomer ran straight up to the queen. She swept a low, elaborate curtsey. 'Your Majesty,' she exclaimed, batting her eyelashes, 'we met at Lady Astor's. I was there with Mrs Roosevelt, if you remember.' She flashed a great toothy beam in the direction of the first lady. 'Mrs Roosevelt mentioned this tea today, and suggested I come along.'

Puzzlement now joined embarrassment on Mrs Roosevelt's big, good-natured face. It was clear she had no memory of any such invitation, but could hardly contradict her countrywoman in the queen's presence.

Marion, like everyone else, could only stare in amazed silence. Was the woman unaware, or just simple? This was not the first royal gatecrasher she had seen; people annually tried to slip in uninvited to the palace garden parties. But this, a private gathering where the Queen of England was entertaining the First Lady of the United States, and in wartime too, was on another level. She had never seen anyone attempt anything like it, let alone succeed.

The woman gushed on, completely without embarrassment of any kind. 'I'd have been here earlier,' she exclaimed, 'except that I've had a little trouble with the beefeaters and soldiers and all.'

Marion, glancing round, saw it dawning on everyone that this woman had just fast-talked her way through the entire Windsor Castle guard. Who on earth was she?

The queen was evidently wondering the same thing. She swung her blue eyes enquiringly at Mrs Roosevelt. 'Ma'am,' the embarrassed first lady began, 'allow me to introduce Mrs . . .' She hesitated, evidently struggling to remember.

'Mrs Gould, Beatrice Gould.' The dark-haired woman beamed, utterly unabashed. She turned now to the queen. 'We spoke at Lady Astor's, ma'am. You very kindly agreed to write some articles for my magazine.'

'Your . . . magazine?' the queen repeated, faintly.

'That's right, ma'am. The magazine of which I'm the editor. *The Ladies' Home Journal* of America!'

Marion could only stare, amazed by the sheer scale of the woman's nerve. This was no simpleton, she was sure now. The scatty breathiness was an act. She had caught Beatrice Gould's glance as it switched from the wife of the president to the wife of the king, and something about its black glitter stayed with her. It had been a look of absolute, ruthless determination.

Chapter Fifty-Four

'The Princess Margaret Rose,' Alah said, 'is absolutely pea green.'

'You're joking,' said Marion. But Alah never had, in all the years she had known her. 'Margaret's too ill to act?'

'*Pea green*, Miss Crawford.'

Marion groaned. The Princess Margaret Rose had been absolutely fine earlier. Moreover, everyone was ready. Ivy's evacuees. Peter's Etonians. Toni, whose Gallic flair had come in handy with costumes and make-up. Various of the Windsor Castle guard. Literally hundreds of people were expected. Tickets had been sold at rates ranging from one shilling for the cheapest right up to seven and six. Close to nine hundred pounds – a stupendous sum – had been raised for the Queen's Wool Fund. Lilibet had been shocked. 'No one will pay that to look at *us*!'

'Nonsense!' Margaret had riposted. 'They'll pay anything to see us.'

Except that they might not be seeing Margaret now. Marion wanted to go in and shake her. Why ruin the efforts of so many good people? Because she could, of course.

She returned, frustrated, to the Waterloo Chamber, where the stage put in by Queen Victoria for household theatricals stood pantomime-ready. The beautifully painted set, the work of two volunteers, portrayed a castle kitchen right down to the turnspit. Cinders' broom stood ready in the corner.

She walked across the stage and into the wings. Behind the set, out of sight, stood the racks of elaborate dresses, beribboned peri-wigs and silver buckled shoes, all specially hired from a theatrical costumier's and all labelled and assigned to the different characters. There too was Queen Anne's sedan chair, pressed into service in a way she could never have expected, as Cinderella's pumpkin coach.

And here too, Marion now saw with a start, even more unexpectedly, was His Majesty. Standing in the wings, hands in pockets, looking round with a critical expression.

'Sir!' She bobbed a curtsey.

The king's interest in the show had been minimal until about a week ago, when his inner Cecil B. DeMille had been spectacularly unleashed. He had insisted on going through every aspect as thoroughly as he went through battle plans with Churchill.

The king looked round from his examination of the stage set. 'Everything all right, Crawfie?'

'Actually, sir, we have a problem.'

He laughed shortly. 'Tell me about it. Any n-number. Although things look a b-bit better now, admittedly.' He was, she knew, referring to the recent victory at El Alamein, which represented the first major defeat of German forces.

He heard her out. His smile disappeared. He sat down on Cinders' three-legged stool and thought. Then he stood up. 'I have the answer, Crawfie!'

'Sir?'

'You will replace Margaret. You know the words, after all.'

She considered. The costumes would not fit. She would be twice the size of all the other actors, apart from a couple of the older Etonians and the six-foot Windsor guardsmen marching on for the finale. 'Perhaps one of the other children, sir? I'm not a very good actor.'

The king looked at her. 'You and I are both actors, Crawfie. We s-stand before an audience every day. We have had to learn to be good at it.'

And how the king had learned, Marion thought. His confidence had increased as his stammer had lessened. The queen's sterling example had showed him the way.

He smiled again, the sudden, wide grin so like his daughter's. 'But if you let Her Royal Highness know you are covering for her, it may well be that you don't get your moment in the spotlight after all.'

He was right, of course. Margaret was out of bed in a flash, health miraculously restored, pea-greenness definitively gone.

The production was an astounding success. The audience, made up of townspeople and estate workers, packed even this huge room. Kerald Jelly was there, of course, after a hard day putting yet more 'finishing touches' to the portraits of the king and queen. They sat in the front row, the latter sparkling with some of the huge diamonds left to her by the recently deceased Mrs Ronnie. The Surrey estate may have gone, ultimately, to the National Trust, but these were the consolation prize.

The finale, as reorganised by the king, was the best scene of all, with the Windsor Castle guard, magnificent in red, black boots gleaming, marching and countermarching across the stage while the children unfurled huge Union Jacks and waved them to thunderous applause.

The cast, especially Margaret, bowed endlessly and lapped it up. Her vivid little face, dazzlingly lovely in the stage lights, looked as if it had never had a wicked thought in its life.

Lilibet looked delighted too, but her pink-faced joy, Marion knew, had less to do with the applause than with a certain figure along the front row. It was not her father or mother. It was Philip Mountbatten.

Marion had seen him the moment he had walked in, as had every other woman in the room. His commanding height, crackling energy and spectacular good looks drew all eyes. He had marched straight to the front and sat down, throwing out his long legs and laughing with his companion, who, like himself, was dressed in Navy uniform. The gold braid on his sleeves shone as brightly as his blond hair. He had distinguished himself in the war, having been mentioned in dispatches for a sea battle off the Greek coast. Italian warships had been sunk. Philip had manned the searchlight.

He was manning one now, she thought, and aiming it at Lilibet. She shone; she sparkled. She might be a dashing Prince Charming on the stage, but the person she clearly considered her real-life counterpart was sitting a mere few feet away, staring appreciatively at her legs in their tights.

The king and queen were obviously oblivious. They gave Philip the occasional amused glance, but no more. To them, Lilibet was still their obedient child. That she was a young woman of sixteen, with a mind of her own, and in love, had not yet hit them. But it had hit Marion. Philip's bold gaze, trained on the young girl she had nurtured for a decade, made her shudder. It was more than disapproval, or even dislike. She realised that it was fear.

'Miss Crawford! My congratulations on an excellent production.' Tommy's slightly sardonic voice fell lightly from behind her. Marion took a deep breath, then turned.

Joan was at his side, lipstick immaculate. Her hair was waves of shining gold, and a modish frock of printed silk skimmed an elegant figure. She swept Marion a brief, unimpressed glance before ostentatiously looking around for more interesting and significant people. 'Look, darling, over there. Isn't that the – ?'

'Darling, why don't you go and talk to them? I need to have a quick word with Miss Crawford.'

He took her arm and tried to steer her to an unoccupied corner. She shook off his hand and stood firm. He looked surprised. 'I just wanted to fill you in, that's all.'

'About what?'

'Last time we met was a bit awkward, to say the least.'

He meant the tea party with Mrs Roosevelt, she realised, interrupted by the gatecrasher. 'Delia Peel and I had a very unpleasant quarter of an hour with Their Majesties afterward,' Tommy said ruefully. 'And the trouble's not over yet.'

'How do you mean?' Marion asked, curiously. The first lady had gone home weeks ago. 'Is Mrs . . . what was her name . . . still here?'

'Gould, and yes she is, maddening woman. I had to go and see her at the Ritz, in fact. At the queen's behest.'

'She's still here?' Marion's mouth dropped open. 'Why?' After what had happened, she had imagined Mrs Gould to be a pariah of the first water. Not someone visited at a fine hotel by the king's own private secretary.

'About the articles Mrs Gould mentioned.'

'The queen surely isn't going to write them?'

Tommy shook his sleek dark head. 'I talked to her for an hour.'

'An *hour*?'

'Told her the queen was above and beyond politics. I said that though she sympathises with the mission to make the women of the UK and USA understand each other better, she can't write any articles herself.'

Marion could only stare back. She could not imagine why the queen was even bothering to tell this to the upstart journalist. Via Tommy especially. Via an interview lasting a whole hour. What a waste of time.

'Well, she's gone back to America now, and hopefully that will be the last of it.' Tommy turned away. 'Goodbye, Marion. I wish you a happy Christmas.'

Chapter Fifty-Five

A photograph of Philip had appeared on the mantelpiece in Lilibet's bedroom. Her parents, possibly by a great mutual effort of will, didn't seem to notice. They, who stood fearlessly against Hitler, were all too obviously terrified of acknowledging that their daughter was in love. Marion understood. She felt exactly the same.

Margaret, as ever, had no such scruples. 'Are you going to get married, Lilibet?' she teased. 'Everyone else is. Look at Ivy and Peter.'

They had been engaged and would be married in the same month. The wedding, in the pretty Georgian surroundings of the Windsor Registry Office, was unfussy but delightful. Ivy was gay in serviceable lavender tweed with a bright yellow courgette flower from the allotment in her lapel. Peter, looking amazed at his own good luck, wore an Eton lily in his elegant three-piece dark suit.

'You were always too good for me,' Marion said, hugging him. She meant it: he had got the wife he deserved and wanted; *someone completely normal, with her feet firmly on the ground.*

'You're right,' Ivy quipped, overhearing. 'But anyway, you're married to those bleedin' Windsors.'

Margaret, Lilibet and the rest of the evacuees had saved their sugar rations, but the cake made by the Windsor Castle cook had a bitter taste to Marion after that comment.

Lilibet's passion for a serving officer renewed her old determination to join up. At eighteen, she was finally of age, but the king and queen were reluctant to let her. With their usual adroitness at avoiding unpleasant matters, they changed the subject whenever it arose.

But the princess could no longer be fobbed off so easily. It was rare for her to sulk, but now she stomped about, brows knitted, mouth a cross line. 'Can't you talk to Papa, Crawfie?' she begged. 'He listens to you.'

Marion doubted that this was the case, but the suggestion was flattering. As was Lilibet's imploring face. The request itself dismayed her, even so. She no more wanted Lilibet to join up than she wanted her to marry Philip. The army would take the princess away, possibly forever. She would hardly return to the schoolroom after she had seen active service.

But there was no choice. Lilibet, once she had set her heart on something, was relentless. Marion found herself tracing a reluctant path to the king's office door.

'Might I have five minutes with His Majesty?' she asked the new equerry, the slight, high-cheekboned one with the dark wavy hair.

Peter Townsend glanced at his watch. He was one of the new non-aristocrat equerries, a wing commander in the RAF, much-decorated. He would, she guessed, be in his late twenties, but looked older. While of an almost feminine delicacy, his features had that familiar, weary, war-worn stamp about them. 'The meeting should be over soon,' he said. 'If you could wait here a few minutes.'

Marion nodded. She liked Group Captain Townsend. He was understated and modest, although obviously brave. A Spitfire pilot, he had been shot down several times and been given a DFC.

But however tactfully she approached it, Marion had never got him to talk about his wartime experiences. He stiffened and something came down behind his eyes. She wondered if he opened up to his wife, whom she had never met but who was supposed to be pretty and lively. There was a child too, a son.

Townsend stood awkwardly beside her now in his RAF grey blue, gazing at his brilliantly polished boots. A muscle ticked in his well-defined jaw, as if he were clenching it. He was staring at the king's shining door as if he could open it by sheer force of will.

The king's door remained closed. The rocking horses were still outside, now old and battered, their paint worn and their manes partially bald through much enthusiastic riding. The girls hadn't ridden them for years, but they had been kept there as a memento of the childhood that Lilibet in particular was now so determined to break free of.

Suddenly, the door opened. Townsend stood instantly to attention, saluting smartly as no less a person than Churchill, with the king behind him, emerged between the rocking horses.

Marion stared in awe. The prime minister, jowly and creased, wore a worn pinstriped suit and held his famous bowler hat. A pair of shrewd, bright eyes met hers. Churchill nodded, then passed on with his rolling walk. She gazed after him, dazed.

Something drained from the atmosphere with his departure. The king, left in the doorway, now looked shrunken and grey. A cigarette, as ever, streamed from between his thin fingers. 'Go in, Crawfie. I just need a word with Townsend here.'

In his office, the air was so thick with mixed cigar and cigarette smoke that it made her cough. Maps were fixed to the wall and bristled with many pins. Papers were scattered across the royal desk, stamped all over with the red imprints of secrecy and the title 'Overlord'.

Marion sat down. She could read the topmost one.

SUPREME HEADQUARTERS, ALLIED EXPEDITIONARY FORCE.

Soldiers, Sailors and Airmen of the Allied Expeditionary Force! You are about to embark on the Great Crusade, towards which we have striven these many months. The eyes of the world are upon you . . .

The king had returned. 'Now, C-Crawfie. What can I do for you?'

She explained her mission quickly, with no introduction. With any luck, it would be a straightforward 'no'. The princess would be disappointed, but at least she would still be around. 'Lilibet wants to join one of the forces, sir.'

The king, now back behind his desk, groaned. 'Lilibet never gives up, does she?' He took another drag of his cigarette, then coughed.

His choking, which was violent and extended, had a sticky rattle to it. He took a gulp of water from a cut-crystal tumbler that stood amid other tumblers in which the amber traces of whisky remained. He looked at Marion with streaming eyes. 'Very well, Crawfie. We'll see what can be arranged.'

She stared. 'Is that a yes, sir?'

He nodded and pulled one of the Overlord documents towards him.

She left as quietly as she could. The golden handle fixed in the polished door turned silently in its lock. The well-oiled hinges closed behind her without a squeak.

In the corridor, a murmured conversation was going on. The participants were a little distance away, round a corner. They had obviously not heard her emerge.

'Twenty months of day and night combat,' came a hushed male voice that Marion recognised as Peter Townsend's. 'I was a sleep-starved wreck. I had confronted death so often that life seemed to have little relevance.'

Surprise rippled through her. Townsend had been taciturn when she had pressed him about his war experience. To whom was he unburdening himself so readily?

'Oh, Peter!' came the familiar high voice of Margaret, undercut with breathy admiration. 'It must have been so *dreadful*!'

'Every time I took off I felt sure it was the last time.'

'Oh, Peter! Thank goodness it wasn't!'

Lilibet wasn't the only one growing up, by the looks of things.

The uniform arrived almost immediately. In her bedroom, Lilibet carefully lifted off the lid of the large cardboard box and pulled away the tissue paper. Her gasp of excitement sent dismay through Marion.

Margaret, in the window seat, slid off the cushion and padded over to inspect the garment.

'Hideous colour,' she commented, poking the thick, rough fabric. 'You're going to look horrible in it, Lilibet.'

Her sister, as ever, refused to rise to the provocation. 'It's not meant to be a fashion show,' she remarked, picking up the cap with its shiny black peak. Marion watched her take it to the small oval mirror hanging over the simple dressing table and perch it on her dark curls. 'This is the uniform of the Auxiliary Territorial Service. And I,' she said, turning with the trademark grin of delight, 'am Second Subaltern Elizabeth Windsor.'

Margaret folded her arms, bottom lip protruding, all attempts at indifference abandoned. 'It's not fair. Why must I spend all day in the schoolroom while everyone else does exciting things?'

Lilibet had put on the jacket now. The breast pockets enhanced her generous bosom. The belt, buckled tightly round her small waist, emphasised her hips. It crossed Marion's mind that not the least of the Army's attractions was the scope it offered to finally wear something different than her sister.

'It's *not fair* that Papa let you do this and not me!' Margaret wailed.

'You'll be old enough soon.'

'Yes, but by then the war will be *over!*'

Only for Margaret could it be bad news that, following El Alamein, things seemed finally to be going the Allies' way. Ground had been gained in Italy, Eastern Europe and the Pacific. And something else momentous seemed to be happening; not long ago, Lilibet had counted almost three hundred Flying Fortresses passing over the castle. 'I gave up at two hundred and eighty-four!'

Marion wondered if they were connected to the Overlord documents she had seen.

The eldest princess now bounded out of the room, eager to show the new uniform to her parents. Various excited dogs poured after her, and after them, Margaret. Last of all Marion, heart full of the sudden knowledge that everything was about to change.

It was a warm, sunny, blue-skied day. The king and queen were having tea on the terrace. Below it the castle rose garden was in full and glorious bloom, warm scents wafting up from the massy colour. The long white tablecloth swept to the ground. It was a scene in which war had no part, until the uniformed Lilibet burst into it. She rushed up to her father and saluted. 'Sir!'

The queen, about to pour, held the silver teapot in mid-air as she regarded her now undeniably grown-up daughter. 'Oh, darling!' Her voice was choked, as if she was forced to face something she had long wished to avoid.

The king looked equally distraught, but other voices began to fill the silence. Loud, booming ones with an unmistakable transatlantic twang. The sorrowful expression on the king's face was replaced by shock. 'C-C-Christ! It's Eisenhower!'

'What's he doing here?' asked Lilibet.

'Coming to get his orders from *you*!' teased Margaret. 'Second Subaltern Elizabeth Windsor.'

'We have a m-meeting later,' the king said evasively. 'But at the moment, Eisenhower's being shown round the c-c-castle. If he comes round the corner, he'll see us.'

'Would that be so bad?' asked Margaret, rather longingly. Eisenhower, often pictured in the newspapers with his sunny beam, was famously tall and debonair.

'Yes, because we're up here and he'll be down there,' her mother pointed out. 'We'll have to shout and it'll be terribly embarrassing.'

Lilibet had grasped the problem. Her uniform seemed to have conferred on her a new decisiveness. As her parents dithered, she took charge. 'There's only one thing for it,' she hissed, as the American voices got louder and closer. 'Everyone under the tablecloth!'

And so it was, that when the Supreme Allied Commander in Europe emerged into the rose garden, his hosts were nowhere to be seen.

'Come and see the Maiden's Blush, General.' The voice of Lord Wigram floated up from below.

'Stop it!' Lilibet hissed to her sister, who was shaking with suppressed laughter. 'He'll see the table moving!'

'Madame Hardy and Mrs Finch are also having a wonderful year.'

'I sure am glad to hear that,' came the general's warm Kansas voice. He sounded amused.

'And Queen Elizabeth is quite magnificent.'

'The most dangerous rose in Europe,' quipped Eisenhower, as the flower's real-life counterpart suppressed a snort.

Chapter Fifty-Six

'The Americans have all gone,' Susan wailed. After the departure of Lilibet from the classroom, this was another huge personal blow. 'But we don't know where.'

She soon found out. That night the king rousingly addressed the country. 'Four years ago our Nation and Empire stood alone against an overwhelming enemy with our backs to the wall. Tested as never before in history, in God's providence we survived the test. Now once more a supreme test has to be faced.'

Marion, sitting with the girls in the king's office, watched him turn from the microphone with glittering eyes. The queen, as she rarely was, seemed similarly downcast. Great numbers of lives were at risk, and the responsibility clearly weighed heavily on the commanders.

'It's D-Day,' Reg yelled the next day. 'We've landed in France! The invasion has started! The war's nearly over. We can go home!'

It wasn't, though, and they couldn't. Germany's latest secret weapon was now unleashed: the terrifying pilotless bombs that came over in droves throughout the day, rasping their way across the sky before stopping suddenly and diving to earth. A month after D-Day nearly three thousand people had been killed and eight thousand detained in the hospital.

'Just what is a doodlebug?' asked Margaret. 'A real one, I mean.'

'An insect found in the Mississippi,' supplied Susan, in whom the countryside had developed a passion for natural history. She was hoping to study it at university.

'But the Germans call it the Vergeltungswuffe Ein,' Reg said.

'That means Revenge Weapon Number One. They're twenty-five feet long and they can fly a preset distance of a hundred and forty miles.' For all its dark purpose, he found the engineering behind it fascinating.

According to Peter, he was a gifted mathematician as well as classicist. In the new world beyond the war that people were now starting to glimpse, there would be great opportunities for children like him and Susan. A new Education Act had recently been passed, in which children from humble homes received state aid from primary school right through university. The war, for all its horror, had speeded up progress. It had opened doors that had previously been closed; not just for paupers, but princesses too.

Lilibet took her ATS duties profoundly seriously. Out all day at the Camberley depot, she returned to the palace in the evening to regale everyone about her day. 'We had a talk about mechanics this afternoon.'

'How *boring*,' Margaret interrupted, savagely.

Lilibet, unruffled, cut a neat piece of cheese on toast. 'Then we had a lecture on oil.'

'*Oil?*'

But then, suddenly, Margaret changed her tune.

'Please can we go and see Lilibet at Camberley?' she wheedled.

Marion looked at her, eyebrow raised. 'Isn't it . . . *boring?*'

'Yes, very,' was the lofty reply. 'But I think she'd appreciate the encouragement, poor thing.'

It was meant to be an informal visit, but then the king and queen decided to come too. Lilibet arrived back in the evenings wide-eyed at the amount of preparation. 'Spit, polish and panic,' she said. 'Everyone shines up everything. I had no idea this was what happened when Mummie and Papa visit somewhere.'

'And me,' put in Margaret fiercely. 'Don't forget me.'

They drove out to the depot through glorious early-spring weather. Margaret, following her parents down the inspection line, snorted to see her sister saluting her. In the garage, Lilibet was at pains to show her family her grasp of engine maintenance. But Marion, watching Margaret, saw the younger girl's eyes suddenly gleam.

'Lilibet! The compression!'

Her sister peered at the engine. 'What about it?'

'It's missing,' said Margaret, confidently.

Lilibet glanced at her parents, and the various officers accompanying them, before looking challengingly back at her sister. 'And how would *you* know?'

Margaret cheekily poked one of her sister's buttons. 'Why shouldn't I know?'

Back at Windsor, Marion went straight to the mews, where the royal cars were garaged. 'Oh yes,' the chauffeur confirmed. ''Er Royal 'Ighness's been positively 'aunting us lately. Been full o' questions, she 'as.'

In September the second of Germany's deadly secret weapons arrived: the V2. Their impact was even more devastating. 'A single rocket can cause a crater fifty feet wide and ten feet deep and demolish a whole street of houses,' Reg reported. When a V2 demolished the Woolworths in New Cross, south-east London, Margaret was beside herself with fury.

But the tide had definitely turned. Now the 'dimout' replaced the blackout. The Russians surrounded Berlin. The horrors of Belsen and Buchenwald flooded the newspapers, which Marion did her best to hide from Margaret and Ivy from her pupils.

And now, finally, the evacuees returned. As Lilibet was at Camberley, Margaret and Marion came to see them off.

The small group stood on Windsor station platform. Beside them, the London-bound train snorted and steamed like an impatient horse. Carriage doors slammed. People hurried up and down. The smaller children chattered and squealed with excitement about going home, about seeing their parents again.

But around Reg, Susan and Margaret, an awkward silence hung. A similar one hung about Ivy and Marion. Ivy was not leaving with her charges. She was moving to Eton to be with Peter, which should, Marion knew, have been a source of happiness. They would be able to see more of each other.

And yet a tight, tense feeling seized her these days whenever she saw her old friend. Ivy rarely resisted the opportunity to urge her to leave royal service, especially now the war was coming to an end. 'You should escape, Maz! Find a man! A life! Have kids!'

Ivy didn't understand, Marion thought. She had a life and kids, even if they weren't her own. As for a man, she had finished with them.

Margaret was the first to break the platform's silence. 'Goodbye, then,' she said politely, extending her hand to Reg for it to be shaken.

Reg, in a red jersey, a cardboard suitcase in his hand, looked surprised. He had been accustomed to hugging his friend. Then understanding dawned. The war was nearly over. The social order was about to be restored. Margaret was a princess. Reg's face fell, as if he had been somehow betrayed.

A whistle blew. The London-bound children clambered aboard. 'Ta-ra!' called Ivy. 'Give my love to Bermondsey!'

From the doorway Reg hung back. 'We had fun,' he said to Margaret.

There was a strangled sound from Margaret. Tears were streaming down her face. Reg scrambled down again and the boy and girl hugged hard. They were parted by the station master blowing his whistle. Seconds later the doors had slammed and the locomotive was wheezing out, hands waving wildly from the window.

President Roosevelt's sudden death in April 1945 came before the news of Mussolini's murder and Hitler's suicide. 'Hitler and Mussolini, in forty-eight hours,' Tommy remarked. 'Not a bad right and left.'

And then, after a night of thunder and lightning, on a beautiful Sunday morning in early May, the phone rang in the private apartments at Windsor Castle. The king and queen, about to leave for church, found themselves summoned back to London, and the princesses with them. It was all over. Like the sudden blowing away of a storm, the atmosphere lightened. After years of gloom, the sun came out.

Chapter Fifty-Seven

The roar from outside burst through the open glass doors. Marion looked at the familiar row of figures on the balcony, backs towards her. The king looked frail but relieved in his admiral's uniform with its heavy gold cuffs. Lilibet was wildly proud in her ATS khaki, buckle and buttons blazing. Beside them, the queen in one of her trademark big hats, curved brim thrusting triumphantly upward, waved at the carpet of people below. Margaret, in her frilly collar, looked like the demure schoolgirl she most certainly was not.

And in the middle of them all, a short, round figure in a wonky bow tie and watch chain. When he looked to the side, to catch something the king had said, Marion saw that tears were pouring unashamedly down Churchill's jowly face.

They were pouring down hers too. No one had said anything, but it was surely unlikely that Lilibet would hang up the ATS uniform of which she was so proud and file meekly back into the schoolroom. Margaret, meanwhile, had been restless and inattentive for months. And now she was standing on a balcony looking at a cheering crowd surging round the palace and stretching down the Mall. A boiling sea of ecstatic people yelling, singing and waving flags. How could she return to algebra after this?

Marion turned back into the room. The magnificent gilt-framed mirrors reflected a scene of genteel devastation. Not bombs now, but champagne glasses. Gathered on the tables, along the mantelpieces and everywhere else those recently assembled had stood. She spotted Margaret's abandoned handbag and went towards it. But someone else got there first, someone slight and delicate-featured in an RAF uniform. 'Leave it with me,' he said. 'I'll give it to her.'

She watched him move to the balcony door. He stood there directly behind the younger princess, who seemed to sense him immediately. She turned and smiled dazzlingly. As he handed over the bag, their fingers touched, not briefly, but lingeringly.

It happened so fast Marion wondered if she had imagined it. But the princess's glowing face, as she looked at Townsend, left her in no doubt. Something was afoot.

The festivities within the palace went on long after the balcony appearances. At one stage the king, queen and princesses were leading a conga line through the state apartments. Well-bred shouts of excitement rose into the gilded moulding, while the stamping gently clinked the chandeliers. Tommy was there looking ill at ease and holding gingerly on to the queen, while Peter Townsend happily clasped Margaret. Footmen in war-issue battledress looked on, clearly longing to join in, but not, even in this moment of national unity, quite daring to.

Huge violet eyes, fringed with impossibly long lashes, gazed excitedly into hers, suddenly. Delicate fingers plucked at her sleeve. Margaret's voice was jerky with delight. 'Crawfie! What do you think?'

'What?'

'Papa is to let us out tonight.'

'Us?'

'Lilibet and I.'

'Out? You mean . . . outside the palace?'

The vivid little face nodded. 'Exactly. Properly out, into the crowds. To celebrate with everyone else.'

'How exciting!' Marion felt thrilled too. 'What time are we going?'

Margaret's smile vanished. 'Not *you*, Crawfie. Just us. Oh, and a couple of equerries.'

She could guess exactly which ones, Marion thought, as Margaret danced off in the conga. She stood there, full of an agitation that was a mixture of hurt and genuine fear. How could Margaret speak to her that way? Would the girls be safe in the great victory crowd? With a very married man who had his eye on Margaret?

It occurred to her that perhaps it was not even true, that permission had not been granted. Margaret was more than capable of inventing it, taking advantage of the situation and having others take the blame afterward. She would make sure, Marion decided.

She watched for the king and eventually spotted him, looking somewhat incongruous in the conga line. She hurried alongside. 'Your Majesty. Margaret tells me she and Lilibet are going out this evening . . .'

The king was coughing with the effort, which seemed a strain on his lungs. He nodded, eyes streaming, as he fought for breath. 'Poor darlings,' he conceded. 'They've never had any fun yet.' Then off he went.

Marion thought of all the things she and the girls had done together over the years. Had none of that been fun? She sat down on a chair in the corridor. The dancers continued past her, wild with joy.

Later, alone, she went out into the crowds herself. It seemed as if the whole world was rejoicing. She watched, as if through a thick glass pane, as soldiers, sailors, ATS and Wrens – anyone in uniform – were hugged and mobbed by grateful people in civvies.

'Roll out the barrel!' everyone yelled. The noise was ear-splitting. It seemed that the whole of London was roaring, screaming and shouting its euphoria. People were laughing and crying. Perfect strangers were kissing and hugging. Years of darkness, privation, terror and sorrow had given way to a mighty mass expression of hysterical relief. For everyone but Marion, it seemed. She felt hollow inside, dull, out of step with the mood.

She dodged several vigorous Hokey-Cokeys and a good number of Lambeth Walks until, by the lions in Trafalgar Square, a young man was shoved against her by a surge in the crowd. 'So sorry,' he yelled over the noise.

She shrugged; there was no need to apologise.

'Come for a drink?'

She hesitated, then nodded. A drink might help. Give her some artificial cheer at least. Feeling so unhappy amid all this ecstasy was like being a creature from another planet.

He grabbed her arm. She allowed herself to be pulled through the sea of people. 'I don't even know your name!'

'George!' he shouted over his shoulder. 'Major George Buthlay, at your service!'

In the pub it was crowded and almost too hot to breathe. The noise of drunken people was deafening. A pub piano was pounding out flat notes. The group nearest them were singing so loudly it was impossible to hear any conversation. *Run rabbit run rabbit run run run . . .*

That he was a major was impressive. 'Where's your uniform?' she yelled. His reply was hard to hear. It sounded as if he had served in the Middle East but the unit had been disbanded early. She was ready with another question. 'Where do you live?'

'The silver city with the golden sands.'

She looked at him quizzically.

'Aberdeen.'

Her eyes widened. So he was a Scot, too. Amid the noise, it hadn't been possible to distinguish. 'I've never heard it called that before.'

He grinned. 'Why should you? You're a Sassenach.'

'I'm Scottish!' Marion gasped indignantly.

'Really?' The dark eyes had a mocking look. 'You don't sound it. What's your name?' His brash manner should have annoyed her, but it didn't. Not tonight, when all normal behaviour was suspended.

She pretended not to hear. Where did he work?

'In a bank,' he shouted. 'How about you?'

'I'm a teacher,' she yelled.

He looked her up and down. 'I'll teach you something.' He turned her towards him and kissed her deeply.

Chapter Fifty-Eight

That Christmas, Alah died and was buried in the Hertfordshire village where she was born. Marion, attending the funeral of her old adversary, was struck by the paucity of the congregation. The church's sixteenth-century interior echoed to a few old ladies' reedy voices. None of the family the deceased had served so loyally had come to see her off in person. A card from the queen and a wreath of violets seemed a feeble gesture after a lifetime of such utter devotion. Marion shivered. Was this what awaited her too? Should she leave? She had George now, after all.

They had not, as she had expected, dissolved separately into the crowds after the VE night encounter. There had been many other similar encounters since. And in between he had taken her out, often to concerts. For someone so obviously bold and apparently rough, he had unexpectedly sensitive tastes in music.

From the arena of the Albert Hall, she had stared up in awe. The size of the place was amazing; the tiered balconies, the arches, the sloped seating, the vast curved stage. Then the concert began and she was lost in the music – Elgar – and full of a sweet, sad mystery. It pulled at her and made her yearn. In the second half it was Rachmaninov: great crashes and sweeps which sent her heart soaring. It all helped her feel she was in love, dizzyingly and dazzlingly so.

'I want to leave,' she said to George. It had taken some time to admit who her employers were. But he had taken it entirely in his stride, which made her love him all the more.

He looked nonplussed. 'But the second half's only just started.'

She laughed. 'Not Rachmaninov! The royal family!'

He smiled and ran a loving finger down her cheek. 'There's no rush. Take your time.'

But there wasn't as much time to take as there had been, she thought, as the music swelled again. She was halfway through her thirties now. And while it was not too late to have her own children, to take up her old career, it soon would be.

'Marry me!' she murmured, as they stood in the shadows of Green Park, opposite Buckingham Palace. He had walked her home. As his tongue traced her neck, knowing that her employers were so close gave her pleasure a rebellious edge.

The tongue stopped.

'What?' he said.

She repeated it. 'I thought the man did the proposing,' he said, looking amused but puzzled.

'Welcome to the modern world. Why shouldn't a woman ask a man to marry her?'

He looked at her, then grinned. 'You're right. Why shouldn't she?'

Lilibet, of course, could not ask Philip to marry her, much as she no doubt would have liked to. He must ask permission from her father, and this seemed, at the moment, unlikely to be granted. Now or ever.

His first visit to Balmoral had gone badly. He had loathed the brown water brought in jugs to the bedrooms and had laughed at kilts, calling them 'sissified'. He had turned up to dinner in an ill-fitting jacket and gone shooting in flannels instead of tweeds. None of this endeared him to the king, but it gave Marion great satisfaction. Philip was reaping what he sowed, unpleasant, arrogant creature that he was.

'I'm not allowed to be in love,' the princess stormed, as though this, not Philip's manners, was the problem.

'Don't moan,' said Margaret. 'We're going to South Africa, remember.'

They were in the suite of rooms that Lilibet had recently been given in the palace, a bedroom and sitting room of her own. Another hint, were it needed, that the princess had become an adult. The suite lacked charm, even so; the princess had neither her sister's style nor her mother's talent for making any place a home. She had accepted whatever the palace storerooms chose to send up, and wherever they chose to leave it.

'I don't want to go to South Africa!' Lilibet snapped. 'Mummie and Papa pretend it's because of the war, to thank the South Africans. But I know it's to try and make me forget Philip.' She paused. 'But I *won't*.'

'Crawfie's not complaining,' said Margaret, shooting Marion a wicked glance. 'And she's having to leave *her* boyfriend. Aren't you, Crawfie?'

As the violet eyes dwelled mockingly on her, Marion found herself, maddeningly, blushing. Margaret's penetrating gaze and instinct for people's vulnerabilities had only increased with age.

'Don't be ridiculous,' she snapped, having finally found her voice.

'No, don't be,' Lilibet agreed. 'Crawfie's our governess. How can *she* be in love?'

Much as she tried to forget it, the remark stung. She persuaded herself that Lilibet did not mean it. She was upset about Philip, that was all. And the dismissive way she had said it, so unlike the old Lilibet, echoed his rude and unpleasant ways. The sooner she got rid of him the better.

The route would go from city to city. Cape Town, Port Elizabeth, Grahamstown. Ladysmith, Pietermaritzburg. Durban, Pretoria, Johannesburg. She would travel with the family on the White Train. This astonishing conveyance, an up-to-date version of the royal train to Scotland, had fourteen carriages, lavish suites, a dining room and sitting room with huge, comfortable armchairs and, incredibly, telephones. 'A miracle of science bent to the service of luxury,' as George had said. He felt the tour was a great opportunity and would not hear of her staying in London with him. She had gradually accepted that perhaps he was right.

Hartnell was creating the wardrobe and was a familiar sight about the corridors again, measuring tape slung over his burly shoulders.

He was portlier than once he had been, and silver steaks glinted in his walnut-coloured waves. But he loved to complain just as much as ever.

'It's three times the usual work!' he told Marion. 'Especially with Maggie putting her oar in everywhere, wanting teenage styles. No doubt to impress that pretty pilot of hers!'

Marion shook her head. Nothing got past Norman. Up until now, only she had guessed the reasons why the youngest princess and the former fighter ace went on such long rides together at Windsor. Although perhaps Rosemary Townsend had guessed too; there were rumours of difficulties. Where it would end was not clear. Hopefully, like her sister's dalliance, with the upcoming tour to South Africa.

'Dresses for every occasion and all types of weather,' Norman went on. 'Windy reviewing stands are a particular danger, I've been told.'

'Windy reviewing stands. Well, I never.'

Norman ignored the irony. 'The answer, since you ask, is weights in the hems. And it's not just wind, let me assure you. No materials that attract fabric-eating insects either. Nor pins that might rust in the humidity.'

'The things you have to think about.'

'Let's talk about what you have to think about, then. Any news on the engagement?'

She shook her head. 'We've decided to put it off until I come back from South Africa.'

Norman looked incredulous. 'Not *yours*, dear. I mean Betty and that sex bomb of a sailor of hers. I'm determined to design the wedding gown.'

The year rolled on. Summer gave way to autumn. The days shortened. Soon, late in the afternoon, Marion could go to the schoolroom window and see the yellow glow of cars down on the Mall. That the lights, having gone out all over Europe, were now all back on again was still a source of wonder. But it was wonderful to be in love again, and be loved in return.

'Crawfie! Here you are!' The voice was the queen's, and full of friendly delight. 'I've been looking for you everywhere!'

Behind her, in the doorway, Marion caught the retreating flash of a footman's white-stockinged calf. Someone, certainly, had been looking for her everywhere.

The queen, gracious in chiffon of the eternal misty blue, sat down with a beaming smile. 'At one time,' she said brightly, 'we had thought of taking you with us to South Africa. But there are very few places for staff, and so we're taking an extra equerry instead.'

Marion met the wide blue gaze. This situation felt so familiar. She had expected to do one thing, and the queen told her, in the most charming manner possible, that she was doing the exact opposite. It had happened so many times over the years, and usually after these encounters she felt bruised and resentful. But now she felt nothing but relief. Good. She could stay in London after all. More than that, even – perhaps now was the time to make the break.

'Margaret was especially keen that Peter come. There are apparently such marvellous beaches to ride on, and Peter is such a wonderful rider. You've never been very interested in riding, have you, Crawfie?' The thin red smile was all kind enquiry.

Marion directed her disbelieving gaze at the schoolroom lino. It was obvious that Margaret had used the riding argument to get her off the tour. The acute younger princess knew she had guessed the nature of her interest in Peter. She was not having a disapproving governess spoiling her fun.

But was this not the chance she had been looking for? Lilibet didn't want her, and Margaret didn't either. So what was the point? She raised her head, forcing a smile. 'Do you think, ma'am,' she said brightly, 'that perhaps the time has come to make a break altogether? Margaret's growing up. On her return from this trip I'm not sure she would take to the schoolroom very easily again.'

Now the words were out, she felt light and free. It had been easy, really.

But the queen looked horrified. 'Crawfie! Don't suggest such a thing! Of course she must go back to her lessons. You must not think of leaving us. We could not possibly manage without you.'

'But I'm *not* staying,' she told George later. He was playing with her hair. His touch on her neck made her shiver. 'She is the queen,' he pointed out, humorously. 'You don't want to end up in the Tower.'

She twisted round and glared at him. 'George! Anyone would think that you wanted me to stay there! Don't you want a life of our own?'

He placed a finger on her lips before kissing them. 'Don't worry,' he whispered, slipping a hand inside her blouse. 'There's plenty of time.'

Chapter Fifty-Nine

Nineteen forty-seven was promising to be the worst winter in living memory. Everything was frozen. Roads were either impassable with snow or hopelessly ice-bound. Shops emptied as supplies failed to get through. Marion had woken one morning to find her face bleeding, cut on an icicle that had formed on the sheet from her own breath.

The papers carried pictures of sheep frozen stiff in the fields, some near the Balmoral estate. Marion sent copies to South Africa in reply to the regular letters from the girls. Lilibet's missives were full of distress at what the British people were suffering. She made no mention of her own suffering but Philip's photograph had disappeared from her bedroom, presumably taken with her. Lilibet had been white-faced and sad on departure. All the papers had carried the image of the princess at the ship's rail, face turned wistfully back towards England. They had thought it was the country she would miss.

Margaret's letters, on the other hand, radiated excitement. South Africa was glorious. The White Train was wonderful. But the real excitement was not referred to. There was no mention of Peter Townsend.

'I could leave now, while they're away,' Marion told George. It was Sunday morning and they were in his Earl's Court boarding house. This required ingenuity; Marion evaded the eagle eye of Mrs Batstone, the landlady, by dressing up in one of George's suits and pretending to be a colleague. 'But that might look sneaky,' George pointed out. 'You don't want to leave under a cloud. Not after so many years.'

'Don't I?' But the weeks were slipping by, and with them her chance. Resigning while her royal masters were out of the country was the obvious thing to do. She felt restless. The old urge to make the most of her opportunities had returned. Once, long ago, she had been a modern girl, in what had been a largely old-fashioned world. Now she was a relic of the feudal past in a brave new Britain.

The post-war wind of change had blown through the nation, sweeping away the old deference, sweeping away even Winston Churchill, whose supporters had failed in their arguments to 'Let Him Finish the Job.' He was no longer Prime Minister; Clement Attlee was, and his Labour government was busy founding a free health service, knocking down slums to build decent houses and establishing a welfare state that would help the very poorest in society. There was no place for governesses in a world such as this. Possibly no place even for royalty.

'No you don't,' George said firmly. 'You need to leave with your head held high. Garlanded with gongs and with a nice fat pension.'

'Gongs?' She stared at him. She hadn't even thought about a pension. She would work as a teacher; she had years ahead of her.

'Well, the OBE, a damehood, you know. And there's bound to be some grace-and-favour house they can give you.'

She laughed. 'Don't be silly.'

'I'm not. I'm just thinking of you.'

The family returned. Philip's natty sports car soon became an evening fixture at the palace's little side entrance, and Marion could hear, even from the distance of her bedroom, the uproar in Lilibet's sitting room, where she, Philip and Margaret would have supper and afterward chase one another about the corridors.

She herself was never asked to the suppers. It wasn't that Philip disliked her; it was worse than that — he didn't notice her. To him, she was a servant, of no interest or consequence. Marion did not care what Philip thought. But that Lilibet might, under his influence, start to feel the same way was unbearable.

Marion had no kind feelings towards the Prince of Greece. Philip's sense of humour tended towards the boorish. But Lilibet, previously so sensitive and sensible, clearly found it hilarious. She happily joined in the shooting of balls at the light bulbs – light bulbs that represented the rare luxury of electricity and that someone would have to replace. Lilibet would have cared about all this, once.

One night, against a background of crashing metal trays on which Philip and the princesses were sliding down the staircases, Marion decided to go before she was pushed. As soon as she had passed the note to the footman she ducked out of the palace and called George.

'I've asked to see her on a very important and urgent matter of a personal nature,' she told him.

There was a pause on the other end. 'I see.'

Unease squirmed within Marion. 'Don't you want us to get married?'

'Of course, of course,' he said immediately, soothingly. 'It's a bit awkward, is all. Ulick's just got me a job. As a bank manager.'

Marion was stunned. 'Ulick? Sir Ulick *Alexander?*' The distant, dignified Keeper of the Privy Purse? She hadn't realised George had even met him.

'Well, he offered,' George said. 'Majors together, you know.' It was rare for him to refer to his war record.

She put the receiver down, confused and suspicious. Was this the queen's doing? Drawing George into the royal toils as well, to make it harder for her to go? Time really was running out now.

At the appointed hour, she hurried to the queen's study, churning with panic.

'Crawfie! Do come in!'

She was behind her desk, almost hidden by the clutter of fringed lamps and silver-framed photographs. The room, as ever, was hot and powerfully rose-scented.

As the footman unobtrusively closed the doors behind her, Marion inched forward. She was wearing, to boost her confidence, her newest outfit, a red silk frock that George had urged her to buy. It was flashy and fashionable with a narrow skirt and modishly wide padded shoulders. The spike heels he had also recommended were sinking into the carpet, and maintaining her balance was difficult, especially given that she was carrying a large framed photograph. That too had seemed a good idea at the time, but now she was less sure.

The queen, who was meant to register it immediately, had not even noticed. She had noticed, instead, a bee on one of the roses. 'Something simply too amusing happened with bees in the Orange Free State,' she said brightly. 'When one of the local worthies took off his hat, it was full of them. His hair pomade, apparently. Too amusing!'

Marion was almost at the desk now. Curtseying deeply with a picture under her arm would be even more of a challenge than walking. Slowly, wobblingly, she descended. The queen went on in her breezy way. 'On St Helena we met a two-hundred-year-old tortoise. It must have known Napoleon intimately.'

Marion's fingers crept to the picture frame. The moment could no longer be put off. She rose, and thrust the photograph forward. 'This, ma'am, is the urgent personal matter I have come to see you about.'

The queen stood up, revealing her usual pastel chiffons, and took the picture. She stared at its plain wooden frame. She did not speak, and the silence, or perhaps the bee, buzzed in Marion's ears.

'What's his name?'

'Major George Buthlay. He's from Aberdeen.' She spoke proudly, and with hope. The Scottishness generally and promixity to Balmoral particularly would surely recommend her choice of husband.

The queen handed back the photograph and sat down again behind her screen of silver frames and lampshades. 'You can't leave us,' she said simply. 'A change at this stage for Margaret is not at all desirable.'

Panic swept Marion. 'But Your Majesty. I . . .'

The telephone on the royal desk shrilled. The queen picked it up and exclaimed, beaming, 'Hello, Fatty!'

Later, still stunned by her failure, she was in her room when someone knocked at the door. The hope rose in her, wild but strong, that the queen had come to give her blessing to her departure after all, and would release her immediately. In her creased red silk and stockinged feet, she rushed to answer.

In the entrance stood Lilibet, radiantly beautiful in a dress of optimistic yellow and blazing with happiness like the sun.

'Crawfie!' She came in, closed the door behind her, and held out her left hand. Sparkling on the pale, well-shaped finger was a large square diamond with smaller diamonds either side. 'Isn't it wonderful!' She began excitedly explaining how Philip's mother had sent her tiara from Athens to be broken up to provide the stones. 'Philip was too poor to buy one, you see. Absolutely penniless! So sweet! Don't you think?'

Marion's words would not move from under the stone in her throat. This was interpreted as joy. 'It's finally going to happen!' exulted Lilibet. 'Philip and I are getting married!'

Chapter Sixty

'The glass will be the easiest,' drawled the earl's daughter. 'It only needs a good kick. Getting rid of silver is much more difficult. Walter and I had such luck. All ours was stolen when we were on our honeymoon.'

As the group dissolved into honking laughter, Marion felt a wave of disgust. Most of these people were Philip's friends; he seemed to run with a fast, smart set. Especially, or so the rumours went, after he had dropped Lilibet back at the palace in the evening.

The princess had always avoided people like this before. But she was showing them the exhibition of her wedding presents with every appearance of enjoyment. It was the preview day; tomorrow it would open to the public, admission one shilling. The queues would stretch for miles. Wedding mania had gripped the nation.

A huge table, draped with white, filled up the entire length of St James's Palace ballroom. Arranged on it, against an already ornate background of huge portraits in thick gold frames, were no less than 2,667 gifts. Sent from not just the furthest corners of Empire, but from across the entire world, they gave the heavy ballroom the fantastical aspect of Aladdin's cave. China and glass glittered, silver and gold gleamed. Leatherware, brassware and furniture shone. Pictures and mirrors glowed. There was enough to furnish, not one pair of newly-weds' house, but many, many palaces.

The princess led the way in the corn-coloured frock from which, at the moment, she could scarcely be parted. Philip liked it, Marion suspected. He had good taste, she would give him that; the yellow was the perfect foil for Lilibet's glossy dark hair, rich red lips and creamy skin suffused with rose. She still wore very little make-up. There was something of the innocent girl about her yet.

Not so these sophisticates of the aristocracy stalking round on their colt legs, tossing fur stoles over elegant shoulders. A white-gloved hand brushed, questioningly, a large pile of magnificently bound leather books. 'They're from Mr Churchill,' came Lilibet's high, clear voice. 'He autographed them for us.'

The owner of the white-gloved hand read the gold-stamped title. '*The World Crisis?* Hardly bedtime reading! This is much more like it!' The earl's daughter paused before a mass of magnificent rubies.

'They're from the Burmese nation,' supplied Lilibet.

'Goodness, look at these diamonds,' interrupted a duke's sister. 'They're absolutely amazing.'

'They're from the Nizam of Hyderabad.'

High-pitched titters greeted this. 'The what of where?'

'What on earth is a Nizam?'

'Does it matter?' murmured the white-gloved girl, gazing at the diamonds. More titters.

And so it went on, slowly round the display. Gasps of admiration alternated with exclamations of puzzlement.

'But, my dear, what could this possibly be?'

The fast set had paused before a lump of pinkish stone. Lilibet beamed round at the group. 'It's an uncut diamond.'

'Is this one too?' The duke's daughter had stalked ahead and was gesturing at a large grey boulder.

'That's a bit of Snowdon. An old man from Wales sent it. He said in his letter that it was for luck.'

Luck, thought Marion darkly. None of this had brought any luck that she could identify. As feared, she had become relegated and ignored, dragged along to carry the handbags. She, who had been Lilibet's all in all. Her friend and companion, her trusted teacher, her playmate, her wartime comfort. All forgotten now that Philip had entered the picture.

Beside the piece of mountain was a small lump of gold. 'From the people of Wales for my wedding ring,' came Lilibet's high, trilling voice. The people of Wales strike again, Marion thought, remembering the first visit to The Little House. Sudden tears stung her eyes and she had to turn away.

The group passed on, not bothering to look at the lace Victorian underslip, beautifully hand-embroidered, that had been worn by the brides of an old lady's family for generations. But no more – and Lilibet would not wear it either.

'What's this?' White Gloves was pointing at a piece of plain cloth.

'It's a loincloth. From Mahatma Gandhi. He made it himself, on a spinning wheel.'

'Why ever would he do that?'

'Well, he's renounced all worldly possessions, you see.' Lilibet passed on to a silver ashtray. 'From the Eisenhowers. I rather wish they hadn't though, as Philip's promised to stop smoking.'

There were exclamations of disgust at two misshapen black lumps arranged on a plate. Marion had opened that one too. The lumps were charred toast, sent by two high-spirited young women who had been making it when the news of the royal engagement came over the radio. They had been so excited they had burned their supper.

'Imagine sending toast,' scoffed the duke's daughter.

'Imagine *making* it,' added White Gloves, derisively.

As the princess laughed her high, trilling laugh, Marion thought of the Balmoral bothy. How little Lilibet had loved to make it then.

'It's a nightmare.' Norman had lost weight and was smoking copiously. 'They're bribing all my staff. My packer's actually been offered a yacht.'

Marion clutched her jacket around herself. It was late October and very cold but they were in the palace gardens because Norman thought the rooms he used were bugged. He had taken to checking the corners of ceilings for spy cameras. Marion was reminded, poignantly, of Cameron the royal detective and the trip to the YWCA. Happy, long-ago days.

She tried to concentrate. 'A *yacht?* Really?'

'It's hell, I tell you.' Norman's tone exactly blended hysteria and delight. 'The whole world wants pictures of my dress. I've had to cover all my windows in muslin. My manager is literally sleeping in the salon.' He lit another cigarette and puffed on it agitatedly.

Finding the right design had taken months. It was perfect though, a vision in satin and pearls and featuring the exquisite embroidery that had made the Hartnell name. Marion was one of the tiny handful to have seen the sketches. But the queen, who had ultimate veto, had taken her time to approve them.

A delaying tactic, obviously. Both king and queen were battling valiantly to hide their dread and despair at the coming parting. Showered with congratulations, none of which he wanted, the king was doing his best to seem cheerful. The queen's serene smile no doubt required as much courage as any of her wartime displays of bravado.

Marion looked at the trees, blazing richly with autumn colour. They had, she felt, an elegiac air. As she glanced at the silver lake another memory surfaced, of Lilibet falling in. Of Tommy's muscled torso. She pushed it away, thinking of George's muscled torso instead.

'And of course,' Norman said, 'I've only just got over the worms.'

'I didn't realise you'd been ill.'

'The *silkworms*.' Norman sighed deeply. 'People thought they were Italian, or possibly Japanese. I was accused of using enemy silkworms.' He let out a rush of cigarette smoke.

'I thought the war was over.'

'Not in the field of bridal gowns, my dear.'

Marion snorted. It was good to laugh with Norman again. 'What do you think of Philip?' she asked.

'Godlike.'

She nudged him. 'I'm talking about the sort of *person* he is.'

'Does it matter?' He brushed a fallen leaf from his jacket. A silence followed, punctuated by the twittering and trilling of birds. They would be leaving soon as well. Everyone was, except her.

'I suppose the cake's a bit odd,' Norman said, eventually. 'They're having a battle scene on it. On the third tier. That battle that Philip was in. Operated the searchlight or something.'

'Matapan?'

'Royal icing, I heard. With edible paint.'

She thumped him. 'Not marzipan. Matapan. The name of the battle.'

Norman was huffily straightening his immaculate jacket sleeve. 'If you say so. But what sort of man has a battle on his wedding cake? Rather macho, isn't it?'

Chapter Sixty-One

It was the morning of the wedding. Marion had slept little. Pictures had whirled in her head all the night long. Lilibet catching happy days at Birkhall. Writing carefully in the schoolroom. Rattling Marion's bell-hung reins to deliver bread in Hamilton Gardens.

Sensing the princess hadn't slept either, she had gone to her suite in the dawn, still in her dressing gown. There would be no other opportunity today to see her alone. In the evening she would leave the palace with Philip. This was goodbye. After sixteen years, this was the end.

They stood at the window of Lilibet's sitting room. The dim light of coming day struggled through the long net curtains. Outside, filling the Mall, was a solid mass of people, many of whom had evidently slept out. Mounted policemen were trotting magnificently past small squatting groups cooking bacon on camping stoves. The window was open slightly; a faint smell of coffee floated in with the noise of the crowd.

She looked at the princess, staring out with wonder at the crowd. Diminutive in her dressing gown, hair rumpled from the pillow, the bride-to-be seemed suddenly so close to the little golden-haired girl driving her team round the park with a dressing-gown cord attached to the bedposts. A sudden surge of love threatened to knock Marion off her slippered feet.

As Lilibet was still staring out, she could take one last long look. The tilt of the head, the delicate profile, the pure pale skin. The soft shine of dark hair. At what point had Lilibet changed from blonde to brunette? She had been too close to see. Precious, intimate moments, thousands of them over the years, had gone by almost unremarked. There would always be a next one. But this was the very last.

Lilibet returned to her dressing table and there was about her the unmistakable air of someone who wanted to get on with things. It was time to go.

She had intended a brisk, smiling farewell. But Marion's footsteps felt lead-heavy as she approached the princess. She blinked wet eyes. 'Goodbye,' she managed. From her blocked throat, it came out a whisper.

Lilibet remained with her back turned, looking into the mirror. The blue reflected gaze was dry, even dismissive. 'Goodbye, Crawfie,' she said crisply. 'I'll see you in the abbey.'

They were now engaged, so George had been put on the wedding guest list. Now they sat in Poets' Corner, Marion in velvet of George's favourite colour, red. She wore a broad-brimmed black hat to which black ostrich plumes were fixed with ruby clips. It was bigger than her usual style but cast a shadow over her face, which might come in useful.

The faint light of dawn was now a dull morning. Through the alchemy of stained glass, the watery sun gave off rays of brilliant colour. They glowed on the ancient stonework and danced off the diamonds and pearls, silks and feathers, medals and braid of the waiting guests. How often she had been here, Marion thought. So many weddings, funerals and christenings. She could remember every detail of all of them.

So could Tommy, she guessed. He sat nearby, impeccable in a morning suit, with the inevitable Joan beside him in tiara and long white gloves. Marion nodded to them both. Tommy nodded back, his gaze lingering impassively on George for some seconds.

'Who's that bloody stuffed shirt?' George hissed.

Five kings, eight queens and eight princes and princesses, from Romania to Iraq by way of Denmark, Norway and Holland, had mustered to see the wedding of the heir to the English throne.

Philip, newly minted as a British citizen, had given up his Greek title but had been immediately swamped by British ones ranging from duke to baron and judiciously sprinkled about the islands. His mother, the strange Princess Alice, who sometimes flitted about the palace in convent robes like a dark ghost, sat in the nave. His sisters, all married to former high-ranking Nazis, were not present.

But not all the black sheep were on Philip's side. Also conspicuous by his absence was the Duke of Windsor, now living in Paris. Marion wondered about Wallis, as she rarely did these days. No one did, which must have been the intention. Their exile was as complete as it was deliberate. When the queen wanted to get rid of someone, that person never came back.

She could see the queen from here. She wore an uncharacteristically simple outfit in what was, for her, an equally unusual apricot brocade. Her face wore its usual expression of sweet composure, but Marion could guess what, today of all days, was going through that most cryptic of royal minds.

'Who's the tall bird?' George was nodding towards a brunette in the front row of the nave.

'Edwina Mountbatten.' The willowy, beautiful and astonishingly rich wife of Lord Louis. He stood beside her, looking equally aquiline and haughty, but possibly a little purple under the eyes.

Last night had been Philip's stag night. The group of naval officers had been pursued by photographers to the Dorchester, where Mountbatten had suggested, in the interests of fairness, that the revellers take pictures of the newspapermen first. They had handed over their cameras, whereupon Philip and his friends had smashed them on the lobby's marble floor. The incident had been reported as an example of Mountbatten ingenuity, but Marion had thought it cold and cruel. She wondered if one of the photographers had been Tom.

The organ played softly. From time to time the doors opened to admit latecomers, letting in the shouts of the crowds outside. 'We want Elizabeth! We want Philip!'

'So do we,' George muttered. 'We've been sitting here for bloody ages. Where are they?'

There was a murmur of anticipation as the great doors opened once again. Under the arched entrance that had welcomed monarchs for centuries stood a doughty, instantly recognisable but nonetheless hideously late figure. With the faithful Clementine on his arm, Churchill started to make his way slowly down the aisle to his seat at the front. 'Hasn't the bloke got a clock? Not exactly his finest hour, if you get my meaning.' George chuckled at his own joke.

But now, finally, the moment had come. All eyes swung to the Great West Door. Marion gasped. Lilibet was here.

She came slowly up the aisle on the king's gold-braided arm. Marion felt at once bright with pride and heavy with sorrow. Lilibet looked like a ship, a beautiful, sparkling ship, rising like a mast from her long full skirts with her cloud of veil following like a sail. She glided up the red sea of carpet towards her naval lieutenant.

The non-enemy silkworms had done a good job; the satin shone pure white in the yellow glow of the tall candelabra. The embroidery on the skirts was spectacular, and there was so much of it, great swags of seed pearls and crystals forming roses, syringa and jasmine. It was based on Botticelli's *Primavera*, Norman claimed, but Marion had never seen the resemblance to the loose-haired pagan in the painting. Lilibet, anyway, looked more beautiful even than the Renaissance Spring.

George nudged her. 'Breathe!'

Marion let out a gasp of air. She felt she was descending from a great height.

'Here's Maggie!' whispered George.

Marion's heart went out to Margaret, resplendent in full-skirted tulle, her glossy head held high, walking in dignified solitude down the aisle after the bride and before the bridesmaids. The separation was to emphasise her rank but made her seem a lonely, even vulnerable figure. She was only seventeen. How would she cope without Lilibet in the palace? *And how will I cope with her?* Marion wondered, glumly. It was a bleak prospect.

The service passed in a whirl. The Archbishop of York conjoined the young couple to have 'patience, a ready sympathy and forbearance'.

George snorted. 'What have they got to be forbearing about?'

Plenty, Marion thought, looking at Philip's arrogant, handsome face.

The couple went into the vestry and came out again, Lilibet radiant with happiness. She passed back down the aisle and then, reaching the place where her parents stood, paused and swept them a deep, beautiful curtsey. As the memory of that very first curtsey to the king on his accession day came back with force, Marion fumbled for her handkerchief.

Outside it was all wild pealing of the bells and the cheers of the crowds clustering about the abbey. Margaret emerged with Peter Townsend beside her, dashing in his RAF uniform. She was looking up at him in a manner that could be interpreted only one way.

The queen was coming out now. She paused beside Marion and smiled. 'I think she is happy, Crawfie.' The glassy blue eyes were wistful.

'I know how you feel, ma'am,' Marion said, from her full heart. 'I feel as if I've lost a daughter as well.'

The queen drew back. There was a beat or two before she said, with her usual serene smile, 'I'm sure you do, Crawfie. But they grow up and leave us, and we must make the best of it.'

With that, she passed on to her carriage. Lilibet and Philip's had already set off, glittering in the sunlight, borne by cheers, into their glorious future.

PART FOUR

NOTTINGHAM COTTAGE, 1949

Chapter Sixty-Two

Marion was weeding, pulling long blades of grass from the lavender border. The air was warm, and lively with birdsong.

The cottage behind her was built of old thin red brick with a tiled roof and roses round the door. It looked like a house in a fairy tale, especially when the nearby field was full of white-fleeced sheep and the pigeons cooed in the trees in the evening. Really, she should be content.

Surrounding the garden was a low white fence into which was set a little gate. On it, in neat black capitals, were painted the words 'Nottingham Cottage'. The long red buildings of Kensington Palace stretched all about. But the traffic of the nearby High Street was almost inaudible here. You would never have imagined you were in the centre of one of the biggest cities in the world.

It was the perfect home for a newly married couple. And yet happiness seemed to have eluded them.

George's playing floated out through the little white-painted window, open on the latch because of the warm day. His hands on the piano keys sounded angry and discordant, and sent a responding note of dismay through Marion. Their marriage had had a difficult start.

After an exhausting year trying to keep Margaret in line, Marion had been at her wit's end. 'We are only young once, Crawfie,' had been the queen's serene view. 'We want her to have a good time. With Lilibet gone, it is lonely for her here.'

Marion doubted that lonely was the word. As well as the nights out with the young officers the king had dubbed 'the Bodyguard', there were the driving lessons with the ever-attentive Townsend. Margaret's beauty, always remarkable, had now reached a ripe intensity. Small-waisted, generously breasted, large-mouthed and big-eyed, she dazzled every man who saw her.

George's enforced return to Scotland, as married couples were not allowed at the palace, was made yet worse by Lilibet's letters transmitting wedded bliss. The arrival of a baby prince had twisted the knife still further. With her husband permanently absent, the prospects of her own family seemed to Marion more distant even than Aberdeen.

We are only young once. In royal service, her own youth had ebbed away. Soon she would be forty. Yet she was still not in control of her life.

And then, one day, it was all over.

Marion was summoned to be told that she was to retire, and that the king would bestow upon her, for her lifetime, one of the grace-and-favour houses that were in his personal gift. It had been hard to believe. The king and queen had finally accepted the inevitable. And George could join her at last.

She had finished the lavender border without even realising. She sat back on her heels for a minute, looked up at the blue sky and smiled. Behind her, in the cottage, the angry piano music went on.

George's permanent move to London should have been the beginning of their happiness. But it seemed, for some reason, to have marked its end. The smile faded from Marion's face.

Where once they had laughed, now they argued. He was dissatisfied with everything. He felt the cottage too small, for a start.

'But I love it,' Marion had countered. 'And it's free. We don't have to pay anything. We should be grateful. We – '

'Shouldn't look a gift house in the mouth?' he interrupted. 'But you gave them the best years of your life, what about those old biddies who've been given ten-room apartments round here? Purely because they're relatives?'

It was true that various old princesses had been splendidly accommodated in 'the aunt heap', as Lilibet and Margaret called Kensington

Palace. But Marion was more than happy with what she had been allotted.

George was also savagely critical about her pension, claiming that it should have been more generous. He also felt that the CVO bestowed on her should have been the DCVO. 'A downright insult,' stormed George. 'If you'd been one of those la-di-da courtiers you'd have been a dame.'

Babies would no doubt have made a difference, but they had not come. The possibility that they never would was too dreadful to contemplate, and burdened lovemaking with impossible expectation. At night, where once they had clung together, now they lay apart. Moreover, she had nothing whatsoever to do. Even chivvying Margaret now seemed preferable to the long days she spent waiting for George to come back, or out in the garden.

How had it all gone so wrong? Why had everything she had hoped for turned to dust? Was it her fault? When she looked back, down the chains of events that had led to this decision or that, one person seemed at the end of every one: the queen.

'Mrs Booth?' Clipped tones broke into her reverie. Someone was standing between her and the sunshine. Someone tall, spare and upright.

'Buthlay. Mrs Buthlay.' Marion scrambled to her feet, brushing the grass from her dress and looking to see who was raising his hat at her. 'Tommy!' she exclaimed.

'Of course, do forgive me. I'm so used to thinking of you as Miss Crawford.'

Thinking of you. It sent a ripple through her even now. She tried and failed not to blush.

Behind her, in the cottage, the piano stopped jangling. George appeared at the window in his suspenders, his sleeves rolled up to the elbow. He gave Tommy a hostile stare.

Tommy seemed unperturbed. He raised his bony jaw and removed his bowler hat again. 'Good morning, Mr Buthlay. Not at work today?'

Marion hung her head. As everyone knew, George was never at work, today or any other day. The bank manager job had never materialised, after all.

Lascelles glanced around the garden and at the house. She saw him taking in every detail with his sharp dark eyes. 'It's really a most attractive place you have here, Mrs Buthlay. Quite unlike any other building designed by Christopher Wren, I should think.'

'May I offer you a cup of tea, Tommy?' This prompt, Marion hoped, would encourage him to make his excuses and move on. But the royal private secretary lingered by the fence, his immaculate pinstripes framed by the pointed white palings.

'That would be very welcome,' he said. 'As a matter of fact, there's something I wish to talk to you about.'

'Most charming,' Tommy said, looking round the small kitchen. They had been unable to use the sitting room because George was again crashing away at the piano. 'My husband is a great fan of music,' Marion apologised, closing the connecting door. The piano stopped, and a hornlike blare filled the room.

'Indeed. And he plays the trumpet too?'

'Actually, that's the boiler.' Marion tried her best to ignore George opening the door again. Was he spying on her?

She went on. 'It's rather temperamental. Water gets hot at odd times and you have to draw it off immediately. We have baths at all times of day here.' She tried to make this sound like a delightful eccentricity rather than the inconvenience it actually was. 'I was having one the other day when Lilibet and Philip arrived on my doorstep.' She gave an embarrassed smile. Oh, why had she started this anecdote?

But it seemed just what her visitor wanted to hear. He seized on it instantly. 'Actually, Mrs Buthlay – '

'Marion, please.' She suddenly craved the illusion that the old days weren't quite gone.

'Marion.' Lascelles nodded. 'It's about the princess that I wanted to talk to you. You remember the amazing Mrs Gould?'

'Vaguely. She wanted the queen to write articles for her magazine. You had to go and see her at the Ritz.'

'Your memory is impressive.' Tommy took another sip. 'Which is what I want to talk about, as it happens. Excellent tea, by the way.'

'You want to talk about my memory?'

A furtive expression crossed Tommy's face. 'Mrs Gould wants Princess Elizabeth to write the articles this time.'

Marion frowned, confused. 'You've lost me, Tommy.' The music from next door had stopped altogether. Even the boiler's brass section stilled. 'Lilibet can't possibly do that. And what has it to do with my memory?'

Tommy let pass a beat or two. 'There is some interest in the idea of articles that promote, er, international ties between women.'

Marion stared at him.

'I'm paraphrasing Mrs Gould here,' the private secretary went on, uncomfortably.

He passed a thin hand through his still-thick dark hair. 'She's extremely determined, as you know. She is, if you'll pardon the expression, absolutely hell-bent on these articles and has support in some very high places. Lady Astor is behind her, as is the American ambassador. And the Foreign Office. '

'*The Foreign Office?*' Marion was astonished. 'She's got *them* on side?'

'Indeed, and they've got on to the palace. It's known as lobbying. Persuasion. Pressure.' He sighed.

Marion turned her teacup in her hands. 'I still don't see what any of it has to do with me.'

Tommy bent towards her. A gleam had entered his dark gaze. 'Quite a lot, actually. I've got a plan. Princess Elizabeth can't write these articles personally, you're quite right. The solution that has been hit on is a series of pieces about Princess Elizabeth, but written by someone else.'

The blood beat in Marion's ears. 'You mean me? You want me to write them?' She thought of all the letters she had written to her mother. And her long, purposeless days. It would give her something to so. A purpose in life. 'I'd love to,' she said, feeling a pleasure and excitement unknown for months.

She stopped. He was holding up a long pale hand. 'Not you. Of *course* not.' His tone was mildly incredulous. 'The writer has already been commissioned by Mrs Gould. For quite a considerable sum, I understand.'

Marion stared. She had not even thought about the money angle. 'Who is it?'

'A good friend of mine. Name of Morrah. Dermot Morrah. Excellent chap. We played chess together all the way to South Africa. And back.'

South Africa. So he had gone on the tour she was dropped from. Dermot Morrah. She did not recognise the name. But if Tommy played chess with him he must obviously be of a certain class.

'And the queen wants him to write these pieces?' But what did Morrah know of Lilibet? 'I've been with Princess Elizabeth for sixteen years,' she pointed out. 'I know her better than anyone.'

She had expected Tommy to look irritated; he looked gratified instead. 'Precisely. So you can talk to him, tell him everything you know. Then he can put it all in his articles.'

Chapter Sixty-Three

The journey from Kensington Palace to Buckingham Palace was a short one. Ordinarily, Marion would have walked, but today she called for a car. The reason was not laziness, nor the wish to avail herself of her perquisites, which, besides a free house, included the services of a chauffeur. George used him far more than she did.

It was because today she had something to carry. It was a box, the polished chest made from the scuttled ship that her mother had given her long ago. It had always been a lovely thing but it was even more beautiful now. Over the years, the colour of the wood had deepened and mellowed so her initial on the curved lid, in paler wood, stood out in sharper relief.

It sat on Marion's knee as the car glided along Kensington Gore. She held it carefully in both hands in case a jolt made it tip over and the contents spill out. Inside, neatly tied in separate bundles, were sixteen years' worth of letters from Lilibet and Margaret. All had been written to her during her short holidays with her mother in Scotland. All told her how much they missed her, urged her to come back soon and gave snippets of news.

The handwriting was a calligraphic history of the girls' development, ranging from the very first childish pencilled scrawls, lavishly illustrated with crayon, to rounded early-teenage hands and, latterly, elegant young-lady script. All were on the embossed notepaper of the various royal residences and all ended with lavish expressions of affection, *From Your Loving Lilibet* or *With Lots of Love from Margaret*.

Marion looked in the box often; more and more frequently, in fact. During her years with the girls it had been mainly a repository, a useful place to put things. But now it was her most treasured possession. It held precious memories, assurances of affection from the two beings she had loved most in the world. And still did, there being no children arrived in the interim for her to lavish her affections on.

The chest reminded her that, while George scoffed at her and criticised, she had been truly needed once. Respected, depended upon, sought out, adored. Lifting out the bundles, carefully untying the faded ribbons and smoothing out the paper so she could read the loving words written there, she felt soothed, sad and happy all at the same time.

George had no idea that the box existed. Keeping it from him was no easy task; he had a suspicious, devious streak, which was the reason that, in her purse, there was often less than she expected. He had only to ask for money, but he didn't. Always at the back of her mind was the fear that, should he come across it and realise what it was, he might offer the contents of her precious chest for sale. She hid it on top of her wardrobe, behind a pile of hatboxes.

But now she had taken it down. It was coming with her to see the queen – proof, were it needed, that no one knew the story of Lilibet's childhood better than she.

'Good morning, Miss Crawford,' smiled the Buckingham Palace policeman. 'We haven't seen you for a while.'

Marion, her box held carefully under one arm, drew herself up. 'I'm Mrs Buthlay now, Constable Jenkins. I've left the palace.'

He gave her a wise look. 'You'll always be Miss Crawford to me. And no one ever really leaves the palace. You know that.'

'Too true.' Marion smiled back, hugging her chest to her side.

It felt strange to be back amid the great red corridors and gilded ornamentation. She had forgotten the vast distances, but she had forgotten none of the people. And it seemed, like PC Jenkins, none of them had forgotten her.

Housemaids nodded and smiled. Footmen grinned. Familiar figures appeared in the distance. There was Mr Linnet, who came daily to fill up the flower vases. Round the bend of a corridor she spotted the man – she had never learned his name – whose daily job it was to wind up the hundreds of palace clocks. And, no doubt, somewhere within the vast building, the Vermin Man was going about his business.

A powerful nostalgia seized Marion as she followed the queen's page down the passages. She had lived here for fourteen years. Every corner had an association. She could almost hear the little girls shrieking with joy in the corridors, thundering happily past visiting prime ministers and princes, often with herself in their wake.

It was true. You never really left the palace.

She waited as the queen's page knocked. 'Mrs Marion Buthlay, Your Majesty.'

The queen was sitting not behind her desk as expected but on a chintz sofa in front of a roaring fire. She wore a dress of pale lavender, and several strings of pearls. A near-empty box of chocolates sat on a small polished table beside her.

She laid down her copy of *The Times* with a sigh. 'Such ghastly news, Crawfie! Cripps is devaluing the pound so rationing gets even worse. And this dreadful Mao Tse Tung. He's just declared China a Communist republic, did you know?'

'Yes, ma'am.' She still read the papers. It was one of the few things that filled her day.

The queen smilingly patted the cushions beside her. 'Well, Crawfie, come and sit by me and we can forget for a while the poor torn world and its problems!'

The warm welcome made Marion's heart sink. It was one of the queen's toughest tactics and brought back many memories of similar past encounters. Her heart was hammering hard. She wished that it was her husband, not herself, who now approached the woman on the sofa.

George had been a man of burning purpose from the second Tommy Lascelles had left Nottingham Cottage. All his aimlessness, restlessness and discontent had disappeared with the click of the latch. He had overheard the entire conversation and deplored it.

It was outrageous, he maintained, for anyone but Marion to write about Princess Elizabeth. She must go to the queen and obtain for herself the permission that had been granted Dermot Morrah. He had been given the task not because he knew the first thing about it but because he was a courtier. The implication, George said, was that Marion, despite knowing the subject backward and forward, was of the servant class and unworthy of it. After so many years in loyal service, it was beyond belief.

Marion agreed. George's raging had keyed her up to a similar degree of self-righteous fury. She tried to summon it now as she lowered herself on the edge of the sofa. Her foot made contact with something; the paw of an animal. From under the sofa came a frenzied yapping.

'Crackers as usual,' smiled the queen.

'I'm sorry, Your Majesty.' She must look even more unravelled than she thought.

The blue eyes widened in surprise. 'No, Crackers is his *name*.' She burst into peals of laughter. Had she made a fool of herself, Marion wondered, or had the queen made a fool of her? As ever, it was hard to tell. But it was not a good start, certainly.

Dabbing her eyes, the queen rearranged herself. 'So, what is it that you wanted to talk to me about, Crawfie?'

She was thundering with nerves, but pulled herself together. Briefly, she explained her mission. The queen heard her out in silence. When she had finished, she looked away. The seconds pounded in Marion's anxious ears.

Presently the queen turned back. Her eyes lingered on the box, whose purpose Marion had explained. 'You were with us such a long time, Crawfie,' she began. Her voice was gentle. Hope began to steal into Marion's heart.

'Indeed, ma'am. Sixteen years.'

'You have good sense and have always been affectionate and loyal.'

'Thank you, ma'am!' The relief was almost overpowering.

The queen raised her plump chin slightly. The blue eyes blazed into Marion's like a searchlight, although the voice remained light and pleasant. 'But I do feel most strongly that you must resist the lure of American money. You must ignore persistent editors. You must say no to offers of dollars for articles about something as private and as precious as our family.'

Marion was confused. 'But Mr Morrah . . .' He hadn't resisted any of this. Dollars, editors, the invasion of privacy. He had royal sanction for all of it. As George had pointed out, over and over, why was it different for him?

The high, light voice went pleasantly on. 'It is fine for your memories to be incorporated into his articles. But you can't write under your own name. That might lead to' – the thin red lips twitched – 'embarrassment.'

Marion was aghast. 'But I would never write anything that might upset the family, ma'am. I would never dream of doing such a thing.' She swallowed, blinking back sudden tears. 'I love your daughters as if they were my own, ma'am. And they were very fond of me.' She held the box forward, as proof.

The queen looked away as if from something distasteful. 'You have,' she said to the fireplace, 'been wonderfully discreet all the years you have been with us. But I do feel, most definitely, that you must not write and sign articles about the children. We could never trust anyone again if you did.'

But she trusted Morrah. And had he worked for her devotedly for sixteen years? Given up his youth, his hopes of family life?

The blue searchlight swung round again. 'Crawfie, you must see that people in positions of confidence with us must be utterly oyster.'

This, clearly, was the final word. The page had re-entered the room. The door stood open. She rose and curtsied deeply.

'Perhaps – ' the queen added, suddenly.

Marion whirled back round, hope tearing through her. 'Ma'am?'

'Perhaps you had better leave that box with me. For safekeeping?' The queen gave her a dazzling smile.

Marion swallowed, gripping the chest to her so hard she felt it might break her ribcage. 'It's quite safe with me, ma'am.' Her eyes locked with her former employer's in a mixture of defiance and desperation. *Don't take it from me. Please. It's all I have left of them.*

The queen looked irritated, but did not press the point. As Marion hurried out, from under the sofa, Crackers growled.

George returned almost immediately after she did. There was only just time to replace the box.

'You should write your own story anyway,' he raged, when she told him about the queen's response. She agreed that it was outrageous and unfair that a courtier was allowed to do what she herself was not. But the queen had said no and that was that. There was no point dwelling on it. She must try to put the whole episode behind her. See it as a spur to leave London and finally start a new life elsewhere.

'What else can I do?' she asked George. 'Where would I take my own version, even if I wrote it?'

Chapter Sixty-Four

The champagne hit the bowl of the crystal glass in a shimmering golden stream. Marion watched it swirl round the sugar cube and drown the lemon peel shaving. A bright red cherry spun amid the bubbles.

Around the glass and through it, the lights of the room shone brilliantly. The focal point was a central chandelier whose blaze bounced off the gilded plasterwork. There were cherubs, moulding and friezes, just as in Buckingham Palace, and a dark-haired diminutive woman sat enthroned in the centre of the room. This was not the palace, however, but a suite at the Ritz. And the woman was not the queen, but Beatrice Gould.

Standing in the centre of a carpet rippling with ribbons and swags of flowers, Beatrice had greeted Marion with the warmth of someone who had seen her last week, not seven long years ago. Time had been kind to her; her figure was as trim, her face as vivid and her dark eyes as bright and keen as Marion remembered. The woman last seen crashing a royal tea party had acquired some extra polish since then, though.

Possibly too much polish, applied with too free a hand. Her shining lipstick was of a brilliant red and matched the gleaming scarlet tips of her nails. Her white two-piece, meanwhile, looked almost risibly over-smart, edged with black and overlaid with ropes of pearls.

'Your good health, Marion.' The rich Iowa tones of Bruce Gould boomed above her. He was a cartoon American, broad, genial and tall as the sky, his cocktail lurching from side to side as he raised it. 'It's great to see you, and to be back in England, where we have so many good friends. Lady Astor, the Marchioness of Reading and Baroness Elliot to mention but a few.'

'Not to mention our many good friends in the government,' Beatrice added swiftly. 'And the Foreign Office, and of course the Royal Household.'

'So,' Bruce beamed. 'How are you, Marion? If I may call you Marion?'

George, in the corner, nodded an urgent 'yes.' 'Marion is fine. Are you well, Mrs Gould?'

'Beatrice, please! And I'm great, thank you. More than great. *The Ladies' Home Journal* is going from strength to strength.'

'Beatrice and I have really turned it around,' Bruce put in. 'It's got the biggest circulation in the world.'

'For a magazine of its type,' Beatrice modified.

'*One and a half million* devoted Ladies of America! That's what we call our readers,' Bruce went on.

'Wanna know what our secret is?' Beatrice had leaned forward. Her scarlet-nailed hand lay on Marion's red velvet knee, the same suit she had worn to Lilibet's wedding. 'We give our Ladies what they want to read about. We commission a lot of top literary figures.'

'And you could be one of them,' Bruce chimed in. 'Have your articles about bringing up the little princesses read by one and a half million Ladies of America.' The champagne hissed into her glass as he refilled it.

Marion looked at him. 'But Her Majesty doesn't want me to write them for you. She wants Dermot Morrah to.'

'And that, frankly, is just nuts!' Beatrice exclaimed. '*Nuts!* Dermot's a *terrible* writer. And he doesn't know the princesses like you do. It makes much more sense for you to do it.'

'And much, much more money,' Bruce added, with a wink at George.

Beatrice's hand squeezed her own. 'Honey, it must hurt to be treated this way. You looked after those princesses for sixteen years, right?'

'She did,' put in George, from the back.

Beatrice ignored him. She kept her eyes fixed on Marion. 'You did everything for those girls. You were by their side when their parents were not. Through the war, through everything. Right?'

'Right,' said George.

'Honey, *you* were their mother, not Queen Elizabeth. It was *you* that brought them up. And this is what the Ladies of America want to know about. Princess Elizabeth is going to be a humdinger of a queen, make a difference to the world. Thanks to *you*, honey.'

Marion, a lump in her throat, did not trust herself to speak. It was true – all true. She took refuge in her cocktail.

'International relations,' Bruce continued, 'are a big part of our work on *The Ladies' Home Journal*. We believe in forging links across the sea. We want to bring America and Britain closer together. You'll remember that Beatrice came over with Mrs Roosevelt during the war.'

'We believe passionately in the power of the written word to unite nations,' his wife said, deftly taking over. 'And it is our strong conviction, Marion, our absolute belief, that your story will do an incredible amount to bring Britain and the United States closer in real friendship and understanding.'

Marion stared at the ribbons on the carpet. They seemed to be moving. She took a deep breath. 'But I can't, that's the problem. When I asked the queen for permission, she refused it. Then she sent a letter repeating what she'd said. It was pretty stern, I have to say.'

'And written two months after she saw you,' Beatrice swiftly pointed out. 'So hardly her top priority.'

Marion glanced at George. There were no prizes for guessing how Beatrice had got this information. In return, he gave her a blithe thumbs-up.

'Honey.' Beatrice leaned persuasively forward. 'The queen is mad keen that these articles come out, believe me. The Foreign Office too, and the Royal Household. Everyone's behind them. Lady Astor too. Your friend Tommy came to see you, right?'

'But I've explained. I can't . . .'

It was no use though. Beatrice was like a runaway train. Once she got up momentum, she was unstoppable. 'Our one and a half million Ladies of America will thrill to your account of how you took a young girl and made her into the finest English monarch since Elizabeth the First. She'll be Elizabeth the Third, right?'

'The Second,' Marion put in hastily.

'But her mother's called Elizabeth, and she's the queen?' Bruce's heavy face creased with puzzlement. Then, as Marion explained about the consort system, it cleared. 'You're kidding me. Two different types of queen? That's crazy. And just the kind of thing that would fascinate our Ladies!'

Marion felt herself weakening. The cocktail, her fury, the idea of writing on the subject she knew more about than anyone else, it was all powerfully attractive. 'But Her Majesty has told me not to.'

There was a silence. Finally, it seemed, she had got through to them.

'Honey,' said Beatrice. 'You don't need her permission. You can do it anyway.'

'She can't stop you,' Bruce added. 'And she'll come round in the end, you'll see. This is gonna do so much to increase understanding and friendship between the women of our two nations. The Foreign Office is gonna be thrilled. The Royal Household, the whole darn lot. She'll be grateful too, believe me.'

'It's a patriotic act,' Beatrice pressed. 'You'll be making a fortune and doing your duty to king and country both at the same time.'

'Even if,' Beatrice added, with a look at George, 'they haven't exactly done their duty to you.'

Something flashed in Marion's mind. There was no doubt she had been treated badly, particularly of late. The queen's manipulations, Margaret's arrogance, Lilibet's coolness, even if inspired by Philip. She had been taken for granted, disregarded, ignored. She had seen Lilibet only once since baby Charles had been born. Yet her personal life had been sacrificed for this girl and her sister. She had given them everything. In trying to free them from their prison, she had incarcerated herself. She thought of Alah's lonely coffin, and nausea

414

went through her. She deserved better than that. Certainly, she deserved something.

Beatrice squeezed her hand again. 'We want *you* to write *your* story about the education of the princesses. Under your own name, and with the queen's full approval. That's what the Ladies of America want. We're actually hoping Her Majesty will write a preface for us.'

'We're *sure* she will,' Bruce corrected, 'which is why we went to the trouble of preparing this.' He placed something white on top of the newspapers in front of her.

Marion peered. 'What is it?'

'A contract!' Beatrice said brightly.

Bruce hurried through the clauses. There were a great many of them. Every eventuality seemed to be covered. 'Happy?' he asked, extending in his huge hand a fat black shiny pen.

Marion looked at the three of them. She looked around the room, the palatial imitation, and felt doubtful again.

Beatrice leaned eagerly forward. 'You owe it to yourself!' she declared. 'People should know the amazing story you have to tell.'

'And just think,' Bruce echoed. 'If those behind the scenes were never to put pen to paper, history would lose some of its most valuable documents.'

In Marion's whirling mind, something jumped clear of the fray. Had not Tommy said this exact same thing, one sunny night in Windsor during the war? *If those behind the scenes were never to put pen to paper, history would lose some of its most informative documents. I don't see how history can arrive at the truth if contemporaries aren't allowed to write it.*

And Tommy, of course, with his visit to Nottingham Cottage, had been the instigator of this whole business.

She smiled and took the shiny black pen proffered by Bruce. The gold nib hesitated over the white sheet below.

Gold and white. The colour of the moulding at Buckingham Palace. Of a pearl mounted in a crown. Of Lilibet at six.

The nib descended. She signed.

Beatrice whooped, leaped out of her chair and flung her arms around Marion. The hug was unexpectedly strong, like being clamped in a vice. George rose and shook hands vociferously with Bruce before giving Marion a kiss that left her breathless. Happiness rose inside her like a big red balloon.

Epilogue

Aberdeen, Scotland
July 1987

The gleaming limousines continued steadily onward, along the main road. Soon they were gone. The woman stopped waving and let her hand slowly drop.

Now she seemed to shrivel. Her form slumped and her face sank into creases. She looked her age; even older. Her heavy, drooping eyes looked tired and hopeless, their light extinguished.

Yet still she stood there at the window. The hours passed. The sun moved across the walls. The people on the mantelpiece grew indistinct in the fading light. The box in the corner was lost in the dusk.

In the dining room, the flowers had closed. The polished silverware caught the last of a pink sunset. In the shadows of the kitchen, the edges of the sandwiches dried and curled.

Finally, the old woman moved. Her hands were numb and her legs felt painfully stiff. In her specially bought new shoes she moved slowly across the carpet and left the room without pulling the curtains. From the mantelpiece, over the coroneted heads of her daughters, the queen stared impassively after her.

In a velvet-black sky, a cold silver moon had risen. Its light spread over the sleeping city, drawing the mica glitter out of the granite as the sun had done during the day. The prosperous road was silent.

Moonlight fell on the neat gardens, touched the broad-branched trees, lit the backs of drawn curtains in the big detached houses.

Only the curtains in the old woman's bedroom remained open. The moonlight fell through the window and across the bed. She lay in the centre, in the pink dress, apparently still. But underneath the white cross-shaped brooch pinned over her heart, faint movement could yet be seen. She was still breathing; dreaming still.

A memory surfaced. Lilibet's coronation. She had been in Aberdeen for two years by then, but no invitation to the abbey had dropped through the door. Invitations rarely did; Marion kept herself to herself. No one must know who she had been, or where. And soon, in this street whose residents had the luxury of distance and privacy, people stopped wondering.

Another memory. Margaret and Peter Townsend. Alone of everyone she had seen it coming. The old woman, in her dream, felt the sharp pain of guessing what the girl was going through. But her sympathy was unwanted. All her letters to the palace had been returned unopened. Following the publication of *The Little Princesses*, the only correspondence she ever got was her own.

They had all rejected her – those for whom she had given up her youth. She had never had children of her own. The marriage to George had been miserable. After his death, her later life had been lonely. And now the end was coming. It was, some might say, a tragic one.

But the old woman on the bed was smiling. She felt a light was shining within her. Bright and dazzling, it banished recent shadows and revealed the glittering past.

What a past it had been. Exciting, extraordinary, epic in scale. She had lived, really lived, as few people ever lived. She had seen history unfold. Known kings and made a queen.

She had been needed. She had been happy and fulfilled. She had loved, passionately. Whether it had been reciprocated or deserved no longer mattered. The loving had been the thing. She had loved as few people ever loved. She had been lucky; gloriously so.

Her life was not a tragedy. It was a triumph. She had chosen her own path, followed her star. By anyone's standards, her career had been astonishing. And when, finally, it was over, she had her memories. Wonderful memories, which would outlast her because of the book. Now, at the end, she could not regret even that.

Outside, in the black sky, the moon rose and brightened. The radiance within her seemed outside her too. It was pressing on her lids like the sun of late summer, a summer from the past before all the trouble began. There was warmth and colour, now sharpening into pictures in her mind. She was in a Scottish garden on an August morning. The air was spicy with woodsmoke and sweet with the scent of sun-warmed gorse. Behind were the moors, wine-red, stretching to distant purple mountains.

And before her, coming over the green lawn, were three figures all dressed in blue. They were smiling at her, the duchess and her daughters, as she had first known them, long ago.

Author's Note

I had wanted to write a novel about the Windsors for years when the story of Marion Crawford literally fell at my feet. *The Little Princesses* – the autobiography about her sixteen years with the royal family which landed her in so much trouble – came tumbling from the shelf of a second-hand bookshop on a rainy half-term day in the north of England. Picking it up and flicking through, I slowly realised that this was the perfect way in to a milieu which had fascinated me since childhood.

As a child I had devoured my grandmother's small collection of royal souvenir books, particularly a large gold volume about the 1937 coronation. The sepia photographs showed a cast of larger-than-life personalities. The ever-thunderous-looking Queen Mary; King George V with his huge, tired eyes; the golden-haired, glamorous Prince of Wales and the enigmatic Mrs Simpson, holding a lapdog and displaying an emerald the size of a floor tile (or so it seemed to me). And of course the York family: fragile Prince Albert (later George VI); the sweet but steely Duchess of York (later Queen Elizabeth) and their daughters, Princess Elizabeth and Princess Margaret, with whose childhood this novel is centrally concerned.

None of my grandmother's books had a picture or even a reference to Marion Crawford. The lively, left-wing young Scottish teacher, whose role in the princesses' upbringing was as crucial as it was lengthy, has largely been eradicated from history. References to her in even the scholarly biographies dealing with the period are few and brief. Mostly they subscribe to the orthodoxy that she made a foolish mistake writing a silly book and her subsequent rejection by those she spent her best years caring for was her own fault. Hugo Vickers, in his brilliant *Elizabeth, The Queen Mother* (Arrow) is rare in trying to unravel what actually went on and suggesting that Marion might have been badly treated. More recently Robert Lacey, in his excellent *The Crown: The Inside History* (companion to the TV series) makes many similar points. Perhaps Marion is finally getting the reappraisal she deserves.

What initially drew me to her story is there on the very first page of *The Little Princesses*, when she tells us that she had intended to teach in the Edinburgh slums. How on earth, I wondered, did someone with a vocation among the poor end up teaching some of the wealthiest people in the world? I read on. She was very young, I realised, only twenty-two; moreover, she was *modern*; one of the first-ever generation of women who saw an education and a profession as their right. So why had this sassy trailblazer with her liberal views gone to work for the most patriarchal institution imaginable?

All this was interesting in itself, but the times through which she lived were unbelievably dramatic; some of the most convulsive and colourful in Britain's history. The drama of the Abdication; the glamour of the coronation; the trauma of World War 2. Marion was at the heart of the royal family throughout, as close to the little princesses as a mother and perhaps closer. Yet afterwards, one mistake led to her being cast into the outer darkness forever. Her tale ended tragically, but during her glory years she lived, she really lived. I could hardly believe that her story had never been told before. Now it has.

Wendy Holden, London 2020

Acknowledgements

For my account of Marion Crawford's story, I took all the facts I could lay my hands on and filled in any gaps with my own imagination. The sources I am indebted to are as many as they are varied, ranging from an amusingly outdated *The Complete Book of Etiquette* published by Foulsham & Co. Ltd sometime in the 1950s and by a Mary and John Bolton (who may or may not have actually existed) to the magisterial *Queen Mary* (Phoenix Press) by James Pope-Hennessy, who definitely did exist.

Others I have consulted include *Marcus Adams: Royal Photographer* by Lisa Heighway (Royal Collection Enterprises); *Britain Between The World Wars 1918-1939*, Marion Yass (Wayland); *The Children's War*, Juliet Gardiner (Portrait/IWM) and the same author's magnificent *The Thirties: An Intimate History*. Also *Queen Elizabeth The Queen Mother: The Official Biography,* William Shawcross (Macmillan); *World War II Day By Day*, Anthony Shaw (Spellmount) *The Heart has its Reasons* by The Duchess of Windsor (Michael Joseph) and *A King's Story: The Memoirs of the Duke of Windsor* (Prion). I have already mentioned *The Coronation Souvenir Book 1937*, Gordon Beckes (Daily Express Publications), but I also gained inspiration and information from *Hons and Rebels* by Jessica Mitford (W&N); *King's Counsellor: Abdication and War – The Diaries of Sir Alan Lascelles* ed. Duff Hart-Davis (W&N) and *These Tremendous Years* (Daily Express Publications).

The latter, a vintage photographic scrapbook detailing sensational events of the Twenties and Thirties, is typical of the rich seam of material I picked up at the second-hand book stall in the excellent weekly flea market at Chesterfield, Derbyshire. For several years its proprietor, Richard, kept back for me any and many royal-themed books gathered from local house-clearances and it is thanks to him – and what seems a disproportionately large number of recently departed royalists in the area – that I now have a roomful of hagiographical souvenir publications with titles like *Queen Mary; The Pageant Of Her Wonderful Years* and *Britain's Glorious Navy*. Yet I found that even in the most fulsome account of royal life there would be a hard little nugget of something interesting and revealing that I could use.

My main source was of course Marion Crawford's own ill-fated autobiography, *The Little Princesses* (Odhams Press); along with her other books *Queen Elizabeth II* and *The Queen Mother* (George Newnes).

I would now like to thank all the people without whom *The Governess* would never have seen the light of day. Thank you to my agents Jonathan Lloyd of Curtis Brown and (in the US) Deborah Schneider of Gelfman Schneider; both of whom believed in it from the get-go. To Lucy Morris of Curtis Brown, who came on board later and was an inspiration. To my editor, Jon Elek, and everyone at Welbeck. I am so thrilled and delighted to be with this exciting new force in British publishing.

Finally, thank you to my family, my husband Jon McLeod and children Andrew and Isabella. All have patiently and for years put up with my royal fixation, but given that I'm now writing a novel about Wallis Simpson, I'm afraid it's not over yet!

Image credit: Laurie Fletcher

Sunday Times number one bestseller Wendy Holden was a journalist before becoming an author. She has written ten consecutive top-ten bestselling novels and sold more than 3 million books.